THE SLEEPER

A LANCE SPECTOR THRILLER

SAUL HERZOG

AUTHORCONTACT

1

Bardufoss, Norway

2:24 a.m. Coordinated Universal Time

Fifty miles from the Norwegian port of Narvik, a military installation known as the Bardufoss Infrasound Station sat huddled next to a frigid, craggy coastline. Located deep within the Arctic Circle, it was nearer to Murmansk in Russia than Oslo.

On the top floor of the station, a naval officer named Aksel Øigarden leaned back precariously on his ergonomic chair. He'd been staring at a series of flat green lines on his seismography monitor for eight hours straight, and was so close to falling asleep that when the lines moved, he jerked in shock, lost his balance, and only narrowly avoided falling to the ground. He did manage to knock over his mug, spilling cold, stale coffee all over his keyboard.

"Helvete," he muttered.

This couldn't be right.

A decades-old ringer, as loud as a firehouse alarm and connected to a steel bell three feet from his head, began clanging with the ferocity of a ship's horn. Its flashing yellow light blinded him, and outside, strobes and wailing sirens sent flocks of seabirds into the night sky for a mile in every direction.

He slammed his fist on the yellow button that killed the alarm and began furiously pulling up data feeds on his computer.

The epicenter of the blast was registering from the open ocean north of the Russian naval base at Arkhangelsk. There was no way an explosion of that magnitude made sense at that location.

Maybe during the Cold War, he thought, but now? No way.

He picked up the phone and speed-dialed his counterpart at NORSAR, the agency responsible for operating the Norwegian Seismic Array. This was the most sensitive and advanced seismic detection system on the planet, which was why ARPANET and the US Department of Defense had tasked it with monitoring Russian territory for nuclear detonations. That role began at the height of the Cold War, and for fifty years, like the sentinels in some mythic saga, NORSAR personnel had diligently watched and waited for the first flickering sparks of Armageddon.

"Thorbjørn, it's Aksel," he stammered.

"I have it, Aksel. The readings are off the chart."

"It's real then?"

"It's real," Thorbjørn said.

"And notification has been triggered?"

Under the terms of the Comprehensive Nuclear Test Ban Treaty, any explosion detected by Bardufoss was automatically communicated to the US Seismic Data Analysis

Center in Alexandria, Virginia. This was part of the system NATO had devised to provide early warning protection against nuclear attack, and there were even rumors that at periods of high tension between the superpowers, a NORSAR detection could trigger an automatic US response. The US government strenuously denied that, but given that similar provisions were known to exist in Russia, it was likely the US had matched them.

"Notification is automatic, Aksel."

"Of course," Aksel said, running his hands through his thick hair. He let out a long breath. He'd spent twelve years preparing for this moment, and now that it had arrived, it felt strangely anticlimactic. That was it. His work was done. A nuclear detonation had been detected, and within seconds, a plethora of automatic systems and failsafes, magnetic tape machines, solenoid circuit breakers, copper wires, and lithium batteries, systems developed during the absolute fever pitch of Cold War paranoia, performed the task they'd been built for flawlessly. A signal was sent to Virginia along a cable on the North Atlantic seabed, and within seconds, every NATO monitoring outpost on the planet was aware of it.

The Russians had detonated a nuke.

"What now?" he said into the phone.

"Now," Thorbjørn said, "we wait."

2

Five hundred miles north of Aksel's location, a small flotilla of Russian fishing trawlers battled against a fierce northerly gale. Gusts of seventy miles-per-hour sent temperatures plunging below negative fifty, cold enough to burn off skin with the ferociousness of a flamethrower. The weather at that latitude was so extreme that the sailors, if they needed to go outside for any reason, required protective suits first designed by the Soviet army for use by soldiers in a nuclear war.

The pilothouses on the trawlers were made of a reinforced steel plate usually reserved for armoring naval corvettes, and the sailors were locked in as tightly as any submariners. The hatches and bulkhead doors were built to the specifications of a Granit-class nuclear submarine.

Despite an advanced glass heating system, the windows

overlooking the bows of the boats threatened to ice over completely. When that happened, it would be impossible for anyone to go outside and clear them off.

The waves were twenty, even thirty feet high, and crashed against the hulls of the boats like walls of concrete, buffeting them over and over with the kinetic energy of a sixty-mile-per-hour locomotive.

The trawlers were thirty miles east of the Svalbard archipelago, home to the most northerly permanent human settlement on earth, and had sent multiple distress signals to the Norwegian Coast Guard station at Longyearbyen.

"Will they even come?" a deck officer said to the captain of the lead trawler under his breath.

The captain, a grizzled sea dog named Yuri Tabakov, looked at him gravely but said nothing.

They were in contested waters. Svalbard had long been a source of tension between Norway and Russia. A treaty from 1920 granted sovereignty to Norway, but also guaranteed to Russia a permanent right to inhabit the islands. The Russian government of the time was determined to exercise that right, despite the fact that there was about as much demand from ordinary Soviet citizens to occupy the far-flung, godforsaken place as there was to inhabit the dark side of the moon. In 1920, Russia was in the clutches of a brutal civil war that saw the unleashing of what historians later called the Red Terror. Hundreds of thousands were killed, and millions more lost their lives to typhus, cholera, and some of the most severe famines of the twentieth century. Nevertheless, the new government in Moscow set about establishing three mining colonies on Svalbard, complete with towns laid out to the exacting standards of Soviet Central Committee planners. The archipelago was to prove so hostile to human life, however, that it forced even the creators of the brutally inhospitable Siberian Gulag to eventually admit defeat. Of the three settlements, only one survived today—the town of Barentsburg.

The other towns could still be seen from boats sailing into Barentsburg, their cultural centers, sports complexes, schools, and apartment buildings slowly crumbling to dust. Even the enormous concrete statues of Lenin, erected in the central courtyard of each settlement, were beginning to totter.

It was from Barentsburg that the trawlers had set out the day before. The crew had been granted shore leave, which had been spent drinking a potent, tax-exempt liquor imported by the mining company from a distillery in Arkhangelsk. The label on the bottles looked more like something for a medicine, or a household cleaning chemical, than anything that would be consumed for pleasure, and the taste lived up to that promise. The town had four prostitutes, who were kept very busy by the twenty-eight men who crewed the four trawlers.

It was common custom at the bar in Barentsburg to curse the Norwegians with every shot of vodka consumed, and the sailors, to a man, had dutifully honored the practice.

There were no curses now.

The captain peered through the window at the roiling water like a man watching a disaster unfurl in slow motion, his eyes squinted, his face two inches from the glass, his knuckles as white as the froth on the waves. A cigarette rested in his mouth, burned to the nub, an inch of ash holding on precariously.

It was a night that would see men drown, and he knew it. He'd seen such nights before. He'd seen storms that flung ships around like children's playthings. He'd seen a hundred men die in a single crashing wave. He'd seen steel hulls break in half. He'd seen the ocean do things that no camera had ever recorded, that no man who hadn't been present would believe possible. And what was more, he knew he would yet see worse.

And then a light washed over the bow. It was like an apparition, an archangel come to deliver him from the jaws of catastrophe.

"There she is, boys," he growled. "There she is."

3

The *Svalbard Icebreaker* was the jewel of the Norwegian Coast Guard. At three-hundred-forty feet in length and with a displacement of over six thousand tons, it was the second-largest vessel in the entire Norwegian Navy. It was propelled by two diesel-electric Azipod thrusters, powered by four Rolls-Royce Bergen generators, and could break through ice up to a meter thick, both ahead and astern. It was armed with a Bofors fifty-seven millimeter naval gun, a twelve-millimeter machine gun, and a European-designed Simbad Surface to Air missile system. On its deck were two helicopters, a British Westland Lynx twin-engined naval utility chopper, and a medium-sized NH90 military chopper.

Most importantly at that moment, it had a towing

capacity of one-hundred-thousand tons, enough to bring all four trawlers back to Svalbard.

It was barrelling through the waves at seventeen knots when the beam of its searchlight washed over the Russian trawlers like the lamp of a lighthouse.

"Good God," the captain said. "What were they thinking?"

The trawlers were so laden with ice, so low in the water, that the waves crashed clear over the decks. Russian fishermen often operated in Norwegian waters illegally. Their government practically ordered them to, using the fact to challenge Norwegian sovereignty claims over vast stretches of the Barents and Norwegian Seas.

"Give me the radio," he said to his navigator, then, into the receiver he barked, "Murmansk-registered trawlers, this is captain Stieg Gunnar of the Norwegian Coast Guard vessel *Svalbard,* responding to your SOS."

He waited but got back only static.

He repeated his message and waited again.

This time, in heavily-accented English, he got a crackly response. He had to hold the receiver to his ear to catch the words. "Norwegian Coast Guard vessel *Svalbard*, this is Yuri Tabakov of the Russian trawler *Taurus*, awaiting your immediate assistance."

"Stand by, *Taurus*," Gunnar said. "We're going to see about latching on. Tell your boats to cut their engines."

He put down the radio and issued the order to pull up within range of the *Taurus.*

"Your coffee, sir," the steward said, putting a metal cup on the counter in front of him. Gunnar picked it up and held it in both hands for warmth.

Looking down at the four little boats, it was hard to

believe anyone would go willingly to such extremes to earn a living. He wondered what these men's homes must have been like that they came to such a place to earn their bread.

"They must have saltwater in their veins," he muttered.

An alarm at the navigator's console began to sound, an irritating electronic chime, accompanied by a flashing red light on the bulkhead.

Gunnar looked at the man. "What is it?"

"Sir," the navigator said, "we're picking up a...."

"A what?"

"A surface disturbance, sir."

"A surface disturbance?" Gunnar echoed.

The navigator looked at him, his eyes wide. "It's a wave, sir. It's going to...."

The navigator was a capable man, but he had a habit of letting his words trail off when he didn't want to say what he was thinking.

Gunnar was about to ask him what the hell he was talking about—*surface disturbance* was not a phrase bandied about lightly—when he saw in the distance beyond the trawlers what appeared to be a snow-capped range of mountains.

"Distance?" he said, his voice weaker than he'd intended.

"Miles, sir. Seven miles. Closing fast."

Even from that distance, Gunnar knew this was nothing natural. It was a thing from old sailors' tales, something told of by firelight to scare children. It was a legend, a curse, a hundred-foot wall of water that nothing could hope to withstand.

He gave himself a few seconds to wonder at it, to stare at its immensity, to accept the inevitable and make peace with his Maker. And then he picked up the ship's comms and yelled, "Brace!" as everything around him exploded in a deafening crash of water and glass and fury.

4

L ance Spector sat in the back of a black London cab, his head against the window, watching the glimmer of oncoming headlights in the droplets on the glass. It was a dreary night, and the dreariness had a distinct, British quality. It was raining, but the rain didn't fall from the sky. It seemed to condense from the air itself, a sort of northerly dampness that got inside his coat, got down to his bones and brought him back to every other time he'd been in that city in winter.

He was in a rundown part of the East End, and the cab drove over the wet cobbles of Whitechapel and Brick Lane, past mosques, off-licenses, and an unending stream of book-ies. The businesses were shuttered for the night, and it was rare to see a surface that hadn't been graffitied.

They turned onto a street lined with brick low-rises, and ahead, blocking the sky, was a rectangular concrete mono-lith, a building so vast it could only have been built by a government, a nation. It rose twenty stories like a cold, gray mountain, its face a symmetry of balconies clad in white-painted plywood.

Lance leaned toward the driver and said, "This will do, pal."

He got out of the cab, slung a leather bag over his shoulder, and inhaled deeply. There was an air of diesel fume, and no amount of rain could make it seem cleaner.

He'd arranged the apartment on the phone. A flat, the landlady called it. It had been advertised on a sheet of paper taped to the wall of a phone booth.

Bachelor apartment. Boarding room price.

Lance paid two months' rent in cash without signing any paperwork or showing any identification.

He walked up to the entrance, his key ready, but didn't need it. The lock on the main door was broken. There was an intercom with a keypad, but that was also broken.

He pushed the door open and entered a drab, institutional lobby. It had been painted with thick, high-gloss paint that could be cleaned with the same mop used on the floors. There was a bank of elevators, eight of them, and he stepped into the nearest. It smelled of urine. He pressed the button for the tenth floor, and it creaked and rattled as it rose, like it was a living creature struggling to climb the height of the building. When it stopped, the doors shuddered open.

He stepped out into a long, straight corridor with plastic light fixtures mounted flush to the ceiling every fifteen feet or so. Some of the bulbs were out. Some flickered. A notice on the wall told him that garbage was under no circumstances to be left in the corridor overnight. Someone had hand-drawn a rat on it with a ballpoint pen.

He made his way down the corridor and, as he

approached his apartment, saw a woman sitting on the ground blocking his path. She was about thirty feet from where he stood and, after glancing back in the direction he'd come from, Lance walked up to her.

She had her back to one of the apartment doors and was smoking a cigarette. Her gaze was fixed on the door opposite. As it turned out, that was Lance's door, and he took his key out of his pocket.

She turned to look up at him and exhaled a long plume of white smoke. She was young—early twenties. Her mascara was smeared, but not from crying. It was more like she'd forgotten it was there and had rubbed her eyes.

She said nothing.

Lance stepped over her legs and put his key in the door. It wouldn't turn. There was something wrong with the lock. He fiddled with it, and the woman said, "You have to pull it out a bit."

"What?" Lance said.

"The key. Pull it out a little."

It worked.

"Thanks," he said, opening the door. He entered the apartment and, before shutting the door, looked back down at the woman.

She wasn't strung out. She wasn't high. She wasn't hurt that he could see. It was as if she was just taking a rest from whatever life she had going on inside her apartment, like a waitress at the back of a restaurant taking a smoke break.

"Why don't you take a picture?" she said.

He gave her a curt nod and shut the door on her.

His apartment was as spartan as they came. It smelled of bleach and fresh paint. A thin carpet, like office carpet, had been laid in twelve-inch squares. On the ceiling was a bare, energy-efficient halogen bulb.

There was a glass sliding door that led out to a narrow balcony. A kitchenette occupied one corner. In front of it was a sofa that faced a wall where a television might be. There was no television.

He let out a tired sigh.

There was a plastic thermostat on the wall, and he turned on the heat. Then he went to the balcony, stepped outside, and looked out at the endless city. It was shrouded in a mist that rose twenty feet from the ground. The buildings poked through, and looking out at it, Lance had the same feeling he got when looking at clouds from the window of an airplane.

He lit a cigarette and, as he smoked, wondered how long he would be at this place. No one had told him to be there. As far as he was aware, no one knew he was there.

It was an exile that was self-imposed.

A man could stay ahead of his own soul only so long. Sooner or later, his debts came due. The conscience could only take so much. In the end, one way or another, every deed would be atoned, every sin paid for, every act of violence avenged.

There was a bedroom in the flat. He hadn't looked at it but already wondered if he'd be able to sleep there. He hadn't slept in days. His mind wouldn't let him. It just turned, over and over, rehashing the same things, the same memories.

He flicked his cigarette over the side of the balcony and watched the ember disappear. Then he went back to the front door and looked out the peephole.

The woman was gone.

5

L evi Roth had slept less than an hour when the call came in. It came on a special line, had a special tone on his phone, and if he didn't answer, would have been followed by one of his security detail pounding on the bedroom door like a bailiff.

He rubbed his eyes and grabbed the phone without looking at the screen. Ten minutes later, he was in the back of a government-issue Cadillac Escalade with full police escort, lights flashing, sirens wailing, running red lights and stop signs with the abandon of a fire truck. The cavalcade only slowed when it reached the main security checkpoint at Langley. The driver had Roth's window down before the vehicle even came to a halt. A guard peered in and waved them through. The car entered a tunnel beneath the new CIA headquarters building that brought them down four stories to a maximum-security, reinforced bunker, built of concrete thick enough to withstand a direct nuclear strike.

At the next checkpoint, Roth got out of the car and entered an underground reception area where two specially-cleared agents from the CIA's Office of Security waited for him. They escorted him down a corridor so bright he had to shield his eyes from the fluorescent light. At the end of the hall was an elevator with the seal of the CIA embossed on the doors. The two guards simultaneously swiped keycards and entered a four-digit pin. The doors opened, and Roth entered the elevator alone. There were no buttons inside, no screens telling him how many floors he had descended, and when the elevator stopped, he stepped out into the CIA's new state-of-the-art Emergency Command Center.

It had only just come online and comprised a highly classified aspect of the National Command Authority—the set of protocols governing who ultimately could issue lawful military orders in cases of extreme national distress. The command center had hardline comms connections to the White House, the Pentagon, and the emergency operations centers for the Army, Navy, and Air Force. It also had direct access to the entire NORAD Alert Network, the Defense Department's Global Information Grid, and the Keyhole Satellite Surveillance Network.

Under the terms of a new, classified Operations Plan, there were now situations in which the CIA Director was authorized to order retaliatory strikes against any foe that took out the national leadership in Washington or threatened the nation's ability to maintain continuity of government. That included issuing orders to any part of the National Military Command, the US Strategic Command, or the Air Force Global Strike Command. It specifically included strike commands to the combat-ready units of the US Strategic Nuclear Deterrent at Barksdale Air Force Base in Bossier Parish, Louisiana, and the units of Strategic Command's Deterrence and Global Srike Capability at Offutt Air Force Base, Nebraska.

What that meant was that in the case of catastrophic

attack, Roth could strike back with every weapon the US military possessed.

Including nuclear weapons.

This was the facility from which such orders would be issued.

He was escorted by two more guards from the elevator to the situation room, where everyone was already seated, waiting for him. Those present included the Secretary of Defense, the NSA Director, the Chairman of the Joint Chiefs, the Navy Chief of Staff, and the President's new National Security Advisor, Jared Cutler. They sat at a long conference table in the center of a dark room. The table was illuminated by low-hanging pendant lights. Beyond the orb of their light, various lieutenants, staffers, and analysts sat in tiered benches like spectators in an amphitheater.

Roth's most trusted advisor, director of the Special Operations Group, Laurel Everlane, was also present. She stood at the far end of the table in front of a set of enormous monitors that provided real-time data from satellites and other intelligence assets around the globe.

Roth took his position at the head of the table and cleared his throat. "So, Laurel, what's all this fuss about?" he said. "Please don't tell me it's another North Korean test launch."

Twice in the past, North Korean missile tests over the Sea of Japan had triggered false alarms.

"It's not North Korea, sir," Laurel said.

There was a carafe of coffee on the table, and Roth poured himself some. On the main screen in front of him, ultra-high-resolution imagery of a frothy patch of ocean was showing. The image was from a Keyhole satellite, so clear that even in the darkness he could see debris in the water.

"That's not one of our boats?" he said.

Laurel shook her head. "You're looking at debris from the Norwegian Coast Guard's *Svalbard Icebreaker*. A formidable vessel, three-hundred-forty feet in length, fifty crew, all the latest technology. It was responding to a distress call from a group of Russian fishing trawlers about thirty miles east of the Svalbard archipelago in the Arctic Ocean."

Roth looked at the image on the screen. Floating in the water, he could see pieces of mangled wood and plastic, buoyancy devices, and dead bodies. "What on earth happened to it?"

Laurel nodded to a specialist sitting behind the monitors. "Play the footage," she said.

The image on the screen changed to a zoomed-out view of the ocean. It was shrouded in darkness, but the lights of the Norwegian vessel could be made out. It was approaching four smaller fishing trawlers that were barely visible.

"What you're about to see," she said, "happened less than an hour ago."

The sea was stormy. Enormous waves buffeted the icebreaker as it approached the trawlers. It was moving in closer, attempting a rescue maneuver, when suddenly, out of nowhere, an enormous wave, like the shockwave from old footage of a Manhattan Project test, blasted across the ocean, obliterating everything in its path.

"What the hell was that?" Cutler said.

Laurel looked at him. "That was a shockwave."

The wave must have been a hundred feet high and moving at hundreds of miles per hour. There wasn't a ship in the ocean that could have withstood it, and already, Roth knew there was no way it had come from anything natural.

"What could have caused it?" Cutler asked.

Roth glanced at Elliot Schlesinger, the Chairman of the

Joint Chiefs. Cutler was a new man, an unknown quantity, untested in his role, and, at least to the people seated around that table, untrusted. Everyone in the room knew the answer to his question—none wanted to say it.

"How far were those boats from the epicenter of the blast?" Roth said to Laurel.

"Thirty miles."

"Thirty miles?" Roth echoed.

She nodded gravely.

"What kind of explosion could sink a ship at a distance of thirty miles?" Cutler said.

Everyone looked at him.

"A natural disaster?" he said.

No one spoke.

He looked around the table, at the faces looking back at him. Very quietly, almost in a whisper, he said, "Not nuclear?"

The director of the NSA, Sandra Shrader, nodded her head.

"Nuclear?" Cutler said again as if to confirm what his ears refused to believe.

"What caused it?" Roth said.

Laurel switched the screen to a live satellite surveillance feed, and Roth's face suddenly went pale. His mouth went dry.

He studied satellite pictures of Russian military installations on a daily basis, everyone present did, and they knew this place. It was a testing range in the extreme north of the country.

Part of a network of facilities across Russia that were working all out on the development of a new range of super-weapons.

The testing range was coastal. It had a snow-strewn

runway, aircraft hangars, and a control tower. South of the runway were administrative and scientific buildings, and beyond those, enough barracks to house thousands of soldiers. There were two fences around the compound, separated by a stretch of no man's land less than a hundred yards wide. A string of guard towers monitored the fences, and Roth could make out soldiers with dogs patrolling the gap between them.

"This is the Russian Navy Testing Range at Nyonoksa," Laurel said.

"Poseidon," Roth said quietly.

"Good God," Schlesinger said. "God help us all."

"Poseidon?" Cutler said.

Navy Chief of Staff, Frederick Winnefeld, cleared his throat. "Poseidon is a new Russian superweapon," he said. "We're classifying it as a weapon of last resort. An underwater drone armed with a one-hundred-megaton nuclear bomb that has been purposefully laced with highly toxic cobalt-60."

"An underwater dirty bomb?" Cutler said. "Why on earth would anyone build such a thing?"

"Because we can't defend ourselves against it," Roth said. "It's a weapon of deterrence. Something they want us to know they have, something that will stop us from getting any bright ideas."

"I thought they had nuclear ballistic missiles for that?"

"Nukes," Roth said, letting out a long sigh. "You'd have thought those would be enough. But we've been working for decades on missile defense systems that can shoot those down before they reach their target."

"So they built an underwater version?"

"All our defense systems assume an attack will come from the air," Roth said. "An underwater bomb could explode off the coast, and no one would even know it was coming. We have no missile defense systems down there—no early warning systems. The amount of radiation released by such an explosion would be enough to render vast parts of our coastline uninhabitable. The wave alone would kill tens of thousands of people."

"I had no idea they were working on such a thing," Cutler said.

"The Poseidon is one of a slew of new doomsday weapons the Russians are working on," Laurel said. "But that's not what we're dealing with here. This explosion appears to be the result of another new weapon system."

"*Another*?" Cutler said.

Laurel looked at Roth.

"Petrel?" he said.

She nodded her head slowly.

It was too much for Cutler. "Wait a minute," he said. "I've been informed that we're doing everything in our power to de-escalate tensions with Russia."

"We are," Roth said.

"But now you're telling me that they're working on a slew of new doomsday weapons? That doesn't sound like de-escalation to me."

"It's not," Roth said.

"Well?" Cutler said. "Then explain that to me. How does that add up? We're de-escalating. They're building doomsday machines."

"That's something you'd have to speak to the President about," Roth said.

"I have spoken to the President about it," Cutler said. "He said the State Department's been making progress."

"You mean the group working out of the embassy in

Moscow?" Schlesinger said. "The embassy that was just blown to smithereens? *That* State Department group?"

"There's no evidence the Russian government was involved in that attack," Cutler said.

Schlesinger turned to Roth. "How the hell did this guy get his job? How is he sitting at this table right now?"

Laurel intervened, attempting to dispel the growing tension. "As far as we've been able to discern," she said, "this was an offshore nuclear explosion caused by a failed test launch of a new Petrel prototype."

"Do we have footage of the explosion?" Roth said.

Laurel hit some keys and the screen went pitch black. On the bottom of the screen were coordinates not far from the position of the *Svalbard*. Suddenly, the screen went white, then the feed cut out.

"That's all we got?"

"You mentioned Petrel," Cutler said.

Roth turned to him. "Petrel is another new Russian weapon system."

"It's part of an entire program of new high-budget, mass-casualty superweapons they've got in development," Laurel said.

"Another doomsday weapon?" Cutler said.

She nodded.

"And the President's aware of this?"

Roth rose up in his seat. He wasn't just speaking to Cutler now. He needed everyone in the room to understand the threat they faced. "As Laurel just explained," he said, "the CIA has been tracking a slew of new weapons prototypes being developed by the Russians. As far as we're concerned, what we're looking at are the most devastating, terrifying, horrific weapons of mass annihilation any nation has sought to develop since the very nadir of the Cold War. We're talking about World War Two levels of depravity. Bombs that create tidal waves. Rockets that spew a trail of nuclear waste in their jet stream. I've informed the President, and he agrees that these weapons are intended to be Molotov's last line of defense, his way of ensuring that we never, ever, target him personally, his regime, or the lives of the ruling elite in the Kremlin."

"So this isn't even about defending Russia?" Sandra said. "It's about defending the regime?"

"That's correct," Roth said. "The CIA's codename for the new weapons program is Project Oppenheimer, and we believe it's being run by the Dead Hand. That's the group inside the Kremlin charged solely with maintaining the President's personal grip on power, no matter the cost."

"Oppenheimer?" Cutler said, and then, unable to resist, added, "Now I am become Death, the destroyer of worlds."

"Very good," Roth said.

"We've got a fan of the history channel here," Schlesinger said.

Cutler was about to say something when Laurel said, "The Petrel rocket is an isotope-powered rocket."

"Isotope-powered?" Cutler said.

"It means that it's not just the payload that's nuclear," she said. "The rocket itself is nuclear-powered."

"Doomsday devices," Schlesinger said, shaking his head. "I thought those days were behind us."

"Nothing's behind us," Roth said. "The battle is as it ever was. As it ever will be."

"This is insanity," Cutler said.

Roth nodded. That was something he and Cutler could agree on.

"I mean," Cutler went on, "the risk alone, the risk of catastrophic disaster, even to themselves, it's just...."

"*Unacceptable*?" Roth said.

Laurel spoke up. "The Russians are aware of the risks of the technology. As you can see here," she said, switching the view to a new satellite feed, "recovery vessels were on standby at the launch site."

"Those are Rosatom vessels," Roth said.

"That's correct, sir. They're ships used specifically for handling radioactive material."

"What does that mean?" Cutler said.

"It means they were aware that a nuclear accident was at least a possibility of the test," Laurel said. "They've dispatched those boats to the site of the explosion now."

"What could they possibly be hoping to recover?" Roth said.

"I have no idea," Laurel said. "The prototype would have been vaporized in the blast."

"What can they be hoping to achieve from any of this?" Cutler said. "It makes no sense. A new arms race will destabilize the entire planet."

"As far as they're concerned," Laurel said, "they're already in an arm's race. And it's a race they're losing. If they pull off just one of these new prototypes, if they deploy it successfully, they'll reset the entire global balance of power. They'll undo, in a single stroke, decades of NATO missile defense technology."

"They'll be able to threaten us with annihilation," Roth said. "Just like in the good old days, when they were a super-power and the whole world listened to what they had to say."

"You mentioned Petrel and Poseidon," Schlesinger said. "How many prototypes do we think they're working on?"

"That's the thing," Laurel said. "We only know about

those two, but we've intercepted Dead Hand communications that refer to The Five P's."

"The Five P's?" Cutler said. "Petrel, Poseidon. You're telling me there's three more?"

Schlesinger turned to Roth with a look of exasperation on his face. "Are we really going to spend the night explaining everything to this guy like we're in kindergarten?"

"What did you say?" Cutler said, turning to him. Schlesinger ignored him, and that angered Cutler even more than the comment. "Hey," he said, rising to his feet. "I'm talking to you, *Elliot*."

"Sit down," Schlesinger said derisively, "before you get yourself into something you can't get back out of."

"Is that a threat?" Cutler said.

Schlesinger leveled his gaze on Cutler and said, "It is what it is."

"Look," Cutler said, raising his voice. "I represent the President of the United States here."

"*Represent*?" Schlesinger said, looking at the others. "That's a bit of an exaggeration, wouldn't you say?"

Cutler was livid. He looked like he was about to reach across the table and grab Schlesinger by the throat. "I can't believe this," he spat. "I can't believe you're challenging my right to be here, and I *don't* believe any of you has properly apprised the President of this threat."

"Why?" Schlesinger said, "Because he didn't talk to you about it?"

The meeting was about to descend into a shouting match when the unmistakable New England bellow of the President was heard from the direction of the door, "Gentlemen! That's enough!" It was a voice that never failed to bring to Roth's mind the image of Captain Ahab on board the Pequod, barking orders at his sailors.

Everything about him, from the way he spoke, to his corpulent build, to the cigars that were never far from hand, couldn't have been more custom-made to a man seeking to emulate Winston Churchill.

As he approached, he was accompanied by the strong odor of cigar smoke, and it was the red glow of a cigar's ember that Roth saw first.

"Calm down, the both of you," the President thundered. "This is not a schoolyard."

Both men were aghast.

"Mr. President, sir," Schlesinger said apologetically.

"Like it or not," the President continued, "Cutler is my advisor. He's one of the few appointees I'm free to select entirely at my own discretion. He's inexperienced, but I have my reasons for selecting him."

"Of course, Mr. President," Schlesinger said.

"But that doesn't mean you get to waltz in and start speaking for me," the President said to Cutler. "Your job is to listen, to hear what's said, and come back and report to me. I don't think it's any secret that the greatest mission of my presidency, perhaps the greatest challenge of our time, is the avoidance of all-out war with Russia. I know not everyone in this room sees the world the way I see it, but Cutler does. He understands that his job is to keep us out of a war that can't be won. That's why he's my aide. You people see the world as it is, and that's why you are where you are. If anyone has a problem with that, they can leave right now."

Schlesinger took his seat.

The President looked pointedly at Cutler and, reluctantly, he did the same.

"I was not aware of this latest test launch," the President said, "until a few moments ago, but believe me when I say I am fully apprised of this threat. I know of Operation Oppenheimer. I know of the new superweapons Russian scientists are working on at a furious pace. I know that they breach every disarmament treaty the Russians have ever signed. And I know that if any of them ever graduates from the stage of prototype to actual deployment, it will constitute an existential threat to our nation, to our security, to our very existence."

"Mr. President, sir," Cutler said, but the President ignored him and kept speaking.

"The Petrel system, once perfected, will provide the Russians with a rocket capable of near-infinite loiter time. It will be able to fly around the globe at supersonic speeds for weeks on end, even months, and will have an unlimited range. It will be able to change course. It will crisscross the skies with complete impunity. There's not a thing our missile defense systems can do to stop it." He turned to Laurel. "Am I correct in that assessment, Ms. Everlane?"

Laurel nodded. "That's absolutely correct, sir."

"It wouldn't be the first time we've faced an existential threat from Moscow, would it?"

"It would not, sir," she said.

The President turned back to Schlesinger and Cutler. "Then let's not lose our heads, shall we?" He turned to Roth and said, "Mr. Director?"

"Yes," Roth said, "quite right, sir. As Laurel was just saying, we believe that what we're dealing with here is a failed Petrel test flight. What else do we know, Laurel?"

"Well," Laurel said, "we know that every nuclear monitoring station inside Russia has suddenly stopped sending data to the Comprehensive Nuclear-Test-Ban Treaty Organization network."

"That sounds like an admission of guilt to me," Roth said.

"We also have live footage of the village near the launch site," she said, pulling up another feed on the screen. The view panned to a village a few miles from the testing range. It was night, and the few streetlamps gave off a blue glow that tinged the streets and made the town look like a set from a Tim Burton movie. Snow flitted across the central square, where a crowd of civilians had gathered. There were families, young children, women with strollers. They huddled close to the buildings, grouped together for warmth, pulling their coats around their shoulders.

Soldiers had been dispatched to control the crowd, and they were directing newcomers toward the square and organizing them into lines.

"This is the village of Nyonoksa," Laurel said. "It is located just a few miles from the testing range. Those buses arriving now have been brought in from Arkhangelsk."

"They're evacuating the village," Roth said.

"They are," she said, "and those trucks are bringing in more troops from the base."

She zoomed in closer to where soldiers were getting off the trucks, and Roth suddenly saw that they were wearing hazmat suits.

"This is bad," he said.

"The buses are transporting villagers to the Semashko Medical Center in Arkhangelsk. Our best guess is that they're being checked for signs of radiation exposure."

"They're scared," Roth said. "They're afraid of what they've unleashed."

6

Lance woke with a start. He reached under his pillow and grabbed the Glock 17 pistol he kept there. Someone was at the door, tapping lightly, using the palm of their hand rather than the knuckle.

He made his way across the apartment silently, gun at the ready. From the crack at the bottom of the door, he saw that someone was standing there. Lance was two yards back, next to the kitchen counter, which he could use for cover. He leveled the gun at the center of the door and said, "Who's there?"

A soft woman's voice said, "Open the door."

"Who is it?" he said again, but he recognized the voice.

She stopped tapping. He watched her feet move away from the door. Then he heard crying.

He went to the door and opened it slowly, keeping the gun concealed. Sitting on the floor with her back to the wall, same as before, was the woman he'd seen a few hours earlier. She had her head between her knees and was sobbing.

Lance scanned the corridor in both directions. There was no one else there. "What's wrong?" he said.

"Nothing," the woman said.

"Something's wrong."

She looked up at him, and he saw her face clearly for the first time. He felt sympathy, but it was far outweighed by suspicion. He couldn't help it. He was looking for the catch, measuring the angles.

"What are you doing out here?" he said.

"I can't find my key."

"Your key?"

She nodded at the door opposite Lance's.

He looked at it. A child's drawing was taped to it, a house, a blue sky, a sun, a woman and a girl. It was signed in a child's hand, but he couldn't make out the letters.

He looked at the woman. She'd changed her clothes. She wore a pink latex dress now, fit so tight he could have counted her ribs through it. It was cut low at her breasts and was barely long enough to cover her ass. Her makeup was a mess from crying.

He sighed. He'd made a rule not to get involved with people, to keep to himself. Getting mixed up with other people never worked out. Everything he touched turned to ash. Everyone he got close to ended up dead. He told himself to shut the door, go back to bed, but instead, he found himself saying, "What happened?"

She looked up at him defiantly. "What do you care?"

"I don't care," he said, "but you knocked on my door, so I figure I've got to ask."

She shook her head as if she'd hoped for more from him, as if, somehow, he owed her more than that.

He shifted his weight and leaned against the doorframe.

He lit a cigarette, waiting for her to say something. She said nothing. They just looked at each other, sizing each other up. It took him about two minutes to smoke the cigarette, and when it was done he said, "Well, have a good night then."

He shut the door and went to the kitchen. In the time it took him to get to the trash can and dispose of the cigarette butt, the woman made a decision. She was banging on his door again, harder this time.

Lance was dressed only in a pair of cotton boxer shorts and he went to the bedroom and pulled on a pair of jeans and the white t-shirt he'd worn the day before. He put his gun back where it had been beneath his pillow. The woman was pounding harder on the door. She'd wake the entire floor if he didn't do something about it.

He opened the door, and she pushed her way past him into the apartment. It was the first time he'd seen her standing. She had a good figure, tall, and her stiletto heels made her taller. Her shoes matched the latex dress, like a costume, like something from a fetish website.

He shut the door and turned to face her. She was leaning with her back to the counter. He had his back to the door. She approached, coming up close, pressing her body against his.

"Come on," she said very softly, almost a whisper. "No one needs to know." Her hand touched his leg.

He looked into her eyes and wasn't sure what he was looking at. What was she after? Was this about him, had she been sent to get close to him, or was it about her?

She broke eye contact but remained close, her hand moving slowly up his thigh.

He reached down and stopped her hand.

"Oh, come on," she said, "don't be like that." She put her hand on his crotch and said, "See! You *do* want to play."

She pressed in closer, their eyes locked, and this time she put her mouth on his. He was taller than her and turned away. He took her hand off his jeans.

She took a step back and looked at him. "What's wrong?" she said.

"You need to settle down," he said.

She backed away from him, all the way to the kitchen counter.

Lance looked at her apologetically. It wasn't that he didn't want her. She looked good. But not like this.

"You're a lot less fun than I thought you'd be," she said.

"Sorry to disappoint."

She looked around the room. It looked like what it was, an apartment that had been cleaned up and turned around by a low-budget property management company.

"This place looks awful," she said.

Lance nodded.

"Seriously," she added. "Like a serial killer cleaned up after a murder. All it's missing is the plastic sheet on the floor."

"Well," Lance said, "there's a dozen other doors on this corridor. Maybe if you'd knocked on one of those."

She didn't like him saying that. She was embarrassed. "You know," she said, "you can quit looking so smug."

"What did I say?"

"You think you've been all chivalrous here tonight, don't you?"

"I don't think anything."

"Sure you do," she said. "Like you're a saint for not fucking me. For turning me down."

"I don't think I'm a saint."

"For humiliating me."

"All I did was come to the door."

She nodded. "*Sure* you did. You just came to the door, didn't you? The perfect gentleman. You had no idea who was on the other side."

Lance didn't know what to say to her.

"You saw me sitting out there earlier. I saw the way you looked at me. I didn't imagine that."

"I'm sorry," Lance said.

"And now, you're just banking it, aren't you? You're just postponing it. She's too worked up. She needs to calm down."

"I don't know what you're talking about?"

"I'm talking about you turning me down," she said, and her cheeks flushed as she said it. "You rejected me, but really, what you're thinking is it's just a raincheck. She'll be ready when I want her. I can come back and collect whenever I want."

Lance really didn't know what to say to that. He supposed, at a certain level, she was right. More or less, that was exactly what he'd been thinking. Not tonight, he'd thought. Not like this. But down the road? Who knows? Never say never.

He looked at her more closely. He remembered the first time he'd seen Sam. The same wild eyes. The same pushing and pulling. Like she didn't know whether to tell him to go to hell or beg him never to leave her. Like she was torn between those two poles.

Then the image flashed across his mind of Sam's mutilated body, lying in the snow, covered in blood.

"I think we should call it a night," he said.

"I told you, I can't find my key."

"I don't care."

"I've got no way to get into my apartment."

"Smart girl like you, you'll figure something out."

Her eyes flashed, fierce, like molten rock. She didn't look like she was about to go anywhere.

He let out a long, tired sigh and went to the sink and poured her a glass of water. "Drink this."

She took the glass and drained it in a single go. His cigarettes were on the counter and she helped herself. She offered him one and he took it. He held out a lighter and she leaned in to the flame.

"I'm sorry," she said.

"It's all right."

"No," she said. "I don't know what's wrong with me. I don't know what I wanted from you."

Lance said nothing.

"I'm messed up," she said.

"Everyone's messed up," he said.

She nodded. "I really did lock myself out of my apartment, though," she said. "That's true, and my baby, she's inside."

"Your baby?"

She nodded. "Well, she's five, but she's *my* baby."

"Five years old?"

"She's asleep. She's fine. I just didn't want her to hear me crying."

"Do you cry a lot?"

"You want to be my therapist now?"

"No," he said.

"Then don't start."

He nodded. He led her back out to the corridor and took his wallet from his pocket. He pulled out a thin steel pin, about as long as a toothpick and curved at one end. He slid it into the keyhole on her door, and a minute later, it clicked open.

"Well, that makes me feel safe," she said.

"You should use the chain."

She nodded. They looked at each other for a second, both having the same thought. Then Lance turned and went back into his own apartment.

7

V iktor Lapin took a pack of cigarettes from his shirt pocket and tapped it on the edge of his desk. It was a habit he'd acquired during his years in the navy, where the cheap government cigarettes always required packing before use.

He leaned back on his seat and admired the new office. Not bad for the son of a cop.

He was wearing a short-sleeved shirt, brown with a mustard-yellow triangular pattern on it, and over that, a brown corduroy sport coat. His hair was long and wavy, his glasses large, with thick rims. His style was retro, proletarian, decidedly out of step with a twenty-first-century Kremlin that was obsessed with Tom Ford and Hugo Boss. His colleagues called him Znamenski behind his back, a reference to a police detective from Russian television in the seventies.

He lit the cigarette and sucked hard.

He had a corner office now—a symbol of power, of status. It was a perk that came with his promotion to the very top of the GRU's Main Directorate. There were only a few men left in Russia now who could scare him.

In a silver picture frame on his desk, still waiting to be picked up by the custodial staff, was a photo of his predecessor, the office's previous tenant, Igor Aralov.

Aralov was dead now. Shot in the street outside his apartment while out for a stroll with his wife. And by one of his own agents, no less. A feisty little bitch with dark hair, pale skin, and smoldering eyes. Her name was Tatyana Aleksandrova, and Viktor had heard it more than once since his arrival.

Outside, snow began to fall. He went to the window. The view overlooked the Khodynka, a sprawling parkland where Tsar Nicholas II, the last emperor of Russia, had been crowned. His was a cursed reign if ever there was one. At the height of the First World War, the empire tottering, the army in disarray, he was yanked from his bed by a group of communist revolutionaries. Along with his wife and five children, he was dragged out of the house and unceremoniously shot. The bodies were then bayoneted, burned, doused in sulphuric acid to make them unrecognizable, and dumped into a copper mine shaft next to the Gorno-Uralsk railway line.

In the anteroom outside the office was an enormous oil painting of the coronation. It was a stuffy old thing, in a heavy, gilded frame, and Viktor had wondered why Aralov kept it around. Perhaps as a reminder, he thought now, of how precarious this all was.

He exhaled cigarette smoke, and it dispersed against the windowpane as if searching for a way around it.

People often said the Tsar's end was foreshadowed from the beginning, from the day he received the crown. That day, the crowds in the Khodynka were so thick that a stampede broke out, crushing thirteen hundred people to death.

Viktor was pulled from his thoughts by the clanging metallic chime of the old phone on his desk. A red light indicated an internal call from his secretary.

He picked it up and said, "What is it?"

"A call from the Kremlin, sir."

"The Kremlin?"

"It's the...."

"The what?" Viktor said impatiently, suspecting the answer.

"It's the Prime Directorate, sir."

Viktor stubbed out his cigarette. Corner offices were one thing, but they came at a cost. It was true there was only a handful of men left that Viktor needed to fear. This call, unfortunately, was from one of them—André Suvorov. He was head of the Prime Directorate and, if the rumors were to be believed, a member of the Dead Hand.

"Put him through, put him through, for God's sake," Viktor said.

There was a brief pause, followed by the sickly sweetness of Suvorov's guttural, wavering voice. He spoke as if his larynx was located in a nasal cavity, the result of a bullet wound to the throat he'd supposedly suffered during a game of Russian roulette.

"Found your way to the new office?" he said.

"I have, sir. Yes."

"Everything to your satisfaction, I trust?"

"Absolutely, sir. Very nice."

"You'll want to get rid of Aralov's things as soon as possible, I suspect."

"Not at all."

"Come now, Viktor. We both know the man's tastes were a little, how should we say?"

"Traditional, sir?"

"I was going to say, dated. You'd think we were still in Stalin's days from the way he did up his area. All those plush carpets and velvet curtains. Personally, I think he harbored ambitions to be in the theater. That was why he cultivated his agents the way he did. All so theatrical. All smoke and mirrors and intrigue."

Viktor was nervous. Suvorov was not a man known for his small talk. He was as ruthless a killer as ever walked the halls of the Kremlin, and considering the history, that was saying something.

"Yes," Viktor said weakly.

"Well," Suvorov said, "I'll dispense with the pleasantries, Viktor. There's a reason for my call."

"Of course, sir."

"They tell me there's more to you than meets the eye, Viktor."

"Who told you that, sir?"

Suvorov laughed. "That doesn't matter, Viktor. What matters is that they're correct."

"I hope they are, sir."

"We shall see, Viktor Lapin. We shall see."

Viktor took a fresh cigarette from his pack and tapped it nervously on the desk.

"I take it," Suvorov continued, "that you've heard of the ... *accident* that occurred last night."

Of course he'd heard of it. He'd seen seven separate communiqués. It was being suppressed by state media but was all over the foreign press. In London and Washington and Berlin, it was front-page news. Every seismic monitor in the northern hemisphere had picked it up. Radiation levels were spiking across Europe. Whatever had happened, whatever the cause of the explosion, it was not the type of thing the Prime Directorate would be able to keep secret.

"I've heard, sir. They're evacuating Nyonoksa. Men in hazmat suits are taking the residents to Archangelsk for treatment."

"It was a test launch," Suvorov said.

"I see, sir."

"The system is codenamed Petrel. You should have been granted access to the file in your latest bulletin."

Viktor knew what Petrel was. One of the President's new superweapons. He didn't hold out much hope for them personally, but then, he didn't have the clearance to really look into them. The details were all classified at a clearance above his paygrade. What he did know was that when the Kremlin ever put the word 'super' before anything, it usually paid to be skeptical. The Nazis had prolonged the war for years by promising the German people what they called *Wunderwaffe*—wonder weapons. Viktor saw this as a similar ploy.

"I read the brief, sir," he said. "A nuclear-powered cruise missile."

"Good," Suvorov said.

"Most impressive," Viktor added, tapping his cigarette against the edge of an ashtray.

"Well, as you might have guessed," Suvorov continued, "the launch was a nonsuccess."

Nonsuccess, Viktor thought, was a *nonword*. It was Kremlin-speak. It was also an understatement of gargantuan proportions. They were speaking, after all, of an unintended nuclear detonation. A tsunami had crossed thousands of miles of international waters. This missile had spewed so much radiation along its flight path that entire villages were being evacuated.

"I see, sir," Viktor said. "And how can I be of assistance?"

"I'll tell you how, Viktor. You can find the man responsible. You can find him, and you can kill him."

That sounded simple enough. Viktor wasn't a big believer in scapegoating innocent workers, it would certainly do nothing for the morale of the remaining scientists, but if Suvorov wanted men lined up against a wall, he would get them. Viktor would shoot a hundred of them if that was what was wanted. He would shoot a thousand.

"I'll get on the next flight to Arkhangelsk, sir."

"I'm afraid it's not going to be that easy, Viktor."

"What do you mean, sir? The technology is flawed, is it not? My men can conduct an investigation."

That was another euphemism—*investigation*. They might as well have picked the names of culprits out of a hat.

"As you can imagine," Suvorov said, "the situation on the ground is chaotic. Eighteen scientists are dead. Hundreds more have been exposed to radiation. Not to mention the military personnel."

"I understand, sir."

"No, you don't," Suvorov said, and his voice suddenly dropped an octave. "This was not an accident, Viktor."

"*Not* an accident, sir?"

"It was sabotage."

"I see," Viktor said.

"I'm not telling you to pin this on some schmuck, Viktor. The lead physicist on the project, a man named Sacha Gazinsky, has gone missing."

"Could he be lost in the chaos, sir?"

"He *was* lost in the chaos, Viktor. That's exactly what he

was. And then we realized his nine-year-old daughter is missing too."

"I *see*," Viktor said, suddenly rising in his seat. There it was. A real mission. A real culprit.

"Sacha Gazinsky," Suvorov said, "is a traitor. He sabotaged this launch, but he also accessed classified files not just for the Petrel system, but for the other four prototypes."

"All five?" Viktor said.

"Yes, everything, the blueprints for all five systems, and now he's missing."

8

Tatyana Aleksandrova knew she was breaking the rules. She knew she was taking a risk.

She was a Russian defector. She'd turned her back on the Motherland. That meant entire divisions within the GRU were actively hunting her down. Teams of analysts and hackers with access to facial recognition data from all over the planet were trying to find her. Traffic camera feeds, CCTV systems, even the cell phone and laptop cameras of ordinary people, were being scoured by supercomputers day and night.

They were looking for her, and when they found her, they would send an assassin.

No one took more pleasure in punishing defectors than the Kremlin. It wasn't just vindictiveness. The leadership in Moscow had to be that way. Theirs was a house of cards, and they knew it. If they allowed one person, anyone, to up and walk away, that one person would become an exodus.

Their entire system was so delicate, so fragile, that without fear, without the magnetizing force of raw, unadul-terated terror, their power would slip away like water slipping through fingers. The GRU knew it. The oligarchy knew it.

And President Vladimir Molotov knew it.

He knew it better than anyone, and he knew that the day it happened, he would be truly friendless. He would be alone. He would be torn from his palace as unceremoniously as the last Tsar, and shot like a dog.

Tatyana knew all that. And she knew there were sleeper agents in Washington at that very moment, just waiting for the call that she'd been found. She took precautions, of course—sunglasses, headscarves, changes to her hair and makeup—but those only went so far.

Eventually, she would be found. She knew that.

But she also knew that being cooped up with Laurel Everlane in a hotel suite for the rest of her life, even if it was one of the most luxurious suites in the city, also wasn't an option.

She was taking a risk, Roth would have called it a *needless* risk, but need was subjective. What Tatyana *needed* more than anything was release.

She told herself that if anyone recognized her, if they followed her or came at her, she would be ready, and she would kill them first.

She slipped out the door of the suite and took the elevator to the lobby. There was a bar there, but she wanted something different, something further afield. She left the hotel and allowed the doorman to show her into one of the waiting cabs.

The driver looked back at her and raised an eyebrow when he saw her.

"Don't get any ideas," she said.

"Lady, I didn't say a word."

She was dressed to the nines in a red, satin Valentino

dress and matching stilettos. She looked good, and she knew it. The nightlife in Washington was tame compared to Moscow, but there were still plenty of options.

"Take me to U Street?" she said.

The cab meandered through traffic north on Connecticut Avenue and was just passing Dupont Circle when her phone rang. She was tempted to ignore it, she'd spent the last few hours with Laurel, examining the satellite footage of the explosion in the Arctic in minute detail, and she wanted a break. She looked at her phone, but it wasn't Laurel calling. The call was from an analog phone routing system she'd set up herself years earlier when she still worked for the GRU. The system allowed informants to contact her anonymously, but also meant they couldn't trace her. She'd designed it for her own protection as well as theirs, and most importantly, it was utterly unknown to her superiors at the GRU.

She answered the call and listened carefully to the series of clicks and beeps given out by the routing switches. It took about twenty seconds to make a final connection, and then a man's voice, speaking in Russian, said, "I want to speak to Tatyana Aleksandrova."

"Who is this?" Tatyana said.

"I'm..." the man said. "I'm a...".

"You're a what?" she said.

She knew there were only two types of people who could have reached her like this. Either, this was a person she'd once thought she might be able to cultivate as an asset, someone she'd wanted to keep off the books, to herself. Or it was someone who'd just tortured and killed such a person to get the number from them. She still didn't know which of the two she was speaking to.

"You told me I could use this number."

"Did I?" Tatyana said.

She had a range of numbers, dozens of them, that she'd registered with different cell providers in dozens of different countries. She never wrote them down, never kept a record of them anywhere except in her head, and never gave the same number to two different people.

"You told me if I ever needed you."

"What number did you call?" Tatyana said.

The numbers were always local. She would give a Russian number to a Russian asset, a Syrian number to a Syrian asset. When they were dialed, they were forwarded through switches and exchanges and proxies, routed and rerouted so thoroughly that they circled the globe multiple times before ever reaching her.

The man gave her a Russian cell number, it began 8182, and instantly, Tatyana's blood ran cold. She knew exactly who this was. The area code was for Arkhangelsk. There was only one person it could be.

"You're the scientist," she said. "The physicist from the testing range in Nyonoksa."

"Yes, I am," the man said, his voice trembling with fear.

He knew that this call could be his last. He knew Tatyana could have given him the number as a trap, as bait to test his loyalty. She'd been a GRU agent, after all, and his job was highly sensitive. It was exactly the type of tactic Moscow might have used.

Either this man was not who he said he was, or he was calling Tatyana on blind trust, based on only the briefest of interactions between lectures at a scientific conference in Moscow two years ago.

Tatyana didn't know which he was.

"The explosion has made quite a stir," she said.

The man said nothing for a few seconds, then, "Is it enough of a stir for me to cut a deal?"

"You want to defect?"

"It's not a question of *want*," the man said.

Tatyana knew she shouldn't trust this. The timing was too perfect. It was too juicy a prize. It had to be a trap.

But her gut told her otherwise. The timbre of the man's voice, the way it wavered and trembled like a reeded instrument, that was real fear. And that was something Tatyana understood.

If this man was what he said he was, it would change everything. He was a key figure, not just in Petrel, but in the entire Oppenheimer Project. Getting the information he possessed would be a game-changer.

"Tell me," Tatyana said, "you had a daughter."

"Natasha," the man said cautiously.

Tatyana remembered the child. A beautiful girl. She'd been five or six at the time and had an illness. Something rare, something complicated. "How is she doing?"

"She's fine," the man said.

"What is she now? Eight?"

"Nine."

"Of course. Nine."

The man said nothing.

"They grow up so quickly, don't they?"

Silence filled the line. Tatyana waited five, then ten seconds. At last, as if confessing a mortal sin, the man said, "I brought her with me."

"Brought her with you?"

"To London."

"You're in England?"

"I left Russia. Fled."

Tatyana tapped the driver on the shoulder and made a

circling gesture with her finger, telling him to take her back to the hotel. This was real. She could feel it down to her bones. This guy was defecting, and he would bring with him an information cache that could alter the trajectory of President Molotov's entire armaments agenda.

"I need to ask you," Tatyana said, "if you do this, your life will never be the same again. Anyone you love, anyone you've left behind in Russia...."

"There's no one. Just me and Natasha."

"They'll hunt you down. They'll hunt her down."

"We have no choice," he said. "The die is cast. We can't go back. It's too late for that."

9

Lance woke early. He lit a cigarette and went to the kitchen to make coffee. There was a french press in one of the cupboards, but no coffee to go in it. There was no food of any kind in the apartment.

He took a quick shower and dressed, then let himself out of the apartment, locking the door behind him. In the corridor, he spent a few seconds looking at the door across the hallway, thinking of the woman.

He saw something on the ground where she'd been sitting the night before and picked it up. It was a cigarette lighter—Dunhill—made of gold.

He knocked lightly on her door, but there was no answer. He put the lighter in his pocket and went to the elevator. When he got outside, it was drizzling lightly. He walked to the nearest grocery store where he bought coffee, milk, cereal, cigarettes, two cans of Campbell's soup.

"Do you sell cigars?" he asked the cashier.

"Nothing I'd recommend," the man said, "but we have some."

"Let me see them," Lance said. They were old, slightly gray-tinged, but he bought four of them.

"You ever heard of the food pyramid?" the cashier said as he bagged Lance's things.

"I'll look into it," Lance said, taking the bag from the counter. As he was leaving, he glanced at the newspaper rack. The headlines were all about a massive explosion over the Arctic Ocean. "How much for this?"

"One pound."

He paid and went back to the apartment. When he reached the door, he took the lighter from his pocket and looked at it again. He tested it. It worked perfectly. He knew what those gold Dunhills were worth. People collected them.

He looked at the woman's door and let out a quiet sigh. Then he knocked.

There was no answer. He knocked again.

Then he heard the clicking and jangling of someone fumbling with the latch and chain. It took a minute but the door eventually opened, cautiously, and from behind it, peering around as if afraid of what she might find, was the face of a little girl.

"Oh," Lance said.

"Yes?" the girl said.

"Is your mom home?"

The girl nodded.

"Can you get her?"

The girl looked up at him almost apologetically. "I'm not supposed to answer the door."

"It's okay," Lance said. "Go tell her that the neighbor is here."

The child went running, and Lance let himself inside.

He was curious—nosy, really. The layout was identical to his but mirrored and facing the opposite side of the building. The sun poured through his windows in the morning. This side of the building was still in shade. It was also full to the point of bursting. Books, magazines, clothes, a television, kid's toys, dirty dishes, ashtrays, everything you could think of that a mother and her kid might think to fill a home.

Lance looked for sign of a man but saw none.

He looked in the kitchen. The sink was full of dirty dishes. Bills, postcards, a few drawings were held to the refrigerator door by colored magnets.

The kid came back from the bedroom and found Lance standing in the kitchen. "She's asleep," she said.

"Mommy's asleep?"

She nodded and walked past the kitchen, planting herself on the sofa in front of the TV. Next to her was a ratty-looking stuffed rabbit.

"Is she in bed by herself?" Lance said.

The girl nodded.

Lance went to the door of the bedroom and peeked in. It was a mess. The woman was asleep, her arm hanging over the side of the bed like a vine. The sheets were in knots, pillows and blankets everywhere, and on the wall behind the bed, a string of Christmas lights hung from the ceiling.

At the foot of the bed, a video camera was set up on a tripod. It pointed at the bed, and on a small table beneath it was a laptop computer. Behind the camera on a second tripod was a ring light.

"Hey," Lance said.

The woman showed no sign of life, and Lance went back to the living room. The kid had turned on the TV.

"How long is she going to sleep like that?" Lance said.

The kid looked at him like he was speaking a foreign language.

"Shouldn't you be going to school?"

"I don't know," the girl said.

"Have you eaten breakfast?"

She shook her head.

Lance's groceries were still by the door, and he went to them.

"Did you know I'm a famous chef?" Lance said.

"No."

"Breakfast is my specialty."

The girl looked skeptical.

"Really," he said.

"You're lying."

"I'm going to prove it to you."

He went into the kitchen and found a can opener. He opened a can of the soup, poured it into a saucepan, and put that on the stove. The girl watched.

"Soup?" she said.

"Tomato soup."

"For breakfast?"

"Why not?"

She walked over to him and took the empty can from the counter, and examined the picture.

"Toast, too?"

"I didn't buy bread."

"We have some."

Lance found the bread in the refrigerator and put two slices into the toaster.

"Butter's in the fridge, too," the kid said.

He looked at her. "You're a smart kid, aren't you?"

She nodded. They ate together.

When they were done, the kid said, "We better clean up."

"Let's not get carried away," Lance said, putting the bowls in the sink. "You be sure to tell your mother I stopped by when she wakes up, all right?"

The girl nodded, and Lance let himself out of the apartment. He still had the lighter.

10

Roth sat facing Tatyana in the passenger compartment of a CIA Gulfstream G550 jet. They'd taken off five hours earlier from Andrews Air Force Base and were about an hour out from London.

Tatyana was asleep, and Roth didn't think he could imagine a more flawless face. She reminded him of a painting that hung in the British Ambassador's residence in Washington. It was a painting by Edmund Leighton of a woman with straight black hair and a strikingly pale face, sitting in the crenellations of a medieval castle, stitching a flag. Roth couldn't imagine Tatyana stitching anything, but the look of composure on her face, the serenity, was enchanting.

There'd been a woman in Roth's life once, decades ago, and everything about Tatyana reminded him of her.

She began to wake, and Roth turned to the window.

"How long was I out?" she said.

"Not long."

He got up and poured two cups of coffee, and brought them back to the table.

"Thank you," she said.

They sat and sipped the coffee, and Roth couldn't help looking up at her repeatedly.

"What is it?" she said.

He shook his head. The truth was, a plan had been forming in his head, a plan that he couldn't tell her about, and it pained him. It pained him because it might cost her life.

That was the thing about war—about being in command. His job, at its core, was to decide who got sent out, who was risked, who might die.

He pushed the thought from his mind and said, "Tell me again how you know this scientist."

"I don't know him," she said, taking another sip of coffee.

"But he trusts you."

"Sort of."

"What does that mean?"

"It's hard to explain."

"Try me."

She sighed and stretched out in her seat. She was looking out the window, and Roth followed her gaze. It was a kingdom of clouds out there, like the scattered islands of an archipelago.

"Playing this game," she began.

"You mean the spy game?" he said.

She nodded. "It's about people. Reading them. Their motives. Their thoughts."

"I'd say that's true," Roth said, "as far as it goes."

"It's like poker. There are players who play the cards, and there are players who play the other players. We're the players who play other players. We watch them. Try to guess what they're going to do. Will they raise the bet? Will they call?"

"Will they fold?"

"Right," she said. "At a certain point, it stops mattering what cards you're holding, and all that really matters is your opponent."

"Identifying who's a friend and who's a threat," Roth said.

She nodded, raised her cup to her lips. The plane passed through some turbulence, and she waited for them to pass before taking a sip. "Living in Russia, our system, our government, it trains you to think in the same way."

"To treat life like a game of poker?"

She looked at him over her cup. Her gaze was electric. It made him feel like a gazelle caught in the eyes of a lioness. "To treat life like a zero-sum game," she said. "A game with winners and losers. You don't have to be a spy in Russia," she said, "or a poker player, to start thinking like that. Ordinary people, just to get through their lives, develop an armor. Especially if they have something to hide."

"And does Sacha Gazinsky have something to hide?" Roth said.

She smiled, an inscrutable, impenetrable smile, and said, "Everyone has something to hide, Roth."

Roth smiled. That was the first thing the CIA taught recruits.

"In Russia," Tatyana said, "people evolve the way species evolve. They become either predator or prey. Those are the only options. You must choose. If you don't choose..." She looked at him and ran a finger across her neck.

"You're dead," Roth said.

She nodded. "Especially if you come within the orbit of the Kremlin."

"Like Sacha has?"

"Exactly," she said. "He's a scientist. He never planned to

enter this world. He set out to be a physicist, not a spy. He's a fish, and he's swimming with the biggest sharks in all of Russia."

"With the sharpest teeth."

"Razor-sharp," she said.

Roth knew she was telling him something important—something about herself, her own life, about who she was and where she'd come from. He was forty years older than her, he'd been an operative in the CIA since before she was born, but her life had given her a training even he could learn from.

"So," he said, "this scientist, he has a gut feeling for you? That's why he contacted you?"

Tatyana shook her head. "I don't think he trusts me, if that's what you're asking. He barely knows who I am."

"But he called you."

She nodded. "He did a calculation. I'm a player at the table. He's a player. The men who are after him are players."

"And this was his best option?"

"He's got to make a play. He can't sit out the hand. The cards have been dealt. I'm not his best option. I'm his only option."

"When you met him," Roth said, "what did you say? Did you ask him for anything? Offer anything?"

"I had nothing to offer. Neither did he. We were two fish in a tank of sharks. I knew it. He knew it. But no one came out and said it. All I did was give him a phone number. A number masked in both directions."

"Without explanation?"

"What explanation could I give? I worked for the GRU. He worked for a top-secret weapons program. Saying something could have gotten us both killed."

"You knew he worked for Project Oppenheimer?"

Tatyana nodded.

"You're certain of that?"

"As certain as I can be," she said. "Project Oppenheimer wasn't something that was ever spelled out to me. Even my bosses in the Main Directorate weren't cleared to know the full picture. It was always hush hush."

"Does five P's mean there are five prototypes?"

"I don't know," she said. "I assumed so, but I don't know for certain. My guess is there are only a handful of men in all of Russia who know for sure what the Five P's really refer to."

"And is Sacha Gazinsky one of them?"

Tatyana shrugged. "I don't know, Roth. What I gave you in the file, that's all I know. When I met him, he was head of a project named Petrel. At that time, I had no idea what Petrel was. I didn't need to know. All I knew was that my boss wanted kompromat on Sacha."

"Was that something the Prime Directorate was aware of?"

"That Igor Aralov was digging for dirt on one of their scientists? I doubt it, but that was par for the course. Igor wanted something on everyone. It didn't matter who it was —Russian, Chinese, American. That was how he exerted influence."

"How did you obtain the kompromat?" Roth said.

Tatyana's eyes flashed. She didn't answer for a moment, she sipped some coffee, then she said, "You know how."

Roth looked out the window. He *did* know how. He wasn't even sure why he'd asked the question.

"Did you get any?"

"Kompromat? Not what I was supposed to get," she said.

"What does that mean?"

"It means he wasn't interested in what I had to offer."

"Really?"

Tatyana shrugged. "Is that so hard to believe?"

"I don't know," Roth said.

"I mean, he slept with me," she said, "but that wasn't enough for Igor. Sacha was a widower. His wife was dead. I needed a lot more than plain sex to get leverage over him."

"Plain sex?"

Tatyana nodded. "Vanilla," she said. "You know?"

Roth cleared his throat. She was trying to embarrass him now, intentionally making him uncomfortable. It was no more than he deserved.

"I see," Roth said. "So you left empty-handed?"

"*Officially*, I did."

"Officially?"

"When I filed my report, I said I found nothing compromising."

"But that wasn't true?"

"It was half true," Tatyana said. "I only spent one night with Sacha. He didn't say much, but from what he did say, I was able to read between the lines."

Roth nodded his head. "And what did he tell you?"

"Well, right off the bat, he suspected I was GRU. The Petrel project was highly classified. He was the lead scientist. He knew he was being watched."

"And he still slept with you?"

"He was attending a conference in Moscow. I came on to him in the bar of his hotel. It wasn't a fancy place, and he's not exactly Brad Pitt. There are places in Moscow where women throw themselves at older men, but this wasn't one of them."

"So he figured you were spying on him?"

She nodded. "I got him to drink too much. I brought him up to my room. There was a camera hidden in the vanity, but, like I said, nothing it captured would have been of any use to Igor. It was just plain sex."

"Vanilla."

"Plainer than vanilla, if that's possible."

"So he's no Casanova?"

"No, he's not. I was supposed to tempt him into doing some compromising things, things he wouldn't have wanted the Prime Directorate to know about."

"What things?"

Tatyana looked at him. "Use your imagination, Roth."

"Sorry."

"I didn't even try to tempt him. He knew what it was. He even told me I didn't have to sleep with him. I could leave if I wanted. He was, I suppose, a gentleman."

"That's nice."

"It was rare, Roth. Especially in Moscow."

"But you didn't leave?"

"I was going to, but we ended up talking. He told me about his daughter. She was sick, which was no secret, but he mentioned that it was a very rare genetic condition. He was scared for her. I could see it on his face."

"So that was it? That was what told you he was looking for a way out."

"It gave me an inkling. I mean, he was well looked after by the Prime Directorate. All the scientists were. Very good salaries. The best medical care for their families. His daughter was being treated at the best pediatric hospital in the country. She really was receiving good care. And Sacha himself was on track to receive a massive financial bonus when Petrel delivered. No one would ever think he had a reason to flee the country."

"But you had a feeling?"

"His situation wasn't so different to mine," she said. "I

was also well paid by the state. They wanted to keep me. I had an unlimited expense account. I could buy anything I wanted. But despite all that, and I don't know if I'd even admitted this to myself yet, on some level, I knew I had to get out. Moscow would chew me up if I stayed. And that was what I saw in him. That same fear. That same knowledge. Like we knew that we were in the dining room of the Titanic. Everything looked perfect. Chandeliers on the ceiling. Candles. Silverware. An orchestra playing. But the rats were fleeing."

"Well," Roth said, "your instincts were right. Here he is. And I'll tell you this, whatever he's selling, we want it. No price is too high. If he has high-level knowledge of the Five P's, or even just of Petrel, we need that information."

Despite years of intense effort and the full commitment of the CIA, the NSA, and the Defense Intelligence Agency, the United States remained essentially blind about the new doomsday weapons being developed by the Kremlin. They knew startlingly little for such an ambitious project, and that terrified people. The President had requested it be placed on the absolute top priority level, and every morning, Sandra Shrader, Elliot Schlesinger, and Frederick Winnefeld received a classified memo headed Project Oppenheimer. It was sent every day from Langley, a physical document in a sealed envelope, couriered by armed CIA agents. And every night, Roth approved the content. Always the same.

No new intelligence.

Sandra had directed the enormously powerful Mission

Data Repository in Salt Lake City, Utah to tracking global references to the Five P's. Literally exabytes had been gathered, more data than the nation's largest technology companies were capable of storing, and still, what they knew of Oppenheimer could be summed up in a few pages. Considering that the project posed an existential threat, that was an untenable situation. Roth had to get inside it. There was no price he wouldn't pay to bring in Sacha safely. And there was no risk he would not accept.

Sacha Gazinsky had to be brought in, but Tatyana Aleksandrova couldn't be the one who did it. She was the best person for the job, there was no doubt about that. Sacha was her contact. He'd reached out to her. They'd slept together. If he trusted anyone, it was her.

But the situation, as always, was more complex than that. Roth couldn't put all his eggs in this one basket. He had another plan for getting inside the Kremlin, and it was something he'd been working on for a very long time. It had really been thirty years in the making, and Tatyana was the key to making it happen. If it worked, he would have a mole at the very heart of the Kremlin. It would change everything.

But it wouldn't come cheap. To pull it off, he needed to buy the trust of those he wished to infiltrate, and that price was Tatyana.

Looking at her now, thinking of all the ways she'd proved her loyalty, the risks she'd taken, the sacrifices made, he hated himself. The thought of what had to be done made him sick to his stomach. He was going to commit the one truly unforgivable sin in the espionage game. He was going to sell out a friend.

But what choice did he have? Russia was working on doomsday weapons that, with every passing minute, grew closer to deployment. And what Roth knew, what he knew perhaps better than anyone else on the planet other than the Russian President, was that the world was slipping inexorably toward war. Humanity was slouching toward its own annihilation. The next Great War would not be like the ones that came before. It would be a conflagration of truly biblical proportions, a war that could not be won.

For it would not be survived.

If there was something he could do to steer the world from that outcome, he had to do it. If that meant slaughtering an innocent, so be it. Lambs had been sacrificed to the gods for centuries. Levi Roth would not be the prophet that failed to make that sacrifice.

Moscow could not get into a position where it believed there was something to be gained from war. That could not happen. Not on Levi Roth's watch.

Tatyana was looking at him, sipping her coffee, analyzing. She had the finely-honed instincts of a predator, she was a trained professional, and Roth knew just by the look in her eye that she already suspected something was amiss.

He needed to distract her. She would not like what he was about to say, and he could use that anger to blunt her judgment. He'd made up his mind. He was going to sell her out. He was going to put her life in the balance. But there was something he could do that would give her a fighting chance.

If she was in London, that would make her a field agent. When the Russians found out where she was, they would immediately order her killed.

However, if she was in Washington, working behind the scenes with Laurel, that would make her a potential asset. On the delicate scales of the GRU's bureaucrats, it would give her life weight. It would make her valuable. And that fact alone might just be enough to save her.

Roth cleared his throat and readied himself for the exchange that would follow. It would be a fight. He took a breath and said, "Of course, there's always the risk this is all some intricate trap."

Tatyana's eyes narrowed. "This is no trap."

Roth chose his words carefully, "Your instincts are telling you this guy is legit."

"This is not just my gut, Levi."

"I know."

"Look at the facts," she said. "Look at the timing. The explosion. They're still pulling bodies from the wreckage. They've got soldiers in hazmat suits evacuating villages. They just let off an unintentional nuclear detonation. If Sacha Gazinsky was ever going to run, this is the moment."

"I know that."

"And he brought his daughter, Levi. Do you really think he would bring her with him if this were some sort of ploy?"

"No, of course not."

"All this, just to get to me? To catch one defector?" She shook her head. "No way."

Roth let out a long sigh. He knew his words wouldn't ring true, but it was the best he could come up with. "There are other types of trap, Tatyana. Maybe he doesn't know what he's a part of. Maybe he's being used."

She was getting angry. He'd just blindsided her with this. She had no idea where it was coming from or why.

"I just want to make sure we're taking every precaution," he said. "I've seen how vindictive the GRU can be. There's no end to what they'll do if they catch you."

"*You're* telling *me* that?" she said. "That's rich."

"Maybe it is, but I'm the one who makes the calls, and I

don't want you in London. Someone else will bring in Sacha."

"Levi, are you out of your mind?"

"That's final."

"If I'm not bringing in Sacha, then why the hell did you bring me on this flight?"

"I wanted..."

The truth was, he'd been selfish. He'd wanted this last clutch of time with her. He'd wanted to say goodbye. She didn't know what this time meant to him. But for him, the pain of it, of knowing what he was going to do, was very real.

"You wanted *what*?" she said, her voice rising with every word she uttered.

"I don't want you in London," he said, "You've got to trust me on this."

Her eyes were so narrow she was squinting. She was measuring him up, his words, his motives. She smelled a rat. She just didn't know where to find it. "What do you *know*, Roth? What are you hiding?"

What he was about to say would anger her, it would hurt her, she would take it personally. But if it kept her alive, if it helped her survive the next few days, it would be worth it. "The truth is, I'm worried about your performance, Tatyana. You've been letting your guard down. You're getting sloppy."

Her eyes flashed like lightning. She knew what he was referring to.

"You've been watching me," she said. "Following me."

"Of course I've been watching you. And you've been taking risks."

"What sort of risks? Leaving the hotel? I'm twenty-nine years old, Roth. I'm not going to spend the rest of my life hiding."

"You gave up your right to a normal life a long time ago."

"Did I? Did I give up my right to sex, too? Is that what's bothering you? My taste in men?"

"You know that's not what this is."

"You sad little man."

"Tatyana!"

"Tell me this," she said. "How are you any different from my bosses at the Main Directorate? You want to use me when you need me, and you want to lock me up in a box when you're done with me."

Roth said nothing. The truth was worse than she knew. The GRU prostituted her. They sent her naked after some of the most dangerous men on the planet. But Roth was going to hang her out to dry. He was going to let them come and kill her. And he was going to tell them exactly how to get to her.

"You know," she said, "I thought things would be different on this side."

She took a deep breath. She was worked up. There was some coffee left in her cup, and she drained it and slammed it on the table. Then she composed herself. Calmed down. Her head was moving slowly from left to right as if she still couldn't believe what he was doing, but she was calm.

Roth didn't know if she was scarier now or before.

She wasn't just angry at him. She was angry at herself. She'd known she was breaking protocol when she went out at night. That made her conflicted, which made it easier for Roth to deceive her.

The pilot announced that they were on their final approach. They put on their seat belts, and Roth said, "When you get back to Washington, take every precaution. Watch your back. Don't let your guard down. Sleep with one eye open."

She narrowed her eyes and fixed him in her gaze. "You know something," she said.

"No, I don't."

"What have you heard, Roth? Why are you holding back?"

"I'm not," he said. "I just want you to be careful. We know they're hunting you."

"Sacha Gazinsky's my contact. I brought him to you."

"I know, Tatyana."

She shook her head in that way only a woman could. Such scorn in her expression. Such contempt.

"You're going to lose him."

11

R oth stepped onto the tarmac at Farnborough Airport in London and looked back at the plane. Tatyana was standing at the top of the steps, lighting a cigarette.

"I'm sorry," he said.

She looked down at him with an intensity that left no doubt as to her feelings and said, "Don't lose him, Roth."

"I won't."

"He's going to be very scared."

Roth nodded.

"He came here because of me," she said. "He's expecting me. One wrong move, and he'll spook."

"I know."

"If anything happens to him...."

"I know, Tatyana."

"Or his daughter."

Roth didn't know what to say. Tatyana herself might not see this through. "I know what I'm doing," he said, turning toward the car. "I'll bring him in."

The car had been sent by the embassy, a Mercedes S-

Class sedan, black, with tinted windows and civilian plates. The driver wore a navy business suit. Roth shivered as he climbed into the back seat, then said, "We're going to Blackfriars. The Old Hamlet."

The car pulled away, and Roth resisted the temptation to look back at the plane. It joined the M3 motorway, which was slow in the heavy morning traffic, and Roth leaned back and shut his eyes. He tried to relax but couldn't. The fight with Tatyana had rattled him. There'd been a time when he would not have considered selling out one of his own. Those days were gone.

He fiddled with the heat controls in front of him and couldn't get it to work. "Damn thing," he muttered.

"You cold, sir?"

"Freezing."

He was wearing a black Burberry trench, and he pulled up the collar. London had a habit of making him feel this way. He hated being there. The weather was part of it, the city had a dampness that seemed to seep into his bones, but there was something else. Something personal. Memories. Too many of them.

London had been Roth's first field assignment, decades earlier, back when the superpowers were closer to all-out nuclear war than they'd ever been. In some ways, it was a time of promise, of optimism. It was the late eighties, the Cold War was waning, and the Soviet Union was on the brink of collapse. Everyone knew it. People in the street knew it. The mood was pregnant with what was possible— what the future might hold. A free Europe. An era of cooperation and friendship. Peace in our time.

Bottles of champagne were opened by the caseload. The ambassador in London hosted so many celebratory dinners that the State Department sent a financial auditor to find out how one embassy could go through thirty-two cases of Amontillado Sherry and twenty-four of Graham's Port in a single month.

In Berlin, people took to the streets, and they took their sledgehammers with them. The wall came down, the iron curtain was opened, and every radio station in the world was playing the same song—*Wind of Change*.

That was all a part of history now. Fate had its own plans. For a brief moment, a younger, more naive Levi Roth had thought the world might actually change. He'd actually allowed himself to believe such a thing was possible.

He'd been mistaken, and that mistake had cost him dearly. There were not many left in the agency from those days, and of those that were, few remembered the immense personal sacrifices that were made in those heady years of flux. The Soviet Union had ended, to borrow the words of Roth's favorite poet, not with a bang but a whimper. The most ruinous war in all of history had been averted. The Cold War never climaxed.

But there had been casualties. Roth had tasted their bitterness, and so had the man he was on his way to meet, the CIA's London station chief, Richmond Tenet.

Forty years ago, when Roth first arrived in London, it had been Tenet who made first contact. He wasn't station chief then, of course. He was out of the academy just a year ahead of Roth, and handling Roth was his first real assignment. The asset Roth brought in for him became the stuff of agency legend, the very backbone of both men's careers, and, to this day, the single highest-ranking member of the Russian security apparatus to defect to the CIA.

At that time, the agency officially operated out of the embassy on Grosvenor Square, but because of Roth's deep cover, he and Tenet couldn't meet there. Tenet sent him instead to a dingy, four-hundred-year-old pub in Blackfriars called the Old Hamlet. Purportedly, its medieval façade, with enormous half-timbers visible through wattle and daub plaster, had only narrowly escaped the Great Fire of 1666.

Roth still remembered his first time seeing it.

Its situation, with only one entrance at the end of a long cobbled alley too narrow for vehicles, made it extremely easy to monitor. It offered privacy, discretion, and no small share of conviviality, and became the regular meeting place for Roth and Tenet during those years.

The assignment was top priority, and the only person in the CIA other than Tenet to know Roth's identity was the director himself in Langley. London oversight was bypassed entirely, and the mission was assigned to Roth and Tenet precisely because they were so new to the agency. They were untainted, unknown to the Russians, untampered with by anyone, friend or foe.

The director could trust them.

And that trust became the difference between life and death. The informant they handled, with Roth doing the face-to-face and Tenet liaising back to Langley, was no ordinary double agent. He was the highest-ranking Soviet spy in London at that time—the *Rezident,* as they called him, and the most respected overseas operative in all of the KGB. His name was Gregor Gorky, and the information he passed on to Roth and Tenet was the most sensitive and arguably the most valuable that US intelligence services had ever received. It encompassed not only Soviet troop dispositions but the attitudes and intentions of their commanders, the schematics and vulnerabilities of new weapons systems, even the methods of decryption for codes in use by the KGB, the Politburo, and the Soviet Strategic Missile Force.

Gorky gave the CIA director, and through him, the US President, a clear window into the mind of the Russian leadership. There was no way of fathoming the value of that insight. At the time, the Soviet system had already begun to unravel. At any moment, the tension and instability, the atmosphere of intense paranoia inside the Kremlin as well as the White House, could have led to disaster.

Both sides saw threats everywhere. They were investing at unprecedented levels not only in nuclear weapons but also biological, chemical, and radiological weapons that threatened to wipe out all life on the planet. Insects were being developed that could cause famines. NATO and the Kremlin were both considering the pros and cons of launching preemptive nuclear strikes against the other side.

Tensions were ratcheted so high that one misinterpreted troop movement, one misconstrued word, one stray spy plane, one shadow, one specter, one rumor could have led to a war the human race would not survive.

In the corridors of power, among those who knew it had ever happened, the information shepherded by Roth and Tenet from Gregor Gorky, and the information purposefully fed back to the Kremlin through him, was credited with having allowed the West to navigate the minefield of Soviet collapse without so much as a single shot being fired.

But there'd been a personal cost. There'd been a woman —the only woman Levi Roth had ever loved. She was a Mossad agent, she had porcelain-white skin and pitch-black features, and her name was Alona Almagor.

12

L ance stood at the window, a mug of coffee in his hand, and looked down at the street below. It was raining again, and the traffic ebbed from one stoplight to the next like water being released from sluice gates.

No one knew where he was. No one even knew he was alive—not the CIA, not Levi Roth, not Laurel. He was in self-imposed exile, and it could last as long as he wanted. If he chose, he could disappear completely, and it could be forever.

A new man could be born in his place, with a new date of birth and nationality—a man with no past, no family, no friends.

He was almost tempted, except he knew life didn't work that way. He was past the point of fresh starts. The dice had been rolled too many times. Too much blood had been spilled.

He knew who he was—what he was—and no matter how many lies he told himself, his soul would not forget that truth. He was a predator. He was a killer. It was written and could not be changed. A wolf hunted. There was no logic to it. No reason.

He opened the door and stepped out onto the balcony. There really were only two choices for a man. Admit what he was, embrace it, or end his life. He looked out over the edge of the balcony and imagined what it would feel like to jump. He reached out over the edge and poured some coffee. He wondered. To feel the building slip away behind him, to feel the air rushing upward like a gale, and then for darkness and an interminable silence to reach up and snatch him down to its depths.

A rap on the door yanked him from his thoughts.

"Hey," someone said. "Open up right now. I know you're in there."

It was the woman, his neighbor, his one friend in the world.

He walked to the door, reaching for his gun as he passed the counter, and placing it in a drawer.

"Hold on," he said as he unlocked the door.

The moment he opened it, the woman said, "Were you inside my apartment?"

Lance raised his hands in a gesture of surrender. "Hey, I was just...."

"Were you messing with my kid?"

"What? No."

"Is that what it was?"

"Hold on a second," Lance said. "I heated up a can of soup. That's all I did."

He'd known entering her home was a violation of her privacy, he knew it was unacceptable, but he'd had his reasons. She'd come to his door first. She'd made contact with him. He had to make sure she was what she said she was.

"How do I know what you did?"

"What are you talking about? What do you think I did?"

He knew what she thought. The question on his mind was what must have happened in her past that her mind went to that place so directly.

"I don't know," she said, and her eyes filled with tears as she realized he wasn't fighting back. "How would I know. I was…"

"Unconscious."

"Asleep," she said.

He knew she'd knocked herself out with something. Maybe a bottle of wine, maybe a couple of pills. There was no way she'd have slept through his visit otherwise.

The kid wasn't with her now, and he wondered if she could hear them from inside the other apartment.

"Look," Lance said, "I'm sorry. I shouldn't have come in without permission."

"You're damn right you shouldn't."

"But I have to ask this."

"Ask what?" she said, suddenly defensive.

"Tell me you never put her in front of that video camera."

She looked at him, her mind taking an instant to process what he'd just said, then she slapped him hard across the face.

"That's no business of yours," she said.

He nodded. He could see that he'd hit a nerve. Something wasn't right. Something about her situation, about her life, was putting the daughter in danger, and she knew it. He could read it on her face.

He clenched his jaw and said what he had to say next. "I'm making it my business." He knew she wouldn't like it, he knew this wasn't fair to her, but there was nothing he could do about that. He'd seen enough to see this for what it was. And what it was, was a plea for help. Knocking on his door at night, coming here now, he'd thought she'd wanted sex. Now he saw that it was something else that she was looking for.

"What did you say?"

"I said I'm making it my business."

She put both her hands on his chest and shoved him back into the apartment. "You're *making* it your business? What's that supposed to mean? Is that supposed to scare me?"

"Tell me she's never been in front of that camera," Lance said again.

The woman started crying. "You're serious? You're actually asking me that?"

"I'm asking you that."

"Of course she hasn't been in front of the camera. She's five years old. I would die before that happened."

"What is it then?" he said.

"What do you mean, what is it?"

"What are you afraid of? Why are you here?"

"I'm here because you came into my apartment while I was asleep and were alone with her."

"She sleeps in your bed," Lance said. "I know she does because it was the only bed in the place."

"The camera's off when we sleep. What kind of mother do you think I am?"

"I don't know what kind of mother you are."

"I lock the door when the camera's on, okay? She watches TV. She doesn't know anything about it."

"What about school? It's a school day today?"

The woman stepped back from him.

"Go fuck yourself," she said. She pulled the door, slamming it shut, and Lance stood there, looking at it. A few seconds passed, and then she knocked again. He opened the door.

"You found it, didn't you?"

"Found what?"

"My lighter."

He took it from his pocket and handed it to her. The way she held it, she was almost cradling it. "Thank you," she said.

He nodded.

"This lighter," she said. "It belonged to my mother."

13

The car arrived at the Old Hamlet, and Roth put on a pair of dark sunglasses. The high collar of his coat was raised above his chin, and he pulled a gray cashmere scarf up over his mouth. When he looked up at the intricate building, he was hit by a pang of nostalgia. Its very existence, like his own, was something it seemed all of history had conspired against. And yet, the Great Fire, the Blitz of the Second World War, even the frenetic development of London's financial center all failed to leave their mark. This old pub remained standing as it ever had against the odds.

To Roth, it was a symbol of resilience—a lone tree standing in a field of ash after a fire. If it ever failed to be there, if he ever walked down the narrow, cobbled alley and found in its place a shiny new office tower, he would take it as a sign that his own time had come also.

This was the place his career had begun. It was the place he'd been formed as a man and a spy, the place he'd first met Tenet, and also Alona. In those years, it had been the one place they'd felt safe, unwatched. Roth let his guard down there. It was off-limits, beyond the bounds of the interminable battle raging between the great powers.

Roth entered the bar, and the scent of old leather, wood polish, and strong ale instantly brought him back. The passing of decades had changed nothing—not with the place, not with himself. Roth had put the CIA above everything else in his life, and this was the place where he'd made that decision. No close connections. No chinks in the armor. No weaknesses. It was here he'd turned away the one woman he'd ever loved. And it would be here, today, that he betrayed Tatyana Aleksandrova.

The bartender, a two-hundred-fifty-pound, six-foot-six, giant of a man named Harry Staples, was standing behind a row of beer taps, in the same spot, with virtually the same expression on his face, as Roth had seen forty years earlier when he'd first walked in.

"Well, well, well," the bartender said when he saw Roth, "look what the cat's dragged in."

"Harry Staples," Roth said, walking up to the bar. "I see the years have not been kind to you."

A grin crossed Harry's face. He reached across the bar and gripped Roth's hand and forearm in both of his. "Good to see you, old pal."

Roth smiled. "I wish I could say the same."

Harry shook his head. "You should be a comedian."

It had been a few years since they'd seen each other, though not forty. Roth and Tenet met at the Old Hamlet periodically, sometimes for old time's sake, sometimes because the nature of their business prevented them from meeting at the embassy. It was a place no one had ever infiltrated. Even now, as director, Roth could walk in and meet his London station chief without fear of being observed.

"It's been too long," Roth said.

If there was anyone in the world who had seen the arc of Roth's life, it was perhaps, more than anyone else, this bartender. He'd seen all of it, the decisions, the sacrifices, the mistakes.

Roth valued Harry's discretion above all else. He had a bartender's knack for knowing what to say and, more importantly, what not to say. He gave Roth and Tenet their privacy. After forty years, that more than anything was the luxury the Old Hamlet afforded.

"You're meeting your pal, aren't you?" Harry said.

Roth nodded.

"The usual booth, then?"

"Usual booth, usual drink," Roth said, following Harry to a table at the back of the bar. The booth was on its own. Its occupants couldn't be listened in on. It had a view of the bar while itself being hidden from every angle but head-on. Above it, a single, low-watt bulb hung from the ceiling in a metal shade. When Roth and Tenet sat there, one of them always reached up and unscrewed it. Roth did that now, as Harry fetched him a pint of strong, amber ale.

Roth took a long sip and nodded his approval. "That's the stuff," he said.

Harry gave him a slap on the arm, almost strong enough to make him spill the drink, and said, "Good man."

There were no other customers in the bar, it might not even have been open for the day yet, but Harry had plenty to keep him busy. He did his job diligently, took no shortcuts. He was about sixty, Cockney, and spoke that strange aberration that saw some Londoners replace perfectly ordinary words with utterly unrelated ones. He'd once told Roth his bill for a drink was a *Lady Godiva*, which someone had to explain to Roth translated to five pounds.

Roth sipped his beer, watched Harry work, and kept an

eye on the door. He looked at his watch a few times. This was his first meeting with Tenet since being made director. He'd started his career as the junior. Now he was the boss.

When Tenet entered, a cold gust accompanied him. He looked toward the booth and saw Roth already there. Roth got to his feet.

"Tenet," he said and thought his greeting sounded oddly formal.

"Don't get up on my account," Tenet said, sliding into the booth.

The two men looked at each other for a moment. There was much that remained unsaid between them. Forty years was a long time. A lot had happened.

Tenet broke the silence. "I think congratulations are in order."

Roth smiled awkwardly.

Tenet turned to the bar. "Harry," he said, "your finest Scotch. None of the cheap stuff. My friend here looks like he could use a little loosening up."

Roth began to protest, but it was too late. Harry brought two crystal glasses and a green bottle that looked like it belonged in a maritime museum.

"This will warm your cockles," he said, placing the bottle on the table and removing Roth's empty pint glass. "I'll let you serve yourselves."

The bottle was half-full, stopped with a cork, and Tenet opened it and poured two generous measures of the viscous liquid. An aroma of peat smoke and what could only be described as iodine overwhelmed Roth's senses.

He raised his glass and took a deep quaff. Tenet did the same and exhaled enthusiastically. "Good stuff," he said.

Roth nodded.

Tenet took another sip, and Roth watched him. The

moment's silence created a sense of suspense. Roth had called the meeting, and it was clear that something important needed to be said. He wondered if Tenet had guessed what it was.

Roth cleared his throat. "The time's come," he said.

Tenet held his eye. He was going to say something but instead picked up the bottle. He'd drained his glass and refilled it.

Roth watched him, analyzing his reaction, gauging him. When Tenet spoke, his words came almost as a surprise. He said simply, "You're sure?"

No resistance. No argument. Always the consummate professional.

Roth admired that, the stoicism. He knew what he was asking, and he knew that no matter what face Tenet put on it, there was pain in this decision for him. To say goodbye to one's family, one's country, to everything he'd ever known and held dear, that took a toll. This was a one-way ticket—a journey from which he would not return.

It reminded Roth of a conversation he'd had once with someone else at that very same booth almost forty years earlier. That time, it had been Alona sitting across from him and Roth who was paying the toll.

"Levi," she'd said, "You're making the biggest mistake of your life. The day will come when you regret this."

It wasn't a threat. She spoke with tears in her eyes. Her heart was breaking, crumbling, slipping away from him forever like so much sand between his fingers. She'd been so beautiful that day. He could hardly bear to think of it. Her skin, so pale it seemed almost translucent, and the darkness of her eyes, smoldering, like soot. There'd been such anger in those eyes, a glint of fierce light, and tears Roth had remembered for four decades.

"I love you," she whispered.

Roth shook his head, almost imperceptibly.

"I choose you," she said.

"You'll find..." he said and then stopped himself.

She grew angry then. "I'll find what? Someone else? How can you say that to me? I love you, Levi. Only you."

Roth couldn't speak. His voice refused to make a sound.

She looked at him and said, "How can you do this?" Tears fell over her cheeks and landed on the table. "How can you throw this away?"

He saw it in her face. She literally couldn't believe what he was doing, the decision he was making.

"Alona," he'd said, his voice a harsh rasp. "I can't...."

"Don't tell me you can't."

"You know I have to do this."

She only shook her head. "Are you mad, Levi? Are you insane?"

"We can still..." he began but stopped. The words were hollow, ash before they even left his mouth.

"I would have loved you so dearly," she said, "for the rest of my life. You would have been everything to me."

He knew she was speaking the truth.

"Do you know how rare that is? How precious?"

He was making a mistake that would define his entire life, he knew it even then, but that knowledge didn't stop him. He was young, idealistic, fanatical even. He'd seen how love could be used against a man. How it could make him vulnerable. Sooner or later, if he said yes to her, someone would use it against him. He could not let that happen. Would not.

He leaned back in his seat and let out a long sigh. Those words, those emotions, had all been exchanged at that very same booth, the same wooden table beneath his hands, the same metal shade above his head, and the same bartender looking on from across the room.

That was the strange thing about a man's life—something Roth had come to realize as he grew older. There was a pattern to it, a strange symmetry, a resonance. Some men died in the same hospital they were born in. Some men met their second wife at their first wedding. And Levi Roth and Richmond Tenet would each give up the same woman, a woman they both loved, sitting at that same booth in that same bar.

Roth forty years ago. Tenet today.

"I suppose we're not getting any younger," Tenet said.

"No," Roth said. "We're not."

"And Igor Aralov is dead."

Roth nodded. That was crucial.

Tenet let out a sigh. "It's now or never, then."

"You're sure you're ready," Roth said. "I wouldn't judge...."

"I'm ready, Levi."

"You don't have to...."

"I know what I'm agreeing to, Levi."

Roth cleared his throat. What he was about to say would cross a line. It would bring him out onto the ice. Certain subjects were off-limits, but he owed Tenet this one last chance to reconsider. It was a chance Roth had never been given himself.

"You'll never see her again," he said, holding Tenet's eye.

Tenet drained his glass. Roth did the same and refilled both.

"She'll hate you," Roth added. "She'll curse your name."

Roth and Alona had always kept their relationship secret, even from Tenet. They had no choice. There was no way it would have been permitted, not as long as she was a Mossad agent.

What Roth still didn't know, even now, was how much Tenet had been able to piece together for himself. And if he hadn't read between the lines then, how much Alona might have told him in the years since? Alona and Tenet had been married almost four decades now. It was hard to keep a secret that long, even for a spy.

Tenet took another sip, then said, "I know that, Levi."

"And that's a price you're willing to pay?"

Tenet nodded.

"You're sure?" Roth insisted.

Tenet looked at him a minute, choosing his words, then said, "We're slipping toward war, aren't we?"

Roth looked toward the bar. Harry was well out of earshot, the bar was empty, but Roth lowered his voice anyway. "Yes, we are."

"And there's nothing we can do to forestall it?"

Roth shook his head. "Maybe if Aralov was still alive," he said. "But even then..." He shrugged. "This is a clock that's been ticking a long time. It's got to run out eventually."

Tenet nodded. "That's what I thought."

Roth sighed. They both knew what this meant. They were going to put into action a plan they'd been hatching for over thirty years, something they'd been laying the foundation of ever since Gregor Gorky was captured by the KGB and killed. They were going to plant Tenet inside the Kremlin. Not immediately, not all at once, but their next steps would put in motion a course of events that could not be reversed.

Tenet had been playing the role of double agent for years, feeding an unwitting handler at the Main Directorate tidbits of information that he and Roth carefully worked out in advance. His handler was Igor Aralov, the same man who had operated Tatyana Aleksandrova before she put a bullet in his skull. Naturally, he'd been wary of Tenet's information for a long time, but Tenet and Roth were patient, they were skillful, and in the end, pulled off their part flawlessly. They started with details and pieces of information that would barely register as valuable but which always turned out to be true. They built trust slowly over the course of years. It took time, but it worked. Tenet became Aralov's best-kept secret, a resource he used skillfully to advance his own career and eventually rise up from the very bowels of the GRU to the heights of the Main Directorate. The key to Aralov's ascent, the weapon he'd developed to outwit his opponents and superiors alike, was keeping Tenet to himself. He buried Tenet's identity so deep in his files that no one would ever find him.

Igor wanted his successes to appear the result of cunning and instinct. He wanted to be known for his trade-craft, honed over years of practice, and for his iron will. If his superiors saw in him a willingness to do what others would not, and if he had a string of successes to back it up, his ascent was assured.

He understood that if anyone ever found out his successes were based on a single source inside the CIA's London office, the illusion would be broken in an instant.

He went to extraordinary lengths to keep his source secret. Any time he sought to rely on intel provided by Tenet, he took pains to ensure he had an alternative explanation for where it had come from. If he couldn't come up with a plausible alternative, he didn't use the information. He was disciplined. He made sure there was no financial trail between him and Tenet. He paid by wire only from secret funds, dark accounts, that he'd amassed without the knowledge of his superiors. It was money no one knew he had—he could have kept it—it was, in essence, his own money. The fact that he sent so much of it to Tenet showed the value he placed on his information, and how jealously he would guard it. Igor had even killed members of his own staff who came too close to the truth.

None of this had been fully foreseen by Roth. He hadn't predicted a handler who would stake his entire career on keeping Tenet a secret from his own bosses. It was a ballsy move by Igor and had caused Roth and Tenet to rethink their plan. It had delayed their objective but had also afforded them certain benefits.

For one thing, it meant no one in Moscow other than Igor ever knew of Tenet's existence. With Roth being the only person in Washington to know, it meant Tenet's identity was essentially bulletproof. There was no one to spill the beans, no one to let slip that the CIA had a problem in its London office, and so, no one to interfere with the plan.

That gave Roth the time he needed, decades, in fact, to perfect his plan. And with that much time, there was nothing he couldn't dream up. He fed information to Igor the way a wife might feed poison to a cheating husband, doing it so piecemeal, taking such an excruciatingly long time that no one ever saw it coming. And gradually, Roth realized the immensity of the influence he'd gained.

Tenet, for his part, did everything asked of him and more. He did the unsavory things that guaranteed that when the investigators and lawyers came pouring in later, everything they found would only confirm his status as a traitor. He wasted money. He racked up secret gambling debts. He cultivated some of the skeletons in his closet that would be expected of a man selling out his own country, including the purchase of certain illegal forms of pornography that would make him highly susceptible to blackmail. And he did so without his own wife, or any oversight agency within the CIA, ever suspecting a thing.

As Tenet rose through the ranks of the CIA, and as Igor climbed to the very top of the Main Directorate, Roth's ability to influence the Kremlin only grew. In Moscow, Igor began to be treated as someone whose word, whose hunches and theories, even if he refused to divulge their source, was gold-plated—beyond reproach.

Everything Roth fed him, President Molotov swallowed without question. As a result, Roth had been able to move the Kremlin in directions it never even suspected. He made Molotov believe US forces in Syria, Iraq, and Afghanistan were far stronger than they had been during periods of vulnerability. Whole offensives were canceled as a result. He also convinced him that US submarines outside the Russian naval facility at Tartus in Syria were ready to fire on supply vessels. Molotov stopped all deliveries to the base, and as a result, Bashar al-Assad was forced to cancel a massive offensive against US ground forces in the east of the country. Had the offensive gone ahead, Assad's army would have overwhelmed the two-hundred soldiers from the First Infantry Division that were guarding the oil fields there. Roth had convinced Molotov to back down from countless aggressive actions in the Crimea and Donets Basin based on threats of US retaliation that existed nowhere but in Roth's imagination.

It was a powerful tool at Roth's disposal, and increasingly vital given President Montgomery's reluctance to stand up to Molotov and draw a hard line. By making Molotov believe in ghosts and chimeras, Roth could make him hesitate. He could make him second guess his most aggressive impulses. He could amplify his fears and reinforce them.

It was power, but it only went so far. Roth could only use it when he knew exactly what Molotov was planning to do.

If Roth could get inside Molotov's head, if he could know exactly what he wanted at all times and how far he was willing to go to get it, that would open a whole new world of possibilities. Armed with that knowledge, Roth was certain he would be able to lead Molotov down a path of delusion and self-destruction that would draw him into devastating missteps, leading not only to his complete downfall, but the utter demise of his entire regime.

That was the plan in any case, but it required taking his operation with Tenet to a whole new level. It required placing Tenet inside the Kremlin.

And that was something that now suddenly seemed possible. For years, Igor had kept Tenet to himself. That had afforded Tenet a degree of protection, but it also meant Roth could never take the plan to its next stage.

Now, Tatyana had not only killed Igor, but had also given Roth a whole new level of insight into Igor's inner workings, his methods, his thinking, and his deepest secrets. She'd worked closely with him for years, and in that time, developed the suspicion that he had a secret source, deep within the CIA, that he would do anything to protect. Igor's secretary kept a file on the source, but Tatyana had never been able to access it. She did, however, know the name of the file.

It was Gray Coat.

Roth still remembered the look on her face when she told him. She knew it was important. She'd revealed it with a flourish, like a magician uncovering a rabbit, and Roth had wanted to reach across the table and kiss her.

According to Tatyana, Gray Coat was Igor's most precious treasure, and now that he was dead, there would be no one to claim him. As a matter of course, responsibility for the file would be transferred to Igor's replacement, an unimpressive career-man in the Main Directorate named Viktor Lapin. But Igor had taken such pains to cover his steps that Viktor would never find the file. He wouldn't even know Gray Coat existed.

Tatyana was adamant on that point. "Igor wasn't generous," she said. "He didn't care about the big picture. He certainly didn't give a damn about his successor. Why would he? Anyone taking over Gray Coat would mess it up. Igor knew that. They would use the information in such a way that the CIA would be immediately tipped off. Then, they would find their rat, and everyone would know the secret to Igor's success."

"So this Viktor," Roth had said, "he'll have no idea what he's sitting on?"

"Believe me," Tatyana said, "Igor Aralov will have left no instructions for Viktor. If you want to keep Gray Coat alive, you're going to have to lead Viktor to him yourself."

It was very risky, it would be putting Tenet's life on a knife-edge, but every time Roth thought about it, his heart pounded like a galloping horse. He had no choice. The stakes were simply too high.

Roth knew in the very core of his being that if he did not stop Molotov, sooner or later, their two nations would come to war. It was inevitable. Molotov was hell-bent on taking the world down that path. Stoking nationalism, promoting militarism, that was the only way he could remain in power. It meant constantly provoking the West, and that pattern, once in motion, only escalated. Vladimir Molotov was a man who would bring the entire world to its knees before letting slip his grip on power.

And it wasn't a question of killing him. He'd seen to that.

There was an entire secret organization in Moscow known as the Dead Hand. It encompassed the top echelon of Molotov's clique, the military leadership, and the intelligence service. And it guaranteed that any strike at the regime, or the person of the President, would trigger a massive nuclear response. In order to prevent a war, Vladimir Molotov and his entire system had to be torn out by the root at the same time.

And that required this plan. There was no other option.

In Roth's mind, the plan had been delayed for so long, had been maturing for so many decades, that it had taken on proportions at once vast and intricate, simultaneously bold and subtle. It was a masterpiece on a grand scale. And it was too ambitious not to at least strive for.

It was irresistible.

And Tenet... Tenet would be a casualty one way or another. It could be no other way. Even if they pulled this off, even if Tenet succeeded in getting inside the Kremlin, the cost to him would be severe.

The only person who knew the truth about what he was doing was Roth. When the dust settled, Tenet would go down as the highest-level defector in CIA history. And he knew that. He accepted it. It was a tough pill to swallow, and he swallowed it.

Roth never sought to pull the wool over his eyes. He'd never pretended things were anything other than what they were. And he'd never asked of Tenet anything he wouldn't have asked of himself had their positions been reversed.

And yet, when all was said and done, it was Tenet's name, and not Roth's, that would be dirt. Tenet would go down in the annals of history as a traitor, a turncoat. The world would curse his memory. Even Alona, his own wife, would think he was a monster she'd never known, a gambler, a pedophile, and a rat. That was the reason Tenet had never had children despite Alona's wanting them. Tenet knew the pain that would follow in the wake of this plan, and the shame that would be heaped on anyone who bore his name.

Tenet's eyes were open. He knew what was being asked of him. He understood what he was giving up, and he was ready to do it.

"We're going to make a move on this new guy?" he said. "Viktor Lapin?"

"I've looked into him," Roth said. "He's ambitious."

"He'll take the bait?"

Roth nodded. "I think he will."

"We'll have to give him something big. Something irresistible."

Roth nodded again. "When we do, it will begin a timer," he said. "You understand that?" The information Roth had in mind was something that could only have originated from him or someone in his inner circle. Tenet's position would quickly become untenable. Even Roth would be unable to stop the CIA's internal investigative machinery from honing in on the source of the leak. They would find Tenet. They would know he was their rat.

"No turning back," Tenet said.

"You'll be fleeing to Moscow as a fugitive. You'll be on the run."

"I understand," Tenet said.

"But when you get there," Roth said, and he knew that what he was about to say was as much wishful thinking as anything, "they're going to welcome you with open arms."

"So the plan goes," Tenet said.

"They'll pry open Igor's files and see the decades of

intelligence you've given them. Your loyalty will be beyond question."

"I hope so," Tenet said.

"And with your operational experience, your institutional knowledge, your domain expertise, and understanding of virtually every aspect of our intelligence system, they're going to give you a seat at the table, Tenet. Mark my words. They'll give you a seat right next to Molotov."

"And that's when the real fun begins," Tenet said.

Roth smiled, but only slightly. "That's when the work begins." He refilled both their glasses, and they touched them before drinking.

"So," Tenet said, "what's our bait?"

"It's big," Roth said. "A part of me wishes it was less so, but there it is."

"What is it?" Tenet said again.

"It's not what," Roth said sadly. He pictured Tatyana, the look on her face when she told him about Gray Coat. All of this was possible only because of her, but Roth had nothing to offer the Russians that would excite them as much as the prospect of getting her back. Her and their missing scientist. The combination was irresistible. They would be after it like bloodhounds on a scent. And when they caught Tatyana, like hounds, they would rip her to shreds.

"Then who?" Tenet said.

Roth looked back at him for a few seconds, saying nothing. He waited. Then Tenet pieced it together. Roth saw the realization in his eyes.

"I'm sorry," Tenet said. "I know you're fond of her."

"I'm fond of you too," Roth said.

Tenet sighed. He finished his drink and then shook his head. "No," he said. "Maybe once, a long time ago, but you haven't been fond of me for a long time."

14

Lance stared at the page. There'd been a truly massive explosion over the Arctic Ocean, and the story filled the front page of his newspaper. Global monitors were picking up huge increases in atmospheric radiation, with some stations showing spikes that hadn't been seen since the days of the *Castle Bravo* test over the Pacific in 1954, or the *Tsar Bomba* test over the Arctic in 1962. The *Tsar Bomba* remained the single most powerful man-made explosion in history, and was dropped by a Tupolev Tu-95 strategic bomber over Severny Island, a few hundred miles north of Arkhangelsk. Lance noticed how close that was to the suspected epicenter of this current blast.

According to the newspaper, the emerging consensus was that the explosion was caused by a failed test of a new Russian ICBM, the Satan-2. The Satan-2 was a traditional, liquid-fuel design that was being introduced to replace the aging SS-18 rocket. The SS-18 had entered service before Lance was born and was in desperate need of modernization.

Lance understood why the analysts thought this was a

Satan-2 test, but based on what he'd seen while still at the
Special Operations Group, he knew the truth was likely
something far more sinister. He'd seen with his own eyes
intercepted GRU communications referring to a number of
terrifying new Russian superweapons. These were literal
doomsday devices, weapons that could only be used by a
nation facing annihilation, after all objectives, including
national survival, had been abandoned. They were, in effect,
self-destruction devices for the planet.

Lance had only spent a few minutes with the documents, they weren't intended for his eyes, but one thing he'd
noticed was that they all originated from the same source—
a single, highly secretive research facility at the Russian
Navy testing range at Nyonoksa, just outside Arkhangelsk.
The Satan-2, on the other hand, was being developed in
Chelyabinsk, thousands of miles away on the Russian
border with Kazakhstan. Any tests of that system would
have been conducted there. Also, Lance suspected, the
Satan-2, based as it was on a well-documented, tried-and-
true predecessor, would look nothing like this when it was
tested.

This explosion was something else entirely, a catastrophe of epic proportions. The detonation had drawn the
attention of every nuclear monitoring post on the planet.
The eyes of the world were focused now on the Nyonoksa
testing range, an outcome the Kremlin would have sought to
avoid at all costs, given the nature of what they were doing
there.

What worried Lance, though, and what he knew would
be worrying Levi Roth too, was what this test showed about
Russia's progress. This was a live-fire test, and even though it
had clearly been a failure, it showed that they were now
entering the final stages of development of their new

doomsday machines. These weapons weren't imaginary, they weren't just some theoretical blueprints on a scientist's drawing board, they were real, and it was only a matter of time before they were deployed.

Roth had been grappling with this threat even before Lance's departure from the CIA. He'd codenamed it *Project Oppenheimer*, and had been trying desperately to raise the alarm. The thing that hampered him was, as usual, politics. The last thing President Montgomery wanted at the time was to give his opponents another justification for war with Russia. He'd buttoned the entire thing up and told Roth to put a sock in it.

That was two years ago, and things had changed. Roth was CIA director now, and Russia was much more of a clear and present danger than it had been. Lance wouldn't have been surprised at all if Roth had succeeded in establishing the Joint Task Force he'd been calling for back then. That group was to be a carefully calibrated tool that included not just the CIA, but the Secretary of Defense, the NSA, the Chairman of the Joint Chiefs, the Navy Chief of Staff, and the President's National Security Advisor. It would be based at the new state-of-the-art Command Center deep beneath Langley, and would be tied in directly to NORAD, the DoD's Global Information Grid, and the Keyhole Satellite Network. From what Lance had seen, Roth had even drafted provisional Operation Plans for the DoD seeking to grant the task force with authority to deploy units stationed at Barksdale and Offutt Air Force Bases. Those bases housed the combat-ready units responsible for US nuclear deterrence and global strike capability.

If Roth had gotten his way, and Lance had no reason to doubt him, it would mean his finger was now on the trigger of a nuclear strike capability that was locked, loaded, and ready to fire.

Lance flipped the page and saw photos of villagers from Nyonoksa being loaded into buses for evacuation. In Arkhangelsk, armed men in ski masks had broken into pharmacies and hospital dispensaries and seized their iodine stockpile at gunpoint. They knew what they needed. They remembered what happened following Chernobyl when the authorities refused to distribute potassium iodide to the local population. Only those who knew how to protect themselves had self-administered iodine. Thousands of others died of thyroid cancer and other forms of radiation poisoning that could have been prevented.

On the next page was a long column about the design of the Satan-2, written by one of the lead scientists working on Britain's implementation of the US Trident II missile. Lance was about to skim it when he was interrupted by yet another knock on the door. He didn't have to open the door to know who it was. He sighed and got up.

"Yes?" he said when he saw her, unable to hide a hint of impatience in his voice.

She was standing with the child, and the child was holding a Tupperware container.

"What's this?" Lance said, softening his tone slightly.

The child looked at her mother, who nudged her encouragingly. "It's brownies."

"It's a thank you," the mother said.

"That's not necessary."

"For cooking my breakfast," the child said, holding the container forward.

"No," Lance said. "Really. You shouldn't have done this." He remained motionless, one hand on the door, the other by his side.

"Aren't you going to take them?" the woman said, looking at him pointedly.

Reluctantly, Lance took the container from the child and held it in front of him like he wasn't sure it didn't contain an explosive. "Thank you," he said stiffly.

"You're welcome," the child said, then turned and went back into her own apartment, leaving Lance and the mother looking at each other.

Lance was about to shut the door when she said, "I wanted to apologize."

"You don't need to apologize."

"Things..." she began, "it's just been a little crazy for us lately."

"That's all right. I shouldn't have entered your apartment."

There was a moment of pregnant silence, then the woman said, "I know she deserves better."

Lance looked down at the Tupperware. He didn't want to get into all this. The woman was scarcely an adult herself. She was doing her best with the hand she'd been dealt. "It's none of my business," he said. "Really."

"No," she said. "What you said earlier. It touched a nerve. I shouldn't have lost my temper."

"It really doesn't matter."

"I'm fucking everything up," she said.

She was looking at the Tupperware too, and Lance didn't know what to say. The silence grew again, and he knew he needed to fill it.

"You're doing your best," he offered, but something about the way he said it made her look up at him suddenly. "I should go," he added weakly.

He was going to shut the door, draw a line under the conversation before her emotions rose again, but she reached up and put her hand on it. "I know what you're thinking," she said.

"Really, I'm not thinking anything."

"You think you've seen enough of me to make up your mind."

"I assure you..." he began, but she interrupted him.

"They never touch me," she said. "They're never in the same room as me. Everything is through the camera."

"Really," Lance said. "I shouldn't have...."

"It's safe."

He nodded. He'd made a mistake entering her apartment. He should have left well enough alone. He knew that.

"It's safe for my child."

"Okay," he said.

"That's the truth," she said.

Lance knew it was the truth, as far as it went, but looking in her eyes, he could see something else. A silent plea, a plea that said all was not well, all was not as it was meant to be. He shouldn't have cared, he was truly trying not to care, not to get involved, but his mind was already running. Something was wrong here—maybe something big, maybe something small. But this woman, and he knew it with a certainty, was asking for his help.

"I believe you," he said quietly.

She sighed. Shook her head. "I'm sorry. I don't know why I'm here. I'll let you get back to your," she glanced past him into the apartment, "newspaper."

"Okay," he said.

She should have left then. She could see he was impatient for the conversation to end. "If you ever need anything," she said, stepping back from the door.

"Thank you."

"Milk or sugar or what have you."

He nodded.

"Or, you know...."

He nodded again. She was wearing yoga pants and a white button-up shirt. The top few buttons of the shirt were open, and he could see the very edge of a black lace bra at her cleavage.

"I'm right across the hall," she added.

"Thank you," Lance said again.

He was about to shut the door when she said, "We're both right across the hall."

Lance looked at her then—really looked at her. He would have been surprised if she was any older than twenty-one. He knew that he was making a mistake. It was a mistake he'd made before, and he couldn't believe he was about to go down this path again. But against all better judgment, he said, "Is someone hurting her?"

The woman took a moment to register his words, and when she did, they seemed to come as a shock to her.

"What are you talking about?"

He shook his head. "Never mind."

"No, really, what the hell are you talking about? Who do you think you are?"

"Forget I said that," he said and tried to shut the door.

She stopped it with her foot. They looked at each other, their eyes locked, and there was some mix of terror and fury and pleading in her eyes that he was certain he understood. Then she reached out, snatched the Tupperware from his hands, and left.

15

Viktor sat at his desk, examining a two-inch rectangular piece of plastic. He turned it over in his hand. He even smelled it. He knew what it was —an Olympus-brand micro-cassette containing thirty minutes of high-fidelity, metal-coated, magnetic recording tape. It was a product that had never been popular in civilian use, not even in the eighties when it was introduced.

He hadn't listened to it yet, he was still waiting for his secretary to bring the tape recorder from the supply room, but whoever had sent it was an artist, a connoisseur. Someone who took pleasure in the details of their craft.

The micro-cassette brought Viktor back to the early days of his career when those tapes were in regular use. Even then, they'd been a nightmare to work with. They were difficult to obtain, nowhere stocked them, and they wore down the batteries on recorders twice as fast as other tapes.

But among spies, they were practically a calling card, a symbol of professionalism, a mark of panache when so many other aspects of the job had to be performed with complete anonymity. The CIA, Mossad, MI6, the French Direction Générale all used them for everything—memos, messages, field surveillance, covert recordings.

Even when they didn't need the *high-fidelity* of the metal-coated tape, agents used them because of what they stood for, because they had class, and because everyone else used them.

Whoever had sent this one was sending him a signal. It was a flair designed to get attention.

The secretary entered the room with the tape recorder and placed it on his desk.

"Plug it in," Viktor said.

He watched her bend over and wondered if she'd sleep with him. She was new, young. There'd been a time when he could have taken such a thing for granted, he was her boss after all, but those days seemed to be gone.

She hurried from the room, and he removed a cigarette from his pack and began tapping it against the desk. He was going to relish this. He inserted the tape into the recorder and lit the cigarette. After inhaling deeply, he pressed play.

It was a man speaking English, with what Viktor thought was American intonation. It was hard to tell. A modulator had been used to distort the voice.

You don't know who I am, but I assure you, your predecessor knew me very well. He called me Gray Coat. I'm sending this message to tell you that your missing scientist has made contact with Tatyana Aleksandrova. I can lead you right to her.

Viktor had a pen in his hand and had begun jotting

down the message as it played. He looked up. He'd been expecting more, but it stopped. That was it.

Even still, the effect of those few words was such that his hand was shaking. He couldn't believe what he'd just heard. He leaned back in his seat and sucked his cigarette, then played the message again and again, listening for any other clues it might contain. He would send it to the lab for analysis, but already, he knew it would reveal only what its sender intended.

There could be no doubt this had been sent by a professional. Everything on that tape would be intentional. Every sound, from the birds tweeting in the background, to the church bells, to the distant sound of an airplane taking off, would be deliberate.

And the message itself, well, it was a bombshell—almost *too* good. Igor Aralov had a secret source? That source wanted to continue working with Viktor? And he had access to the most valuable information Viktor could have wished for?

It was suspicious, certainly, but the more Viktor thought about it, the more he sensed an aura of legitimacy. For one thing, the number of people who knew Sacha Gazinsky was missing was vanishingly small. Overlap that with the set of people who knew of Tatyana Aleksandrova's defection, and well, there really was only a handful of people who could have made this tape. And whoever it was, they were intimately acquainted with events of critical importance to the Kremlin, essentially as they were unfolding.

Viktor had read Igor's files. He'd gone back years. There was no mention of a Gray Coat in any of them, that much was certain, but that didn't mean no such source existed.

As he read the files, Viktor couldn't shake the feeling that he was missing something. None of them painted a complete picture. The dots didn't connect. Maybe what he was seeing was that famous, inscrutable logic that Igor had been so known for. But Viktor was too sly to really buy that. He knew how people operated, he'd studied human nature, he'd conducted enough interrogations to know when someone was holding back. In short, he knew how to sniff out a rat.

Since his earliest days in the GRU, he'd been taught that whenever there were multiple explanations for a thing, the simplest, the most mundane, was the correct one. One explanation here required him to believe that Igor was an uncommonly intelligent operative, a man with such subtle insight and keen intellect that he'd seen connections and drawn conclusions that other men couldn't see, even when they knew they were there. The second explanation was simply that Igor had kept a mole to himself.

When faced with those options, Viktor knew exactly where the smart money lay. He also saw that this wasn't just another bet. It wasn't some matter of small account. This was a moment that, if it came at all, came just once in a man's lifetime. It was a ticket.

Viktor had spent his entire career cultivating the persona of an outsider, a nonconformist. The way he dressed, the way he spoke, it gave the impression of his being a man of the people, of the rank-and-file. If the GRU had a union, he would have been shop steward. He calibrated everything to appear as a bureaucrat, a career man, utterly unthreatening to his superiors. He was diligent, competent, but gave the impression that an office, a good car, and a decent retirement package were the extent of his ambition.

All of that, however, could not have been further from the truth. Viktor Lapin, whose name in French translated to rabbit, was in fact a wolf. His sheep's clothing concealed a truly colossal ambition, and that ambition was all the more dangerous because it was hidden.

It was true his father had been a city cop. It was true too that he fit in seamlessly with the blue-collar, working-classes of the Moscow suburbs. He spoke like them. He dressed like them. He drank their brand of beer and smoked their brand of cigarettes.

But he was not one of them.

He was forty-five years old, and in the time he'd spent climbing the ranks of the GRU, he'd paid particular attention to one thing—where exactly the power in President Molotov's Russia lay. Over the years, he'd developed a startlingly complete view of Moscow's Byzantine oligarchy. Like the blueprints of a machine, he'd drawn out how the various players fit together and fed off each other and where cracks and weaknesses might be exploited. He saw that there was a group in Moscow that occupied a rarefied stratosphere. They formed the very pinnacle of the regime, a pantheon of lesser gods circling and worshipping one almighty center. For them, the rules other people lived by, the ordinances, the laws of man and nature, ceased to apply. Things were possible for them that others could scarcely dream.

Viktor wanted to become one of them. After all, the President himself had risen from within the ranks of the KGB. With enough skill, with the right kind of cunning, why could the same not happen for him?

Gray Coat had taken a risk in sending this message. On the American side, it would be a small group indeed who knew of Tatyana's location. If Viktor acted on it, Gray Coat would be exposed. Someone in the CIA would realize they had a stranger in the house. In the bowels of its internal oversight apparatus, some technocrat would immediately begin triangulating Gray Coat's location. Gray Coat must have known that.

What reason could he have for taking such a risk then? What objective? What desire? Perhaps some promise Igor had made? The Kremlin rewarded its servants, after all. As President Molotov was fond of saying—the Devil looked after his own.

Protocol was clear that Viktor had to pass this information up the chain. There was no way he was authorized to keep it to himself. He should have packaged it up and sent it directly to Suvorov.

But he had no intention of doing anything of the sort. Why should he? This source had been Igor's golden goose for years. Now he would be Viktor's.

He lit another cigarette and sucked hard. When something like this came your way, a treasure that literally fell in your lap, you kept your mouth shut. To do otherwise would be a sin against your own good fortune.

Viktor would treat this the way the Allies treated *Ultra*. When you cracked a machine like the Enigma, you protected that fact. You didn't squander it. Viktor would rely on Gray Coat only when he could explain it as having come from other sources. Sources his superiors were aware of.

If he passed this message up the chain now, Suvorov would go after the scientist immediately, he'd order a hit on Tatyana, and Gray Coat would be burned, lost forever.

A secret was a dangerous thing to have in Moscow, but if Viktor couldn't keep this one, he was in the wrong profession. He told himself that while sucking his cigarette and savoring what already tasted like the heady, intoxicating elixir of where this might take him.

Sacha Gazinsky threatened the President's entire

weapons program. That meant he threatened the President. If Viktor was the one to deliver Sacha's head, well, that was the kind of thing destinies were made of.

Viktor stubbed out his cigarette. He ejected the tape and put it back in its envelope. With his pen, he marked it Top Priority and tagged it with his personal identifier. Then he called in his secretary and told her to personally deliver it to the lab.

He watched her leave, then picked up his lighter. It was steel, petrol-burning. He'd gotten it in the army. He flicked it open and shut, over and over, a maneuver he'd practiced tens of thousands of times. His handwritten transcript of the recording was on the desk, and he stared at it. He gazed at it, almost as one would gaze on a lover.

Then he held it over his ashtray and lit it on fire.

16

L ance woke with a start. There was screaming out in the corridor—a woman's screams, and then a child's.

He grabbed his gun and went straight to the door, yanking it open. In the corridor, a big man with a beard, he looked like Bluto from the old Popeye cartoons, was half carrying, half dragging the child toward the elevators. He had his arm around her neck, and she kicked and flailed in terror as he jerked her from the ground with each step. The woman chased after them, screaming, striking the man and pulling desperately at the child. The man backhanded her with a sudden ferociousness that sent her flying. Lance saw her head hit the wall hard, and then she slumped to the ground.

"Hey," Lance cried.

The man stopped and looked up at him. The woman hadn't lost consciousness, but she'd come close to it. She was wearing nothing but underwear.

"Who the fuck are you?" the man said.

Lance strode toward him. He let go of the child and

pulled a gun from his coat. The kid ran to her mother. Lance stepped over them as he passed.

"Stop," the man yelled, holding the gun inexpertly, "or I swear to God, I'll blow your head off."

Lance reached him in two more strides and, with a single smack, knocked the gun from his hand. It discharged as it fell, and Lance simultaneously swung his fist. The man ducked, but Lance's punch was a feint. He hit the man with an uppercut to the mouth, letting the handle of his own gun make contact. The man stumbled backward, and Lance grabbed him before he fell, pulling him in closer. Then he hit him again, bringing down the butt of his pistol like a hammer.

The man collapsed, and Lance was on him before he hit the ground, punching his face over and over, letting the gun add to the weight of his fist. The man was out cold, his face a bloody pulp. The fight was over. But Lance didn't stop hitting him. He couldn't. There was a rage inside him that blocked out all else. He hit the man over and over. Blood spattered. The structure of his face began to give way.

The woman grabbed Lance by the arm and screamed at him, begging him to stop. It was only her screams that brought him back to his senses.

He took a breath. He looked down at what he'd done. If he hadn't stopped, he'd have crushed the man's skull completely.

He looked at the woman. She was crying. She had the kid in her arms and had covered her face to block what Lance had done.

"I was..." Lance said.

Her head was shaking. She was looking at him now like he was the monster. "What's wrong with you?" she said.

"I don't know," he said quietly.

"You were going to kill him."

Lance got to his feet slowly. "Who is he?" he said.

"He's no one," the woman said. "It doesn't matter."

"Is he her father?"

She shook her head.

"He was going to take her," Lance said.

The woman said nothing. Lance realized his fists were still clenched. He opened them and saw that his hands were quivering.

"Where was he taking her?"

"Nowhere."

"They were going somewhere."

"I..." she stammered, "I don't know where they were going."

"Did he ever take her before?"

The woman had her hands over the child's ears as well now, covering her entire head as if blocking her senses would somehow protect her from the world. The child clung to her like a frightened animal.

"Who is he?" Lance said again. "I need to know."

"He's... I work for him."

"You work for him?"

She nodded.

"On the camera?"

She nodded again.

"He takes the money?"

"He gets a cut."

Lance crouched down to her level. "I bet he does," he said, then he took her chin in his hand, making her look at him. "Listen to me very carefully," he said.

Her eyes were wide. She knew what he was going to ask. There was only one thing that mattered, and they both knew what it was.

"Did he ever lay a finger on your girl?"

The woman looked at the little girl and began to cry. Then she said, "It wasn't like that."

"What was it like?"

"He was threatening me."

"How?"

"He said social services would take her away from me."

"Why?"

"Because I tried to quit."

"You tried to quit working for him?"

"He said if I didn't keep working, he'd tell social services how I made my money. He said I'd lose custody."

"So that's where he was taking her?"

She nodded.

"You're sure?"

"I'm sure," she said. "If he ever so much as laid a finger on her, believe me, I'd say."

Lance nodded. He could tell by the look on her face that she meant it.

"Did he ever try to take her before?" he said.

She shook her head. "He threatened it. Every time I tried to quit, he told me I was unfit to be a mother. He said all he had to do was tell social services about me, and I'd lose her."

"But he never actually took her away?"

"Not until tonight."

"What was different about tonight?"

"Tonight..." she said, and her words trailed off.

"Tonight what?"

"I didn't back down tonight."

"You always backed down before?"

She nodded her head.

"Why not tonight?" Lance said, suspecting the answer before she said it.

"Because... because of you."

He clenched his jaw.

"I don't know why," she said, "but knowing you were there, across the hall, it made me feel...." She looked at him and just shook her head.

Lance breathed in deeply and exhaled. "Emboldened?" he said, finishing her sentence.

She nodded.

Lance grabbed the man and heaved him up onto his shoulder like a sack of potatoes.

"Where are you taking him?"

He looked at her and said, "Take the kid inside. Put her to bed. This is over."

He walked to the elevator and pushed the button. When the doors opened, he got in and rode it to the top floor. The man was beginning to come back to consciousness, he tried to struggle, but Lance kept a firm grip on him.

The elevator stopped, and Lance carried him out to the corridor. He found the door to the service stairwell and tried it. It was locked, but a single, firm kick to its base split the frame. He pushed it open and climbed one flight of stairs to the roof.

"What's going on?" the man mumbled.

The door to the roof was steel with a deadbolt, and Lance drew his gun and fired a single bullet through the lock. The sound reverberated in the concrete stairwell, and the door swung open.

On the roof, a thin coat of snow shimmered in the moonlight. Wind whipped over it, and Lance, in his underwear and white shirt, shivered.

He threw the man on the ground, where the cold soon roused him. When he came to, he looked up to see Lance pointing a gun at him.

"Give me your boots," Lance said.

"What?"

"You heard me."

"What are you going to do with me?"

"Take off your boots," Lance said again.

The man's face was so mangled it looked like he'd been through a meat grinder. He would need hospital treatment.

Lance watched him open his laces and kick off the boots. They were a few sizes larger than Lance's. He put them on and said, "Now your coat."

"What?"

Lance fired the gun. The bullet hit the roof about a foot from the man's legs. "Say what again."

The man took off his coat and threw it to Lance. Lance put it on, then took a step forward. The man backed away from him. Lance stepped forward again. As Lance advanced, the man kept backing away, scrambling across the roof until he reached the edge. They were fourteen floors up, and the wind hit the north face of the building head-on, sending a wall of icy air rushing upward.

"Take off your pants," Lance said.

"What?"

Lance fired the gun again. The shot struck just inches from the man's knee. "Next shot maims you," he said.

"Please," the man said, "why are you doing this?"

"Take them off," Lance said.

The man slipped out of his pants.

Lance nodded toward the edge of the building.

"No," the man said, shaking his head.

"Throw them."

Reluctantly, the man let the wall of wind catch the pants and take them into the sky like a plastic bag in a gale.

"Now, the shirt."

The man shook his head but took off his shirt and let the wind take it as it took the pants. He was down to his underwear now, terrified of what was coming, shivering visibly.

"Give me one reason why I don't throw you off the side of this building right now," Lance said.

"No," the man begged, "please. I didn't do anything."

"What was that fight about?"

"Nothing. She owes me money. I was collecting."

Lance fired the gun again.

"Please," the man screamed. "She didn't want to work. She was trying to quit."

"Why?"

"She said her kid deserved better. She said she deserved better. You know how they are."

"And you wouldn't let her quit."

"It's my business not to let her quit."

"You ever lay a finger on the kid?"

"What? No," the man said.

"Stand up."

"Please, I'm begging you."

"Stand up. Come on. Don't make me say it again."

The man got to his feet slowly. Reluctantly.

"Turn around," Lance said.

"Please," the man wailed again. He was crying now, blubbering freely.

"Turn around."

The man turned around to face the abyss. His shoulders heaved up and down as he cried.

Lance fired the gun. The bullet flew by the man's head, so close he would have felt the air from it. He soiled himself, the piss running down his leg and staining the snow on the ground.

"Admit it," Lance said. "Tell me what you did."

"What I did?" the man cried.

"To the kid."

"I swear to God. I never laid a finger on that child."

Lance stepped forward and pressed the gun to the back of the man's head.

"You tell me one more time you didn't touch that girl, and I'm going to blow your head off."

The man was close to collapsing. His whole body shook. "I swear to God I didn't touch that child."

"You're going to die for it anyway," Lance said. "You might as well own up to it."

"I fucked the woman," the man stammered. "I swear to God that's all I did."

"I ought to shoot you just for that."

"Please," the man begged. "I made her work the camera. I slapped her around."

"And you fucked her."

"She let me."

Lance took a deep breath and looked over the edge of the building. The snow swirled fiercely as if caught in a vortex. The man was so close to the edge he might have fallen over. All it would take was a light push.

Lance stepped back. "Don't you move a muscle," he said. "You move, I shoot."

The man nodded frantically, crying like a child, shaking.

Lance backed all the way to the door. The man remained exactly where he was.

"I ever see you around that woman or kid again," Lance said, "I swear to God you'll wish you never were born."

"I swear to God you'll never see me again."

Lance opened the door. From the stairwell, he looked back at the man one last time, standing there, barefoot, nothing on him but his piss-stained underwear.

When he got back to his own floor, the corridor was empty. The door to the woman's apartment was shut. He walked up to it and checked it. It was locked.

Then he entered his own apartment and shut the door behind him.

17

Viktor leaned back in his seat and rubbed his eyes. He'd been staring at the screen all night and could feel himself beginning to doze off.

He picked up the phone and called his secretary. Her phone clanged just outside his door, but there was no answer. He didn't remember dismissing her but wasn't surprised she'd slipped out at some point. It was almost dawn.

He pulled himself up from his chair and went to her desk. Her phone had a direct line to the building's service department, and he pushed a button with a picture of a man holding a tray on it.

A groggy, half-hearted voice said, "Catering."

"I'm sorry," Viktor said in mock sympathy. "Did I wake you?"

"Oh, no, not at all, sir."

"Good. Bring me fresh coffee. Very strong. Bring it right in." He put down the phone and went back to his desk.

He'd been poring over the lab analysis of the micro-cassette for hours. As he'd suspected, there'd been a significant amount of additional data embedded in the high-fidelity frequency.

The lab isolated it and sent it back as a long series of letters and numbers that looked like garbled gibberish. Viktor knew there was something there, and began the painstaking process of sifting through it. He sent it to his tech team in Saint Petersburg to see what they would make of it, but it was Viktor himself who first noticed a pattern.

He saw that some of the numbers were preceded by the same tag—SK-42. The SK characters were Cyrillic, and Viktor had seen the tag before. It was used on older, printed Russian military maps. SK stood for *Systema Koordinat,* or Coordinate System. The 42 referred to the *Krasovsky* standard, introduced in 1942. It was used by the Russian army for determining the location of high-value assets, enemy targets, and state borders. It was an extremely accurate Cartesian plotting system, capable of pinpointing locations anywhere on earth to within an eighth of an inch. Even the most modern GPS standards, utilizing the latest L5 communications bands, could only claim an accuracy of about thirty centimeters.

Viktor plotted out the points and found that they were all locations in Washington. The highest concentration was around Lafayette Square, just north of the White House, but there were points also at U Street, Dupont Circle, the US Capitol, and other locations around the city. He'd sent the coordinate data to Saint Petersburg hours ago and, with a sigh, checked his email. Still nothing.

There was a knock on the door.

"Come in," he said.

A woman in her fifties wearing a gray dress and apron came in with a tray. On it was a stainless steel coffee carafe with sugar, milk, and a few cookies.

"Leave it there," Viktor said, nodding toward the sideboard.

He was about to tell her to pour him a cup when the phone rang. He almost knocked it off the table as he grabbed the receiver.

"Finally," he said. "Tell me you found something."

"We did, boss. We called the embassy in Washington and had them send someone out to the locations you plotted."

"And?"

"At every spot, they found a camera."

"What sort of camera?"

"Traffic, CCTV, security. They took pictures, and we were able to determine that they all belong to the same contractor."

"What contractor?"

"Piscataway Security, a large firm based out of Alexandria, Virginia."

"Okay," Viktor said.

The woman in the apron was standing by the door, and he made the motion of bringing a cup to his mouth.

"While we were running the firm through our system, we also figured out that part of the data contained database access keys and IP whitelisting instructions."

"No milk," Viktor said to the woman. "Just black."

"So we tried the keys against Piscataway's servers."

"And?" Viktor said, taking the cup of coffee from the woman.

"We're inside their cluster right now, sir."

"So, what does that get us?"

"Well, sir, the company's largest client is the DC Metropolitan Police Department, which contracts them to operate traffic and CCTV cameras all over the city. They operate over three thousand cameras for the city."

"Including the ones that were located at the coordinates I sent?"

"Yes, sir."

The woman was waiting by the door again, and Viktor waved her out of the office. "So we've got access to three thousand camera feeds across Washington?" he said.

"Right now, we do, yes. But Piscataway ships the data to a Glaciar Archive every twenty-four hours. At that time, all the encryption keys get re-hashed."

"And we get kicked off the server?"

"Correct, sir."

"So we have access to three thousand video feeds, but only for the next twenty-four hours?"

"The passwords are reset at two AM local time, sir. That's in six hours."

"Well," Viktor said, "I guess we can start with the cameras they gave us the coordinates for."

"Well, sir, the last part of the data contains not only the serial numbers for those cameras but also timestamps."

"So they're telling us where to look, and when?"

"Yes, sir. The timestamps are all from the last few hours. It's all footage we still have access to."

"Copy it and send it to me immediately."

"Already done, sir."

Viktor hung up the phone and checked his computer. He accepted the file transfer and opened the first clip. The footage was surprisingly clear, not the grainy, black and white he'd been expecting. It showed the entrance of a luxury hotel. A brass plaque identified it as the Saint Royal on Lafayette Square in Washington. A uniformed doorman and bellhop stood at attention by the door. A cab pulled up, and the doorman spoke to the driver.

Then a woman came out of the hotel through the large revolving door. She was slim with dark hair, lightly disguised in sunglasses and a silk scarf.

Viktor paused the clip. He zoomed in on the woman's face and stared at it. He couldn't believe it.

In a flash, this confirmed that Gray Coat wasn't just *a* source—he was *the* source—someone connected to the very heart of the US intelligence apparatus. He didn't just have access to classified information—he knew how to use it. He knew how to kick the CIA right in the nuts.

Viktor clicked through the files, watching each in turn, and he knew exactly what he was looking at. If he handled Gray Coat correctly, and if he managed to keep him secret, it would be his ticket to the very top.

But that meant finding Igor's file as soon as possible. He needed to dig up everything he could. Igor must have known Gray Coat's identity. He must have had a way of contacting him, communicating in both directions. He must have kept a file.

Viktor picked up his coffee cup and brought it slowly to his lips. This was going to change everything.

da Hudson's phone woke her. She reached for it blindly, almost knocking over a lamp in the process.

"This is Ada."

"You're needed at the office."

"I just..." she said, then let out a sigh. "All right."

She hung up and looked at the digital clock by her bed. It was almost hard to believe there'd been a time, and not that long ago, when eight hour's sleep was something she took for granted.

Those days were gone.

Maybe they were testing her, she thought. Wasn't sleep deprivation one of the CIA's methods?

She went to the kitchen and pushed the start button on her coffee maker, then stumbled into the bathroom and took a hot shower. Fifteen minutes later, she was washed, dressed, had on a smattering of makeup, and had even given her hair a quick blow-dry.

She went to the kitchen and filled her Starbucks thermos with coffee, wondering what they could possibly want her for at this hour. A lot was going on, the whole embassy was abuzz since the Arctic explosion, but it was all above her paygrade. Certainly not something that required her to be dragged from bed. She wrapped herself in a long, tan cashmere coat and left the house. It was still dark out, and she didn't find a cab until she'd walked halfway to the Embankment.

"Where to, love?" the driver said.

"US embassy," she said and still felt a thrill as she said the words. Despite the long hours, the ridiculously meager salary, and her complete lack of social life, she was exactly where she needed to be.

When she first got to Langley, they assigned her a desk on the sixth floor of the new headquarters building and told her to get comfortable. It seemed that for the time being, the interests of national security would best be served by her document formatting and Microsoft Excel skills.

"How long before I get assigned to the field?" she'd asked her line manager, Laurel Everlane.

Laurel looked at her through squinted eyes, weighing her up. "Scrawny thing like you?" she'd said. "Two years minimum."

That was three months ago, and a lot had changed. The world had changed. The US embassies in Moscow and Beijing had been blown to smithereens. Hundreds were killed. For a lot of people, including Ada, nothing would ever be the same again.

Ada's mother worked for the State Department in Moscow. She'd been posted there a year earlier and was at the embassy when the bomb exploded.

Ada was sitting at her desk when she got the news. She tried her mother's cell, over and over, and told herself that the worst hadn't happened. When she still hadn't reached her mother three days later, she accepted the truth. Her mother's body hadn't been found, and the State Department didn't officially give up on her for a few more days, but Ada already knew. She already felt it in her bones. She would never see her mother again.

She didn't shed a tear, not then and not later. Her mother was all the family she had in the world, but Ada didn't cry. She didn't grieve.

She wondered what that meant. She knew she needed to see someone, a shrink or therapist or whatever, but she was afraid of what the agency would make of that. She'd worked too hard to allow some pencil pusher to write her off as a basket case.

She traveled to Moscow alone to escort her mother's body home. The coffin was empty, but Ada didn't know what else to do.

The funeral was a quiet, sedate affair. She stood alone beneath an umbrella while a priest her mother never knew rattled through a liturgy she wouldn't have believed.

As soon as it was over, she got in her car and drove to the ravine near her old high school. At the bridge, she pulled over and slammed her fists on the steering wheel. If she was going to get through this, she knew there was only one option. There was only one therapy that would soothe her, only one balm for her soul.

Revenge.

She no longer reported to Laurel Everlane—Laurel had been whisked off by Levi Roth himself—but whatever she worked on now, Ada knew it was high level. It was hush-hush.

Paramilitary.

She called Laurel from the car, right there on the bridge, while overlooking a sixty-foot drop into a gorge.

"Laurel," she said, "it's me. It's Ada."

"Ada," Laurel gasped, and from her voice, Ada knew how the conversation would go. It would be all sympathy and condolences, apologies for not sending flowers, for not having called. She didn't want that.

"Don't..." she said, but Laurel couldn't stop herself.

"I'm so sorry, Ada. When I heard...."

"I don't want sympathy, Laurel. That's not why I called."

"Of course," Laurel said.

"I called about work."

"If there's anything you need, anything I can do."

"I want you to put me in the field."

"What?"

"You heard me."

"Ada, that's not what I do."

"You can make it happen, Laurel. I know you can."

"It's not that simple."

"They killed my mother," Ada said, and her voice cracked.

"I know they did," Laurel said. "And you need time to process that."

"I don't need time for anything."

"You're grieving, Ada."

"I'm not grieving. That's the thing. I can't."

"You're in shock."

"I'm mad, Laurel. That's what I am. I'm mad as hell."

"I know you are, Ada. And I know you feel like...."

"Laurel," Ada said, and she knew what she was about to say was crossing the line, "I read your file."

Laurel went quiet then.

Ada was clenching the phone so tightly she thought she might break it. She tried to take a deep breath. She shouldn't have been speaking like this, bringing this up. It was personal. Private.

"I read your file," she said again, "so I know you understand this. I can't sit at a desk for two years and click on my computer. If I don't do something, I'm going to lose my mind."

She waited, giving Laurel a chance to respond, but Laurel didn't say anything.

"Laurel?" she said tentatively.

This was it—the end of her career. The CIA was an organization that tended to put a lot of stock in self-control, and Ada had just shown a flagrant lack of it.

Then Laurel spoke. "Claymore," she said.

"What?"

"I can't make any promises, Ada. You know things are complicated. My position is complicated."

"Claymore," Ada said, feeling the word in her mouth.

"You hear that word, you think of me, okay? You think of this conversation."

"What does it mean?" Ada said, but the line had already gone dead.

19

V iktor's phone rang, and for once he didn't jump at the sound. He picked it up calmly, ready to luxuriate in his moment of glory.

"This is Viktor Lapin," he said, not even trying to hide his self-satisfaction.

"You found our little whore," Suvorov said, and Viktor could practically hear him salivating.

Viktor had spent what remained of the night drafting a very carefully worded report to Suvorov. He knew exactly where Suvorov's mind would go when he read it. He would want Tatyana Aleksandrova killed immediately. She was a rat and deserved a rat's death. That was why Viktor had given him the Sacha Gazinsky connection also. He had no choice.

"You got the memo," Viktor said.

"It made for some interesting reading," Suvorov said. "How did you find her?"

"We got lucky, sir. She was picked up in Washington by police CCTV cameras. My team was in the database for an unrelated file, running facial recognition algorithms, trawling."

"And it spit out Tatyana Aleksandrova?"

"Yes, it did, sir."

"Remarkable," Suvorov said.

"Indeed, sir."

"And you're sure it's her."

"We have her from multiple angles, multiple cameras. It's her all right."

"So careless of her."

"Out for a stroll without a care in the world, sir."

"I expected more of her. She wouldn't have been caught like this when she worked for us."

"We wouldn't have tolerated it."

"No," Suvorov agreed, "we would not."

Viktor sought to keep the conversation moving. The faster Suvorov's attention was drawn from one point to the next, the less time he would have to dwell on any particular detail that might trip Viktor up.

"So, sir," he said, "we tracked her to the Saint Royal Hotel and began running every type of surveillance we could throw at her."

"This says you pinpointed the hotel just two hours ago."

"Correct, sir. She's inside as we speak. Drinking at the bar, in fact."

"And this says you ran a what? A stack trace?"

"The team in Saint Petersburg performed an SMTP stack trace, that's correct, sir."

Viktor was lying now—spinning yarn out of whole cloth. It made him vulnerable, but good news was always something people were eager to believe. If he wanted to keep Gray Coat to himself as Igor had done, he would have to get used to telling a lot more lies.

"And you found messages between her and Sacha Gazinsky?"

"Not exactly, sir. The messages are gone, deleted on both ends, and the caches erased. But what they weren't able to get rid of was the SMTP trail."

"And the SMTP trail shows us..."

"That the communication took place."

"So we know she was speaking to Sacha Gazinsky."

"Yes, sir."

"Do we know who contacted who first?"

"Unfortunately not, sir. Either she's systematically trying to lure people to the other side, or Sacha knew what she'd done and turned to her for help."

"She and Sacha," Suvorov said, "they've met."

"When?"

"She was assigned to look into him by Igor Aralov. One of his fishing expeditions."

"I didn't know that, sir."

"She filed a report. It's in Igor's database."

"What does it say?"

"Not much. Have a read for yourself. In any case, this is good work. I'll pass it along, see that you get credit."

That was a bald-faced lie, and they both knew it, but it didn't matter. Suvorov didn't need to pretend otherwise. It was the pecking order, the way things were done. The President was interested in the scientist personally. There was no way Suvorov would share the credit for finding him.

"Tell me," Suvorov said, "how many assets do you have in Washington right now?"

"I'd have to check the directory, sir, but definitely more than a few. What are you thinking?"

"We must find Gazinsky. That's the President's priority, which means it's our priority. Tatyana is our lead to him."

"I've got assets that can get close to people, sir."

"She's a trained operative, Viktor. She won't be easy to get close to."

"I assure you," Viktor said, a thin smile crossing his face, "the man I have in mind, he's *uncommonly* good at what he does."

"And what is it that he does, exactly?" Suvorov said.

"I don't know how to describe it, sir. He suffered a trauma in his early childhood, something involving his father that led to a jail sentence, a suicide. It seems to have caused him to develop an ability to pick up on certain psychological cues in other people."

"In women?"

"He's got an instinct, sir. He's dangerous. He can frighten them."

"He can frighten women?"

"Yes, sir."

"Half the creeps in Moscow can frighten women."

"This guy does it in a way that attracts them, sir. Like moths to a flame, he draws them in."

"What is this horseshit?"

"Sir, all I can say is that women of a certain *psychological profile* are attracted to him."

"This is a crock of shit, Viktor."

"It's not, sir."

"You expect me to believe you have some sort of mesmerist who can hypnotize women?"

"It's more complicated, sir."

"I've never heard such nonsense."

"The President has approved it, sir."

"What do you mean?"

"The President has used him."

"The President has?"

"Yes, sir."

"Personally?"

"He's endorsed it, sir. It works."

Suvorov sighed, he was wavering, but Viktor had done his homework. He'd read Tatyana's file. This was a long shot, a huge risk, but it was their only chance of getting within a million miles of her in the time available.

"This profile, then?" Suvorov said.

"The psychological profile."

"Tatyana Aleksandrova fits it?"

"Well, sir, I've looked at her history. There are certain...."

"What?"

"*Incidents,* sir."

"Viktor, if you don't stop speaking in riddles...."

"Perhaps if I send you the kompromat we've got on the asset."

"Just tell me what it is."

"Sir, it's footage from a suite in the Moscow Ritz Carlton hotel. It shows a sexual encounter he had with one of Igor's honeytraps."

"And?"

"Well, sir, he's *hurting* the woman."

"What do you mean, hurting her?"

"Not just hurting her, sir. There's something going on between the two of them. Some sort of subconscious manipulation. The footage is difficult to watch, sir. It's disturbing. Even for me."

"He's a sadomasochist?"

"Sir, if he is, he's taken it to a level I've never seen."

"I don't think this is what's going to get...."

"Sir, the woman, she participates willingly."

"I've heard enough."

"All the way to the end, sir."

"The end?"

"He kills her, sir."

"He kills her? She lets him?"

"He's done it more than once, sir. He doesn't just kill the women. They let him."

"And he finds them?"

"He can pick up on certain cues, sir. If there's a woman with a certain...."

"*Psychological profile*?"

"Exactly, sir."

"He finds them?"

"Sir, he wasn't a target of Igor's. He just happened to be staying at the same hotel as her. They met in the bar. He honed in on her, knew what she would let him do, and got her to take him up to her room."

"He found *her*?"

"It was just his dumb misfortune that Igor had a camera in the room."

"He picked up one of Igor's widows...."

"And strangled her to death on camera while Igor watched. That's what happened, sir."

"And ever since...."

"Igor's used him repeatedly, sir. He's some sort of psychopath."

"So, you think Tatyana is susceptible to this?"

"I think it's our best shot."

"Based on what?"

"Just give him a chance, sir. If he doesn't see it, he'll back off."

"I don't know, Viktor."

"Let me forward you his file, sir. Read Igor's case notes. He's been tried and tested."

"Tatyana's going to look at him with a microscope,"

Suvorov said. "You know she is. She'll run every background check in existence. If there's anything there, she'll find it."

"His background is clean, sir. There's nothing to find. He's not just a US citizen. He's a war hero, a decorated veteran. He's a military contractor now, with the highest-level political connections. He's even got a security clearance."

Suvorov sighed. "I don't know," he said.

"Sir, let me get him to scope her out. If he doesn't think she'll crack, he'll let me know."

"Tell him to tread softly, Viktor. If he spooks her, we lose Gazinsky for good."

"That won't happen, sir."

"The President is watching us."

"I understand, sir."

Viktor realized how nervous Suvorov was. The President's attention had him on edge. His neck was on the line every bit as much as Viktor's. If he let Sacha Gazinsky slip through his fingers, well, he wouldn't come out unscathed. Not this time.

"Viktor," he said, "before you go."

"Yes, sir."

"There's potential here. There's scope for you. Don't think I haven't noticed."

"Noticed what, sir?"

"I see that you're a climber. I see you're a reacher."

"Sir, I don't think...."

"Your little act doesn't fool me, Viktor. The shabby clothes. The pathetic demeanor. The cheap car. I see where your eye is."

"Sir, truly..."

"Don't forget who you work for, Viktor Lapin. You understand me? Don't forget who butters your bread."

"I won't, sir."

"You answer to me. If you want to rise up in the world, the only path is through me."

"I understand that, sir."

"I am the way. I am the truth. Isn't that what they say?"

"Yes, sir."

"So don't fuck this up. Use your mesmerist if you think he can get close to the whore, but bring me Sacha Gazinsky. If you lose him, it's both our heads, mark my words. I won't go down alone. The slightest hint of blowback, and I'm pulling you down with me. I'll pull you all the way to hell."

"I understand, sir."

"I've shat bigger turds than you, Viktor. I'll fucking string you up like a dog."

20

D eclan Haines sat on his sofa and stared at the forged, carbon steel barrel of a Springfield 1911 Tactical Response Pistol. It was chambered for a .45 ACP, and he'd just loaded it. Now he sat looking at it, the way the light played off the matte black surface, the intricate checkering on the handle, the subtle isotopic glow of the tritium sight. It was an object he knew intimately. He knew it better than parts of his own body—the weight of it, the recoil. It was the tool of his craft. It was his livelihood.

And so, it would be apt if it was the gun that blew his brains out.

He swished scotch around in a glass and took a sip. The ice had melted, weakening the spirit. In his other hand was a cigarette, the ash so long it threatened to fall to the carpet. He wouldn't have liked that. He was a stickler for neatness. His apartment looked like a condo developer's brochure, all white leather and tinted glass and stainless steel.

When he raised the cigarette to his mouth and sucked, it singed audibly.

He was thirty-eight years old and had achieved many of the milestones to which a man his age might reasonably aspire. He was a decorated veteran, had served his country with honor, obtained a degree from Harvard Business School, and built a successful company. He was at the top of his field and the top of his game. That very day, he'd been on Capitol Hill testifying before the House Oversight Committee. Congressmen from eight districts were vying for his attention, and a raft of multi-million-dollar military contracts were poised to come his way.

He should have been on top of the world. He had everything. All that was left was to find a nice girl, settle down, and start a family. He'd even purchased an acreage overlooking the Potomac for that very purpose.

But he wasn't thinking of that. He wasn't thinking of his success, of his future. He was a man with a tortured soul. He had an addiction. He had blood on his hands, and it was getting harder and harder to live with himself. He couldn't control it—couldn't blunt his impulses. He killed people, women, and he couldn't stop.

More and more often, he sat staring at the gun, imagining putting the end of the barrel in his mouth and pulling the trigger.

He drained the scotch and got up. He had somewhere to be. There'd been a chalk mark on the door of his mailbox when he got home. That meant only one thing—Igor fucking Aralov.

He put his gun in his coat and took the elevator to the basement level, where his driver waited with the car.

"Where we headed, boss?" he said as Declan got into the back seat.

"Union Station."

"You taking a trip?"

Declan shook his head. "No," he said. "I'm not taking a trip."

They drove down Massachusetts Avenue in silence. At Columbus Circle, Declan told him to stop. He got out and crossed the plaza, entering the station through the East Hall. He passed the Amtrak ticket booths and the enormous Christmas Tree that still towered over the central concourse. Just outside the Columbus Club was a wrought iron staircase leading to a mezzanine, and he looked around before climbing the steps. At the top, on a marble landing overlooking the main floor, was a set of payphones.

Declan sighed. Sooner or later, this was going to get him killed, and he knew it. He looked around the station, the monumental architecture, the vaulted marble ceilings. The entire place was empty, and yet someone was watching him. Someone was always watching. He knew because as soon as he got there, leaning on the rail above the concourse in his long coat and black gloves, one of the phones began to ring. It didn't matter when he came—whether he was summoned or not. Day or night, if he came to this spot, as soon as he was alone, the phone rang. The clanging filled the cavernous hall, and he snatched it, as much to stop the noise as any other reason.

On the other end of the line was a man's voice, Russian, raspy, as if carved from granite. "Declan Haines?"

It wasn't the voice he'd been expecting. He hadn't heard it before.

"Where's Aralov?" he said. "I deal with Aralov."

"You deal with me now." The tone brooked no debate.

Declan's jaw tightened. "What happened to him?"

"What do you care?"

Igor Aralov had been the bane of Declan's life for two

years. There was no one on earth he would have killed more gladly. But this change, this new voice, was not good.

"I don't know you," he said.

"You listen to me very carefully," the voice said. "Aralov's dead. You work for me now."

"Why would I?"

"Because I've got the footage. I know your secret, you sick fuck."

Declan balled his fist. He wanted to punch something. They had him by the balls, and they were never going to let him go. They would use him until there was nothing left to use. Then they would leave his body to rot in the open like the carcass it was.

"Did you hear what I said, Declan?"

Declan said nothing. This was just one more symptom of his powerlessness, one more byproduct of his addiction. Sometimes he wondered if he should just let them release the footage. It would be easier that way. That was when he looked most closely, most longingly, at the pistol.

Igor Aralov had manipulated him like a puppet. Now Igor was dead, something Declan had fantasized about a million times, and there was a new man in his place. Sooner or later, and this he knew with every ounce of his being, he would have to eat a bullet—he would have to die by his own hand.

"Did you hear me?" the man said again.

"I heard you," Declan said.

"Good, now go to the Saint Royal Hotel and get a room. Instructions will follow."

21

The embassy in London was at Nine Elms, directly across the river from MI6. When Ada first arrived, she spent an entire weekend rewatching all the Bond movies. Now, every time she crossed the Vauxhall Bridge, she half-expected to run into Judi Dench.

Her cab pulled up at the sidewalk, and she entered through the west pavilion staff entrance.

"Back already?" the Marine said as she cleared security.

He'd been there a few hours earlier when she left for the night. She made note that he remembered her and eyed him cagily. He had the build of a linebacker. He'd throw her around a bedroom like a rag doll if she let him.

"No rest for the wicked," she said and immediately berated herself.

No rest for the wicked?

She couldn't have thought of a lamer response if she tried. She avoided making eye contact with him while buying her coffee but stole a glance on her way to the elevators.

Ada's official cover was as an attaché with the Department of Agriculture, and, as she made her way to her desk, she wondered if this after-hours errand might even be related to that role.

"Hello?" she called as she passed the reception, but it seemed no one was there. The other desks in her section were empty. She got up and made a round of the entire department. All the offices, all the desks—empty.

She realized then that she didn't know who'd been on the other end of the line when she'd picked up earlier. For all she knew, the message hadn't been meant for her. She looked at her watch and wondered if she could steal an hour's sleep in the conference room. She was seriously considering when the light above the elevator came on.

She took a sip of her coffee and waited, arms crossed, watching as if it was her job to make sure no one got off when the doors opened.

When they did open, a man she didn't recognize, dressed in a tailored black suit and crisp shirt, stepped out and looked at her. He looked around to make sure no one else was there and said, "Are you Ada Hudson?"

Ada nodded.

"I need your codeword."

"My what?"

"Your codeword," he repeated, offering no explanation.

He was holding a drab, brown, tamper-proof envelope, and Ada wondered what in the world he was talking about.

"Your SOG word," he said, lowering his voice.

"SOG?" she said.

The man said nothing. She could tell the envelope was for her, but she wouldn't be seeing it until she gave him what he wanted. Then she realized what he wanted—what SOG was.

Special Operations Group.

"Is this?" she said, but the man's face was so still, so blank, that she knew there was no point asking him for details. "Claymore," she said quietly.

He handed her the envelope and, without another word, turned and got back in the elevator.

"Wait," Ada said.

He looked at her but said nothing. When the doors started to shut, he did nothing to stop them. Then he was gone.

Ada looked at the closed doors for a moment, then went to her desk and sat down. She took a sip of her coffee.

Claymore, she thought. Laurel.

She examined the envelope. She'd seen the kind before, they were common at Langley, but she'd never received one herself. It was designed with the same intent as a wax seal, not to protect the contents, so much as to make it obvious if someone else had looked at them.

She used a letter opener to cut through a holographic panel and then tipped the contents of the envelope onto her desk. It contained an ordinary-looking Amex credit card and a single piece of paper. On the paper was a brief, typed message.

Go to Victoria Station.

From the payphones in the central concourse, call the Saint Royal Hotel in Washington.

Ask for the penthouse.

When they ask who's calling, give your codeword.

Destroy this message right now.

Ada glanced around the room as if suddenly wary of someone sneaking up on her. There was no one there. She read the message again, then tore it up, brought the scraps to the women's washroom, and flushed them down the drain.

22

Declan stood by the window of his thirteen-hundred-dollar-a-night suite and looked out at Lafayette Square. With the soft snow and the glow of the street lamps, he could have been looking back in time a century. There was even a horse and carriage out there.

He lit a cigarette and wondered what was coming. What would they make him do? If there was one thing the GRU knew, it was that desperation could make a man do anything. It was all they needed to know.

He went to the minibar and grabbed the miniature bottle of scotch, unscrewed the top, and drained the contents. He was about to do the same to the vodka when the hotel phone rang.

He stared at it. He didn't want to answer.

Declan had done terrible things in his life, unspeakable things, things that made him sick to his stomach when he thought of them. He'd done them before the GRU found him, and he would have continued to do them had he never come on their radar. But that didn't make them any easier to stomach.

He was a man with a rotten soul, and he knew it. The anima of the world would breathe a sigh of relief when he died. His very existence was a burden to it. But knowing that didn't change anything. He was what he was. A viper, a scorpion, a rat.

He picked up the phone and said, "What is it?"

It was the hotel concierge. "Mr. Haines, we have a package for you."

"A package?"

"Yes, sir."

"What is it?"

"I can't say, sir."

"What does it look like?"

"It's an envelope, sir."

"An envelope?"

"Yes, sir."

Declan sighed. "All right, send it up."

He hung up the phone, went back to the minibar, and drained the vodka and the gin. When the knock came on the door, he checked the peephole. It was a slight man in a bellhop's uniform. He opened the door.

"Your package, sir."

The bellhop handed him an envelope. It was rigid, like the ones used to protect photographs.

"Thank you," Declan said.

The bellhop made no sign of leaving, and Declan reached into his pocket and pulled out a five-dollar bill.

"Thank you, sir."

"Send someone to restock the minibar, would you?" Declan said before shutting the door.

Then he sat on the bed and opened the envelope. It contained photographs, black and white, enlarged. The first was a clear shot of a woman's face. She was pale with dark features, extremely attractive. Others showed her from different angles at different spots around the city. She dressed as if trying to conceal herself, sunglasses, a scarf on her hair. The stills had been lifted from security camera footage but were very clear. A number showed her entering the Saint Royal Hotel. The timestamp was from just a few hours earlier. She was probably in the hotel at that very moment.

The next set of photos showed her in various bedrooms, usually hotel rooms, having sex with different men. Declan flipped through them quickly, then went back and re-examined each closely in turn.

"Son of a bitch," he said to himself.

The footage was distinctive. He recognized it instantly. The positioning of the camera directly in front of the bed, tilted downward at a forty-five-degree angle. The four-to-three aspect ratio, like old Hasselblad or Rolleiflex medium-format cameras. The ultra-high resolution.

The camera Igor Aralov used was a military-grade Imperx model with a sixty-four-megapixel feed at twenty-four frames-per-second. Declan had seen footage of himself taken with the very same model, he'd watched it a thousand times, and there was zero doubt in his mind these pictures were a match.

This woman was one of Igor Aralov's. She was a Main Directorate widow, charged with obtaining kompromat from targets all over the world. She was a professional, highly trained in deception, and any attempt to approach her would be extremely dangerous.

But Declan could already see why she'd been assigned to him.

In each of the encounters, she was allowing the man to *mishandle* her in a specific way. *Allowing* was, of course, a term Declan understood loosely. She wasn't consenting to the treatment, not in any moral or legal sense. In some, she was struggling, perhaps for real, perhaps acting. In others, she was genuinely frightened. He could see it in her eyes. It thrilled him.

In every one of the photos, the man had both hands on her neck, and in at least one, her life was in real danger.

That wasn't a coincidence. Declan knew that. The same woman, over and over, in exactly the same predicament? That didn't just happen.

She was a GRU operative. It was in her power to kill any of those men. But instead, again and again, she writhed on a bed while he held her down and, at the very least, toyed with the idea of strangling her.

To a man of Declan's predilection, that was a signal as subtle as a foghorn. He saw right into her primitive, atavistic unconscious. He looked at the closeups of the men's hands on her throat. Declan had a *modus operandi*. Whoever had sent him this envelope knew what it was. What these photos showed was that this woman was susceptible to it.

There was no way to know for certain until he met her in person, but Declan was aroused. He understood this woman or thought he did. He felt he could handle her—tame her. He thought he could break her will beneath the force of his own.

And he wanted to.

23

A da left the embassy and got in one of the cabs waiting outside.

"Victoria station," she said. "And step on it."

"I'll go as fast as I'm allowed," the driver said, but there was so little traffic that she was getting out at Grosvenor Gardens scarcely three minutes later. The bronze statue of Ferdinand Foch loomed over her as she hurried across the street and into the station's central concourse. The stores were still closed, the station all but empty, and she found the payphones quickly.

Using her cell, she looked up the number of the Saint Royal Hotel, then dialed it on the payphone. An automated voice came on, asking her to insert a credit card and accept an exorbitant international rate. She entered one of her personal cards, and a moment later, a man's voice said, "Saint Royal, Washington DC."

"Penthouse, please," Ada said.

"Please hold."

Ada lit a cigarette and glanced around the concourse.

The man came back on the line and said, "Who may I say is calling?"

Ada swallowed. "Claymore," she said.

She was put back on hold, then heard the clicking of a call being transferred. She waited and a woman's voice, young with a slight Russian accent, said, "Who is this?"

Ada sucked on the cigarette and exhaled. "This is Claymore."

"Claymore?" the woman said.

"Yes."

"Hudson?" the woman said. "Is that correct?"

"Ada," Ada said.

Ada told herself to breathe—to speak calmly. She'd been training for this moment her entire life and wanted it with every fiber of her being.

"Ada Hudson," the woman said, "you've been activated as a paramilitary operative by the Special Operations Group of the Central Intelligence Agency. Do you understand what I just said?"

"I understand," Ada said, struggling to believe what she was hearing. She'd known Laurel was in deep, she wouldn't have been rubbing shoulders with Levi Roth if she wasn't, but the Special Operations Group? It didn't get any deeper than that.

"The information I'm about to give you is classified under Executive Order 13526 of and protected under US federal law by the Espionage Act of 1917 and the Intelligence Identities Protection Act of 1982."

"I understand," Ada said.

"You no longer work for the Central Intelligence Agency, the US Department of Agriculture, or the United States government in any capacity, and your status and access at the

US embassy has been revoked. You are not to return to the US embassy, nor are you to return to the apartment issued to you by the US Department of State. Do you understand?"

Ada's head was spinning. "I understand," she said, "and I waive my right to be informed of my...."

"If you are captured, Ada, you will be disavowed. You will be on your own."

"I understand everything," Ada said. "I signed up for this with my eyes open. I waive my right to further disclosures. I'm ready."

"All right," the woman said. "Just remember, no going back to your old life. No personal calls. No personal activities. You're a paramilitary operative now. Ada Hudson no longer exists."

"Off the grid," Ada said. "Completely off the grid."

"Okay. Your codename is Claymore. Your line operative is Laurel Everlane. If you need to make contact with her or anyone else, you do so through me the same way you made this phone call."

"From this phone?"

"From any ordinary British payphone."

"All right."

"No cell phones. No private landlines. No hotel room phones."

"Okay," Ada said.

Payphones weren't quite as ubiquitous as they'd once been, but she'd find one when she needed one.

She looked across the concourse. A girl in a navy apron was opening a coffee shop, sweeping the seating area. She glanced in Ada's direction, and Ada had to tell herself there was nothing suspicious about it.

"You're going to need to remember your training for this," the woman said. "Everything you know about craft.

Every trick of the trade. Every covert tactic."

"Okay," Ada said.

"Once engaged, your life will be in immediate danger. There are GRU assets across London at this very moment who will be authorized to kill you."

"I'm ready," Ada said.

The woman's voice changed then, became less robotic, more human. "This is a dangerous mission, Ada."

"I understand," Ada said.

"I mean it."

"I'm a CIA operative," Ada said firmly. "I've trained for this moment my entire life."

"Take a moment," the woman said.

"I've had plenty of time to think this over."

"You've recently suffered a personal tragedy," the woman said.

"Excuse me?"

"It was very recent," the woman said. "It would be understandable if you were, for any reason...."

"If I were what?"

"*Unready.*"

"*Unready*?" Ada said. "Would you feel *unready* if your mother had just been blown to bits and someone gave you the chance to do something about it?"

The woman was quiet for a moment, then said, "No, Ada. I would not."

"Then let's get on with this. I'm ready for the mission. I want this."

"Okay," the woman said. "There's a Russian defector coming in."

"All right."

"A scientist. Very important."

"He's in London?"

"Yes, hiding. We still don't know where and he wants to keep it that way."

"Okay."

"His name is Gazinsky. Sacha Gazinsky. Remember it. He's traveling with his nine-year-old daughter."

"Okay."

"He's terrified of the GRU."

"Of course."

"At some point in the next few hours, he's going to give us his location. When he does, it will be passed to you."

"And I'll make contact?"

"Yes. He has scientific information. Tell him Roth is willing to cut a deal for it."

"This has something to do with the explosion in the Arctic," Ada said.

The woman ignored the comment. "This is a dark mission of the Special Operations Group. It has been authorized secretly by the director of the CIA, Levi Roth, and President Ingram Montgomery. No one else knows of it—not in London, not in Langley. The London embassy, the State Department, and all CIA resources globally are off-limits to you from this moment onward."

"I understand."

"You have me, you have Laurel, you have the Group. That's it. We operate alone."

"I understand."

"You need backup, you come to us."

"Okay."

"You need access to a resource...."

"I come to you."

"Right."

"I get it," Ada said.

"At no point do you report in. Not to Langley, not to the station chief, not to your line manager. Is that clear?"

"Crystal."

"Don't go to your apartment. Don't use your cell. Don't use your car."

"I don't have a car."

The woman sighed. Her voice was strained. Ada could tell she was stressed. "Laurel says you're good for this," the woman said.

The comment took Ada by surprise. "I am good for it," she said.

"The GRU is looking for this guy, Ada. They want him back, bad. The Russian President wants him back."

"Okay."

"That means no mistakes. Even a single slip and they'll find you. Believe me. And if they find you, they find him."

"Okay," Ada said, her heart pounding.

"Not leaks. Not flags. No slips. You can't trust our side either."

"I understand," Ada said again.

"Do you have the credit card I sent?"

"Yes."

"Get rid of your personal cards. Get rid of your cell."

"Okay."

"If you carry them, you'll use them, so don't carry them. As soon as we hang up, go to a post office and you put your wallet, your cell, anything electronic, in an envelope and mail it to your apartment. When you need money, use the card I sent. Hotel rooms, restaurants, cabs, phone calls, everything. That card is the only trail you leave. It can't be traced."

"All right."

"The card is also how Sacha's location will be transmitted to you."

"Okay."

"Put the card in an ATM like normal. Any ATM, it doesn't matter. The PIN is your birthday. Two-digit month, two-digit day."

"Okay."

"It's a regular bank card. You can get cash with it. You can see your recent transactions."

"Okay."

"Sacha's location will be entered on the account as a transaction detail. When you view the transactions, you'll see it. At that point, you'll be the only person on earth who knows the information. You and Sacha. It's completely secure. I won't even know it."

"Who'll enter the transaction?"

"Don't worry about that."

"How often should I check for it?"

"Every hour."

"Okay."

"Any questions?"

"What do I do when I find him?"

"First off, you approach him very cautiously. You understand?"

"Yes."

"We don't know for sure what this guy is thinking. It could be a GRU trap for all we know. Don't walk blind into anything, okay. Approach with extreme caution."

"I understand."

"Also, whatever you do, don't scare him off. He'll be jumpy as hell. He'll be terrified someone's going to find him, find his daughter."

"I understand."

"If he is who we think he is, Roth really wants his information. It's *very* valuable."

"Okay. I'll approach softly."

"When you speak to him, tell him the CIA is ready to cut a deal for information relating to the Five P's."

"Five P's."

"Correct. Say that and see what he has to offer. Also get an idea of what he wants in return, money, asylum, a new identity, whatnot."

"Okay."

"Try to get something from him that proves good faith."

"Good faith?"

"Roth's going to want to know what he's offering. How valuable it is. He's also going to want proof the guy is for real. Find out if Sacha has anything like that. It will help Roth if he needs approval for some aspect of the deal."

"Okay."

"Afterward, create some distance. Don't call me from his hotel. Don't call me from anywhere too near him."

"And to call you?"

"Same as before. Use a payphone. Call the Saint Royal. Ask for the penthouse."

"Okay," Ada said. "And now? When I hang up. Where do I go?"

"Lay low. Steer clear of anyone who might recognize you. Disappear."

"Okay."

"Like you trained for."

"Got it."

"Check the card hourly. The address will show there."

"Okay," Ada said.

"And make sure you don't create some sort of trail

leading the GRU to Sacha. Watch your back. Be evasive. You're the only person who'll know where he is."

"I understand."

"All right, Ada. I'm going to hang up. God speed."

God speed," Ada said and was about to hang up when she added, "Wait."

"What is it?"

"What do I call you?"

"You call me Tatyana," the woman said, and the line went dead.

24

Sacha Gazinsky was a man who'd suffered loss in his life. He was fifty-five, thin, with gray hair and an unruly silver stubble on his cheeks and chin. When she was alive, his wife was often mistaken for his daughter. She'd died giving birth to their daughter, Natasha, and now, Natasha was mistaken for his granddaughter.

That didn't bother Sacha. He wasn't impressing anyone. He lived for two things—his work and his daughter. Neither was hampered by his appearance.

He looked across the bed at Natasha. She was sleeping soundly, exhausted by the trip. The room was warm and a lock of hair stuck to her forehead. He reached out and put his hand on her back, feeling the rise and fall of her breath. He would die a thousand times to save her.

They were in a cheap hotel in Soho, a place that accepted cash for the room. They'd arrived the night before, late, on the last Finnair flight from Helsinki. At Heathrow, he withdrew as much money as he could from his cards, over a thousand pounds, and then discarded his wallet, cell, Natasha's iPad, and their passports. From the airport, they took the tube into Central London, changed trains three times, and got off at Oxford Circus.

Sacha was out of his depth. He knew nothing of the GRU's tactics or how to evade them. All he knew was that he had something valuable, something he could trade. If he could stay off the radar long enough to cut a deal with the Americans, Natasha would be safe.

He could have gone to the embassy directly, he'd thought about it, but he knew it was too dangerous. The place was under constant surveillance. The moment he got within half of mile of it, the GRU would know. And even if he made it inside, what then? No one there had the slightest idea who he was. They would see a scruffy Russian off the street with a briefcase in one hand and a nine-year-old daughter in the other. Not exactly the type of thing they were trained to accept. Why would they listen to him? Why would they believe what he said? He wouldn't make it past the lobby, and if he did, it would be to a windowless interrogation room where he explained his case to some disinterested, low-level CIA analyst who had no context, no knowledge of Russia's weapons program, and no power whatsoever to cut him a deal. Without notifying the CIA in advance, without having a senior contact ready to receive him, the risk of his being turned away was too great.

And what then? He would walk right out the front door of the embassy, Natasha in tow, and a bunch of GRU thugs would pick them up at the bottom of the steps.

The only way he had any leverage, the only way he would be met by someone who understood the value of what he had to trade, was if he laid the groundwork.

That required time, and it required explaining his case to Tatyana Aleksandrova before he went anywhere near the embassy.

He'd racked his brain trying to think of all the ways the GRU might find someone on the run, someone alone in a hotel room with no cell phone, no credit card, no electronics. He couldn't think of any, but he knew they existed. There were entire divisions of the GRU that specialized in such things. He wouldn't make the mistake of underestimating them.

The greatest point of vulnerability would be right after he made contact with the Americans. Right now, as far as he could tell, he and Natasha were the only two people alive who knew where they were. When he told Tatyana, that would make three. And who would she tell? How quickly would the circle grow? How careful would each member of that circle be? How confident was he that no one in the CIA, or the London embassy, was in the pocket of the Kremlin?

That was the moment of risk, the moment of extreme danger, but what choice did he have? He'd come to London to cut a deal with the CIA, to get the protection of the CIA. If he couldn't trust them, the plan had already failed.

And what was the plan? Simply to stay off the radar long enough to make the deal. He didn't think an agreement would be difficult to reach, not once the CIA realized who he was. He could give them the Kremlin's entire super-weapons program, every design detail, every technical innovation, and every flaw and vulnerability. Sacha had drawings, blueprints, thousands of gigabytes of technical data and analysis. The new weapons were terrifying, but Sacha was one of the few people alive to know exactly how flawed they were. Their technology contained so many vulnerabilities that, with Sacha's guidance, the US military could readily develop countermeasures that rendered every one of them utterly unusable.

What was the cost of one child's medical treatment when weighed against that?

One *innocent* child's medical treatment.

If they objected to Sacha, and he could see how they might, that was all right. They could do whatever they wanted with him. They could imprison him for contravening every nuclear weapons convention on the planet. They could put him publicly on trial. They could use him for their political purposes. He'd say anything they wanted him to say. He'd plead guilty to any crime. He'd discredit the Kremlin and its doomsday weapons program until he was blue in the face. He'd even let them throw him back to the wolves at the Lubyanka if that was what they wanted.

As long as they took Natasha. She was all that mattered. She was all that had ever mattered to him.

He'd done his best for her. She'd received the very best medical treatment Russia had to offer. Sacha was valuable to the government, his role was critical, and that meant Natasha had been treated for years by the best pediatric geneticists in the country. They took her to the State Clinical Institute No. 6 in Moscow and gave her every test in the book. The eventual conclusion was that she suffered from a vanishingly rare genetic disorder, something so rare it affected only a few hundred children on the entire planet and had never before been diagnosed in Russia.

A team of the most respected doctors in the country swore to Sacha that they could treat her, but Sacha knew enough not to take them at their word. He knew the government would tell him anything. They needed him to keep working on the weapons program, to finish his research, to perfect the prototypes. His daughter's treatment was how they would ensure his cooperation.

But Sacha was a scientist, and his mind worked on

Natasha's predicament by focusing on the science. He began poring over all the available research on her condition. He read everything he could, accessing western medical journals using prepaid credit cards so that no one would know what he was doing. He printed the articles from public computers and put them in the paper binders used by his own research team so they looked like his other work documents. When he was done with the articles, he burned them in a small iron stove behind his house.

He learned that there was nothing the doctors in Moscow could do for Natasha. She was nine years old, and if she kept on the path she was on, she would be dead before her twelfth birthday.

The GRU kept a close eye on Sacha, as they did with all their top scientists. Defections were a constant threat, and they were always vigilant for the signs. If they'd realized what he learned, that there was a potential treatment for her condition, but it was only available outside Russia, both their lives would have been in grave danger. What father could be trusted to remain in a place like Arkhangelsk and continue his job when there was a doctor in the United States who could save his daughter?

The treatment that was being developed was highly experimental and relied on advanced gene therapies that were being developed by a single team at the renowned Children's Research Hospital in Boston, Massachusetts. The team, led by an incredibly talented geneticist named Charles Hannson, hadn't announced a cure for the condition. That was why the GRU hadn't picked up on it. But Sacha, with the single-mindedness of a desperate parent, had been able to piece together from the data that a growing proportion of the patients in Boston were older than twelve. One, a girl of fifteen, had ceased showing symptoms.

For Sacha, the scientist who believed only in what the data could support, that was enough. That was the deal he wanted.

He would give the CIA anything, and in return, they would see to it that Natasha became a patient of Charles Hannson. They didn't have to treat her in Boston, they could keep her somewhere less conspicuous so that she would be safe from GRU revenge-seekers, but Hannson had to oversee her care. That was the deal he was willing to give his life for.

He kissed her on the forehead and left a note on the pillow next to her. He didn't think she would wake before he got back, but if she did, it said he would be back soon and not to leave the room. He'd disconnected the landline from the wall the night before but now jerked it from the back of the receiver as well, breaking the cord. Natasha had no one to call, but he didn't want to risk her unwittingly using the phone for some reason.

He put on a brimmed hat and dark glasses and went down to the lobby in the hotel's rickety old elevator. Even there, he found himself looking around it suspiciously for hidden cameras. As he left the hotel, he expected with every step that someone would stop him. No one did.

It was dawn, the light was dim, and low cloud hung over the street like a fog. He walked quickly to Piccadilly Circus, a major intersection, and took the stairs down to the underground station. There, from a payphone, he dialed the number Tatyana had given him.

"Hello," he said in Russian when it answered, glancing at every passerby suspiciously.

"Hello," a voice said. It was a woman's voice, but not Tatyana.

"Where's Tatyana?" he said.

The woman spoke Russian, but he could tell from the accent she was American.

"Don't give me any names," she said.

"I need to speak to her."

"The number you dialed has been redirected to an operator for a division of the Central Intelligence Agency that is expecting a message from you."

"What?"

"Please limit your message to only the essential information required."

"What is this?"

"This conversation will not be acknowledged by the government of the United States, cannot be relied on in legal proceedings in any jurisdiction, and is not protected by federal law or the constitution of the United States. Do you understand?"

Sacha's head was spinning. The woman's Russian was serviceable, but what she was saying made absolutely no sense to him.

"Do you understand?" she said again.

"Yes," he lied.

"This conversation does not represent an agreement or an intention to form an agreement with the government of the United States or its agents. Do you understand?"

Sacha didn't know what this was. He'd told Tatyana he wanted to defect and had assumed, perhaps naively, that he would continue dealing with her personally. He had no idea who this woman was.

"Sir," the woman said. "Do you understand what I have told you?"

He didn't know what to say. "I can't speak to Tatyana?"

"Sir, I don't know who that is. I don't know who you are. I'm a conduit. What you tell me will be passed to the appropriate destination. This is for your protection and the protection of our assets."

"I don't..." Sacha said, "I'm not an...."

"Sir, if there's no message, I must hang up."

"No," Sacha said. "Don't hang up. I have a message."

"Proceed."

Sacha swallowed. What he was about to tell this woman, this complete stranger, was information that could end his life—end his daughter's life.

"Sir, what's the message?"

But if he didn't tell her, it was only a matter of time before the GRU found him.

"Sir?"

He had no other option.

"I'm hanging up."

"Wait. I'm in Soho. Mildred Arms Hotel. Room 470."

L aurel sat in the back of Roth's Cadillac Escalade, waiting while his plane taxied to a stop outside the hangar.

"How sweet," he said when he saw her. "You didn't have to come."

She smiled thinly. "What can I say? I missed you."

Andrews Air Force Base was ten miles from Central DC, and Roth told the driver to take them to the Saint Royal. It was early, before dawn, and traffic was light. Laurel was holding a cup of coffee in a to-go cup. On the seat next to her was a copy of *The Post*.

"The agent has Sacha's location," she said.

"The agent?"

"The agent you insisted take over."

Roth nodded. He didn't want to get into all that, not with Laurel. He'd done what he had to.

"Tatyana's upset, Roth."

"I'm sure she is."

"She doesn't understand why you sent her back."

"Well, luckily, our nation's security doesn't rely on her understanding."

"I don't understand it either. Sacha Gazinsky is her contact. She knows him. They've met."

"I know that."

"Slept together."

"Laurel, I know."

"Sending a different agent, that risks spooking him. He was expecting her."

"Your other agent is more than capable."

"Is she?"

"Yes."

Laurel shook her head. "You don't even know the name of the other agent."

"Of course I do."

She was pissed off. He'd known she would be, but that didn't make it any more comfortable. He looked out the window. It was going to be another long day.

"I don't suppose you picked me up one of those," he said, looking at her coffee.

"You can get your own."

"And here I was, thinking you'd come out to welcome me home."

She rolled her eyes.

Roth pushed the button to speak to the driver. "There's a Starbucks up ahead," he said.

"You got it, boss."

He looked again at Laurel, but the ferocity of her eyes made him look away. If she was this angry over this, what would it be like if she ever found out he'd thrown Tatyana to the wolves?

"Hudson," he said.

"What?"

"That's the agent's name. Ada Hudson."

Laurel wasn't impressed. "Have you met her?"

"You vouched for her. That's enough for me."

"This is her first mission."

Roth shrugged. "Meet a guy, verify he is what he says he is, find out what he's got to trade. It's hardly *rocket science*."

"Oh, you're hilarious."

"I try."

"If something happens to her, Roth."

"To Tatyana?"

"To Ada."

"Right."

"I swear to God."

Roth understood why she was mad. What he'd done, under any normal circumstances, was the wrong call. But these weren't normal circumstances. This was a stab in the back, a betrayal, one that Laurel and Tatyana would never see coming. And the guilt ate at Roth.

Laurel looked out as they pulled into the drive-through. "You really think he's going to give us a backdoor to Petrel?" she said.

"I live in hope, Laurel. I live in hope," he said, opening the window. "You want anything?"

She didn't answer. He asked the driver, who took a latte.

"You're nervous about something," he said as they pulled up to the payment window.

Her eyes flashed back at him. "I was just forced to risk the life of an agent, and I'm not sure why."

"There's something else."

"I'm mad at you, Roth. I'm very mad."

"Something else, though."

She sighed. "It's Tatyana."

"What about her."

"She's pissed at you. I mean *really* pissed."

"I can handle that."

"And, well..."

"Laurel, what happened?"

"She let a stranger into her...."

"Into her..."

Laurel nodded.

"Into her *what*, Laurel?"

"Don't make me spell it out."

"Her bed?"

"Yes."

Roth had known this was coming. He'd given Tenet the greenlight before getting on the plane. The footage led right to Tatyana. What surprised him was how quickly the GRU had moved. Igor Aralov's successor was more dangerous than he'd been given credit for. Viktor Lapin, the name meant rabbit, but Roth saw him now for the shark he was.

And it broke his heart because he knew he was betraying all of them—Laurel, Tatyana, Ada. He'd thrown all three in the water, and now, no matter how close the shark's jaws got, he would have to let it play out. He would have to watch, motionless, even as the water turned crimson with their blood.

There was no other way.

Getting Tenet into the Kremlin was the final move, the checkmate, the death blow. It was the culmination of decades of preparation, and if it allowed Roth to depose Molotov and avoid a war, then any price was worth paying. It was painful, but he was willing to sacrifice any of them, Sacha Gazinsky included, if it got Tenet into the Kremlin.

He took a sip of his coffee. It scalded him.

"Damn it."

Laurel was surprised. The reaction wasn't like him.

"Is everything all right?"

"It's fine."

"You sure?"

"Just got some on my shirt," he said before bringing the subject back to Tatyana. "This isn't the first time she's done something like this."

"No," Laurel said, "but it's the first time she's been this angry."

"It's because of the flight. What I said to her."

"What did you say to her?"

"I said she was getting careless."

"How did she take that?"

"How do you think?"

Laurel nodded, then said, "You know, this isn't something that's going to stop happening."

"I know that."

"Not for her, and not for me either."

Roth looked at her but said nothing.

"We're not your prisoners, Roth. You can't expect us to act like we are."

"Can I expect you to be discreet?"

"Were you discreet?" Laurel said.

"What does that mean?"

"When you were our age? When you were in our position?"

Roth pictured Alona. "When I was in your position," he said, "I acted like discretion was the difference between life and death."

Laurel looked away. She sensed she might have crossed a line. She said, "Well, I ran the guy."

"And?"

"It could have been worse."

"Oh, could it?"

"Declan Haines. Late-thirties. He's a US citizen. A veteran, actually."

"State databases?"

"I ran every federal database and all fifty states."

"Five eyes? MI6?"

"He's clean," she said. "He travels a lot, but he's clean."

"What sort of travels?"

"Business. He's been to Moscow."

"You're kidding me."

"He's got the Silver Star, Roth. His company is a contractor for the DoD. He's got a security clearance."

"Well, there's nothing to worry about then, is there?" he said sarcastically.

"He's been to over seventy countries. Moscow twice in six years. That's not an unusual pattern. It's not a flag."

"Like hell, it's not."

"This could be a lot worse," she said again. "All things considered."

"I'm glad you think so."

Laurel took a sip of her coffee, and Roth could see something was still bothering her. "The thing is," she said, "she found him at the hotel."

"The Saint Royal?"

"Yes."

Roth had opened the lid of his coffee and was blowing on it.

The hotel was problematic, and Laurel knew it. It wasn't just that their penthouse was there, which was a breach in itself, but rather the fact that it was predictable. It was part of a pattern. Patterns were dangerous. Habits. Daily routines. That was where they got you.

"Maybe you should have a word with her."

"I will."

"She knows better than this."

"I know."

"I mean, come on."

"I know, Roth."

Roth sighed. They were pulling up in front of the hotel. "She's doing this to piss me off," he said.

Laurel nodded.

"A big fuck you to the boss."

"She knows how to get her point across."

26

A da hailed a cab outside the train station.

"Berkeley Square," she said to the driver.

It was a short ride, and the cab dropped her outside an antiquarian bookstore on the corner of Hill Street. As she rounded the corner, the sycamores in the park before her exuded a mist that clouded the air and made it softer. The buildings were neat, Pre-Raphaelite townhouses. Winston Churchill once lived at number forty-eight. Charles Royce, at twenty-one. William Waldorf Astor, richest man in America, lived at Lansdowne House on the square's south end.

It was all very prim and handsome, the epitome of Mayfair chic, with the residences gradually giving way to hedge fund offices, wealth managers, and private banks.

Ada looked around the square carefully. It would soon be bustling with people, but for now, it was empty. A bus passed but didn't stop. She walked through the park to the other side of the square and entered the Café L'Express, an elegant coffee shop that was just being opened up for the morning.

She ordered an Americano and found a seat outside, overlooking the street. She was the only customer, and took the liberty of lighting herself a cigarette. As she watched the street, she thought back to her training, the telltale signs she was being followed.

When she finished the coffee she got up and went to the ATM at the building next door. The square was getting busier, people arriving in smart, tailored suits with leather briefcases and expensive shoes. She put the card in the machine and followed the prompts to view transactions.

Her heart thudded when she saw the message.

Room 470
Mildred Arms Hotel, Soho

This was it, the moment she'd been waiting for. She was in play. And if she was in play, she needed a gun.

One of the less advertised facts about Berkeley Square was that it was home to a higher density of private banks and obscure European finance houses than any other patch of real estate on the planet. It was a miniature Switzerland, a Liechtenstein, right in the center of Mayfair, where financial regulations and tax laws disappeared for those clients rich enough to afford it.

On the square's east face, between an opulent private club called Annabel's, and a traditional pub called The Footman, was the London branch of a small Gibraltor-based banking house called Saffron & Saracen. It wasn't a bank in the ordinary sense of the word. In centuries past, it provided financing to merchants and ship-owners. Today, Ada wasn't sure what it did. All she knew was that it offered some of the most secure safe deposit boxes in the city, and they were available to clients at any hour of the day or night.

She walked up to its imposing door and rapped the brass knocker. The door opened, and she entered an anteroom of paneled wood and a smooth, marble floor. When the door behind her shut, the next opened, leading her into a large hall with a ceiling three stories high.

An officious woman in a black and white tweed suit came into the hall from a side room and said, "Ms. Hudson, how nice to see you."

Ada had been to the bank only once before, back when she first arrived in the city. This woman hadn't been there that day but knew her name now.

"Thank you," Ada said.

Ada felt out of her depth in the place. It was all a far cry from her Wells Fargo branch back home.

It was Laurel Everlane she had to thank for this.

"You need a cache," Laurel told her.

"The CIA has caches."

"You need your own."

"For what?"

"*Emergencies.*"

At the time, Ada had struggled to imagine a situation in which CIA drop boxes would be off-limits. Now, she was dark-channeled, she'd been told not to use anything that could be tracked by London Station, and she saw the wisdom of Laurel's advice.

"What can I do for you this morning?" the woman said.

"You can tell me where you bought that suit," Ada said.

The woman smiled very thinly, unamused.

"I need to access my box," Ada said, clearing her throat.

"Of course. If you'll follow me."

The woman led her through a set of heavy doors, inlaid

with deep carvings, and told her to have a seat. The chairs were mahogany. They looked like they'd come out of a church. The whole place smelled of furniture polish.

"Can I get you anything?"

"I'm fine," Ada said.

The woman disappeared, and a minute later, a man dressed like the head waiter of the Ritz appeared holding a silver tray. On the tray was a black electronic device that looked like an old Blackberry cell phone.

"If you would be so kind," he said, handing her the device.

He turned away, and Ada entered the sixteen-digit code she'd chosen when she'd set up the box. When she was done, the device chimed softly, and the man took it from her.

"If you would be so kind," he said again, leading the way to another set of doors. He spoke theatrically, putting all the emphasis on the first syllable of the sentence.

Ada followed him into a wide corridor, decorated in the same nineteenth-century fashion as the rooms she'd already passed. The only difference was that every ten feet or so, they passed a set of ultra-modern, stainless steel doors. At the fifth set of these, they stopped. The man was wearing white leather gloves, and he removed them very deliberately, then placed his fingertips on a scanner next to the door. The door opened to reveal a sterile room, harshly lit with bright fluorescent bulbs. In the center of the room, directly beneath the light, was a stainless steel table, and on the table was a metal box, about the size of a microwave oven, textured like the surface of a golf ball.

"When you're ready to leave," the man said, emphasis on the *when,* "or if you require assistance for any reason, press the green button on the table."

"Thank you," Ada said.

She entered the room and the doors shut behind her with the whoosh of an air seal being formed. She felt a slight change in air pressure and instinctively looked for the ventilation source. On the wall in front of her, just below the ceiling, was a black metal grill, about six inches by twenty-four. From it came a steady stream of conditioned air.

That, the light above her head, the table, the box, and the green button, were the only items in the room.

She opened the box for the first time since she'd packed it. It contained cash in a number of currencies, identity documents from various countries bearing her image but false aliases, some prescription medications that would be useful in an emergency, two guns, a suppressor, and ammo. The larger of the guns was a Heckler & Koch MP5 submachine gun. The smaller was a Mark 23 semi-automatic pistol, chambered for a .45 ACP.

That pistol packed a punch, more than a standard-issue sidearm, which was why she'd packed it. She took it out of the box and examined it, attached the suppressor, and loaded it. Then she put it in her coat, along with extra ammo, some cash, and a false US passport. Then she shut the box, locked it, and pressed the green button.

The street was a little busier when she got back out. She crossed into the park and walked through it slowly, taking time to look over her shoulder in case she was being followed. On New Bond Street, she hailed a cab and had it take her to Chinatown Gate. From there, she walked briskly through the busier, pedestrianized area of Chinatown as far as Leicester Square. There, she hailed another cab and said to the driver, "Mildred Arms, Soho."

She was nervous. This was it—the defector's location. If she led anyone to him, his blood would be on her hands.

"This will do," she said to the driver when she was a few hundred yards shy of the hotel.

She got out and looked around. There were no other cars on the street. Her cab pulled away, and she watched until it rounded the corner. Then she made her way slowly down the street, taking time to look in the store windows as she passed.

Soho had a distinct character. It was a place where prostitutes and brothels and sex shops rubbed shoulders with hipsters and advertising agencies and trendy clothing stores. She stopped at a store selling fetish costumes and looked in the window. Inside, the store was dark, and the glass created a mirror. Behind her, the street was empty. She glanced skyward. Unless someone was watching from above, she was in the clear.

She'd intended to enter the hotel but, when she got there, decided to take one final precaution. This time for her own safety as much as Sacha's. Tatyana had warned her not to walk in blind. She crossed the street and entered a small café.

"An espresso," she said.

"For here?" the barista said.

She nodded. She was the only customer and took a seat by the window. Outside, some cars passed—a FedEx van, a man with an umbrella. No one went in or out of the hotel, which was a dilapidated place with a set of concrete steps leading to brass doors. Above the steps, an overhang lined with light bulbs created what might once have passed as a snazzy entrance. Now, it looked more like a rundown movie theater.

She looked at the barista, a guy about her age in a black t-shirt and brown apron, and waited until he noticed her looking. "Would you mind terribly doing me a favor?" she said.

"That depends?" he said, a sly grin crossing his face.

"Phone the hotel across the street and tell them room 470's order is ready."

"What order?"

Ada gave the guy a mischievous smile. She wasn't above using charm to get what she wanted.

"You can use the phone if you like," he said.

"No thanks," she said as if he was the one asking the favor. "You do it."

27

"Declan Haines," Viktor said into the phone. "How nice of you to call."

"I bedded your little whore," Declan said.

"I'm looking at the tape now, Declan."

Viktor had, in fact, watched it over a dozen times. The first time he watched it, he'd been holding a cigarette, and when he heard Tatyana tell him what she wanted, he dropped it in his lap. He had to stand up to brush it off before it burned him.

"How do you like it?"

"Very nice work," Viktor said, "but it doesn't show whether you managed to plant a device."

"I couldn't."

"All you had to do was slip it in her purse."

"She was too careful. She didn't let me out of her sight the entire time."

"Did she drink?"

"Only in the bar."

Declan had laced the wine in his room with a very small amount of gamma-hydroxybutyric acid and a crushed

Rohypnol tablet. Not so much that she would have been able to tell she'd been drugged, but enough to get her guard down a little.

"And she didn't sleep?"

"She did not," Declan said. "It was wham, bam, thank you, ma'am. Then she was gone."

Viktor sighed. Declan had performed *admirably*, but the truth was, there was very little chance of him getting any meaningful intelligence from someone like Tatyana Aleksandrova. She was a professional. Her GRU training file showed one of the highest test scores of her entire cohort. Her service record was as near flawless as Viktor had seen. She may have been straying from the straight and narrow after hours, she shouldn't have been in that bar, and she certainly shouldn't have been bedding strangers, but planting a bug on her? That wasn't happening, and Viktor knew it.

"The most important thing is that you don't tip her off," Viktor said. "Get as close as you can, see her as often as she lets you, but don't do anything rash."

"Understood," Declan said.

"Keep giving her what she wants."

"My pleasure," Declan said.

"Yes," Viktor said. "I'll bet it is."

He hung up the phone, and his mind went to Gray Coat. The Kremlin was watching. The President was watching. Suvorov had tapped him to deliver the goods. It wouldn't do to come up empty-handed.

He lit another cigarette and called in his secretary. She opened the door and stood by it hesitantly, reluctant to enter. She was wearing a rather stern dress, black with a white collar framing her face as if she'd just stepped out of a Vermeer portrait. Her hair was tied back, and her legs were covered in opaque black stockings.

"I prefer you with your hair down," he said.

She'd gone out of her way to discourage his advances and looked now at the floor, avoiding eye contact. He was quite sure the very sight of him made her skin crawl.

"Place a call with the Prime Directorate," he said. "I need to speak to Suvorov."

"Very good, sir."

"And bring fresh coffee," he said. "This pot's cold."

A moment later, his phone rang. Suvorov's secretary was on the line waiting to connect him. And then, Suvorov's sickly voice. "I hope it's good news, Viktor."

"My guy made contact."

"The masochist?"

"Sadomasochist."

"That was fast."

"Like a fly to shit, sir."

"I can see why you put so much stock in him."

"I'm not the only one."

"Did he get anything?"

"He found out how she likes it."

"Very funny, Viktor."

"Sorry, sir."

"Nothing about the scientist?"

"Not yet, sir."

"And a bug? Did he plant a bug?"

"No, sir, but he's going to maintain contact. She'll let her guard down sooner or later."

"You make sure she does, Viktor."

"Yes, sir."

"And make sure he treads very lightly. If we lose her, we lose Sacha Gazinsky."

"I'll notify you the moment I have more to report, sir."

Viktor was about to hang up when Suvorov said, "Oh, Viktor."

"Yes, sir?"

"Is your man filming these encounters?"

"He is, sir, yes."

"I'm going to need the tapes."

Viktor hesitated only a second, then said, "Very good, sir."

He hung up and stared at the phone. There was no reason for Suvorov to ask for the tapes, he thought, other than titillation.

The secretary arrived with the coffee and placed it on his desk.

"Pour it," Viktor said, and while she did so, he pressed play on Declan's footage once more.

She glanced at the screen, then looked away immediately.

"Is there anything else, sir?"

"Hmm," he said languidly, leaning back in his seat. "Anything else?" His eyes moved from her to the screen and back again. Very gradually, she began backing away from him.

"If there's nothing else...."

She was about to reach the door when he said, "Tell me, Varvara...." He'd never addressed her by name before, and the sound of it caught her attention. "Did you ever work under Igor Aralov?"

She answered quickly, nervously, plainly uncomfortable.

"I did not, sir. Agniya was always his girl. They didn't have time to replace her after...."

"After?"

Varvara swallowed. "Her death, sir."

Viktor wasn't surprised she was uncomfortable. A

woman named Agniya Bunina had been Igor's secretary. She'd occupied the position for years. There'd even been rumor of a relationship between them. It all ended when Igor strangled her to death on her living room floor. She'd been keeping secrets, a dangerous thing in their world.

"Ah yes," Viktor said, smiling lustily. He was enjoying this. "Rumor has it, she was his *girl*, as you put it, in more ways than one."

"I wouldn't know anything about that, sir."

"Come, Varvara. I know you all chatter and chirp like little birds."

"Agniya was very discreet, sir."

"She was, she was," Viktor said. "So discreet, in fact, that she kept secrets even from him."

Varvara nodded.

"A private database, from what I hear. Something she was sharing with the Prime Directorate."

"I know nothing of it, sir."

"Of course," Viktor said. "Of course."

She inched closer to the door. Her discomfort was such a pleasure to him.

"The man she answered to at the Prime Directorate," Viktor said, "his name was Davidov."

Varvara's face remained motionless.

"Evgraf Davidov," Viktor said. "A distinctive name if ever I heard one."

She was like a fly in a spider's web.

"Such an old-fashioned name," Viktor said. "Don't you think?"

She nodded.

"I'd remember it if I ever heard it," he said.

She shifted on her feet uncomfortably. He could tell she

knew. These secretaries, they were as thick as thieves. They had no secrets from each other.

"He's dead, of course."

"I didn't know that," Varvara said.

"Of course you didn't. Why would you?"

She was as still as a deer caught in a wolf's gaze.

"There's no reason to hold back from me, sweetheart. Igor's dead. Davidov's dead. Agniya's dead."

"I'm not holding back."

He shook his head slowly as if her reticence disappointed him greatly. "Things can get a whole lot *uglier* around here," he said.

"Sir, truly…" she stammered.

"A whole lot uglier," he said again and then pressed play on the video of Tatyana and Declan. "Come closer, my dear. Come and see."

She took a small step in his direction, and he turned the monitor toward her. He let it play for a minute. Tatyana restrained. Declan's hands tightening on her throat for a longer and longer time between breaths.

"It really is quite thrilling, don't you think?" Viktor said.

Varvara said nothing. She was scared.

"Quite beautiful."

"Sir, please, I really don't…."

"As you can see," Viktor said, nodding to the growing bulge in his lap, "I certainly think so."

"Agniya kept tabs on Igor for the Prime Directorate," Varvara said.

"She kept the files on Davidov's server," Viktor said. "I've read them all. They're incomplete."

"Incomplete, sir?"

"Something's missing, Varvara. Something Agniya didn't

share with the Prime Directorate. Something she kept for herself."

"I don't know...."

"Igor was running someone else. His deepest secret of all."

"Why would Agniya keep...."

"Why would she keep what? Igor's secret?"

"Sir, truly, I keep my head down. I don't want any trouble."

"It was her insurance, Varvara. It was her way out. Something she could hold over Igor's head when the time came."

"Please, sir. I swear to you...."

"I mean," Viktor said, "I can sort of understand why Igor finally snapped and did what he did. Secrets can be so very damaging to *healthy* working relationships."

He looked at her closely. She wasn't as innocent as she pretended. She knew.

"Sit down, Varvara."

"Sir?"

"Have a seat, dear."

Reluctantly, she took the seat across the desk from him. He looked at her for a moment, reading her.

"I know you girls talk," he said. "Little secrets. Little whispers. Little bits of leverage for when the time comes for bargaining."

Her lip was trembling. She was close to breaking.

"Well, Varvara. Let me tell you this. Your time for bargaining has arrived."

"Bargaining, sir?"

"For your dignity, my sweet. For your body."

"Sir?"

"For your soul."

"For my soul?"

"For your life, Varvara."

"Are you saying...."

"I assure you, Varvara. Everyone you're afraid of is already dead. The only one left to fear is me."

"Agniya had a file," she said, so quietly it was almost inaudible.

"Ah, well done, my dear. Was that so difficult?"

Varvara shook her head. "She never told anyone where she kept it."

"But you're a smart girl. You figured it out."

There was a notepad and pen on the desk, and Varvara reached for it timidly.

"That's it," Viktor said. "That's a good girl." As the pen began moving across the pad, his lips curled into a smile.

She put the pad back on the desk and stood up.

"Not so fast," Viktor said.

She looked at him, the fear in her eyes so thick he could almost taste it. "Refill my cup."

She poured him another cup of coffee and then practically ran from the room. Only when she was gone did he look at the pad. This was it, his prize, his moment of victory.

He sipped the coffee and began tapping a cigarette on the desk.

What she'd written was a series of SQL queries, as well as the database identifiers and login credentials necessary to run them. Viktor didn't recognize the database but opened his SQL terminal and entered the information anyway.

He lit his cigarette and inhaled deeply, then hit enter.

The search ran for a few seconds, then returned a single match.

Identifier: USP_002336

Codename: Gray Coat
Name: Richmond Tenet
Loyalty: (Compromised)
Agency: Central Intelligence Agency
Lead Agent: Igor Aralov
Status: Double Agent—Reliable
Restricted Database

_____

Beneath the entry, outlined in precise details, were the steps to be taken if direct contact was required.

28

Ada sat by the window, sipping her coffee. Ten minutes passed, and she was considering her next step when a frail man in a tan trench coat and a ridiculous brimmed hat came out of the hotel. Ada had been expecting someone in his mid-fifties. This guy looked older.

He came into the café and stood timidly at the door. Ada and the barista were the only other people there, and he stared at each of them in turn.

"What can I get you?" the barista said.

"Yes," the man said, his accent as thick as the villain from a low-budget spy movie. "I received call."

The barista nodded in Ada's direction, and the man turned and looked at her again. She looked back at him a moment, made eye contact, then returned to looking out the window, saying nothing.

"Thank you," the man said, "it's a mistake. I have no order." He hurried back out of the café, and Ada watched him cross to the hotel.

"That was weird," the barista said.

"*You* called him," Ada said, putting on her coat. She left some money on the counter and followed the man into the hotel.

From the lobby, she could tell the hotel had once been grand, but those days were long gone. The high ceiling and marble pillars were faded with age, and the plush red carpet was thin along the high-traffic path from the elevator to the door.

The man was waiting for an elevator, and when he saw Ada, his eyes filled with fear. She walked toward him. The only other person in the lobby was the concierge, sitting disinterestedly behind his desk.

Ada stood next to the man, and they waited. The elevator was brass with deco accenting, and when it arrived, it chimed like a lunch order at a diner.

"Get in," Ada said to him quietly.

"If you're going to kill me, do it here. My daughter's upstairs."

"Don't talk until we're in the elevator."

He stepped inside, and Ada got in next to him. The doors closed, and she pushed the button for the fourth floor. The man was visibly agitated.

"Calm down," she said.

"My daughter's in the room."

"I'm not here to hurt you."

"Where's Tatyana Aleksandrova?"

"You know Tatyana?"

"Yes, I know her. I was expecting her."

"My name is Ada Hudson."

"You're with the CIA?"

"Yes."

She looked at him more closely now, the aged features, the tremble in his hand, the ridiculous outfit that made him look, quite literally, like a man on the run. It was a marvel he'd made it this far.

"Are you going to help us?" he said, his voice almost a whisper.

"I'm going to find out what you have to offer and bring it back to them."

"To the CIA?"

"To my handler."

"He'll say if we have a deal?"

"*She.*"

Sacha nodded. "How long will that take?"

"Not long."

"The Kremlin is looking for me."

"I know."

"It's only a matter of time before they find me."

"I'm the only person in London who knows your location."

"I'll make a mistake."

She looked at him again and shook her head. "That hat and coat are the mistake. I'll bring you some clothes next time I come."

"I thought I should hide my face."

"You look like Dick Tracy."

The elevator stopped, and the doors opened. Ada drew her gun and let him step into the corridor first. They walked to his room and stopped.

"Is the gun necessary?"

"Is this a trap?"

Sacha shook his head. "My daughter...."

"Anyone else?"

"No."

"Any weapons?"

"No."

"You go in first, leave the door wide open. I'll be right behind you."

"Natasha's only...."

"I won't hurt your daughter."

He opened the door, giving Ada a clear view inside. The television was on. A child was sitting on the bed, her eyes glued to the screen. Next to her was an empty breakfast tray.

"We have a visitor," Sacha said in Russian.

Ada entered the room.

"Shut the door," she said to Sacha, speaking Russian now. She turned to the child and gave her a thin smile.

The girl was frightened.

"My name is Ada," Ada said, feeling awkward. It didn't feel right to have the gun in a child's presence. She made sure no one else was in the room then put it back in its holster.

"She's a friend," Sacha said. "She's going to help us get to America."

Ada went to the window and pulled back the lace curtain. The street below was as it had been. She looked at the phone.

"I pulled out the cord," Sacha said.

"Good. Don't use it under any circumstances."

"I won't," Sacha said.

The three of them stood for a moment, staring at each other. Every time the child made eye contact, Ada looked away.

"Why don't I make tea?" Sacha said.

Ada nodded.

"Turn off the television," Sacha said to the child.

"Papa," she said in protest.

He gave her a look, and reluctantly she turned it off with the remote.

There was an electric kettle, and Sacha filled it from a sink in the bathroom.

"Have a seat," he said to Ada.

She hesitated, then sat by the window where she could see the street.

Sacha sat on the bed next to the child. They listened to the sound of the kettle heating up.

"I shouldn't stay long," Ada said. "I need to find out what you're offering the US government and what you want in return. The sooner I get back to them with that, the sooner we'll know how to proceed.

"Okay," Sacha said. He was hesitant, afraid he wasn't going to get what he wanted, and he stalled by getting up to finish making the tea.

"Let's start with what you want," Ada said. "What are you asking for?"

He cleared his throat and brought her a cup of the tea. He also gave one to the child before sitting back down.

"I have," he began in English, "how you say, a *checkered* history."

Ada looked at the child.

"She doesn't understand us."

"You're sure?"

He nodded.

Ada turned to the child. "You must be very excited to be in England," she said in English.

The child looked at her father.

"Have you been here before?"

"She's seen Buckingham Palace," Sacha said. "Haven't you?"

She shrugged.

"Tell the lady what you saw."

"Did you see the soldiers?" Ada said.

She nodded.

"Were they handsome?"

She said nothing.

"Did you learn English in school?"

"A little," the child said.

Ada turned back to Sacha. "Okay," she said.

Sacha nodded. "My work," he said hesitantly, "it was very *private*."

"Why don't you tell me who you reported to?"

"There's an organization within the Kremlin, very close to the President, known as the Dead Hand."

"The Dead Hand?" Ada said.

"Their job is to protect the President. Protect the regime."

"I see."

"Not to protect Russia, you understand. Only the regime. It's not the same thing."

"I understand," Ada said.

"The regime was afraid of..." he searched for the word.

"In Russian?" Ada said.

He said a word that translated to decapitation.

"I see," Ada said.

"He was afraid the CIA would try to kill him."

"The President?"

"Yes. It's much easier to kill one man than to defeat a nation."

"Yes, it is," Ada said, sipping her tea.

"Regime change," Sacha said.

"Right."

"He saw what happened to Milošović, to Saddam, to Bashar Al-Assad."

"Regime change has been a part of CIA strategic doctrine," Ada said. "I get it."

"So the Dead Hand, they look for ways to create insurance policy."

"Okay."

"Weapons," Sacha said. "Weapons so destructive that a decapitation strike is not worth the risk."

"And you worked on those weapons?"

"Yes, I did."

"And you have documents? Data? Proof?"

"My daughter," Sacha said, changing the subject, "she has a very rare health condition."

"I see," Ada said.

"Genetic."

"And that's what you want to trade for?"

Sacha looked at the child. "She's my life," he said. "She's all I have."

Ada nodded. She didn't think a child's medical treatment would be too much to ask.

"The treatment she needs," Sacha said, "it's only available at Children's Research Hospital in Boston."

"Okay," Ada said.

"The doctor's name is Hannson. Charles Hannson."

"I see."

"That's what I'm trading for."

"You want your daughter to be treated by Charles Hannson's team in Boston."

"That is correct," Sacha said.

"That's it?"

"That's it."

"Okay," Ada said.

"Do you think that will be possible?"

"Doctors are expensive," Ada said.

"I understand that," Sacha said.

"And, as you said, you have a *checkered* past."

"I understand that also, but I ask nothing for myself. All I want is that my daughter is safe."

"The US government can put you in a protection program," Ada said, "but the GRU will be after you for the rest of your life."

"I know that."

"Your daughter will be at risk, especially if the GRU knows she needs treatment in Boston."

Sacha nodded. "I just want the best deal I can get for her," he said.

"All right," Ada said.

"The details I leave to you."

"It won't be me who decides."

"Somehow, she can be helped," Sacha said. "If we make deal."

Ada nodded. "I'll pass on your request."

"And if they don't want to help me," Sacha said, looking at her, "I understand."

"They won't hang you out to dry," Ada said.

"They can do with me as they want."

"And what are you offering them?" Ada said. "We were speaking of documents."

Sacha got up and went to the wardrobe in the corner of the room. Inside the door was a cardboard poster tube. He brought it to the desk and pulled out large, rolled-up, xerographic sheets. On them were schematics, diagrams, mathematical equations, and handwritten notes in a scrawled Cyrillic script that Ada assumed was Sacha's.

Ada lifted one of the sheets to look at it more closely.

"These are the original prototype schematics of the Petrel rocket system," Sacha said.

"Are they real?" Ada said.

Sacha was taken aback. "Are they real?"

Ada nodded. "I'm going to be risking my life for these," she said. "I want you to tell me they're the real deal before I do that."

"Of course they're real. I drew the blueprints with my own hand."

"Our analysts will go over them with a fine-tooth comb."

"I give you my word," Sacha said.

She looked at them again. They certainly looked valuable.

"Look here," Sacha said. "Petrel system uses a nuclear-powered ramjet engine. That means the air from the forward thrust of the rocket is compressed here," he pointed to a spot on the drawing, "and used to power further forward thrust here."

"Okay," Ada said.

"It's my design," Sacha said. "The rocket must be brought to Mach Two by a launch vehicle, but once it reaches speed, it powers itself. It can loiter indefinitely. It can stay in the air for months if it wants. Maybe for years."

"For years?" Ada said.

"This is a five-hundred-megawatt nuclear reactor," he said, pointing at something that looked like an anatomical drawing of a heart chamber.

"Okay," Ada said.

"It exhausts fission product along the flight trajectory."

"It exhausts fission product? That doesn't sound good."

"It's very bad," Sacha said. "Petrel leaks so much radiation that the Kremlin forbade testing over Russian territory. That's why we launch them out of Nyonoksa. Directly north. Tell your analysts to look for the radiation. They'll find it over Arkhangelsk. This equation," he pointed at some scrawls, "shows the signature to look for."

"That will confirm that the drawings are real?"

"Yes, it will."

"Why would anyone want a rocket that leaks radiation?" Ada said.

"You're thinking like an American," Sacha said.

"What's that supposed to mean?"

"These rockets, they're not designed to win a war. They're not designed to protect anyone. They're like thorns on a rose."

"Thorns on a rose?"

"Or poison on the back of a frog."

"They're a deterrent," Ada said.

"These rockets, they're insurance policies. They paint a picture."

"Of Armageddon?"

"Of what happens if anyone tries to take out the President. The enemy is everyone. The CIA. Other foreign powers. Domestic opposition."

"Domestic opposition?"

"Would you try to depose a man who had weapons like these?"

"I think that I would," Ada said.

Sacha shook his head. "How you think President Molotov stays in power so long? He's not popular. He has done nothing for the Russian people. Their lives are more precarious now than they were twenty years ago. But there is no opposition. No protests. The people say they love him."

"He oppresses opposition."

Sacha gave her a look that made her feel obtuse. "People from your country..." he said.

"Explain it to me, then."

Sacha sighed. "It's like this," he said. "In Soviet times, when I was a boy, we supported the government because we were afraid of American nukes."

"Right."

"We were terrified of them."

"Of course."

"They made us hide under our desks at school. They showed us cartoons of detonations. Everyone was afraid."

"It was the same in the US."

"Right," Sacha said, "but we're not afraid anymore. America is a democracy. America is Tom Cruise. It's Top Gun. They would never blow us up."

"So Molotov needs a new enemy?"

"Molotov *is* the new enemy," Sacha said. "He's in the Kremlin, and he's sitting on weapons that are so horrible, so self-destructive, that even if America restrains itself, even if no foreign nation ever fired back, our own weapons would be so destructive, to us, that we're more terrified than ever."

"That makes no sense," Ada said.

"It makes perfect sense."

"It's so...."

"Nihilistic?" Sacha said, using the Russian word.

"Yes."

"Welcome to Russia," he said, spreading his hands.

"How do you fight that?" she said.

"How do you fight a suicide bomber?" Sacha said.

"You shoot him."

"You run," Sacha said.

"Or that."

"How do you fight a kamikaze pilot?"

"You shoot him too," Ada said.

Sacha spread his hands again. "They're hard to hit."

"Yes."

"America has all the power," Sacha said. "It has democracy. It has freedom. It has bigger population, greater military power, more advanced technology. It has oil. It is silicon. It has bitcoin."

"It's holding the aces," Ada said.

"It's the nexus of all global networks," Sacha said. "The only other country even close to meeting it on any front is China, and it's still far behind."

"It's gaining," Ada said.

"Russia, on the other hand, now has an economy smaller than Texas, did you know that?"

"I did not."

"And Texas is just one state."

"It's a big state."

"It's just one state," Sacha said again, "and still, Molotov stays in power, and not just that, but the world, including Washington and Beijing, listens very closely every time he makes a sound."

"That's true."

"And not just that. None of them would ever dare try to depose him."

"Because you built these weapons for him?" Ada said.

Sacha nodded.

"Why?"

"Why?" Sacha said. "That's an American question."

"It's a human question."

"Only someone who knows choice can ask why. If there is no choice, there is no why."

Ada began rolling up the blueprints. "Well," she said, "if these drawings are what you say they are...."

"They are what I say they are."

"Then they'll speak for themselves."

"That's not all I have. That's just a taste."

"What else do you have?"

"Petrel is just one weapon system. There are many, and they're all terrifying."

"You created the poison," Ada said. "Now you're selling the antidote."

Sacha shrugged. "I know what you must think of me."

Ada said nothing.

"But this is the deal," he said. "They don't have to take me. Just take the child."

"Okay."

"I've been intimately involved with all the new weapons systems, and every one of them has serious flaws."

"And you can point them out?"

"I can point them out in such detail that these *super-weapons* won't look so super at all. They'll lose all their bite."

"That's a big claim, Sacha."

"Listen to me," he said. "Petrel. It can only be produced close to uranium enrichment sites. That's the only way to make the reactors, and those only exist near major Russian cities.."

"Okay," Ada said.

"There's only a few places in all of Russia that can do it."

"I'm sure our analysts are aware of that."

"But are they aware that the rockets, once they're ready, are so large and so volatile, they can only be transported on specially built rail cars?"

"They'd figure it out."

"And only for a certain number of kilometers."

"Okay."

"And would they figure out that the launch vehicle cannot be attached to Petrel until just prior to the launch? The two of them together are too dangerous."

"What are you getting at?" Ada said.

"They have to attach Petrel to the launch vehicle, then fuel the launch vehicle, then launch it."

"Okay."

"From a rail-accessible launch site within a certain distance of a few major reactors."

"And Petrel's leaking radioactivity the whole time," Ada said, beginning to see what he was getting at.

"If I tell your analysts the signature of that radiation, they will have enough time, using Keyhole satellite, to detect any Petrel rocket before it ever leaves the ground."

"Meaning...."

"Meaning it will nullify the threat," Sacha said. "A rocket like this, it's like a grenade with the pin pulled. If you find it while it's still on the ground, it's so vulnerable as to be worthless. Worse than worthless. It's a liability."

"It's a nuclear weapon on the ground," Ada said.

Sacha shook his head. "This is no conventional nuclear weapon. Every missile contains a 500-thermal-megawatt reactor. That's about a sixth of the size of a city power plant."

"Okay."

"Bigger than Chernobyl," Sacha said. "And with zero containment. Zero shielding."

"There must be something."

"Shielding is made from lead. That's too heavy to launch."

"Okay," Ada said, "and this is all in your drawings?"

"Those drawings are enough to dismantle Petrel completely as a threat. The Kremlin might as well scrap the entire project."

Ada knew this was big. Bigger than the CIA was expecting.

"Like I said," Sacha said, "it's a grenade with the pin

pulled. All you have to do is stop the man from throwing it, and he blows his own arm off."

"Thank you for the very graphic picture."

"And that's just Petrel. There are other weapons. Weapons worse than Petrel. And the flaws are less obvious. There's no way the Pentagon will be able to nullify them without my knowledge."

"And you're offering to dismantle all of them?"

"I designed them," Sacha said. "I can break them."

29

Richmond Tenet had been stationed in London for forty years. He'd been selling secrets to the Kremlin for almost as long. He did so now under the protection of CIA Director Roth, but that hadn't always been the case. For decades, he and Roth had acted without the knowledge of Agency leadership. During that time, had anyone found out what they were doing, they would have been tried and shot for treason.

But no one did find out, and that wasn't an accident.

Their plan had survived multiple White House administration changes, shifts in CIA leadership, and the immense upheavals that accompanied the collapse of the Soviet Union, the dissolution of the KGB, and the rise of its successor agency.

Roth and Tenet had done their part. They'd held their nerve, kept their cool, and maintained extremely exacting standards of tradecraft for decades without ever slipping up. But it would have all been in vain were it not for Igor Aralov. Their ruse required an ideal partner on the Russian side, and Igor was that partner. He was a master at keeping secrets, and he kept Gray Coat so deeply buried that no one in Moscow even suspected he existed.

But now he was dead, and the deepest vaults of his files were being opened by a new man. If the new man wasn't up to par, it would be Tenet's neck.

That was unavoidable, it was a risk that had been accepted, but it still made Tenet nervous as he walked along the Mall next to Saint James's Park. He had his dog with him, a scruffy Bedlington Terrier named Winston, who tried to run ahead as they climbed the steps behind the King George Memorial. The steps led to a warren of little streets around Carlton Gardens, and it was there, in the shadow cast by a bronze statue of Charles De Gaulle, that he stopped. A large oak hung over the statue, its branches making observation from above impossible. There was a wooden bench under the tree, and Tenet sat on it and took a leather cigar case from inside his coat.

He leaned back on the bench and lit the cigar. The moistness of the air seemed to absorb the smoke that billowed around him.

He was there to meet the new man, Viktor Lapin. The fact Viktor wanted to meet face to face, and so soon after taking him on, was cause for concern. It was extremely risky —reckless even. Sitting there, waiting, Tenet felt like a closeted gay man from decades past, waiting for some surreptitious encounter.

Three decades ago, Tenet and Igor had agreed on a signal for face-to-face meetings. In the intervening years, Igor had used it just once.

The signal was dated now, anachronistic even, and had not been updated because Igor didn't intend on ever using it again. It involved Tenet's car, at the time a red Jaguar E-Type, that he parked on the street in front of his apartment.

Now he drove an F-Type in British racing green, but parked it in the same spot. A flier would be placed on his windshield. To avoid suspicion, it would be placed on the windshield of every car on the street. It would be for a public meeting organized by the Socialist Workers Party, to take place at the Bethesda Congregational Church at a time of Igor's choosing. It was the type of flier that would not have looked out of place during the heightened political atmosphere of the eighties but now stood out like a sore thumb.

Viktor's choice to use it showed a recklessness, a lack of patience, that would bring Tenet's position to a head. He would have to flee the country soon, and the time had come for him to reconcile himself to the fact. He couldn't say goodbye, of course. Not to anyone. But he could prepare himself to let go.

He'd been smoking for about ten minutes when a man approached. He was the only other person on the street, and he stopped at the base of the statue to read the plaque. He was younger than Tenet, in his mid-forties, and wore a brown corduroy jacket with elbow patches.

He glanced at Tenet. "Gray suits you," he said.

Tenet's heart pounded. This was him, the new handler, Viktor Lapin. "I should have worn a warmer coat," he said, completing the pre-arranged words.

Viktor lit a cigarette with a match. He shook the match and threw it away. Tenet watched him closely. Every move he made, every gesture, was a signal. The success of the plan was in this man's hands. Tenet's life was in his hands.

"What happened to Igor?" he said.

Viktor turned back to the statue before answering. "A widow bit him."

Tenet nodded. "I take it his files are secure."

"If anyone knew about you," Viktor said, "you wouldn't be sitting here."

"Sitting here is what I'm concerned about."

Viktor sucked his cigarette. "I needed to see you for myself."

"And?" Tenet said. "Does the famous Gray Coat live up to expectations?"

"I know I've put you at risk."

"Yes," Tenet said. "You have."

Viktor flicked some ash. "I'm going to keep you intact."

"And if you can't?"

"Then I'll look after you."

"Why doesn't that give me a warm, fuzzy feeling?"

Viktor eyed him. "Let's not waste time," he said. "Something's afoot in London."

Tenet hesitated a moment, as if considering his options, then said, "Levi Roth was here."

"What was he doing?"

"He didn't tell me," Tenet said. He exhaled a white cloud of smoke, and it hung in the air in front of him, "but one of my agents was tapped by the Group."

"The Special Operations Group?"

Tennet nodded. "She's gone dark."

"Why would they do that?"

"Why do you think?"

A smile crossed Viktor's face. "Sacha Gazinsky?"

Tenet puffed smoke and said, "Someone's got to bring him in from the cold."

"Who's the agent they tapped?"

"A new girl. Ada Hudson."

"Under your command?"

"Not now."

"But you know her?"

"No one really knows her. She just arrived."

"She's clean then."

"Virginal," Tenet said.

"Well," Viktor said, glancing up and down the street to make sure they were still alone, "where is she now?"

"I told you," Tenet said. "She's gone off-grid."

"Don't play coy with me. You wouldn't be here if you didn't have something."

"I'm here because *you* asked for a meeting. Not me."

It was Viktor's turn to smile. He sucked his cigarette, and Tenet thought there was something very effeminate about the way he did it. "This is *your* house," he said. "With all due respect, if Sacha Gazinsky is here, you're going to have to find him."

"Is that a threat?"

"It's a fact. The President is watching. If we don't lock this down, heads are going to roll."

"Not my head."

Viktor blew smoke at him. "If I go down, Richmond Tenet, I assure you I won't go down alone."

Tenet shook his head. "No," he said, "I'm sure you wouldn't."

"So, can you find her?"

"She's made a mistake," Tenet said, "but if I follow it up, I'll be leaving myself exposed."

"I told you I'd look after you."

"Aren't you sweet?" Tenet said. "But I'm going to need more than words."

"You want some sort of assurance?"

"An assurance is exactly what I want."

"What would put your mind at ease?"

"Safe passage to Moscow."

"If you give me Sacha Gazinsky," Viktor said, "I can get you a suite in the Tsar's palace if you want."

"You need to start making the arrangements now."

"You're married, are you not?"

"I'll be traveling alone," Tenet said, and he was surprised at how easily the words came to him. Forty years of marriage, forty years of life, written off in just four words.

"All right. You have my word."

"A few weeks ago, Ada Hudson visited a private bank in Mayfair."

"She won't go near a dropbox now. Not if she's been dark-channeled."

"There's no CIA drop box at this bank."

"So this is something she's set it up by herself?"

"Yes. And she used embassy credentials."

"What does that mean?"

"It means I can look into it for you, but the water's going to get very choppy, very fast."

"I told you," Viktor said, flicking the butt of his cigarette vaguely in Tenet's direction. "I'll make the arrangements. I'll take care of you."

30

George Chapman was a strange creature. Politically, he was an atheist. A nihilist, really. He didn't believe any of it. He'd served in the Royal Marines, but what he'd seen there had changed his view of the world not a bit. To him, Britain was no city on a hill. It was no beacon of light upon the world. It was a striving, clinging, clutching nation, just like all the others. If there was oil, or the whiff of it, in went the army. In went the boys. Home came the coffins. Simple as that.

Find something you're good at, was what he'd always been told. Not, find something true. Not, find something you believe in. Find something you're good at.

Being a sniper was something he was good at. The L115A1 Long Range Rifle, as the Ministry of Defense called it, had become almost an extension of his body. He could hit targets from one, two, sometimes three kilometers distance.

The transformation from boy to man had been fast. One minute he'd been playing football on the green behind Sainsbury's, sneaking cigarettes from his mum's purse, and the next, he was on the roof of a squat, brick building in

Umm Qasr, Iraq, looking through the old-style night-sights of a rifle. It was as if he'd been transported to another planet. Even at night, Umm Qasr was hotter than anything he'd ever experienced. And it was drier. Just breathing made him feel like he'd been up all night, smoking.

GOPLATs.

That was why he was there. GOPLAT was short for Gas and Oil Platform. That was what Her Majesty's Government was interested in.

In a whisper, Chapman's spotter said, "Take the shot."

"Could be anyone," Chapman said.

From that distance, in that light, all targets could be anyone. Indeed, they were *anyone*.

"Come on," the spotter said. "Get it done."

It was his first real shot. His first shot in anger, as they called it. If he made it, it would be his first kill. Not two days earlier, he'd been fingering a girl from his secondary school named Tish, in the bathroom of the pub in Clapham where he'd had his first legal beer.

Chapman depressed the trigger.

Time stretched. He heard his mother's voice. Her face flashed before his eyes.

And then the spotter said, "Good kill."

Turned out, Chapman's good kill was a twelve-year-old boy. That shook Chapman, but Her Majesty's Government assured him it was legitimate. Nothing to lose sleep over. He'd been carrying an explosive device.

In the coming months, Chapman got dozens more kills, all in pursuance of the same objective. It turned out there was a lot more to Her Majesty than palaces and royal weddings and waving from motorcades.

There were GOPLATs.

Now, twenty years later, Chapman knew what only a

man with his number of kills could know. That all kills were the same. And whether you pulled the trigger for the Queen of England, the Crown Prince of Saudi Arabia, or the President of Russia, made no difference whatever.

Find something you're good at, they told him. And he had. He got in and out, he covered his tracks, and he got paid. That was what he was good at. Chapman's crew was one of the few operations in London willing to take a job from anyone, against anyone. He wasn't cheap, but he didn't ask questions. Muslim, Hindu, Christian, Jew, who they were, what they'd done—made no difference. Chapman had killed Russians for Saudis, Americans for Russians, Saudis for Yemenis, and twelve-year-olds for the Queen of England.

Tehran was a client. Damascus was a client. Pyongyang was a client.

But client number one, his best-paying, most regular, most reliable, was Viktor Lapin.

Chapman was on his way home from the pub when he saw the signal—a chalk 'X' on the postbox in front of his house. He walked past the house, got in a white Ford Transit, and drove to the warehouse space he and his crew operated out of in Lambeth. The location of the warehouse was good, central, with the river on one side and the train tracks leading into Waterloo Station on the other. By road, there were only two approaches, one east, one west. He had cameras on both.

He parked in the yard in front of the warehouse and made his way to the office at the back. The office was actually a steel-walled shipping container with a bolted door on one end. Unlocking it required three separate keys, and Chapmen went through the laborious process of opening them. Inside, there was no light, and he used a cigarette lighter as he entered.

On the floor in the corner of the container was a standard-issue Ricoh fax machine from the 1980s. As a precaution, Chapman had removed the machine's memory chip and bypassed that part of the circuitry with a piece of copper wire. That meant the only record of messages, coming or going, was the paper they were printed on.

Additionally, Chapman had replaced the ink in the cartridge with an all-purpose cleaning ammonia from a hardware store. The ammonia was invisible on paper but could be revealed by dabbing vinegar on it. If this was not done within a couple of hours, the ammonia would evaporate, and the message would be lost.

The precautions were simple. They wouldn't stump the security services for long. They simply allowed Chapman to be sure that there was no digital record being stored on the machine and that, unless the paper had been brushed with vinegar, no one had read the message.

There was a sheet of paper in the tray now, and he picked it up. He had a packet of vinegar in his pocket, and he ripped it open with his teeth and wet the message. He wiped the vinegar around with his sleeve. The message was from Viktor.

Target: Ada Hudson—CIA Officer

Location: Saffron & Saracen Bank, Berkeley Square

31

A da left the hotel and walked in the direction of Leicester Square, the poster tube containing the blueprints under her arm. After a few blocks, when she was confident she wasn't being followed, she hailed a cab and told the driver to take her back to the hotel.

He pulled over about a hundred yards from the hotel entrance, and she said, "Can we wait here a minute?"

"What's going on, love?"

"I'll give you fifty quid if we can just sit here for ten minutes."

"Let's see it," the driver said.

She handed him the money, and he looked at her carefully. "This better not be some funny business."

"It's not," she said.

He had a copy of a tabloid newspaper on the seat next to him and picked it up.

"Can I smoke?" she said.

He looked back at her again, took in her nice clothes, her expensive purse, and said, "For a pony, you can."

"You'll have to translate that."

"Twenty-five quid, miss. Cleaning fee."

She offered him a twenty, and he took it. Then they both lit cigarettes and cracked their windows.

From where they were parked, she could clearly see the entrance of the hotel.

"Would you phone that hotel for me?" she said to the driver.

"You phone them."

"I don't have a phone."

"I don't have the number."

"I'll give it to you."

He shook his head as she handed him another twenty. "What am I asking?" he said.

"Tell them you're a cabbie, and your fare hasn't shown. Ask if anyone's left in the last few minutes."

He asked and then hung up.

"Well?" she said.

"They said a woman in a long coat left a few minutes ago."

"That was me," Ada said.

"Look, whatever your game is, I don't need no funny business."

"We're just going to sit here a few more minutes," she said.

They sat tight for about fifteen more minutes, and no one went in or out of the hotel. Everything was quiet.

"All right, love. I ain't got all day."

"Take me to Berkeley Square," she said.

He dropped her by the Café L'Express, and she went in and had another coffee. She sat again on the patio, taking her time, watching the square, the traffic, the people. She sat there for the best part of an hour, and nothing looked out of the ordinary at all.

She got up and left the café, crossed the street, and walked through the park. On the other side of the park, she took another moment to observe, then went up to the bank entrance.

She went through the same process to get into the bank as she had before, the brass knocker on the door, the paneled anteroom, the marble floor. Once inside, the same officious woman met her, and Ada eyed her for any sign that something was amiss.

"Ms. Hudson," the woman said, "I'm afraid you just missed him."

"Missed him?" Ada said.

"The man from the embassy."

Ada glanced around the hall, the high ceiling, the wraparound staircase. "What embassy?" she said, reaching into her coat and pulling out her gun.

The woman gasped.

"Who was here?" Ada said. "What was his name?"

"He said he knew you," the woman stammered. "He had credentials. Our office called the embassy to verify."

"Someone was here from the embassy?"

"That's correct."

"Looking for me?"

"Please put away the gun."

"Where is he now?"

"He left, not fifteen minutes ago."

Ada looked at the door she'd just come through. "That way?"

The woman nodded. "I'm sorry," she said. "He had diplomatic credentials, the same as yours."

Saffron & Saracen wasn't the type of bank that did business with just anyone. Ada had used her embassy credentials to open her account. She didn't see how that information had gotten back to the embassy, but apparently, it had.

"What was his name?" Ada said.

"You know I can't tell you that."

"You told him about me."

"I told him nothing of the sort."

"Then how did he know I was here? How did he know to look for me here."

The woman looked at her helplessly, shaking her head, her eyes fixed on the gun.

"This was a mistake," Ada said, more to herself than to the woman. She should not have come there. Tatyana had warned her not to use anything familiar.

She pointed her gun at the woman and said, "What was the man's name?"

The woman began to cry, but Ada felt no sympathy for her. "You said you ran his credentials with the embassy. What name did you run?"

"Parker," the woman said. "Peter Parker."

"Peter Parker?"

She nodded frantically.

"Like Spider-Man?"

"A coincidence," the woman said.

"Right."

"The embassy confirmed he was who he said he was."

"And he asked for me by name?"

The woman nodded again.

"How did he know where to look for me?"

"I have no idea," the woman said.

"How did he know I'd been here?"

The woman didn't know what to say.

"Perhaps he used his spidey senses," Ada muttered.

"I'm sorry, miss?"

Ada shook her head. Her mind was reeling. She'd fucked up. She shouldn't have come there. And worse— there was a rat in the London Embassy.

"Ms. Hudson?" the woman said, still staring at the gun.

"Is there another way out of this bank?"

32

C hapman was directly across the square from the bank, watching the entrance through his rifle scope from the third story of a five-story office building. The bank backed onto the street behind, Hay's Mews, and he'd stationed a man there. That man's name was Hamish McLaren. He was a burly Scotsman with arms like tree trunks and a belly like the hood of a Volkswagon Beetle. He was in a white Ford Transit with false plates.

There was a third man also—a drone operator who'd served with Chapman in the Royal Marines named Stan Morel. He was working from another Transit van parked a block away next to Lansdowne House.

Stan's job was to track the target from above. The drone was military-grade and carried four high-resolution cameras with different focal-length lenses. The four-hundred-millimeter could resolve faces from half a mile. The biggest risk was losing the target in the underground. Six stations, Green Park, Marble Arch, Hyde Park Corner, Bond Street, Oxford Circus, and Piccadilly Circus, were all within about a quarter-mile of the square.

The target was a CIA agent, trained in evasive measures and likely armed. Viktor's instructions were clear. They were not to kill her. The Kremlin wanted her alive.

Chapman's rifle was chambered for a .338 Lapua Magnum, but he'd crafted his own non-lethal, rubber impact rounds. A well-aimed shot should bring her down without killing her.

Stan's voice came over the radio. "Hold on. I've got movement on the mews."

"Is it her?"

"We've got a man and a woman coming out of a door. I'm trying to get a visual on the face."

"I see them," Hamish said.

"Stay where you are, Hamish," Chapman said, getting ready to abandon his position. "Don't spook her."

"I've got visual," Stan said. "The female's a match."

"Can you tell if she's armed?" Hamish said.

"Can you?" Stan said.

"What's the order, boss? I can ram her."

"Which way is she moving?"

"South."

"Follow her," Chapman said, throwing his rifle in its case. "And Stan, stick on her like glue."

Chapman had a car on the street below, a black, seven series BMW with tinted windows. The plates were false, and nothing in the vehicle led back to him. When he got to it, a parking attendant was writing him a ticket.

Chapman ignored him and got in the car. He fired up the engine and almost caused an accident when he pulled into the traffic lane. He rounded the park and turned south onto Fitzmaurice. "Where is she now?"

"Coming your way, boss," Stan said.

"Running?"

"Walking. Briskly."

"Good," Chapman said, pulling into a parking spot on Fitzmaurice.

He wouldn't have chosen the spot. It was an expensive street, home to a number of high-profile private clubs. Chapman was outside one of them now, its blue and gold flag mounted to the wall above the door, and from where he sat, he counted six different security cameras.

"I'm guessing she's headed for Green Park," Stan said.

"Hamish?"

"Still walking."

Traffic was busy—a lot of pedestrians.

"I'm right outside the Lansdowne," Chapman said. "Right side of the street with my hazards on."

"We'll be there in thirty seconds."

"As soon as you round the corner, charge her with the van, Hamish."

"I won't be able to hit her. Not with these barriers."

"She'll run my way. I'll shoot her below the waist. Then we throw her in the van and patch her up at the warehouse."

Chapman opened the glove compartment and took out a Glock 17 nine-millimeter pistol. He watched the sidewalk in his rearview mirror. The woman came around the corner, walking at a quick pace but not panicked.

Hamish came around the corner behind her in the van. As soon as he had a clear run at her, he gunned the engine, and the van lurched onto the footpath, bouncing over the curb. Pedestrians leaped in every direction. He hit a garbage can, lost both wing mirrors, charging headlong for the woman.

She was supposed to panic. She was supposed to run toward Chapman and his nine-millimeter.

But she didn't.

Instead, she turned to face Hamish's direction, staring down the charging van. Hamish rammed another bin, crushed a bank of locked bicycles, then hit a sturdy lampost, coming to a halt not ten feet from her.

Chapman watched Hamish fumble for his gun, but before he found it, the woman had hers drawn. She raised it up, pointed it at the windshield, and fired three shots through the windshield.

"Fuck me," Stan yelled over the radio.

Chapman didn't hesitate. He aimed for her legs and fired three shots. The woman dived for cover, then began running back in the direction of the square. Chapman got in the car and put his foot down.

"Hamish," Stan shouted into the radio. "Hamish."

There was no answer other than Hamish's gurgling. One of the bullets must have missed his vest.

Chapman pulled the handbrake and let the car spin back in a one-eighty. It crashed up onto the curb in the process, hitting garbage cans, bicycles, even an empty stroller as he charged down the street against the direction of the traffic. He dodged oncoming cars by ramping back up onto the footpath, smashing into anything that came in his path. He didn't care what he hit and accelerated, speeding back toward the square.

The woman reached the square, crossed the street, leaped over the two-foot-high iron railing, and ran through the park.

Chapman had to go around the park to stay after her.

"Stan?" he yelled.

"I've got her, boss. She's headed for Bruton Street."

The street was narrow, lined with expensive boutiques and even more pedestrians.

"Where's she going, Stan?"

"I don't know, boss. Oxford Circus? Bond Street?"

Chapman jammed on the brakes again and careened onto Bruton Street, his tires screeching as he steered into more oncoming traffic.

He passed the Westbury Hotel and Sotheby's auction house, gaining on the woman, lurching onto the footpaths to get around cars, sending pedestrians diving for their lives out of his path.

The street cleared momentarily of traffic, and he gained speed. He pulled up alongside the woman, she running on the footpath, he driving in the street next to her. He raised his gun and pointed it out the window. She wasn't ten feet from him. There was nowhere for her to dive for cover. He had her and was about to fire.

"Boss, watch out."

The warning came too late.

Chapman slammed head-on into an oncoming bus, slamming his head forward as an airbag filled the cabin.

"Fuck," he yelled, slamming his fists against it.

"She's getting away," Stan cried.

"Stay on her, Stan."

Chapman pushed the door of the car open and stumbled out into the street. Dozens of people in every direction stared in horror. The second he put weight on his leg, it buckled.

"Fuck," he yelled again as he hit the ground.

33

Ada stood on the platform at Oxford Circus tube station. She was breathless, her heart pounding, her hair and clothes in disarray. The other passengers on the platform looked at her warily.

She kept looking at the escalator, expecting armed men to appear at any moment and open fire. When the first train arrived, she got on. She stood by the door, eyeing everyone closely, and the moment the doors shut, she stopped them and jumped off.

She looked up and down the platform. No one else got off the train.

A minute later, a westbound train pulled in, and she boarded it. Again she stood by the door, watching along the train in both directions for anyone who might be coming her way. Her hand gripped the rail so tightly her knuckles hurt.

She realized that she'd lost her shoes in the chase. Her tights were torn. Her feet were cold and wet. She looked at her reflection in the window. She needed to straighten herself out.

She'd shot a man.

She'd seen the bullet land above his collar bone, the blood gushing out. She thought he was dead.

Her first kill.

After four stops, she got off of the train and realized her entire body was trembling. She was cold. She was in shock. She had to hold on to the wall to steady herself.

She took in deep breaths while commuters rushed past her in every direction.

It was only then that she realized she didn't have the blueprints. The cardboard tube was gone. Everything Sacha had risked his life for, his daughter's life for, lost.

And it was her fault.

They found her at her bank.

She was burned. She thought of Sacha and Natasha, the two of them lying on the bed in the hotel room, already dead, blood soaking into the mattress.

Something had gone seriously wrong, but her head was spinning too fast to figure out what it was.

She didn't know what station she was at but disembarked and followed a sign for the District Line. She got on a train in the direction of Wimbledon and got off again after one stop at High Street Kensington. She exited the station. It was raining outside, but she didn't care. She walked a block from the station in her bare feet, watching every passing vehicle, every pedestrian as if they might try to kill her.

She stopped at the first set of payphones she passed and inserted her card. When she got through to the Saint Royal, her throat was so dry she had to clear her throat to speak.

"Penthouse," she said.

"Please hold."

She pulled a pack of cigarettes from her pocket and dropped the first cigarette she tried to light on the ground.

"Who's calling?"

"What?"

"Who's calling?"

"Claymore."

She took out another cigarette and put it in her mouth, then fumbled with her lighter but couldn't get it lit.

Tatyana's voice came on the line. "Ada, what's going on?"

"You tell me what the fuck's going on."

"Ada, calm down. What happened?"

"We have a rat in our house, Tatyana. That's what happened."

"What?"

"They were waiting for me. They tried to kill me."

"Ada, I'm looking at Keyhole footage from Berkeley Park right now. Tell me that wasn't a CIA dropbox you were accessing."

"It was my own box," Ada said. "I set it up myself. No one knew about it."

"Someone knew."

"Someone from the embassy," Ada said.

"That's not possible."

"Then you tell me what that was."

"Ada, you need to calm down."

"I am calm," Ada cried.

"Where's Sacha now?"

"You..." Ada said and realized she was speaking too loudly. She dropped her voice, checking over her shoulder to see if anyone was looking at her. "Tatyana, there's a rat in our house, and he's trying to kill me."

"All right," Tatyana said. "I'll start a sweep. But right now, we need to focus on the mission."

Ada's mind was still reeling. The rain was soaking into

her coat. Her feet were bare against the cold ground. Nothing was right.

"He knew you," she said.

"Who did?"

"You know who. Sacha Gazinsky."

"That's correct," Tatyana said. "So what?"

"He was expecting you to bring him in."

"Okay?"

"So what the hell is going on, Tatyana? Why am I here and not you?"

"Ada," Tatyana said, "don't do this."

"Don't do what?"

"You can trust me."

"Can I?"

"You know you can."

"I don't know what I know."

"Just breathe."

"There's a rat in our embassy, and you need to find him," Ada said. "Otherwise, there's no chance in hell of bringing Sacha in alive."

"You need to stay away from Sacha," Tatyana said. "You're burned now. You're out. I'm sorry."

Ada had finally gotten her cigarette lit, and the nicotine was beginning to calm her.

"Where's Sacha now?" Tatyana said. "He wasn't at Berkeley Square."

"I left him at his hotel," Ada said. "Oh God, what if I led them to him? I have to call."

"Don't call anyone."

"I have to get him out of there. I could have led them right to him."

"Ada, don't go near him. You need to cut loose."

"I'm not leaving him," Ada said, barely listening.

She had to go back. If that little girl died because of a mistake she'd made, she'd never forgive herself.

"I had blueprints," Ada said.

"From Sacha?"

"Yes. Blueprints for the Petrel rocket system. They showed design flaws the Pentagon could exploit."

"And you lost them?"

Ada glanced around the street. Everywhere she looked, she saw threats. She sucked on the cigarette and flicked the ash against the side of the phone. "He's got more information. On the other weapons systems. I have to get back to him."

"Ada, wait."

Ada hung up. A car up the street jammed on its brakes, and she almost drew her gun. She was too jumpy. Too agitated. Someone at the embassy had just tried to kill her. Who?

She was outside a Marks and Spencer store, and she went inside and bought some fresh tights and a pair of sneakers. Then she hailed a cab from the street.

"Where to?" the driver said.

Why wasn't Tatyana bringing in Sacha? If she knew him, if he expected her, a source that valuable?

She needed to straighten out her thoughts. It was questions, things that didn't add up, that got people killed. But she didn't have time for that. Someone had found her, and if they'd found her, they could find Sacha.

"Hey, lady," the driver said.

"Sorry."

"Where are we going?"

"Soho. Mildred Arms Hotel."

34

S acha was getting restless. It had been hours since Ada left the hotel, and still no word. He hadn't expected her to be gone so long.

He was on the bed next to Natasha, and she turned to him from the television.

"I'm hungry," she said.

The hotel offered room service, it was what they'd had for breakfast, and the food was passable.

"I can go down and order you something," he said.

"I want to come with you," she said.

Of course she did. They'd been cooped up in the room all morning. There were only so many cartoons a girl could watch.

She was flipping through channels when an image flashed across the screen that caught Sacha's attention.

"Go back," he said.

She went back to a local news channel. There'd been some sort of incident not far from where they were. Gunshots had been fired. A woman was seen fleeing. The reporter was standing in front of a black BMW that had crashed headlong into a bus. There was still blood visible on the asphalt. The view switched to a CCTV camera. A woman was running across a street, people dashed out of her way, then she hopped a fence into a small park. The camera was a hundred yards from her, and she had her back to it, but one detail jumped out at Sacha like a bullhorn— the woman's long, camel-colored coat.

He looked at Natasha, his heart pounding.

"Sweetheart, we need to pack up our things."

"What? Why?"

"We have to go to another hotel."

"But we just got to this hotel."

"Pack your things," he said again, trying and failing to keep his voice calm.

She got up and went to the window where she'd laid out her clothes from the day before.

"Get away from there," he snapped.

She looked at him in surprise. "Papa," she said.

He went to the window and pulled the blind. He was scaring her, but he couldn't help it. He was spooked.

A few minutes later, they'd packed their meager possessions.

"Come on, Natasha," he said, opening the door to the room. "Let's go."

"I haven't showered."

"That's okay," he said, checking the corridor before leading her out of the room.

The elevator seemed to take an eternity, and when it arrived, he practically shoved her into it.

"Papa," she said again, "what's going on?"

He shook his head, and when they arrived at the lobby, he said, "Come on, darling," and pulled her out after him.

He'd paid for the room with cash the night before and

threw his room key on the check-in counter as they rushed past. "Checking out," he said to the concierge.

Practically at a run, he rushed Natasha through the lobby.

The bellhop held the door for them, and Sacha said, "Taxi?"

"I can call you one," the bellhop said.

"No," Sacha said and began hurrying down the street, yanking Natasha by the arm with each step.

"Papa," she protested, but he didn't listen. There was a car approaching, a black cab, and he could already tell it was slowing down.

In a panic, he grabbed Natasha and was about to throw his arms around her to shield her when he heard a voice.

It was Ada.

"Get in," she said, beckoning them toward the cab. "Come on. Hurry."

Sacha didn't know what was going on. The cab pulled up next to them, and, acting purely on adrenaline, he put Natasha into the car and followed.

"Go," Ada said to the driver. "King's Cross. Step on it."

Sacha looked at her. Her appearance had changed dramatically in the hours since he'd seen her. Her hair was disheveled, her cashmere coat was sodden with rain, and her elegant heels had been replaced with a pair of white sneakers. There was a gash on her thigh, and the stocking was torn.

"What happened?" he said.

"I was attacked."

"By who?"

"I don't know, but we need to get out of the city. The embassy is compromised."

"Compromised?"

"I'm going to keep you safe, Sacha," she said. "I swear to you."

Sacha didn't know what to think. He glanced at Natasha, then out the window at the crowded London streets. "Where are we going to go?" he said.

"We'll find someplace safe," Ada said.

"How did they find you?"

"I don't know, but they won't get a second chance. We'll stay completely off the radar. We'll blend in. We'll look like a family."

"Someone tried to kill you."

"I know, Sacha."

"If they found you once, they'll find you again."

"Someone betrayed me," she said. "Someone at the embassy. That's not going to happen again."

"If there's a mole at the embassy, how are we going to make a deal with them? How can we trust anyone there? How can we trust what they say?"

"We'll cross that bridge when we come to it."

"We're at that bridge now," Sacha said.

"Your deal will be made with the Special Operations Group in DC directly," Ada said.

"What if they have the mole?"

"God help us if they do," Ada said, and then, when she saw the alarm that caused on his face, added, "We'll get your daughter to safety, Sacha. Believe me. I'll die before I let anything happen to her. You have my word."

Sacha put his arm around Natasha.

"Papa, where are we going?"

Sacha looked to Ada.

"We're going to get on a train," Ada said in Russian. "Get out of this busy city."

"I'm scared," Natasha said.

"I know," Ada said. "I am too."

The cab brought them to the Pancras Road plaza in front of the train station and pulled over.

Ada got out first. The square was full of people and a line of cabs waited by the station entrance for riders.

"Come on," Ada said.

Sacha held Natasha's hand tightly as they made their way up the steps to the station's west concourse. Inside was even busier than the plaza had been. The station was a major regional train hub, a commuter station, a busy metro station, a shopping mall, and a food court all rolled into one. Every person in the place was in a hurry.

"Stay close," Sacha said to Natasha as Ada examined the departure board above the concourse.

"Where will we go?" Sacha said, looking up at the board. In just the next thirty minutes, there were over forty trains leaving the station, most of them to cities Sacha had never heard of. As well as stations across Britain, there were services to Paris, Amsterdam, Brussels, and more.

"There's a train leaving for Inverness in ten minutes," Ada said.

"Where's Inverness?" Sacha said.

"Scotland."

"Scotland?"

"It's as far as we can get from here," Ada said. "It will give us time to get our bearings."

"Okay," Sacha said. He reached for Natasha's hand but didn't find it. When he turned, she wasn't there. "Natasha," he called, turning a full circle. "She was right here," he said to Ada desperately.

"Natasha?" Ada called.

"I let go of her hand for a split second," Sacha said.

He swung in every direction. People everywhere hurried by him.

"Natasha," he cried again, growing increasingly frantic.

Ada tried to take his arm, but he pulled himself free.

"Sacha, we need to remain calm."

"Natasha," he cried. "Natasha."

There was an escalator nearby, and he ran to it and let it carry him upward. The added height gave him a view above the crowd. He strained to see through the people.

And then, miraculously, in a flood of relief, his eyes filling with tears, he saw her. She was fine, completely oblivious, not twenty feet from where Ada was standing. She was looking at a display of pastries.

"Natasha," he cried, and in his relief, began rushing back down the escalator, pushing his way through people, running to keep pace with the rising steps.

"Watch it, pal," someone grunted as he shoved past.

"Natasha," Sacha cried over the head of the man. "My daughter. Please. Let me pass."

Ada saw him and followed his line of sight to Natasha. Only when Ada got to her did Sacha allow himself to be brought up the escalator before coming back down the other side.

35

C hapman stumbled into the warehouse and collapsed onto a chair. His leg was gashed badly where it struck the side of the car in the crash. Walking was agony. He was bleeding badly, but he'd made it back. He was pretty sure Hamish was dead, and he hadn't heard from Stan since they broke off comms.

He tore off the silicone mask he'd been wearing and threw it on the ground. The operation, a simple snatch, had been a complete and utter disaster. And it was a GRU job— the very last client Chapman would choose to disappoint. He had to make contact with Viktor. If he didn't fix this, and he wasn't even sure that he could, then he and Stan were as good as dead.

He had an emergency contact for Viktor but didn't want to use it. He looked at the phone on the desk and sighed. All calls, no matter what precautions he took, came with risks. The Russians were masters at telephonic masking. They had the most advanced concealment techniques on the planet for both analog and digital network traffic. But Chapman knew British intelligence agencies were close on their tail. If he made this call, he'd have to tear down his entire operation—the warehouse, vehicles, networked electronics, all of it.

But it didn't matter. He was screwed either way. He'd survived in his business longer than most, and one of the main reasons for that was, to put it plainly, his ability to handle his clients. When things went right, he accepted payment and remained discreet. He didn't hike prices in an emergency. And when things went wrong, he didn't go dark. He called in.

A fact he was always painfully aware of was that, when all was said and done, he was more likely to be killed by one of his own clients than by anyone else. And if he was taking bets, he'd have said the GRU was the client to do it.

This was not the time to cut and run.

He picked up the receiver and dialed the number he had for Viktor. It clicked and buzzed and rerouted more than a dozen times before giving him a dial tone.

"Pick up, pick up, pick up," he muttered while he waited. Every second the connection was live put him at risk of detection.

When Viktor's voice came on the line, he did not sound happy. "Where the fuck have you been?"

"You know where I've been," Chapman said. "I was lucky to get back alive."

Viktor let out a laugh, and Chapman took it to mean he'd be lucky to stay alive much longer. "Who was that woman?" he said.

"I ask the questions," Viktor said.

"I would have been more careful, Viktor. I would have been a lot more fucking careful if I'd known she was going to react like that."

"She's a CIA agent. I told you that before you went in."

"You never told me she was that trigger happy. She killed Hamish."

"She's a child, Chapman. Fresh from the Farm. She can barely drink legally where she's from."

"She can fire a gun," Chapman said.

"Is this why you called? To make excuses?"

Chapman sighed. He'd opened his jeans and was examining the gash on his thigh. It was still bleeding and hurt like a son of a bitch, but as far as he could tell, it was only a flesh wound.

"I'm calling because I need another shot at her."

"I think you've done enough for one day, don't you?"

"Let me make this right, Viktor."

"You shot up half of London. Television crews. Police everywhere. That's a lot of shit to blow back on me."

"Viktor."

"I think it's time for you and me to sever ties."

"I can fix this."

"It's a shame," Viktor said. "You and I go back a long way."

"Viktor, please."

The line went dead. Chapman listened to the tone, looked at the receiver in his hand, then slammed it against the table. He did it again and again, over and over until the rugged plastic housing came apart.

He didn't stop until a voice interrupted him.

"Hamish is gone."

It was Stan.

"Where were you?" Chapman said.

"Picking up the body," Stan said.

"Dumped?"

"Hamish sleeps with the fishes now," Stan said.

"We'll all be sleeping with the fishes if we don't fix this."

"You should call in."

"I already called in."

"You spoke to Viktor?"

"He doesn't want anything to do with us."

Stan nodded. Chapman looked him in the eye.

"I'm sorry," Chapman said.

Stan was born in London, spoke with a thick London accent, but his people came from Haiti, and he still had a certain nonchalant *je ne sais quoi* about him. He gave Chapman now a small shrug, as if he'd just been told his toast was burned, and Chapman said, "We have two options."

"Run and hide?"

"And we both know what hiding from the GRU means."

Stan nodded. "She was a feisty one, wasn't she?"

Chapman let a quiet laugh. He had a bottle of cheap scotch in the desk, and he took it out and opened it.

"To Hamish," he said and took a swig.

He passed the bottle to Stan, who did the same, and then Stan said, "There's one other option."

"What option?"

"The American."

"From the embassy?"

"I got drone footage of him when he entered the bank."

"He's Viktor's source."

Stan nodded.

"If we burn him, Viktor will...." Chapman let his words trail off.

"Kill us?" Stan said, taking another swig of the scotch. "He's going to do that anyway."

"Do we know how to contact him?" Chapman said, taking the bottle.

Stan smiled. He nodded at the phone receiver that Chapman had just smashed. "I can get you a number."

"His calls will be audited. He'll be burned."

"Eventually," Stan said. "Not right away."

Chapman shrugged. "I don't see a lot of other options." He tried to stand up.

"Slow down," Stan said. "Let me get a look at that leg for you."

Chapman stretched out his leg, and Stan doused it with whiskey and bandaged it. Then he helped Chapman get dressed in fresh clothes and a new silicone mask.

"I'll make the call from a payphone," he said. "We should at least make an effort not to burn all our bridges."

"I'll start packing my toys," Stan said. "There's a lot of tech here I can salvage."

Chapman put on a large, fleece-lined sheepskin coat and pulled up the hood. "How do I look?"

Stan gave him a bemused smile. "Million bucks," he said and made his way to the locker where he kept the drones, cameras, radio transmitters, and other military-grade equipment he'd amassed over the years.

Chapman pulled himself into the driver's seat of their last van and fired up the engine. He drove through the industrial park and out the set of chainlink gates. He needed to be near the embassy when he made the call. He drove to Oval, double-parked by the gas works next to the Beefeater distillery, and walked from there to Oval tube station. Walking hurt, and by the time he found the payphones, his leg throbbed. He dialed the number Stan had given him. It was a number he'd never in a million years have imagined he'd be calling—the cell phone of the CIA's London Station Chief.

"Mr. Tenet?" he said as soon as the phone picked up.

"Who is this?"

"Your dry cleaning's ready."

"What?"

"You can pick it up immediately. We're at Kennington Park by the tennis courts."

"What are you talking about?"

"No delay," Chapman said and hung up.

enet was worried. The call broke every protocol and safeguard that he and Igor had put in place over the course of decades.

He'd known the events he'd set in motion would leave him exposed, but he hadn't counted on Viktor Lapin being so flagrant about it. The plan only worked if it got him to Moscow. If the CIA zeroed in on him before he got out, then it would all be for nothing.

And Roth couldn't help. His hands were tied. He wouldn't help Tatyana and Laurel either. He had to let things play out. He had to let the chips fall where they may. Any interference risked tipping off Viktor.

Something had certainly gone wrong. Viktor should have caught Ada by now. Tenet had given him everything he needed. He'd even gone to the bank in person to confirm she'd been there, guaranteeing the CIA would link him to the leak. Now, a call to his personal cell phone? The Agency's internal auditing process would hone in on him in a matter of days.

But he had no choice now but to keep going on the path

he'd started. He was in for the proverbial penny, as the British said. To stop now would leave him in the worst of both worlds. He needed to prove to the GRU, beyond any doubt, that he was absolutely indispensable, and he needed them to get him to Moscow. Otherwise, the whole intricately laid plan would go up in smoke.

The good news for Viktor was that Tenet had what he needed. Ada Hudson had just been detected by a facial recognition algorithm running on CCTV footage from King's Cross Station. The footage was British, gathered by MI6. The algorithm was American, processed by the NSA at Mission Data Repository in Salt Lake City, Utah.

Tenet, by virtue of his position as London Station Chief, was privy to the top-secret agreement between London and Washington that made the collaboration possible. Under the agreement, an unfathomable amount of British surveillance data was routed to the NSA, where it was merged with the PRISM data already being tracked by the US government. The information included petabytes of emails, cell phone records, Internet traffic, financial transactions, CCTV footage, and GPS data. In order to facilitate the quantities of data being shared, a Swedish Tier-One Internet backbone with its own Autonomous System designation and Internet exchange points was contracted to lay physical cables directly between Scapa Flow, Scotland, and Churchill, Manitoba on the Hudson Bay in Canada. The work was disguised as commercial, and increased the amount of traffic that could flow between Europe and North America by more than thirty percent. Its sole purpose was surveillance.

The agreement was top-secret for security reasons naturally, but it was also illegal. It contravened fundamental aspects of both British and American constitutional law, including the US Constitution's Fourth Amendment, and the UK's Human Rights Act. If the press ever got wind of it, the news would topple the government in Whitehall and could possibly bring down President Montgomery's administration in Washington also.

Ostensibly, the data-sharing allowed the NSA to track American citizens while they were in the United Kingdom. In practice, what it allowed was PRISM-level surveillance of all of the UK, with the results being shared by the CIA, the NSA, and MI6.

Tenet had put a System Trace Request on Ada as soon as Roth told him she'd been tapped to bring in Sacha. That request had just returned a match.

He looked at the footage one final time before erasing it and removing the request from the log.

Then he put on his coat and told his secretary he'd be back in half an hour.

He went down to the ground floor and got a cab outside the consulate entrance. "Kennington Park," he said to the driver. "By the tennis courts."

The cab brought him to the corner of Brixton and Harleyford, not five minutes from the embassy, and Tenet entered the park through the iron gates facing Saint Mark's church.

He was tense. He had no idea who he was meeting. He also knew that very soon, in a matter of days, a week at the most, CIA auditors would know this meeting had taken place.

The park was quiet. It was cold, and there was still a light dusting of snow on the ground. He pulled his coat around his neck and went up to a kiosk overlooking the lawn.

"Do you have coffee?" he said.

"Of course we do," the woman in the kiosk said. "What do you want?"

"One milk, one sugar."

She pressed a button on a machine and handed him a small plastic cup. "Two quid, love."

He paid her with two coins and made his way to the bench facing the tennis courts. A minute later, a man in a hooded coat sat down next to him and lit a cigarette.

"You're Viktor's source," the man said, looking forward. He was British.

"You've compromised me," Tenet said.

"I know."

"You know? Do you?"

"I'm sorry," the man said.

"Viktor told you to do this? To call my cell? To meet out in the open like this?"

"How else would I be here?"

Tenet sighed. "Well," he said. "I hope it's worth it."

"That depends on what you've got to tell me."

"All you had to do was pick her up at the bank. One young woman."

"Well, that didn't go according to plan, did it?"

"No," Tenet said. "It didn't."

"She killed my man."

"Darwinism in action," Tenet said.

The man shook his head. He flicked away the butt of his cigarette and said, "Well, clock's ticking."

"I can tell you where Ada is," Tenet said, "but I need you to pass on a message to Viktor."

"Anything."

"I need out, now."

"You and me both, mate."

"Will you pass on the message?"

"I'll tell him."

"The CIA's going to close in on me very quickly now. I need to get out. Whatever time frame he was thinking, this meeting just accelerated it."

The man nodded. He was lighting another cigarette. This was what it had come to, decades of painstaking trade-craft, of tortuous attention to detail—a meeting on a park bench with a common thug.

"So," the man said, "where is she?"

"She left King's Cross forty minutes ago. Inverness train. The scientist is with her."

da sat facing the direction of travel. Across the table, Natasha sat by the window, her head on Sacha's shoulder.

"She's sleeping," Ada said.

Sacha nodded. "It's the rhythm of the train. It calmed her."

"The sleep will do her good."

He nodded.

Ada looked at him. He had an expression on his face like he wanted to tell her something.

"What is it?" she said.

"She's the only thing that matters," he said.

It was something he'd told her before. "I know," Ada said.

"The *only* thing," he said again.

The stress was getting to him, she thought. "I'm sorry this has been so difficult," she said.

"It's not your fault," Sacha said. "I knew it wouldn't be easy."

"I made a mistake," she said. "I shouldn't have gone to

that bank. That's how they found me. That's why I was attacked."

"We all make mistakes," Sacha said, and she got the impression he was talking about more than her attack.

"Well, my mistake could have got you both killed."

"Who were the men who attacked you?"

"I don't know, but they were connected to the embassy."

"That makes our job a whole lot more difficult, doesn't it?"

She nodded.

"I...."

"You what?"

She shook her head.

"Tell me," he said. "It will lessen the burden."

"The man I shot. He was my first."

"Your first kill?"

She nodded.

He reached across the table and took her hand in his. She was surprised. This man developed weapons of unimaginable horror, weapons designed to destroy the earth as much as to perform any military objective, but he didn't seem a monster. He had a daughter he wanted to protect.

They were alone in the carriage, and neither of them spoke for a few minutes.

Outside the window, England sped by. They passed through Peterborough, Doncaster, York, Darlington. About an hour into the journey, a man came down the aisle with a snack cart.

"We'll have two coffees," Sacha said, "and two cakes."

The man gave them two cups of coffee, and two frosted cakes, individually wrapped in foil.

"Thank you," Ada said.

She watched him as she sipped her coffee. He was staring out the window at something. She followed his gaze but couldn't see what it was that had his attention.

At Durham, the conductor told them they would have a ten-minute stop.

Natasha was still asleep, and Ada asked Sacha if he smoked. He did not.

"I'll be back in a minute," she said and went out to the platform. She lit a cigarette and smoked it right outside Sacha's window so that they could maintain sight of each other. The station was quiet. Snow whipped around in the wind and piled up against the wall of a vending machine. There were only a few passengers coming and going. Six in total boarded the train. Ada looked at all of them closely. None seemed a threat.

She finished the cigarette and went back to her seat. Natasha was still asleep. She'd moved so that her head was on Sacha's lap.

"The blueprints you gave me," Ada said, taking her seat. "I lost them when I was attacked."

"Then the GRU knows for certain why I'm here."

She nodded.

"Although, I suppose they already knew."

"If they needed any proof," Ada said, "they have it now."

Sacha smiled sadly. "They didn't need proof."

"Will you be able to recreate them?" she said.

Sacha nodded. "I can redraw them."

"I would have taken photos," Ada said, "but I don't have a phone."

"I don't either."

"We better not lose each other then."

He smiled again.

"How did they let someone like you slip through their fingers?" she said.

"They were distracted."

"The explosion?"

"It wasn't an accident," Sacha said.

"Sabotage?"

He nodded.

"You?"

"Who else?"

She shook her head. She was looking at a man who'd sabotaged a nuclear rocket. She wasn't quite sure what to make of that—what that said about him. He clearly had some sort of moral code, he was risking his life for his daughter, and he was trading his life's work to the CIA so that they could counteract the weapons he'd developed, but he'd also caused a nuclear detonation that had led to casualties across the Arctic, as well as untold devastation.

"What kind of person does a thing like that?" she said. It wasn't an accusation. She just wanted to know.

"I'm already dead," Sacha said. "I knew that before I ever left Nyonoksa. There will be no rest for me. Not in CIA protection. Not in hiding."

"The GRU has to kill you," she said. "Don't they?"

He nodded. "They have to send a message. If I get away, what does that say to the other scientists who have... *misgivings*?"

"Is that what you had?"

He smiled. "It's hard to develop weapons of mass destruction and not have misgivings of some kind."

"I don't know how anyone could work on the weapons you developed," she said.

Sacha shrugged. "Like I said earlier, when you have no

choice, a lot of things lose their complexity. They lose their nuance."

"But no one can force you to do a thing."

"The scientists on the Manhattan Project," Sacha said, "did anyone ever question how they could do what they did?"

"People questioned it."

"That work was carried out by your government. The government you serve."

"Their work brought the War to an end."

"The *good* guys," Sacha said. "The Allies."

"What are you saying? That they shouldn't have done it?"

"The men involved," Sacha said, "all professed to regret the work after it was done."

"They didn't know how destructive it would be."

"They had the models," Sacha said. "They had the equations. They knew."

"So you're equating your work with theirs?"

"I don't know," Sacha said. "I don't ever want to see the weapons I built in use. That's the truth."

"I should hope so," Ada said.

"But at the same time, if it wasn't for Natasha's illness, if she could have been treated in Moscow, I never would have defected."

"You'd still be there?"

"I'd still be there."

"But why?

"Why?" he let out a mirthless laugh. "I'm Russian. It's Russia. I didn't choose to be born there. I didn't choose my fate."

"And the Nazis didn't choose to be born in Germany when they were. Is that what you're saying?"

"I don't know," Sacha said. "Isn't there some truth in that? If you'd been born in a different place, at a different time, would you be the same person you are?"

"I suppose not," Ada said.

Sacha began opening the wrapper on his cake. Ada did the same. They ate their cake, and Sacha said, "After I'm gone...."

Ada stopped him. "Hold your horses. We don't know how this is going to play out."

He shook his head. "I know what's coming for me," he said. "You don't get to walk away from the things I've seen. They'll get me."

"You're resigned to that?"

He looked down at his daughter's head on his lap, moving some stray locks from her face. "When I'm gone," he said, "promise me you'll look out for her."

Ada looked him in the eye. "I will," she said, "for whatever it's worth."

"It's worth a great deal," Sacha said.

38

When Chapman got back to the warehouse, Stan was reviewing the drone footage from the attack.

"I confirmed about Hamish," he said. "He was pronounced dead on the scene."

"One less loose end," Chapman said, getting out of the van.

Stan looked up at him.

"What?"

"You're a heartless bastard. You know that?"

"You have permission to say the same about me when I'm dead," he said.

Stan had piled their equipment on three skids, ready to load into the van, and Chapman went over to it. He examined the crates of guns, grenades, plastic explosives, scopes, night sights, drones, cameras, sensors, and just about every other piece of hardware a contractor in their business might need.

"All ready to go?" he said.

Stan was looking at his computer screen and didn't answer.

Chapman picked up two SIG Sauer P250 pistols, chambered in the 9x19 Parabellum, and put them in the pocket of his coat. It was a gun widely used by police forces in the United Kingdom and would be difficult to trace.

He also picked up the case containing his L115A3 long-range rifle, still loaded with rubber impact rounds. In addition to the gun, the case contained a Schmidt and Bender 25x scope and a sound suppressor.

"I need a drone," he said to Stan.

"What?"

Chapman nodded his head.

"You know where they are?" Stan said.

"Gray Coat found them."

"So quickly?"

"They left King's Cross by train less than an hour ago."

"Headed where?"

"Scotland."

"If they're on a train, we're going to need satellite surveillance," Stan said. "There'll be half-a-dozen stops along the way. We need to know where they get off."

"Put in a request with Viktor," Chapman said. "He'll approve it."

"He doesn't know you spoke to his man."

"He won't care if it gets him a second shot at the prize."

"All right," Stan said.

"And select a drone. I'll take it with me."

Stan got up and came back with an Aeryon SkyRanger quadcopter. It weighed about five pounds and could be controlled remotely using a laptop.

"What's the range of that thing?" Chapman said.

"You'll have an hour on the batteries," Stan said. "Range is five kilometers from the laptop."

"Speed?"

"Fifty miles-per-hour."

Chapman began packing the equipment into the van while Stan sent a satellite requisition request to Viktor.

"You following the train by chopper?" Stan said.

Chapman nodded. He shut the van and turned to Stan. "I shouldn't have said that about Hamish."

"It's all right," Stan said.

"I'm as rattled as you are."

"I'll get over it."

"Okay," Chapman said. "We'll get a drink when I get back."

"A drink or three," Stan said.

Chapman was about to get in the van when Stan said, "By the way, what are we going to do about the cardboard tube?"

"What tube?"

"The target, she was carrying a cardboard tube like you'd use to hold a rolled-up document."

"I didn't see that."

"She dropped it in the street when we attacked. Police picked it up."

"You clever boy," Chapman said.

Stan nodded. "The police won't have a clue how valuable it is. I'll check their logs and find out where it is."

"Be careful," Chapman said.

Stan raised two fingers to his forehead and gave Chapman a salute.

Chapman pulled out of the warehouse and joined the traffic on Peckham Road. The heliport was on the Isle of

Dogs, south of Canary Wharf, and he crossed the river at the Blackwall Tunnel. Traffic was a bastard as usual. When he reached the heliport, the pilot had a Eurocopter EC155 fueled and ready for take-off. The chopper had a top speed of two hundred miles per hour and a range of over five hundred.

"Someone help me with these bags," Chapman said.

A porter loaded the bags while Chapman told the pilot they were headed north toward Scotland and needed to make up time.

"We can get as far as Edinburgh without refueling," the pilot said.

Chapman nodded, and five minutes later, they were airborne. They flew rapidly north over the brick-colored expanse of Hackney and Bethnal Green, and it wasn't long before the enormous city was receding behind them.

Chapman sat back in the plush leather chair and watched the landscape pass below. He needed to collect his thoughts. The train had a two-hour jump on him. If the targets remained on it long enough, the chopper would make up the lost ground and pass them. If they got off too soon, he would lose them unless Stan got the satellite surveillance up and running in time.

He lit a cigarette and looked at his watch. The chopper was equipped with a phone, and he dialed Viktor's number again.

"I just got a request from your man for satellite surveillance on a train," Viktor said.

"Did you give it to him?"

"He didn't say what it was for."

"You know what it's for."

"I told you to stand down," Viktor said. "I believe I was very clear on that point."

"She's on that train," Chapman said.

"How did you find her?"

"I have my ways," Chapman said.

He'd been wrestling with whether or not to tell Viktor he'd spoken to his source at the embassy. Viktor would find out soon enough, but Chapman was gambling that he wouldn't care, so long as the job was completed successfully.

"I think it's time you and I parted ways," Viktor said.

Chapman's breath caught in his throat. "Not so fast," he said.

"Not so fast?"

"Viktor, listen to me."

"You don't speak to me like that."

"Your scientist is on that train with her," Chapman said. It was his last chance.

"Scientist?" Viktor said.

"Yes."

"I never told you about a scientist."

Chapman swallowed. "I spoke to your source at the embassy."

"You did what?"

This had all been a mistake. Chapman could feel it. He was fucked.

"The man who visited the bank."

"You spoke to him?"

"Yes," Chapman said.

"He's been a GRU source for decades. Do you have any idea how valuable he is?"

"Viktor," Chapman said, but Viktor cut him off.

"Of course you don't."

"Sir."

"Sir? It's too late for *sir*, don't you think?"

"I'm in the air, following the train. I can finish this job."

Viktor was quiet for a minute, and Chapman could literally feel the seconds slip by. He was aware that his life was in the balance, and it had a strange effect on him. He thought back to the twelve-year-old boy in Umm Qasr. Everything that had happened in his life was a direct result of that moment—that bullet. Everything that followed could be traced back to it. He felt it in his soul. He'd pulled the trigger and dropped that boy. A boy he didn't know. A boy no one cared about.

But he might as well have been holding the gun to his own head. Sometimes, you think you're killing, when in fact, what you're really doing is dying.

"Ada Hudson is on the train with the scientist?" Viktor said.

"That's what your source told me."

"Is the girl with them?"

"What girl?"

"The daughter. The child."

"He didn't say."

"You listen to me very carefully, Chapman."

39

S tan watched the drone footage of the attack over and over, honing in on the exact moment Ada Hudson dropped the cardboard tube. He got a face capture of the police officer who picked it up and ran facial recognition on him against the Metropolitan Police database. He found out the officer's home station was West End Central on Saville Row and checked their evidence log. The officer had turned in something just thirty minutes earlier.

"There you are," Stan said to himself.

The tube was still awaiting processing. That meant no one knew what it was and that it hadn't been flagged as critical.

Stan quickly forged a Met Police evidence requisition form, keeping it deliberately vague.

Cardboard poster tube. Two feet long. Found on Fitzmaurice Place.

He made it a transfer request to the New Scotland Yard evidence repository and entered it into the system, complete with tracking information and a barcode. He added a note that a private courier would come by to pick it up.

He printed out the form and put on a pair of leather gloves before handling it. He took it from the printer, scrawled a signature on it, and folded it twice. Then he put on his helmet and leather jacket, as well as a reflective yellow safety vest that always had the effect of making him look more official.

He was about to head out the door when Chapman's fax machine started going off. It had to be Viktor's reply to the satellite requisition request. Stan went and grabbed the sheet of paper and brushed it with vinegar.

Identifier: RSR_043403

Hardware: Glonass-KM   High-Resolution Surveillance

Location: United Kingdom

Target 1: Sacha Gazinsky

Target 2: Ada Hudson

Target 3: Natasha Gazinsky

Lead Agent: Viktor Lapin

Agency: Prime Directorate

Status: Approved

The message was followed with instructions on how to access the hardware remotely. He went back to the computer and logged in. Extremely clear footage of a train speeding along the English countryside filled the screen.

He called Chapman.

"You making good time?" he said when Chapman picked up.

"Yes," Chapman said.

"I'm looking at the train now. Viktor approved the request."

"I spoke to him. He knows I met with the source."

"And?"

"He wasn't happy."

"Is he ever?"

"Listen," Chapman said, "I think she's headed for Edinburgh. That's four hours from now. I'll be there well ahead of her."

"If they get off before Edinburgh," Stan said, "I'll follow them on satellite. I have three faces locked into the facial recognition system."

"Right," Chapman said. "She's traveling with a Russian defector and his daughter. He's the real target."

"So that's her objective? Bringing in a defector?"

"Right."

"She's doing a fine job of it."

"She's being fucked by Viktor's source. She doesn't know what she's up against."

"What about the daughter?"

"Natasha Gazinsky. You should have imagery there."

"She looks very young, Chapman."

"Stan, come on."

"What do you mean, come on?"

"We've got our orders. We took this job. We have to finish it."

"We didn't know it involved a kid."

"I know, Stan."

"What have you gotten us into?"

"I don't know, but I'm going to get us out of it."

Stan let out a long breath through his teeth. He ran his hand through his hair and leaned back.

"You all right?" Chapman said.

"Just tell me what age this girl is."

"Nine."

"Fuck me."

"Listen, Stan. You don't have to worry about it. Just make sure we don't lose them."

"Chapman," Stan said, but whatever he was going to say, Chapman didn't want to hear it.

"The other thing is the tube. Viktor wants it."

"Chapman, what did we always say? If things got hairy. If things started to cross a line."

"Stan, we have to finish this job. We have no choice."

"We could...."

"We could what?"

"You know."

"Cut and run?"

"We've got money. We've got...."

"What have we got?"

"*Survival* skills."

"Survival skills? Stan, you're in la-la land."

"Nine years old, Chap."

"And what about your mother? What about your little daughter? Do *they* have survival skills?"

"What's this got to do with them?"

"I just got off the phone with Viktor," Chapman said. "He was pretty clear about what he expected."

"He threatened my daughter?"

"Not in so many words."

"I'll kill the fucker."

"Not before we finish this job, Stan. So get your head in the game. This isn't the time to start getting squeamish."

Stan tapped the pockets of his jacket, searching for his smokes.

"If Viktor monitors the satellite on his end, can you get the tube?"

Stan sucked deeply on a cigarette. "The tube's at the police station. West End Central."

"Do they know what they've got?"

"They don't have a clue. I could get them to hand it over the counter right now, no questions asked."

"All right," Chapman said. "Go get it."

The phone went dead. Stan put it down and flicked ash from his cigarette onto the floor. He didn't have a good feeling about this. He and Chapman had been through a lot together, they'd done things Stan wasn't exactly proud of, but he'd always been able to justify it to himself. He figured, if someone was stupid enough to get themselves in trouble with the Russians, or the Syrians, or the Iranians, then they'd probably done something bad. That logic didn't apply so neatly when the target was a nine-year-old girl.

He stubbed out his cigarette and forced himself to get up. There would be time enough later to be racked by guilt.

It was a short motorcycle ride to Saville Row, and he pulled up right in front of the station. The police had no idea the contents of the tube they'd recovered were valuable. Because of that, and the fact Stan had access to their database, stealing it would be surprisingly easy.

He entered the station with his gloves and helmet on and opened the visor to speak. There was a line of people waiting to speak to the administrator, and he skipped past all of them as if he'd been there so many times before that the rules didn't apply to him. Confidence was key. He threw the evidence requisition on the counter while the administrator was helping someone else and said, "Cheers, love."

"Hey," she said, "you need to wait your turn."

"This one's from HQ, love."

"Don't *love* me."

Stan raised his hands as if it made no difference to him what she did. "Listen, I'm just the courier. They tell me urgent, I tell you urgent. Simple as that."

The woman sighed and asked the man she was serving to excuse her. She disappeared into the back of the station, and when she returned, she was holding the cardboard tube. It was in a clear, plastic bag, and there was a police tracking sticker on it. She scanned the form Stan had forged, then scanned the sticker on the bag.

The scanner beeped, and she handed him back his form.

"Sign here," she said.

Stan signed, and she passed him the tube.

40

The first thing Chapman did after landing in Edinburgh was call Stan.

"I'm in Edinburgh," he said.

"Good," Stan said. "The train's two hours behind you, and we got a visual confirmation."

"Really?"

"Ada Hudson got off the train at Durham. She smoked a cigarette on the platform and got back on."

"Sacha's still with her?"

"We have to assume he is," Stan said.

"Okay," Chapman said.

He was relieved. The only confirmation he'd had that they were on the train at all was from Viktor's source at the embassy. And there'd been a gap of over an hour before Viktor got the satellite surveillance set up. That was a lot of time.

"The train stops at Waverley, right?" Chapman said.

"Yeah. It'll be there for twenty minutes."

Edinburgh was the largest city on the train's route. Waverley was the most important station. Chapman was sure they'd get off there. It was their best chance of disappearing, laying low, and he would be ready.

"My chopper's refueling here," Chapman said. "If they get off before Waverley, I need to know immediately."

"I'll be on them like glue, boss."

"What stations do they pass after Waverley?"

"Only Perth and Inverness."

"I'm going to bet she gets off in Edinburgh."

"It's a safe bet."

"I'll set up a shot at the station."

"You sure?"

Edinburgh Waverley wasn't the easiest place to arrange a shot. The station was crowded, in the middle of the city, and the train platforms were covered, meaning Chapman would have to be inside the station. He had a few options. He could wait on the platform. That had the advantage that if they didn't get off, he could get on board and catch them in their seats. He didn't love that idea, however. After what he'd seen of Ada Hudson and what she was capable of, a shot from a distance would be safer for him.

"I'm sure," he said. "Did you recover the tube?"

"Yes," Stan said.

"Thank God."

Chapman walked through the executive lounge and hailed a cab out front.

"Waverley station," he said to the driver, heaving his two heavy carryalls in with him. The airport was south of the city, about twenty minutes from the city center, and traffic was light.

Chapman was familiar with Waverley station and thought of the ways he could set up a shot on the drive. Trains entered the city through the large, landscaped gardens in front of the castle. There was a tunnel beneath the Scottish National Gallery that re-emerged on the other side before entering the station.

One option was to take the shot from the paved pedestrian area behind the National Gallery. The tracks could be seen from there, and it was just a hundred yards from the western end of the platforms. The problem was that he wasn't guaranteed a line of sight along the entire length of the platforms. The angle was oblique, and at the far end of the platforms, his view would be obstructed by a bridge crossing the width of the tracks.

That was Waverley Bridge, wide enough for two traffic lanes, bus lanes, footpaths. It was directly above the center of the platforms, but there was no way Chapman could set up a shot from it. It was crowded with people, brightly lit, and in any case, he would have only been able to see the platforms from its western side. On the other side, the station and platforms were covered by a Victorian-era roof of steel trusses and opaque glass.

"Drop me off on Princes Street," he said to the driver. "At the Balmoral."

The cab pulled up outside the hotel, and Chapman unloaded the bags.

"Can I help you, sir?" a hotel bellhop said, approaching the cab.

"Yes," Chapman said, looking at his watch.

He followed the bellhop into the sumptuous lobby of the hotel and went up to the desk.

"I'd like a room on the top floor?" he said to the woman at the desk.

"Fond of the view?" she said.

He nodded.

"Stunning, isn't it?" she said in her Scottish accent.

She typed on her computer and told him she had a west-facing room on the top floor for seven hundred pounds per night. In all likelihood, it was the most expensive hotel room then available in the city.

"I'll take it," Chapman said, taking a credit card and his driver's license from his wallet.

He was giving up his identity. The intelligence services would have no trouble connecting him to all this once the job was done and the dust had settled. But there was nothing he could do about that. He'd already resigned himself to going into hiding when this job was done. He and Stan would have to burn everything, flee the country, perhaps for the rest of their lives. The thing about the GRU, though, as it operated under President Molotov, was that they would look after him. They would make it worth his while.

If he succeeded.

If he failed, it was a different story. Viktor had left him in no doubt about that.

The girl swiped his credit card and checked him in. "Would you like some help with your bags?" she asked.

"No thanks," he said, taking his key.

He took the elevator to the top floor and found his room. It was well appointed with wide views over the Princes Street Gardens and the castle.

Chapman went to the minibar and poured himself a coke. There was about an hour's daylight left. He made sure the door to the room was locked then opened the carryall containing the drone and laptop. He unpacked them, connected the laptop to the Internet through a specially modified cell he'd brought for the purpose, and called Stan.

"Where are you calling from?" Stan said.

"The Balmoral Hotel. Top floor."

"That's a good location," Stan said. "Good signal. Can you open the windows?"

Chapman doubted he'd be able to open them without breaking them. "I'll call you back," he said.

He'd chosen the top floor for a reason. The windows opened onto an extended sill around the top of the building that acted like a rooftop balcony. It wasn't intended for the purpose, it was purely ornamental, but it was three feet wide, just about large enough to step out onto, and was protected from view by a stone rail about two feet high. The windows had been adjusted for safety and only opened a few inches for ventilation. Chapman took out his toolkit and removed the stoppers on one of the windows that prevented it from opening further.

When he was done, it swung open all the way.

He got the drone and set it up on the sill. He powered it on and ran through the diagnostics. Then he went to the laptop and connected it to the signal emitted by the drone.

He called Stan.

"All right," he said. "You should be picking it up."

"I have it," Stan said.

"The drone's on the balcony. Take off straight up."

"Will do."

"I'll have to leave the laptop here. I might not be able to come back for it."

"Understood," Stan said. "I can wipe everything from my end."

Chapman left the drone on the balcony, and the laptop open on the desk. On the door, he put up the 'do not disturb' sign, then he left the room, taking the other carryall with him.

With the drone set up, all that remained was for him to find a shooting position. He left the hotel and took the steps down into Waverley Station's main arrivals concourse. At the far end of the concourse, conductors stood at gates, checking tickets and ensuring that only passengers went onto the platforms. Above the concourse was a large, electronic arrivals board. Pigeons stood on the board, and their droppings smeared the front of it. The train from King's Cross would be arriving at platform seven.

The station was busy with office workers and other commuters making their way home from the city, and Chapman just stood there in the middle of the crowd, watching. Along the back of the concourse was a raised steel walkway that led out of the station toward the Fruitmarket Gallery and Market Street. The walkway was closed for repairs, and the wall behind it was covered with netted scaffolding, three floors high.

The workers had already clocked off for the night, and Chapman went up to the barrier and slipped in behind the netted mesh that covered the scaffolding. He climbed to the second level and checked to see what sort of vantage it gave him. From the position, he could see out over the crowded concourse and down the length of each of the platforms.

He walked along the scaffold until he was directly across the concourse from platform seven. The sightline was perfect. He sat on the wooden planks with his legs over the edge and watched the platform through the netted mesh for a few minutes. He lit a cigarette and tried to calm his nerves. No one could see him.

41

It was dusk when the train finally pulled into Haymarket station in Edinburgh. Slightly more than half the passengers disembarked there, and Sacha asked Ada if they were getting off too.

She shook her head. "Waverley's just a few minutes down the track. We'll get off there."

Natasha was awake. She'd been patient during the journey, but it was clear she was eager to get off the train.

"What will we do when we get there?" she said to Ada.

Ada didn't know what she was supposed to say to her. Every time she looked at the child, she felt an overwhelming sense of responsibility. Ada knew her life depended on the decisions she made, and with the GRU tracking them, she'd only be able to stay ahead of them for so long.

"We'll find a hotel," she said.

"How long will we stay there?"

"I don't know," Ada said. "I think just one night."

The train pulled out of Haymarket, and a few minutes later, the driver announced Edinburgh Waverley.

"This is us," Ada said.

They gathered up their things and made their way to the door of the carriage. Two other passengers got off ahead of them.

"We'll buy some supplies once we find a hotel," she said to Sacha. "Some toiletries, some clean clothes."

"Dinner?" Natasha said.

"Dinner too," Ada said, stepping down onto the platform ahead of the others. Sacha helped Natasha with the steps, then followed her.

"I don't know if my coat is up to the task here," Ada said, doing up the button at her neck. It was a good few degrees colder than London had been. The others did up their coats too.

They hurried along the platform toward the concourse. Ada scanned the crowd. A homeless man asked passers for change. A police officer stood with his thumbs in the straps of his vest.

Ada saw a drug store across the concourse. She thought they would check in to one of the hotels near the station, and she would come back for toiletries and some snacks.

She looked back at Sacha and Natasha to make sure they were still following. Sacha seemed lighter, like a weight had been lifted from his shoulders. Being in Edinburgh, farther away from the tentacles of the GRU, was a relief to him.

Ada turned back ahead and felt a sudden concussion in the air, as if the atmosphere had suddenly compressed. She realized later it was the feeling of the bullet breaking the sound barrier.

She didn't know what was happening at first. It was all too fast. Sacha was there, confident, Natasha's hand clenched tightly in his own, and then, so suddenly it didn't seem real, he was flung backward onto the concrete platform as if thrown by an explosion.

Ada stared at him. For a second, she didn't know what she was looking at. Then her vision focused on his hand. He'd been holding Natasha's hand so tightly that her mitten was still in his grip.

Natasha looked at her hand, then at her father on the ground behind her, and let out a high-pitched scream, a single note, like something emitted from an electrical device.

On the ground, twelve feet from where he'd been standing, Sacha Gazinsky was lying on his back, his head carved open as if cleaved by a two-handed ax.

Ada wasn't thinking. Instinct took over. She was running before she knew it, before she was even consciously aware of the direction of the bullet or its angle. There was scaffolding across the concourse, three floors high and draped in a green mesh, and she ran toward it.

The mesh meant anyone behind it could see out but couldn't be seen, and she knew instinctively that it was where the shooter was positioned.

Across the concourse, a set of steps led to a raised walkway. The area was closed to the public, and Ada jumped a barrier and ran up the steps. Halfway up, she jumped the handrail and landed on the second level of the scaffolding behind the mesh. It was dark but just light enough for her to see that no one was there. There was another level to the scaffolding above her, and she heard the boards of it groan under the weight of someone running.

She drew her gun and began sprinting the length of the platform, watching the level above while simultaneously keeping an eye on the ground, making sure she didn't fall. The shooter reached the end of the scaffold and jumped out from it onto the steel walkway, and kept running. He'd been above it. Ada was below and about twenty yards behind him. She leaped up and grabbed the edge of the walkway, and pulled herself up. The walkway led to a set of steep, stone steps. Ada dashed up the four flights of them and reached the street above just in time to see a well-built man in tight clothing enter a narrow, stone archway across the street. She kept after him, and the moment she entered the archway, four bullets hit the wall right next to her head, sending shards of stone into her face.

She dropped to the ground and put her hands over her head. Three more bullets struck stone, and she glanced up. She was in a long, upward sloping alley, the walls covered in graffiti. The stench of urine was overwhelming. The shooter had reached the next set of stone steps and was bounding up them, three at a time, sending periodic, un-aimed shots back in Ada's direction.

Ada got up and continued the chase, oblivious to the wild bullets that were hitting the walls around her. This man had just killed Sacha, and she was going to catch him or die trying. She didn't care which. The steps led up to the narrow medieval warren of streets of Edinburgh's Old Town.

The shooter reached the top and took cover behind the wall, then he emptied his gun, firing more blind shots down the narrow stairway. Ada didn't even duck. She kept up the chase, gaining on him with every step.

The shooter flung his empty gun to the ground and kept running. Ada followed, passing the archway. It opened onto a cobbled street leading up toward the castle. The street was lined with tall, gothic buildings, dark with soot, and as she ran past the spire of Saint Giles' Cathedral, she realized in the edge of her mind that a drone was buzzing somewhere overhead.

The street was quiet but not devoid of pedestrians, and Ada dropped to one knee and took aim. She held out her pistol with both arms, drew a bead on the man's head, and depressed the trigger—a single shot.

A mist of blood sprayed the air. The man stumbled and fell forward, crashing to the ground. The people on the street realized what was happening and began to run in panic.

Ada, barely aware of them, rose slowly to her feet and, breathless, walked calmly to the man's body.

She stood over him and looked down. Her bullet had hit him squarely in the back of the head. There was no question he was dead. Even still, she put two more bullets in his back.

She looked up and down the street. There were multiple witnesses to what had just happened. In the distance, she could already hear the sound of police sirens.

She checked her gun, reloaded, then looked up at the sky. The narrow, stone streets meant the drone was lower than it should have been, and she could just about make out the glint of its metallic shell. She aimed, then, as if in warning to the world, unloaded her gun into the sky at it.

42

Viktor was in his favorite restaurant, sitting alone, a bowl of hot borscht in front of him. He dipped his spoon into the sour cream and placed a large dollop in the middle of the bowl. He did it daintily, with finesse, as if applying the final touch to an oil painting. The restaurant was a traditional place with wooden tables and simple furnishings. It was on Leningradsky Avenue, across from the Belorusskaya, and was popular with GRU staffers because of its proximity to headquarters.

"Hey," he said, raising his hand to get the attention of the waitress. "I need more dill over here."

The waitress gave him a sideways glance.

He picked up the pepper grinder and was about to begin grinding it when his phone started to ring.

He sighed and pulled it from his pocket. It was an unrecognized number, international. Ordinarily, he wouldn't have answered, but with so many balls in the air, he didn't dare ignore it.

"Viktor Lapin," he said impatiently.

"Viktor?"

"Who's this?"

"Is this Viktor?" someone said in English.

"The question," Viktor said, "is not who I am, but who you are?"

The man cleared his throat. His voice was deep, and he spoke with a strong London accent. "This is Chapman's man. Stan."

"The one who put through the satellite requisition?"

"Correct."

"Why isn't Chapman calling me himself?"

"Chapman's dead."

The waitress came over with the dill, and Viktor pointed at the soup. She sprinkled it on top of the sour cream, and he pointed at his beer glass, which was empty. She took it with her when she left.

"Who killed him?" he said.

"The CIA woman, Ada Hudson, but not before he hit his target."

"Sacha Gazinsky?"

"That's right."

"He killed him?"

"Near blew his head off."

"And the child?"

"The child?"

"The daughter? Gazinsky's daughter?"

"She's still with Ada Hudson."

"I see," Viktor said. "Well, Chapman's man...."

"Stan," he said.

"Stan," Viktor repeated, emphasizing the plosive as if savoring a flavor, "you have some nerve calling me, don't you think?"

"I thought this was good news," Stan said.

"Good news? Chapman burned my most valuable asset

in London to find out where Gazinsky was."

"But he got him. He's dead."

"And I suppose you're calling now to collect his payment?"

There was a pause on the other end of the line, then Stan said, "There's something else."

"Oh, is there?" Viktor said. "Why am I not surprised?"

"The blueprints."

"What blueprints?"

"Sacha gave Ada Hudson a cardboard tube containing technical drawings for some sort of missile."

"How do you know that?"

"Because I have them."

Viktor leaned back in his seat and pulled out his cigarettes. "This conversation just gets more and more interesting, doesn't it, Stan?"

"I have your drawings. Gazinsky's dead. I'd say that counts for something, wouldn't you?"

"And what would you say it counts for?"

"Chapman always said the GRU looked after its own."

"Did he, indeed?"

"I'm not cattle trading with you, Viktor. I have what's yours, and I need to come in."

"The loyal soldier."

"Exactly."

"What about Chapman's operation? I don't want any loose ends."

"I've already torn it down. Hardrives, records, everything's been burned."

"And now you want an extraction?"

"Chapman went all out on this. He didn't just burn your man in the embassy. He made calls from his cell. He used his own credit cards. Someone's going to piece this back to him pretty quickly."

"I can get you out, Stan. Don't sound so worried."

"You can get me to Moscow?"

"If that's what you want."

"And payment?"

"I'll give you Chapman's contract."

"The full share?"

"I'm not going to swindle you, Stan. Like your friend said, the GRU looks after its own."

"Like the devil?"

"Exactly like the devil."

"Okay," Stan said. "And what about these blueprints? I can burn them if you want."

"No, no," Viktor said. "Don't burn them."

"You want to see them?"

"You take very good care of them, Stan. They're your ticket out."

"So what happens now?"

"Just calm down, Stan. Why don't you tell me where you are, and I'll see about getting you taken care of."

43

Ada made her way down the steps of Carrubber's Close back toward the station in a state of shock. Only vaguely was she aware of the police sirens. They were coming from every direction. Edinburgh was not a city accustomed to multiple shootings in a single night, and every police officer in the city had been called to the area.

Luckily for Ada, they still didn't know who they were looking for, a fact that was demonstrated when she walked right past a group of four officers as she descended the steps back into the station. They didn't give her a second glance.

The station was in chaos. There were police everywhere. Four ambulances had arrived on the scene. Some police tried to stop her from entering the platforms, but she pointed to Natasha. "My daughter," she said. "That's my daughter."

They let her pass, and she hurried over to Natasha, who was numb with shock, and threw her arms around her.

In the chaos, no one had pieced together that Natasha was the victim's daughter. None of the paramedics or police officers had taken an interest in her. She'd been corralled with the rest of the people in the station away from the body, and Ada was able to take her back through the concourse to the Princes Street exit. There were more police at the entrance who paid them no mind, and a moment later, they were out in the cold air of Edinburgh's Princes Street. It was a busy shopping street, and there were a lot of people on it.

Ada walked up to the nearest cab and opened the door.

"Where to, love?" the driver said.

"The department store," Ada said. "What's it called, again?"

"Harvey Nick's?"

"Yes," Ada said.

She needed to clear her head. She needed to think fast. The shooter had been a step ahead of her again. How did he know where to wait for her? She hadn't even known herself that she was getting off there. The Russians had been a step ahead of her at every turn. They even had a drone in the air. She didn't know if she'd shot it down or if it was still up there. All she knew was that she needed to take evasive measures.

The cab brought them to the Harvey Nichols entrance on Saint Andrew Square, and they got out. She kept tight hold of Natasha's hand as they hurried through the crowds. The store was a high-end place, and a girl in a pink suit offered them a perfume spritz as they entered. Ada waved her away.

Natasha was still in shock, and Ada was grateful for that. If she'd been able to process what was going on, what had just happened to her father, she wouldn't have been able to keep going.

They hurried through the store and exited to the pedestrianized area known as Multrees Walk. It was dark outside, but the area was busy and amply lit. Ada avoided looking upward as they hurried down the street and entered the Saint James Mall.

She was in shock herself. She wasn't sure what she was doing. Her training had taken over. She was going through the motions now, unthinking, acting on muscle memory. How could they have known where she'd be before she even knew it herself? Did they have a team at every stop the train made, waiting for her? How could she hope to get ahead of an opponent like that?

And Sacha, her main objective, was dead. She was a complete failure.

But she couldn't afford to give up. Not while Natasha was still relying on her. That was something she could still do. It was also something she'd promised Sacha. Something she owed him.

She followed the signs for the mall's multistory parking lot. "Come on, Natasha," she said, hurrying her into the stairwell that led to the lot.

Once in the lot, Ada led them along the rows of cars, trying to look as casual as possible. She tried the handles of some of the older cars, trying to find one that wasn't locked. The third car she tried, an old Toyota with bald tires and rust spots, opened.

"Quickly," she said to Natasha, putting her in the back. "Lie down," she said to her, covering her with her coat. "Stay covered."

Natasha did as she was told, her face blank, and Ada got in the front. She reached beneath the steering column, searching for the starter and ignition wires. When she found them, she pulled them loose, removed the insulation on the first half-inch of each wire, and touched them against each other. The engine cranked to life and fired up.

She exited the parking lot onto Leith Street and drove north out of the city. The traffic was slow, and it took almost twenty minutes to get to the Forth Bridge that took them north over the Forth and out into open country. Traffic remained heavy until Dunfermline, where they abandoned the stolen vehicle in the parking lot of a suburban shopping mall. The mall was just closing, but Ada was able to use a payphone at the entrance to call a cab.

They waited for it in the cold, and when it arrived, she said to the driver, "Is there a car rental place near here?"

"There's an Enterprise," the driver said.

"Take us there."

The Enterprise rental office wasn't far, and Ada used the credit card Tatyana had given her and a false ID to rent a Volvo SUV.

"You can sit upfront with me now," she said to Natasha as they got into the car.

Natasha got in next to her, and Ada took her coat off and put it on the child like a blanket.

"Natasha, are you okay?"

Natasha looked at her but was unable to speak.

Ada rubbed her cheek with the back of her hand, then drove them out of the parking lot. Before getting on the highway, they stopped at a drive-through, and Ada ordered two burgers with fries.

"You want a milkshake?" she said to Natasha, and Natasha said nothing.

She got Natasha a coke and herself a large coffee, then they got onto the motorway, headed north in the direction of the remote mountains of the Scottish Highlands.

Ada ate from her lap as she drove. Natasha fell asleep without so much as looking at her food.

44

Viktor read over his final report to the Prime Directorate one last time. He was nervous. It was a bold document, and Suvorov would not like it, but that was the nature of the game. The distribution list was wider than Viktor had ever had access to before and included the President himself. If he was ever to make a power play, this was the moment.

By convention, he should have cleared the report with Suvorov first. Suvorov was the lead agent. It was his operation.

But that would have taken all the power out of Viktor's hands, it would have put Suvorov in the driver's seat, and he would have taken all the credit.

"Fuck it," he said, tapping a cigarette against the desk. He lit it, sucked deeply, and pressed the send button.

That was it. Done. He leaned back in the chair and tried not to think about it. There was a bottle of XO Calvados in the drawer beneath his desk, and he brought it out. If there was ever a time for a drink, it was now.

He filled the small glass and downed the shot, then

refilled it and stood up. He went to the window. It was an impressive skyline, the city at night, the towers of President Molotov's capital glittering in the distance like jewels. Indeed, eight of Europe's ten tallest buildings were clustered together in Moscow's new International Business Center. They were the cream of an economy that was designed to put the wealth of one-tenth of the planet's landmass into the pockets of just a handful of men. Those soaring spires were symbols of more than money. They were an embodiment of modern feudalism, of the raw power the strong could exert over the weak.

The Tsar emancipated the serfs in 1861, but those towers were the proof that such documents changed nothing. They were pieces of paper, in a world of blood, and bone, and steel.

Things didn't change. Russia was as it had ever been. The world was as it had ever been. Anyone who thought the West was different was fooling himself.

Viktor gazed out the window and wondered what he'd just done. Had he just signed his own death warrant? Nothing worth having ever came without risk, he told himself, and downed the second shot.

He was about to refill the glass when the phone on his desk began clanging. It was the middle of the night. If it was Suvorov, the response was swifter than he'd expected.

"Viktor Lapin," he said.

"You sly little fuck," Suvorov snarled.

"Suvorov, I don't understand."

"Don't piss in my ear, Viktor. You understand perfectly. Let's not play pretend."

"I was simply...."

"You saw your chance, you worm. The President's name on the distribution list. It was too much for you to resist."

Viktor didn't know what to say. He'd known this was coming. It was pointless to deny it. He'd made a move. He was gunning to rise up the ranks.

"You're not the only one who wishes to leave his mark, Suvorov," he said. He could hardly believe he'd uttered the words.

"Oh, you'll leave a mark, Viktor. Believe me. A smear of blood."

Viktor's hand was shaking so hard he could barely hold his cigarette. He raised it to his mouth and sucked.

"Isn't this good news?" he said. "Gazinsky's dead. That's what you wanted, wasn't it?"

"Gazinsky's just the start of our worries, Viktor. The President is adamant we get the girl too."

"The child," Viktor said quietly.

"We can't let her slip away. What message does that send all our other scientists in these rotten, godforsaken outposts if we let that happen?"

"I understand, sir."

"There's a price to taking credit for a job too soon, Viktor. You need to put a bullet in that child and let every scientist in Russia see what happens to defectors."

"I just lost my best man in London."

"There must be someone else there who can take care of a little girl for you."

"There's Chapman's man."

"The one who recovered the blueprints?"

"He requested an extraction."

"And what did you tell him?"

"I told him the GRU paid its debts."

"He's going to have to take care of this for us before he gets what he wants."

"He's not going to be happy."

"I could give a shit about his happiness."

"Yes," Viktor said, "but he might cut and run. He's already burned down Chapman's operation."

"You'll have to figure out a way to incentivize him."

"I told him I'd get him out."

"You want to impress the President?" Suvorov said. "You want to play with the big boys? Get him to get the girl."

"How's he going to find her?"

"How did he find Gazinsky? Your masochist friend, I believe?"

"Right," Viktor said, swallowing. His masochist friend, as Suvorov put it, Declan Haines, had yet to come up with a single piece of actionable intel. Everything of value had come from Gray Coat, and Gray Coat was getting antsy now too. There were only so many times Viktor could keep going back to the same well. Gray Coat had taken risks. He'd been brought out into the open by Chapman. He needed to get out of London soon, or it would be too late.

"I don't know if the masochist can still get to her."

"You better hope it's at least one more time, Viktor, because let me make this very clear for you. You're not out of the woods yet. Not by a long shot. You got the President's attention, but that's only the beginning. The last thing you want to do is fail, now that he's watching."

"I'll call him," Viktor said.

"You do that," Suvorov said, "and when you're done, get yourself to an airport."

"Why? Where am I going?"

"Where do you think?"

"Not Arkhangelsk."

"You've got loose ends to tie up, Viktor. Lots of loose ends."

45

Tenet watched the sun rise over the birch trees at the end of his street. It was the last time he would do it, he thought. Alona was still asleep, sprawled in the bed like a young child, the sheets in knots around her. She'd always been a tosser and a turner. That was something that hadn't changed through the years.

He put on the coffee as he always did and dressed quietly while it brewed. Then he kissed his wife as if this morning were no different to a thousand others and told her he'd bring back a bottle of wine to go with dinner. There was a wine merchant at Battersea Park. It stocked the finest vintages in the city. He would pay it one last visit before he left.

"What's the occasion?" she said, her voice thick with sleep.

"I always loved you, Alona, in my way."

Her eyes didn't open. He didn't know if she'd heard him. She'd fallen back asleep.

He filled his thermos with coffee, slipped out of the room, and left the apartment. Outside, the temperature had risen a few degrees since the day before. It made the air feel pregnant. He usually drove to the embassy, and Viktor had told him to keep his habits as close to normal as possible.

He got in the car and fired up the engine. As he was pulling out of his spot, his phone rang.

"Richmond Tenet," he said, checking his wing mirror for traffic.

"It's Viktor."

Tenet's heart immediately began to thump. Just hearing his voice made Tenet uneasy, and yet, this man was to be his entire future. This man was where he was going to make his home. This man would be the only friend he would ever know, perhaps for the rest of his life. Tenet would be a false friend, he would funnel information back to Roth, he would serve his country, but it would be Viktor he saw out his days with.

"Can't you give me this final morning in peace?"

"There's something we need to take care of before you leave."

"My train..."

"You won't miss your train."

Tenet was so distracted he almost missed a stop sign. He slammed on the brakes, and the car behind him blared its horn.

"I need you to meet someone for me."

"I've got a sword over my head, Viktor. The CIA's tentacles are closing in."

"This won't take long."

"If I don't get out now, I'm going to miss my window."

"One of Chapman's men," Viktor said. "I need you to pass him one tiny message. Then you can get on your train."

"Chapman?"

"The man you met in the park yesterday."

Tenet had seen the bulletins before he left the embassy the night before. He'd pieced together what had happened in Edinburgh. Gunshots fired, a Russian national gunned down in public. The gunman also dead. He knew Chapman had killed Gazinsky. And he knew Ada had killed Chapman. It was one of the reasons he was so desperate to get out of the city.

"Yes," he said, "and a fine mess he made."

"The man's going to be at King's Cross in an hour. You can meet him there, then get on your train to Paris."

Tenet sighed. This increased his risk.

"Cheer up, Tenet. I'll get you out of there. You're too valuable to leave behind."

"And how will I recognize him?"

"He speaks with a London accent."

"A London accent? That narrows it down at Kings Cross, doesn't it?"

"He'll find you. Sit at the café under the clock and wait for him."

"What's his name?"

"Stan."

"Just Stan?"

"Just Stan," Viktor said.

"And how will he recognize me?"

"Because he found you yesterday."

"He did that?"

"Yes. He tracked you from that private bank."

"I see."

"Plus, you'll have a briefcase on the table."

"I don't carry a briefcase," Tenet said.

"I'm sending you details for a locker at the station now. Access the locker, and you'll find the briefcase."

"What's inside it?"

"What do you think is inside it?"

"I don't know, Viktor."

"What difference does it make?"

Tenet sighed. "All this dicking around," he said. "It's going to end up screwing me in the end. I can feel it."

"There's money in it," Viktor said. "When have you ever handed over a briefcase that held anything but money?"

"I've never handed over a briefcase," Tenet said. "Igor had the sense to use a lackey for that. I'm the CIA's London station chief. He knew how to value that."

"Well, I'm not Igor," Viktor said.

"No," Tenet said. "You're not."

"Stan's going to give you some documents."

"What documents?"

"That doesn't concern you. Just get them from him and bring them with you to Paris."

"That's it? A simple swap?"

"Almost," Viktor said. "He thinks he's going to Paris with you."

"*Thinks?*" Tenet said.

"We have one more job for him before he leaves the city."

"He's not going to like that, is he, Viktor?"

"If there was an alternative, I would take it."

"He's the only man who can do this job for you?"

"That's what I said, isn't it?"

"All right. I'll tell him that. And what's the job?"

"Sacha's daughter."

"What?"

"This is from the Prime Directorate. It's got to be done."

"Sacha's daughter is a...."

"Child. I know."

"Nine years old," Tenet said.

"I know what age she is."

"Has this man ever done something like that for you before?"

"Of course not. But this is from the President of Russia himself. And if he doesn't do it, it won't only be his head on the cutting block, Tenet."

"No," Tenet said, "it will be yours, too."

"Careful," Viktor said testily.

"All right," Tenet said. "Give him the briefcase, give him the message, and that's it?"

"That's it."

"And you think that's all it will take?"

"Oh, you make sure that's all it takes, Tenet, or your reception here in Moscow won't be quite as warm as you're expecting."

"Warmth is not something I'm expecting, Viktor. I assure you."

"Just make sure he knows what's at stake, Tenet. If he looks like he needs a push, give your regards to his mother and daughter."

"So that's it? That's how you do business now? Threaten his family?"

"Don't pretend to be shocked, Tenet. I've seen the file Igor left on you. You've gotten your hands dirty."

"Not like this."

"Just pass on the message, then catch your train. We'll be waiting for you on the other side."

"Fine," Tenet said, hanging up.

He was at Battersea Park, and he took a pen and notebook from his glovebox before getting out of the car. He crossed the street to the wine merchant, Archibald's, and wrote a brief note on the paper.

Richmond Tenet
    One case Château Lafite-Rothschild '68.
    Usual address.

It was a small gesture, the wine he and Alona drank together on the night of their first date. It wouldn't make up for anything. It wouldn't soften the blow. But he thought she'd understand, in a way.

He and Alona had never been overly sentimental. The truth was, and he'd always known it, she hadn't married him out of love. At least, not a passionate sort of love. There was affection between them, certainly. There was friendship. And from Tenet's side, for what it was worth, there was love. But Alona's heart had always belonged to someone else. Sometimes that was the way of it.

Tenet slipped the note in the frame of the door and went back to the car. He drove straight to King's Cross and parked legally in a multistory lot across the street. The CIA would know he was missing soon enough. There was no need to alert them sooner because of a double-parked car.

On his phone, Viktor had sent him the name of a private locker company that operated out of the lower level of the main arrivals concourse of the station, as well as a locker number and access code. Tenet went to the attendant and told him his locker number. The attendant pointed disinterestedly at a bank of lockers behind him. Tenet found his locker and entered the code. Inside was a single steel briefcase. It had a traditional-looking code entry wheel, but there was something electronic attached, a small black cube about the size of a dice with a single red light on it.

He looked at his watch, then went back up to the main

level where he found the café beneath the clock. He went in and ordered a coffee and found a seat overlooking the concourse. He scared off the pigeons with the briefcase, then made sure to place it on the table in front of him.

He waited about thirty minutes, and a handful of other customers came and went. It was still early, and the concourse was relatively empty.

At eight on the dot, a man in an Adidas tracksuit and jacket approached him. He sat down at Tenet's table as if they were old friends.

Tenet looked up at him from his newspaper. "You're Stan," he said.

The man nodded.

"The man who tracked me from the bank?" Tenet said.

"The one and only," Stan said with a slight shrug.

"Well, thanks for that."

Stan looked at the briefcase. "I hope that's not for me?"

"Yes, it is," Tenet said.

Stan understood immediately what it meant. "Money?"

Tenet smiled. He raised his hand and rubbed his thumb and index finger.

"I thought I was going to Paris."

"There's been a change of plan."

Stan's jaw clenched. He took the briefcase and placed it on the ground between his feet. "What sort of change?"

A server came over and asked if she could get them anything. Tenet waved her away, but she said, "You've got to order if you're going to sit."

"Fuck me," Stan muttered.

"Two coffees," Tenet said.

She left, and Tenet returned his attention to Stan. "Look," he said, "Viktor's got one last thing he needs you to take care of."

"And then I get out?"

"Then you get out."

Stan nodded, resignation on his face. "I suppose he threatened my kid."

Tenet didn't answer. The girl came out with the coffees, and he watched her leave before taking a sip.

Stan leaned back in the chair and ran his hands through his hair. "Fuck me," he said again. "What's the job?"

Tenet sipped his coffee again. He looked around the concourse. It was quickly filling with morning commuters. It was a strange world, he thought. He'd given his life to the Central Intelligence Agency, an organization designed to protect the interests and security of the greatest democracy on the planet. And now, he was leaving his wife of forty years and telling this man, who appeared decent, that he had to murder a child or his own child would be murdered. And he was doing it on behalf of Levi Roth, Director of the CIA.

He couldn't help suspect that somewhere along the way, somewhere in all their plans and plots, their decades of moves and countermoves, he and Roth had lost the plot.

"I think you know what the job is," he said.

Stan looked at the ground. He reached into his pocket and pulled out a packet of cigarettes.

"I don't think...." Tenet said, but his words trailed off.

"You can't smoke here," the waitress said, completing Tenet's thought.

Stan ignored her. Tenet wasn't even certain he'd heard her.

"The girl?" Stan said, dropping his voice.

Tenet felt shame as he nodded, as if the order had come from him.

"Take the briefcase," Tenet said. "It will be useful."

Stan was looking in the distance. The waitress was coming back over, and he took one last drag of the cigarette before she arrived. He threw it to the ground and crushed it under his shoe.

"I need the blueprints."

Stan sighed. He handed over the cardboard tube. "So this is what it's come to?" he said.

Tenet didn't know what to say.

"This is how it starts," Stan continued.

"How what starts?" Tenet said, looking at his watch. There was a train leaving for Paris in twenty minutes, and he intended to be on it.

"The slippery slope," Stan said.

"You can claw your way back," Tenet said.

"Is that what you did?" Stan said.

Tenet shook his head.

"If your government ever finds out what you've done, you'll go down as the biggest traitor in CIA history."

"They'll find out," Tenet said.

"You say that like you don't care."

Tenet shrugged. He finished his coffee and rose to his feet. "Just do the job, Stan."

"I just burned down the whole operation, didn't I? The police will be all over Chapman's case. How am I going to find this girl?"

"I heard finding people's what you do."

46

V iktor stepped out of the plane into the frigidly cold Siberian night. There was a black Mercedes sedan waiting for him on the runway, and he hurried down the steps toward it. A soldier got out of the driver's seat to hold the door for him.

"Welcome to Arkhangelsk, Mr. Director," he said when he got back into his seat.

"It's colder than a witch's tit up here," Viktor said.

The driver nodded and turned up the heat. "To the hotel?"

Viktor leaned back in the sumptuous leather seat and lit a cigarette. "Unfortunately not," he said. "Take me to Naval Command at Severodvinsk."

Severodvinsk was a small city thirty-five kilometers west of Arkhangelsk on the Dvina River Delta. Because of the military shipyards there, which specialized in submarine construction, it was a restricted town requiring a special permit to enter. Despite its bleak location, it had a few claims to fame. *Leninsky Komsomol*, the Soviet Union's first nuclear submarine, was built there in 1957. During the eighties, the largest submarines ever built by man, the Akula-Class nuclear-powered ballistic missile subs, with a displacement of over forty-eight thousand tons and the ability to support a crew of one-hundred-sixty men for months without surfacing, were built there. It was a town that, even now, was dominated by the central government in Moscow and its Northern Fleet naval policies.

Viktor shivered as he looked out the window. They bypassed Arkhangelsk and continued along a stretch of the M-8 highway that was as desolate as any road on earth. It was thirty minutes before the car was passing the military checkpoints outside Severodvinsk. Viktor flashed his GRU credentials, and the guards let them pass.

"Take us to Nyonoksa," he said to the driver. "The Navy testing facility."

The driver nodded, and Viktor lit another cigarette. Outside, enormous concrete monoliths rose up on both sides of the road as symmetrically as if they had been constructed by bees. They passed the shipyards and row after row of identical apartment blocks. Snow was falling heavily, and the wind picked up.

"How far to the naval facility?" Viktor said.

"Sir, it's another thirty-five kilometers west of here."

"I thought it was in the city."

"No, sir."

The weather was so bleak that Viktor asked, "Will we make it?"

"I wouldn't have brought this car, sir, if I'd known we were going so far."

"But the road, will it be passable?"

"The road is not heavily trafficked, sir."

"You're saying you don't think so."

"It's plowed by the military, sir."

"Which means?"

"Sir, there's a naval administration office at the Palace of Culture here in Severodvinsk. I suggest we arrange an escort there."

Viktor nodded.

At the naval office, Viktor left the Mercedes and its driver behind and was taken the rest of the way to the naval facility in a convoy of four UAZ Hunter off-road trucks. The passenger compartment of the trucks was so cold that he was given navy overalls and boots to wear for the drive.

It took another half hour to reach the facility at Nyonoksa, by which time Viktor's hands were so numb with cold that he couldn't smoke. Viktor had intended to surprise the commander of the facility, but he knew the administration office in Severodvinsk would have called ahead.

They passed the front gates of the facility without stopping, and Viktor told the driver to go straight to the commander's office. When they reached the headquarters, orderlies rushed out to escort Viktor into the building. They took him to the anteroom outside the commander's office and told him to make himself comfortable. There was a large, water-fed radiator on the wall, and Viktor sat right on it.

"Can I bring you anything?" the commander's secretary asked.

"Tea," Viktor said. "Very hot."

She hurried off and returned a moment later with black tea and sugar and a plate of very plain cookies. "I'm sorry," she said, putting the plate on the table. "If we'd known you were coming, I'd have made sure to bring something in from Arkhangelsk."

"It's fine," Viktor said, taking a cookie and dipping it in the tea.

He had to wait a few minutes for the commander. When he finally appeared, Viktor saw he was a corpulent man in his forties with short hair and horn-rimmed glasses.

"My name is Anpilov," he said, rushing forward so hurriedly he almost knocked over one of the orderlies.

"I know what your name is," Viktor said.

"And I know why you're here, sir," Anpilov said.

"Why don't you let me do the talking," Viktor said. "It will be easier for you."

Anpilov's face went pale. "Of course," he said.

"In your office," Viktor added.

Anpilov led the way into a spartan office. In the center of the room was a plain wooden desk with a heavy leather chair on either side.

"Can I offer you anything?" Anpilov said.

"No."

"Vodka, cigars?"

"What kind of cigars?"

"Nicaraguan, sir. Maduros."

"Any good?"

"Quite good, sir."

Anpilov offered him the box, and Viktor chose a cigar and sniffed it. Viktor sat down in one of the chairs, and Anpilov produced a lighter. Viktor lit his cigar, and Anpilov picked up the phone on his desk and told the secretary to bring in the vodka.

"I have a feeling I'm going to need it," he said to Viktor.

"I don't need to explain why I'm here, then."

Anpilov shook his head. "Sacha Gazinsky," he said.

Viktor nodded.

"I've prepared a list of names," Anpilov said.

"How many?"

"Twenty-five."

"Twenty-five?" Viktor said in surprise.

"It was a major breach of our protocols, sir."

"That it was," Viktor said, puffing smoke. "That it was."

"The explosion. The casualties. A complete breakdown, sir. He would never have been allowed to slip away otherwise."

Viktor read the label on the cigar. "You got these in Moscow?"

"At the airport, sir, yes."

Viktor would have to remember to pick some up when he got back. "This is a rocket testing site, though, isn't it, Anpilov?"

"Sir?"

"Accidents, explosions, they're a natural part of the process."

"This was a very big explosion, sir."

Viktor blew smoke in Anpilov's direction. He was beginning to become aware of the power he held. It would only grow. He was going to enjoy that.

"It was a nuclear detonation," Viktor said, blowing more smoke at the man. He suddenly felt like a boy blowing smoke in a jar that contained insects—seeing how much they would take before reacting.

Anpilov was worried, as well he should be. He was getting himself worked up. "I can send the list to the Kremlin now," he offered. "I checked it thoroughly. No one on the list is critical to our progress."

Viktor allowed a smile to cross his lips. "If only you'd been this diligent before."

Anpilov nodded.

Viktor sighed. "Well, Anpilov, unfortunately for you, the Kremlin doesn't want a list of names. Not this time."

Anpilov knew what that meant, and to his credit, he took

the news like a man. He simply nodded his head, then lit himself one of the cigars.

The secretary knocked on the door, then entered. She carried a tray with two glasses and a bottle of vodka.

"Thank you, Irina."

They watched her pour the drinks, and as she made her way back to the door, Anpilov said, "Our guest may want ice."

"No," Viktor said. He waited for the girl to leave, then raised his glass to Anpilov. Anpilov did the same, then they drank.

"I suppose..." Anpilov said before his words trailed off. He had nothing to say.

Viktor reached into his jacket and pulled out a service weapon. He put it on the desk with a thud.

"I have four children," Anpilov said.

"I know that," Viktor said, "because, unlike you, I do my homework."

"I thought the child was being treated at the hospital in Moscow."

"Well, apparently Moscow wasn't up to the task."

Anpilov poured two more glasses. His hand was shaking. "Please," he said, "there must be something...."

"Don't lose it all now," Viktor said. "Not at the last moment."

"Of course," Anpilov said, raising his glass again. Viktor didn't join him this time. He let him have his last drink alone. He threw what was left of his cigar in the ashtray. He was about to leave when the secretary came back in with ice. She saw the gun on the desk and stopped in her tracks.

An awkward silence ensued.

"I'll wait outside," Viktor said. "Don't make this harder than it has to be."

"Take your gun with you," Anpilov said. "I have my own."

Viktor nodded. He picked up the gun and went to the door. The secretary made way for him to pass, then asked Anpilov if he still wanted the ice.

"Please, Irina," Anpilov said.

She nodded and left the room, shutting the door firmly behind her. Viktor went back to the heater and watched the secretary. She sat resolutely at her desk, refusing to meet Viktor's eye. A light on her phone came on, and Viktor said, "Outgoing?"

She nodded.

"Who's he calling?"

She looked at the phone and paused a moment.

"Well?" Viktor said.

Her voice caught in her throat when she spoke. "His wife."

Viktor looked away. To the secretary, this was his doing. He was the villain. He didn't mind. Seconds turned to minutes, and the silence between them grew more awkward.

"Your job," Viktor said, "is safe. I'll see to that."

Her eyes flashed daggers at him, and he regretted having spoken. She was about to say something to him, he could see it, but the gunshot beat her to it. It rang out, and she let out a brief scream before immediately smothering it.

Viktor looked at her, then away again. He cleared his throat. He went to the office and opened the door without knocking. Anpilov was on the ground next to his desk. There was a splatter of blood on the wall behind him, and his chair had been knocked over. The back half of the skull was missing.

He went back to the anteroom and lit a cigarette. "Someone's going to have to clean that up," he said to the girl.

47

It was only a few weeks since Roth had been in Lance's town of Deweyville, Montana. The time had done little to calm the Rocky Mountain wind that whipped down from the mountains and blasted the taxi as if trying to prevent it from going further.

"It never lets up, does it?" he said to the driver as they pulled into the lot of the EconoLodge.

"This ain't half of it," the driver said. "You need a hand with the bag?"

"I got it," Roth said, stepping out into the blizzard. The wind almost knocked him over as he hurried inside the motel. A flurry of snow followed him through the door.

"Checking in, sir?" the girl at the desk said.

Roth gave her his credit card. He remembered her from the last time he'd been there.

"How was room 309?" she said.

"Great."

She checked him in and gave him his key. "I put you in 309 again," she said as if expecting the news to please him.

"That's perfect," he said and gave her his driver's license. "Could you arrange a car for me?"

"When do you need it?"

"Right away."

He went up to the room and put his bag on the bed. One thing he could say about Deweyville, it wasn't easy to get to. Long flight, long drive, bitter weather. Maybe that was why Lance had chosen it.

He put on the kettle, then undressed and took a long, very hot shower. When he got out, he made tea and drank it at the small desk in the corner of the room, dressed in the white robe provided by the motel.

Lance Spector was dead. It was a fact that still hadn't quite sunk in. As soon as he'd learned of it, he immediately started to focus on what would come next. The loss was a blow. There was no other way to put it.

It was a blow to his plans for the Special Operations Group, to everything he'd had in mind for Laurel and Tatyana. It was a breach in his lines. And recovery wouldn't be easy. President Molotov was stepping up his antagonisms in every sphere—cyber, crypto, economic, political, military, cultural. He was interfering in US elections, planting ransomware across essential infrastructure, stirring up trouble in the Middle East and Central Europe, and putting pressure on US allies across half the globe. Roth knew that if he didn't respond fast, he would lose the initiative. That was the driving factor behind his decision to push Richmond Tenet into the Kremlin now. Igor Aralov's death provided the opportunity, but Lance Spector's death provided the urgency.

It seemed to always be the case, the large print gave, and the small print took away. An opportunity opened, and a catastrophe struck. Aralov was dead, Tenet was in play, but

Lance was gone, and many of the prospects he'd been cultivating were in disarray as a result.

Nevertheless, the fight went on. The global power game stopped for no man. The world didn't care about Levi Roth and Lance Spector. It was a tempest that would never be tamed. And that was why Roth was there, in that godforsaken town in the middle of the Rockies.

He was there to clean up—to tie up the loose ends. If he didn't do it, Vladimir Molotov surely would. He had to go to Lance's home and root out every document, every thumb drive, every old photograph, and handwritten letter, and software cache, and erase or recover all of it.

He finished his tea and decided to get something to eat before going out to Lance's house. There was a bar down the street, the Eureka, and he dressed, put on his coat, and braved the weather once again.

"What'll it be?" the waitress asked when he sat down.

She was blonde, in her twenties, attractive. Roth wondered if she knew Lance. He wondered if she knew he was dead. "How's the burger?" he said.

"Not as good as the steak."

He ordered the steak and a beer, and when he was done, he went back to the motel and asked if his car was ready.

"It's the blue sedan out front," the girl said. She put a key on the counter.

Roth drove straight to Lance's address. The route was straightforward, and he'd been there a number of times, but he used his phone to navigate anyway. When he got there and saw the lodge, perched high over the mountainous valley, he felt a pang of sadness.

It was hard to believe how recently it was that he'd been there with Laurel, convincing Lance to come back to the Group. And now Lance was gone. For good. Roth wondered sometimes how Lance's life might have turned out if he'd never run into him.

He walked up to the door, he had the key, and let himself in. It was cold inside. The girl who'd been living there with Lance, Sam, was dead too, and there was no one to keep the furnace running.

He turned on the lights and looked around. There was no sign of any break-ins. Nothing was out of place. He listened. Silence.

His search of the house was methodic. Experience had taught him where to look, what things might be hidden, what things might come back to bite him if he didn't find them. He checked for loose floorboards, hidden roof panels, secret compartments built into the furniture. He wasn't working completely in the dark. He'd visited Lance when he was building the house. It hadn't been a purely social visit. The pictures he'd taken gave him information about the structure of the building that he'd had analyzed back at Langley. There were two potential hiding spots that interested him most. One was a heavy safe, built into the stone chimney stack that held up the roof. The other was a hidden compartment beneath the hearth in the living room fireplace that had been carved into the solid rock of the mountain.

He went to the hearth first and cleaned it of soot and ash. He pulled out the iron grate and found the notch in the flagstone that acted as a handle. He gripped it and pulled. The stone was heavy, easily over a hundred pounds. He heaved at it, raising dust that caught in his throat and brought on a fit of coughing. He continued to work, and eventually, with no small effort, the flagstone budged.

Using his phone's flashlight, Roth peered into the

compartment. It contained weapons, ammunition, a scope and tripod for a sniper rifle, some electrical equipment.

That was it. None of the things he was looking for.

He stood up and brushed himself off. He wasn't there for weapons. There were things Lance had, information, that an adversary could use. It was hard to know what might be used, but in the right hands, any bit of personal information would make Roth and the Special Operations Group vulnerable to manipulation and deception.

He went into the kitchen and poured himself a glass of water.

Then he went upstairs to the bedroom, where he knew the safe was located. He didn't expect to be able to get into it. There were some combinations and sets of numbers he could try to unlock it, but in all likelihood, he would have to call out a specialist from Helena to break it open for him. Helena was a three-hour drive away, which would mean coming back tomorrow.

He entered the bedroom, where a large painting that looked like a Rorschach test hung on the wall. Roth took down the painting, and behind it was the steel door of the safe.

Immediately, Roth saw that it was unlocked. The door was ajar about half an inch.

He felt a shiver, as if a window had just been opened, and instinctively looked over his shoulder. He reached inside his coat for his gun. The room was empty. The house remained completely silent.

He looked back at the safe and wondered if the Russians had beaten him to the prize. There were no signs of break-in on the safe. The door and locking mechanisms were intact.

He reached out, and very carefully, opened the door. He half expected the safe to be empty, but it wasn't. Inside, he saw that the safe contained exactly the sort of items he'd expected. There was a nine-millimeter pistol and ammo, a number of passports and other identity documents from various countries under different names, and thick stacks of cash, American, various European currencies, Japanese Yen.

It was clear the safe hadn't been raided.

There was an envelope on top of the cash, and Roth picked it up. Scrawled on it in Lance's handwriting was Roth's name. Roth opened it carefully and, inside, found another envelope. This one was addressed to Lance. It had been sent through the regular mail and had been opened.

Roth removed the contents and looked at them. They were photographs of Lance's old handler, Clarice Snow. They were black and white and had been developed by hand.

Roth went through them one at a time. Clarice getting out of a car. Clarice meeting her Russian handler. Clarice kissing Lance. Clarice naked on a bed in a pornographic pose.

The last photo was an ultrasound. Roth had seen it before and had verified it with the hospital. It was from John's Hopkins Division of Maternal-Fetal Medicine. A doctor had signed it, and Clarice's name was filled out in type on the upper left corner.

Roth looked again at the front of the envelope. The postmark was dated four days before Clarice's death. Someone had sent these photos to Lance just days before he'd carried out the order to kill her.

The order still haunted Roth. It hadn't been easy to issue. Clarice had worked for him. He'd recruited and trained her personally. It had been under his eye that the relationship between her and Lance developed. He'd known there was more going on between Clarice and Lance than met the eye. What he hadn't known, hadn't even suspected, was that Clarice was pregnant. Never, not in a million years, would he have ordered Lance to kill a woman who was carrying his own child.

The thing was, Lance had carried out the order.

Roth shivered again. Something didn't feel right. What was this envelope doing there? Why was Roth's name on it? Why was the safe open?

According to the postmark, Lance had either seen these photos right before he carried out the order to kill Clarice, or soon afterward. The postmark said it had been sent from the post office on Pennsylvania Avenue in Washington.

Roth wondered who'd sent it. Clarice? The Russians? Someone else?

It was certainly someone who knew a lot more about the inner workings of Roth's operations than anyone should have—someone who wanted to drive a wedge between Roth and Lance.

And maybe they'd succeeded. The relationship between Roth and Lance had never been the same since. It never truly recovered. Roth had ordered Lance to kill Clarice. Whether Lance knew she was carrying his child at the time or found out later, the scar that something like that left would run very deep.

There was a sheet of notepaper in the envelope, and Roth took it out. It was folded twice. He unfolded it. When he read it, his blood went cold.

We have things to discuss.
Meet me at the Old Hamlet.

48

S tan sat nervously in a dark corner of a dingy bar in Soho. Every time someone entered, he jumped. He kept expecting to see a CIA kill squad coming for him. It was only now beginning to sink in that Chapman and Hamish were dead, and the realization was making him sweat. He'd burned his cell. He'd torn down the operation at the warehouse. He should have been out of the country by now, putting as much distance between himself and London as possible, but instead he was sitting in this bar, scarcely two miles from MI5 headquarters.

"Another beer?" the waitress said.

"Yeah," Stan said without looking up.

"What's that?" the waitress said.

"I said yeah," he said again.

He knew he needed to figure his shit out and fast. Fear had a way of making people do stupid things. If he didn't find Gazinsky's daughter and finish this job for Viktor soon, he was going to end up in hot water.

The bar was quiet, but he wasn't the only customer. There were two women at the bar, prostitutes, and each had propositioned him in turn. He'd considered taking them up on it. What did he have to lose at this point? But then he learned one of them wasn't actually a woman.

He looked at his watch nervously, and the waitress brought him his drink.

"You're welcome," she said sarcastically when he failed to respond.

He was about to say something to her when the door opened, spilling in light. Stan looked up to see a man's silhouette fill the door.

"Tito," Stan said, getting his attention. To the waitress, he said, "Bring him a beer."

Tito was a big man, and he lumbered over to the booth and sat down.

"Nice spot," he said, eyeing the place.

"It's discreet," Stan said.

Tito was a man whose skill set overlapped somewhat with Stan's. The two men moved in the same circles, provided many of the same services for their clients, but their career paths had diverged when Stan started working for Chapman. Tito worked by a different code. His outlook was more cautious. He worked for more reputable organizations, legal organizations, and the majority of the work he did for them was legal. It might not have paid quite as much, but Tito didn't have to worry about the GRU coming after his daughter the way Stan was.

Tito usually worked disappearances. When a wealthy stockbroker's daughter disappeared while backpacking in South America, or if his wife ran off with the pool boy and the family jewels, Tito tracked them down. Likewise, when someone made off with a priceless Rembrandt, or the wrong set of Tiffany diamonds, Tito tracked them down.

Finding people was what he did, and that was what Stan needed him for.

The waitress brought the beer, and Tito eyed her provocatively. She pretended not to notice.

She left, and Tito turned to Stan. "So," he said, "what's this all about? Why all the cloak and daggers?"

Stan looked away. He let out a sigh and sipped his beer, trying to think of what to say.

"Well?" Tito said.

"I'm in trouble," Stan said.

Tito nodded. He wasn't surprised. Finding people who didn't want to be found was bound to ruffle feathers. The types of clients Stan dealt with only increased the danger. "I figured as much."

"Real trouble," Stan said.

Tito took a sip of his beer. "What have you gotten yourself into, Stanny boy?"

"Russians," Stan said.

Tito blew through his teeth.

Stan nodded.

"I told you this shit would catch up to you," Tito said, shaking his head.

"I know you did, and you were right. I'm really fucked."

Tito got the waitress's attention and held up two fingers. "Vodka," he said to her, then to Stan, "in honor of your Russian friends."

Stan said nothing.

The waitress came over with the shots and left them on the table. Tito raised his, and Stan followed his lead, knocking back the shot.

"What does Chapman have to say about all this?"

"Chapman's dead," Stan said.

Tito looked at him. "What's that?"

Stan nodded.

"What are you into, Stan?"

"I need to find someone."

"What do you mean, you need to find someone?"

"I need to finish the job Chapman started, or I'm going to end up like him."

Tito was shaking his head. "You need to find someone? Then find them."

"It's not that simple. I burned down Chapman's shop. Everything's been wiped. I've got no access."

"So you're thinking?"

Stan nodded.

"Oh, no," Tito said.

"Tito, if there was anyone else."

"I always told you this was going to get you into trouble."

"I know you did."

"I'm going to regret this, aren't I?"

"I'm sorry."

"You're really going to drag me into this?"

"I already have."

"What are you talking about?"

Stan shook his head. He was looking at his beer and refused to look up.

"Stan?" Tito said. "What the fuck are you talking about?"

"I gave your name to the client."

"You did what?"

Stan looked up, catching Tito's gaze.

"You gave my name to the GRU?" Tito said. "You fucking dumb son of a...."

"They threatened my kid, Tito."

Tito was about to say something else but stopped himself.

"I'm sorry," Stan said.

"You're sorry?"

Stan looked back down at his beer.

"You're fucking sorry?"

Stan had the briefcase with him, and he lifted it onto the table.

"What's this?"

"It's all I've got."

"Fuck, Stan," Tito said, grabbing the briefcase off the table and putting it back on the ground. "You've lost your head, you have."

Stan reached into his jacket pocket and took out a thumb drive. It contained images of Ada Hudson and Natasha Gazinsky. He slid it across the table.

"These are the targets."

"Who are they?"

"It's best you don't ask."

Tito was shaking his head. "I ought to go straight to MI5."

"You're not going to do that."

"Watch me."

"They won't just go after you, Tito. They'll go after your family."

Tito's jaw clenched. He knew he had no choice. He was snookered, and it was Stan who'd snookered him.

"We're done, you and me," he said.

Stan nodded. He'd expected it.

"When this is done, you better stay off the grid, my friend. You better tuck yourself away somewhere I never find you because if I ever see your face again, I'm going to kill you."

49

Roth was back in London, back in Blackfriars, back outside the medieval half-timbered façade of the Old Hamlet pub. He couldn't believe it when he'd found Lance's note and didn't waste a moment getting on a plane.

He stepped out of his car and looked up and down the street as if expecting to see Lance standing there, waiting. He went into the pub where Harry, as always, was behind the bar with his apron on and the sleeves of his white shirt rolled up.

"Back so soon?" Harry said, surprised to see him.

"It's been a busy week in my world," Roth said.

"You'll be wanting a drink then."

Roth nodded. Harry began pulling a pint, and Roth waited for it at the bar.

The pub was quiet. There was just one other customer, a man at a table near the window reading a newspaper, paying no mind to Roth and Harry.

"Your friend joining you?" Harry said.

Roth shook his head. "Another guy."

Harry looked surprised.

"What?" Roth said.

"I never pegged you as a man with more than one friend," he said.

Roth shook his head and brought his beer to the usual booth. Harry disappeared behind the bar for a few minutes, then reappeared with a pack of cigarettes.

"Don't anyone steal anything," he announced to his two customers, then went outside for a smoke. Roth watched him light his cigarette through the window, the silhouette of his sloped shoulders visible through the partly obscured glass.

He looked at his beer and took a sip. He realized he was tapping his foot. He was early for the meet, and he was anxious.

Harry finished his cigarette and came back inside. "Freezing out there," he said.

Roth nodded. He looked at his watch. A man was approaching the door, and when he entered the bar, Roth could scarcely believe his eyes. Standing in the doorway, in the flesh, larger than life itself, was Lance Spector.

Lance peered around the room as his eyes adjusted to the dim light, and Roth caught his attention. There was a strange smile on Lance's face, as if he knew he'd gotten away with something, and as he passed the bar, he said to Harry, "I'll have whatever he's having."

He came over to the booth and said, "Levi, you look like you've seen a ghost."

Roth shook his head. "I attended your funeral," he said. Lance slid into the booth, and Roth added, "You look very fucking pleased with yourself."

Lance gave a slight shrug. "Unless you see it happen with your own eyes," he said, "I ain't dead."

"I did see it with my own eyes."

"Not a body, you didn't."

Roth shook his head. "No. Not a body."

Harry came over with Lance's drink and then left them alone. Lance sipped his beer, and Roth watched him. A silence grew, and Roth decided to break it before it got awkward.

He cleared his throat. "I was surprised to get your note."

Lance nodded. "I take it you saw the photos then."

Roth was surprised. He'd expected him to broach the subject more gently. "I did," he said.

"Clarice knew I was coming for her."

Roth nodded. "So she sent the pictures?"

"Yes."

Roth took a sip of his beer. There was an elephant in the room, something he desperately wanted to ask Lance about, but he was reluctant.

"She was hoping the ultrasound would change my mind," Lance said.

Roth nodded. That made sense, as far as it went. *Don't kill me. I'm carrying your baby.*

What made less sense was why it hadn't worked. Lance had killed her. He'd executed the order without so much as a moment's hesitation. The question that burned through Roth's mind was whether at the moment he pulled the trigger, Lance had known she was pregnant.

"Was the ultrasound real?" he said, although he already knew the answer to that question.

Lance nodded.

Roth looked at him, then back at his beer. He reached

behind his head and rubbed the back of his neck. He was sweating, although he wasn't certain why.

"If there's something you want to ask me," Lance said.

"Did you receive the envelope..." Roth said, then his voice trailed off.

"Did I receive it in time?" Lance said.

"Before you killed her. Did you know?"

"No."

Roth let out a sigh almost of relief, as if anything about this could be good news, but something about the look on Lance's face said there was more to it.

"The pictures arrived too late. I'd already killed her," Lance said. "But the truth is, I already knew she was pregnant."

"What?"

"I'd known for weeks."

"What are you talking about?"

"I knew, Roth."

"But how? She wasn't showing."

"She got pregnant on purpose. It was part of the GRU's plan. A way to entrap me."

"How do you know that?"

"You remember how I found out she was a traitor?"

Roth nodded. "She was passing packets to a GRU man."

"That same ultrasound was part of the package I intercepted when you first told me to follow her."

"You never told me that."

"No," Lance said. "I kept it to myself."

"Why?"

"Because I knew what it meant. I knew it was my child. I needed time to decide."

"To decide what?"

Lance sighed. "To decide which side I was on."

Roth nodded. He took another gulp of beer. Few men would have seen the situation in the terms Lance did, but Lance was like few men. He found out a woman was pregnant with his child, and a few weeks later, he executed her without ever telling anyone what he knew. In the question of blood over loyalty, Lance chose loyalty. At least, that was what this sounded like.

"Did you ever find out for certain the baby was yours?"

"It was mine," he said.

"But did you run a DNA test?"

He shook his head.

"It could be arranged," Roth said.

"No."

"Don't you want to know?"

"No," Lance said. "I don't. I made my decision. I know what I did. Digging around doesn't change anything."

"If you find out it was someone else's," Roth said.

"Then I killed someone else's unborn child," Lance said. "Either way, it was a child of God."

"A child of God?"

"It was someone's child, Roth. It had a mother and a father, and no amount of DNA tests now are going to absolve me of my crime."

"It wasn't a crime."

"Sure it wasn't."

"It was an order from your government. From your commanding officer."

Lance gave a slight shrug to show what he thought of that.

"You should have come to me," Roth said. "You should have told me."

"Why?"

"I would have changed the order."

Lance said nothing. He sipped his beer and looked across the bar as if suddenly interested in the other side of the room.

"Why didn't you come to me?" Roth said.

"It wouldn't have changed anything," Lance said. "She was still a traitor. She still needed to be executed."

"If I'd known she was carrying your child, Lance? Of course it would have changed something."

"Would you have countermanded the order?"

"Countermanded?"

Lance nodded.

Roth cleared his throat. "Maybe."

"Maybe?"

"I would have ordered someone else to carry it out," he said.

"That's the thing, though, isn't it?" Lance said.

"What's the thing?"

"The order to kill my child. It was going to stand whether I did it or someone else did. If I told you Clarice was pregnant, you would have just given the order to another asset."

"And spared you this guilt."

"Spared me? You couldn't spare me this."

"Of course I could have."

"You could have told another man to kill my child. Where would that leave me?"

"What are you talking about?"

"How could I live with that? How could I let another man pull the trigger that I was meant to pull."

"You're speaking like it made no difference who killed her."

"I killed her," Lance said. "Whether I pulled the trigger or someone else did. Passing the buck to another man couldn't have changed that. You'd have given him the order, and then I'd have had to kill him too."

"The other assassin?"

"If he killed my child? Hell, yes."

"So your solution was to do it yourself?"

"I'd have had to kill you too, Levi," Lance said. "If you ordered another man to kill my child. How could I have lived with that? I'd have had to come after you."

Roth swallowed. He hadn't thought of it like that. "I'll admit there were times," he said, "when I thought you would."

"There were times I thought I would, too," Lance said.

Roth smiled nervously. He couldn't help it. Lance was telling him he'd thought of killing him, and he believed him.

"But your order was sound," Lance said. "She was a traitor. She sold us out. She had to go."

"If I'd known she was pregnant with your child...." Roth said.

"You'd have given the job to another man," Lance said. "We've already established that."

Roth took a sip of his beer. He wasn't sure what this was about now, where it was going. He'd come hoping to bring Lance back into the fold. Now, he wasn't so sure that was going to be an option.

He looked at Lance. He couldn't understand how anyone could be so unmoved, so cold, talking about this. He'd been ordered to kill his own child, and he'd done it. There was a logic to it, at least for Lance, there was some sort of moral reckoning that was being done, but it was no morality Roth understood. There were things on the earth, mysteries that could only be understood by the men who stood at the center of them.

"So that's what I wanted to tell you," Lance said, leaning back.

"What is?" Roth said.

"That it's behind us. It's on me. Not you. I knew she was pregnant. I knew it when you gave me the order. I knew it when I pulled the trigger. And I chose not to tell you."

Roth let out a sigh of relief. He waved to Harry for two more beers.

"I should get going," Lance said.

"Stay," Roth said.

"Whatever it is you came to ask," Lance said, "the answer's no. I didn't call you here for that."

"How do you know I'm going to ask for something?"

"You didn't cross the ocean just to lay old ghosts to rest."

"No," Roth said, shaking his head. "Old ghosts are all I have, but you're right. It's the new ones I'm worried about now."

Lance started to stand, and Roth reached out and grabbed his hand. It was an uncharacteristic gesture, physical contact, but he needed to get his attention. He couldn't warn Laurel and Tatyana of Tenet's mission. To do so would compromise everything. But with Lance's help, he might just be able to nudge the scales in their favor.

"Please hear me out," he said. "It's important."

"Everything's important."

"It's life and death, Lance."

"Everything's life and death."

"But this time, it's Laurel and Tatyana's life and death we're talking about."

Lance looked at him.

"Give me twenty seconds," Roth said.

"Talk fast," Lance said.

"They don't know what they're up against."

"What do you mean?"

"They're walking into a trap."

"So warn them."

"I can't."

"Why not?"

"Because I helped set it."

50

Back at his apartment, Lance packed two Glock 17 pistols with ammo, some cash, and a cell phone that Roth had given him. He was on his way out, locking the door when he heard a voice behind him.

"Where are you going?"

He turned to see the kid from across the hall, standing in front of her open door, staring at him. "What are you doing out here?"

"Where are you going?" she said again.

"I'm going to work."

"Will you come back?"

"Yes," he said.

She looked at him uncertainly, like she knew he was lying, and he lifted her up and put her back inside her apartment, shutting the door. He walked down the hallway and was waiting for the elevator when she came back out to the corridor.

She didn't say anything, the two of them just stared at each other, then the elevator arrived and he stepped inside.

Outside the building, he caught a cab to the American embassy. There was a McDonnell Douglas MD-530 helicopter waiting for him there, and he boarded as soon as he arrived.

Ten minutes later, they were above Farnborough Airport, twenty-five miles east of the city. Lance looked down at the three steel hangars, laid out in a neat row next to the terminal. The chopper landed in front of the first hangar where a fueled Embraer Praetor 500 jet, capable of a top speed of over seven hundred miles per hour, was waiting on the concrete. The pilot told him everything was ready for takeoff, and Lance climbed into the passenger compartment and buckled up. The jet was configured for six passengers, but he had it to himself.

There was a selection of newspapers and a thermos of coffee on the console by his seat, but he barely had a chance to look over the headlines before the pilot was announcing their approach to Edinburgh. He looked out his window at the lights of the city, twinkling in the darkness.

It was an executive terminal, and he was able to rent a powerful 8-series BMW with five-hundred horsepower and zero to sixty in 3.7 seconds from the concierge desk.

He got in the car and gunned the engine. It growled reassuringly as he pulled out of the airport parking lot. He got on the main road into the city and called Roth.

"It's me," he said. "I've landed. Did you find her?"

"She used a credit card Tatyana gave her at an Enterprise car rental," Roth said.

"Have you tracked the car?"

"We can't. The employee didn't enter it in the system."

"What do you mean? They just gave her a car?"

"It's probably on a paper form at the office."

"Okay," Lance said. "Send me the address of the office. I'll check it out."

Roth sent the address, and Lance used his car's navigation to get to it. It was in Dunfermline, not far, and when he arrived, he entered the parking lot and parked in front of the car rental office. The place had shut for the night. The lights were on the inside, but it didn't seem anyone was there. The parking lot Lance was in was fenced, well lit with two CCTV cameras, and there were gates at the two entrances that could be shut and locked. Both were open. There were a few other commercial units in the building, but none of them were open. Behind the building was a closed parking lot with barbed wire around the top of the fence.

Lance lit a cigarette and watched the office for the length of time it took him to smoke it. Then he got out and threw the butt on the ground. He went up to the door of the Enterprise office and checked the lock. It took him about thirty seconds to pick it open, and then he was inside. There was a silent alarm, and he'd triggered it by opening the door. A small red light flashed on a metal box behind the front desk. He figured he had about five minutes before security arrived.

He went to the computer and hit enter on the keyboard. A terminal opened, showing him a password entry screen.

There was a steel lockbox behind the desk, unlocked, and he opened it. It contained the keys to all the vehicles. For cars still in the lot, there were two sets. For cars that had been rented out, there was just one backup set. A tag on each key identified the vehicles by license plate, make, model, and color. About half of them seemed to be out with customers.

On the desk, someone had written out a list of the three vehicles that left the lot during the last shift. The first was a large van, the second was a Volkswagen sedan, and the third was a Volvo SUV. The Volkswagen went out in the afternoon, the Volvo later in the evening.

Lance took the spare key for the Volvo from the lockbox and wrote down the information from the tag. It contained the model, color, and license plate. He put the piece of paper in his pocket and put the key back in the lockbox, shut it, and then walked out of the office as calmly as if he was an ordinary customer.

He got in his car, fired up the engine, and was pulling out of the lot onto the street just as three private security vehicles, their yellow lights flashing, were approaching the lot. The security vehicles drove right by him, and he headed into Dunfermline, driving normally, obeying the speed limit.

After he'd made a few turns and crossed a few intersections, he called Roth.

"I've got a plate for you."

"All right," Roth said.

Lance read it out, as well as the make and model of the Volvo, and said, "It'll be equipped with tracking technology."

"Let me get back to you," Roth said.

Lance pulled over and got out of the car. There was a convenience store, and he went in and bought smokes and coffee and asked if there was somewhere nearby to pick up food.

"What are you looking for?" the clerk said, and his accent was so thick that Lance thought at first he was speaking another language.

"I'm not picky."

"There's an Indian around the corner."

Lance went there and ordered butter chicken and rice. By the time he got back to the car, Roth was calling.

"The vehicle's on the move," Roth said. "It's about a hundred miles north of your location."

"Can you send the coordinates?"

"They should be on your phone now."

51

It was dark, and it was late, and Ada had no idea where she was supposed to be going. Outside, the temperature was dropping fast. It was already a full ten degrees colder than when they left Edinburgh. She looked at Natasha, dozing fitfully in the seat next to her, and knew the child was in a state of utter shock. She needed to find her a safe, warm place to spend the night—somewhere where she would have a chance to process everything that had happened to her during the past few days.

The terrain they were passing through was mountainous, heavily forested, and according to the road signs, the only town of any substance ahead of them was a place called Aviemore. She followed the signs for it, counting down the miles of windy asphalt, and was struggling to keep her eyes open when they finally reached the town.

It was smaller than she'd expected, little more than a village with a single street, but there was a hotel at the entrance of the town done up in the style of a Swiss ski chalet. She pulled over and entered the reception, where she was told that there were no vacancies.

"Is there another hotel in town?" she said.

"There are a few," the receptionist told her, "but they'll all be full. This is the high season."

"High season for what?"

"Skiing," the receptionist said.

Ada went back to the car and drove on past log cabins and stone lodges and stores with quaintly shuttered windows.

Natasha was beginning to stir. "I'm cold," she muttered, and Ada pulled the coat up over her.

"I know," she said, turning up the heat. "Just sit tight for a few more minutes."

They'd almost come to the end of the town, and Ada was beginning to lose hope of finding anywhere to stay when she saw a bar on the corner with the lights still on.

She pulled up and got out of the car. Inside the pub, a bearded man in a checkered shirt was sweeping the floor. All the chairs had been put up on the tables.

"We're closed," he said, looking up.

"I'm sorry," Ada said, " but I need to ask for some help." She gave him the sweetest smile she could muster.

"Oh?" he said.

"I've got my daughter in the car," Ada said. "She's cold, and we haven't got a place to stay."

"Aviemore's no place to be in wintertime without a place to stay," the man said. "These mountains get awfully chilly."

"I noticed," Ada said. "It was just, well, we left the city in a hurry."

"I see," he said, looking at her a little more closely.

She knew she was a mess. She hadn't had a chance to fix herself up since the shootings, and everything about her was disheveled. "We got in the car and started driving," she said. "We didn't stop until we got here, and now that we're here, I don't know what I'm going to do."

"Are you in some sort of trouble?"

"If a deranged ex-husband counts as trouble," she said, giving him a thin smile.

"Oh, it does," he said, nodding. "Oh, aye, it does."

"This place felt... *remote.*"

"If it's remoteness you're after, you've come to the right spot."

"And if it's lodgings I'm after?" she said.

He sighed. "That might be a little tricky." He went to the bar and picked up the phone.

Ada watched him, listening to every word he said. He called a friend, and when he hung up, he wrote an address on a piece of paper.

"It's not the Ritz," he said, "but it will do."

"I don't know what to say," Ada said.

The bartender shrugged. "Don't go thanking me until you see the place."

"I'm sure it's perfect."

"I wouldn't go that far, but it has the basics—clean towels, warm bed, hot water."

"I really don't know how to thank you," Ada said again.

"It's just the one bed, but it's a double."

"That's fine."

"And there's an access code."

He'd written a four-digit code beneath the address.

"You're sure about this?" Ada said.

"You'll be more than comfortable there."

"And who should I pay?"

"Drop in tomorrow, and we'll sort all that out."

"Thank you so much," Ada said, turning to leave.

"And let us know if there's anything at all you need."

"I will," she said and gave him a last smile before going back to the car. Natasha had dozed off again but woke as soon as she opened the door. She looked up at Ada expectantly, and Ada gave her as comforting a smile as she could manage.

"We've got somewhere to sleep," she said.

Natasha nodded.

She entered the address into the GPS, it was a few miles outside the village, and began driving. The road took them higher into the mountains, up steep inclines, and around sharp switchbacks. Through gaps in the trees, she could see a deep valley between high, snow-capped mountains. It all glimmered in the moonlight as if made of glass.

About two miles from the town, the GPS directed her off the road onto a snow-covered track.

"I hope we don't get stuck," she said to Natasha, trying to keep her spirits up.

They started along the track, the car threatening at every dip in the road to get stuck. Along both sides of the track, the bare branches of trees reached toward the moon like fingers, giving it a sinister feel.

"This is creepy," Natasha said.

"It will be nice when we get there," Ada said.

And then, as if on cue, the road sloped downward, creating a trough between two rises. At the bottom of the trough, the snow was so deep that the car lost traction as it tried to climb back out. Ada put her foot down, but it only made the problem worse as the wheels spun uselessly.

"We're stuck, aren't we?" Natasha said.

Ada tried a few more times, but it was no good. The more she tried, the deeper the tires dug in.

Keeping her voice as comforting as she could, she said,

"We can walk from here." She had no idea how far it would be.

She stepped out of the car and sank instantly into knee-high snow.

The night was still and frigidly cold. In the moonlight, the landscape was almost bright. She grabbed a few essentials from the car, then went around to the other side and helped Natasha out.

"I'm sorry about this," she said as the child sank into the wet snow.

"It's okay," Natasha said.

"Are you scared?"

"Yes."

Ada led her by the hand up the rise. The snow was deep, and it was tough going, but from the top, a few hundred yards ahead of them, they saw the wooden cabin.

"There it is," Ada said.

52

Lance drove late into the night and, when he got tired, pulled into a gas station. He needed coffee and went inside the store, which was pretty well stocked. He filled a paper cup with something that had been brewed many hours earlier and grimaced when he tasted it.

"You got anything hotter than this?" he said to the clerk.

The kid behind the counter shook his head, and Lance paid him, prepaid for a tank of gas, and went back outside. As he filled the car, he leaned on the hood and sipped the coffee, if that was what it was, and let the cold night air clear his head. There were no other cars at the station—none on the road. The sky overhead was very clear, and the cold air around the moon created a halo of refracted, crystalline light.

Lance was thinking about something Roth had said back at the Old Hamlet. He'd said that Laurel and Tatyana were walking headlong into a trap, and that it was a trap of Roth's own making. He refused to go into more detail but said that if it paid off, it would be worth the sacrifice.

"Even Laurel and Tatyana's lives?" Lance said.

Roth simply nodded his head.

Lance couldn't believe it—giving them up so flippantly, like a general looking at a map, waving away lives like they were so many pieces on a chessboard.

"How can you do that?" he said.

"It's my job."

"To get your own people killed?"

"Sometimes."

They locked eyes, and Lance said, "You listen to me very carefully, Levi. If something happens to them because of your plotting, if either of them dies...."

Roth raised a hand to stop him. "I know, Lance. I know."

"I swear to God."

"I know, Lance," Roth said again. "Why do you think I'm here talking to you?"

Lance couldn't figure him out. The detonation over the Arctic was directly tied to Project Oppenheimer, the Kremlin's terrifying new superweapons program. The lead scientist of that entire program, a man named Sacha Gazinsky, was trying desperately to defect to the American side.

The Russians were trying to kill him, of course, but Laurel and Tatyana were more than up to the task of bringing him in alive. Or at least, they should have been.

"Why is this green agent, Ada Hudson, bringing in the scientist?" Lance said.

"She's all we had."

"Bullshit," Lance said. "You had Tatyana."

"Tatyana was ... *indisposed*."

"Indisposed? What does that mean?"

"It's complicated."

Lance eyed Roth carefully. "You double-crossed her, didn't you?" he said. "You double-crossed both of them. Stabbed them in the back."

"You can't win a war without taking on casualties," Roth said.

"And that's all they are?" Lance said. "Casualties in a war?"

Lance could already see the storm brewing. Whatever Roth had done, whatever he was plotting, would creep closer and closer to Laurel and Tatyana until eventually they passed into its gravitational pull, like the event horizon of a black hole, and get sucked in.

Sacha Gazinsky was dead, gunned down in the open at the train station in Edinburgh, and the agent with him, a green recruit fresh out of Langley, was so out of her depth she was lucky to still be alive. The Russians had been a step ahead of her every inch of the way, and might have been even if she wasn't being double-crossed by her own side.

Whatever secrets Sacha Gazinsky had been willing to trade for his freedom were gone now, lost forever, taken with him to his grave.

And somehow, in some twisted, messed up way that was practically his trademark, Roth was behind all of it. Losing Sacha Gazinsky, losing Ada Hudson, even losing Laurel and Tatyana was a price he was willing to pay.

And all Roth would say was that if Lance understood what was at stake, if he had the full picture, he would see that the sacrifice was worth it.

"Worth it?" Lance gasped. "Laurel and Tatyana?"

"Yes, them," Roth said, and he said it so coldly that Lance didn't think he recognized the voice sounding the words.

"Then why bring me in at all?" he said. "If their death is so worth it."

"Because I can."

"You didn't even know I was alive until twelve hours ago."

"Because this is exactly what I *would* do," Roth said, and the way he said it only made Lance more uneasy.

"*Would* do?"

"If I knew only what the Russians think I know, then bringing you in is exactly what I would do now. It's the logical next step."

Lance shook his head. "Always playing with fire," he said. "One of these days, Roth, you're going to get us all burned."

"There's a difference you can make here, Lance," Roth said. "That's why I'm here. You can tip the scale just enough that Laurel and Tatyana can walk away when this is all over, and you can do it without ever jeopardizing my greater mission."

"Your *greater* mission?"

"I don't expect you to understand," Roth said, and he shook his head sadly. "I don't expect anyone to understand."

Lance looked at him, the old spy, the puppetmaster, and saw that even he was beginning to lose track of all the sacrifices that had been made to this false god he called stratagem.

"And are you winning, Roth? Are you ahead? When you reckon up your ledger and cash out your chips, are you up or are you down? Does the house owe you? Or do you owe the house?"

Roth looked at him and thought for a minute, then said, "Sacha Gazinsky has a daughter."

Lance said nothing. He knew what Roth was doing, and he eyed him the way a man eyes a rattlesnake.

"It's true," Roth said. "I'm just telling you the facts."

This wasn't fair. Laurel and Tatyana were one thing.

They were in trouble, even if they didn't know it, but it was trouble they'd agreed to. They were players on the field. They were fair game.

But throwing in a girl like this?

"Just the facts, eh?"

"I didn't put her there," Roth said. "But there she is, and you know as well as I do that the GRU can't let her get a happy ending."

"How old is she?"

"Nine."

"Nine?"

"That's her age, Lance."

"Nine years old? Just like...." He let his words trail off.

"That's the rub, isn't it, Lance?"

Lance's jaw clenched. He was looking at Roth and knew that he was helpless. There was nothing he could do. Roth had every shrink in the CIA get inside his head. He knew the dark cracks and crevices of Lance's mind better than Lance did himself. And he knew exactly what made him tick.

"At the end of the day," Roth said, "that's all you really need to know, isn't it, Lance?"

"One day, Levi, you're going to step on ice, and you're going to hear a crack."

Roth simply shrugged. He knew what he was, he knew what he was doing, and he wasn't backing down.

The thing Lance couldn't wrap his head around, though, and it didn't get any clearer the more he thought about it, was what objective Roth could possibly be pursuing that was worth all this?

Project Oppenheimer was terrifying—literally the stuff of nightmares. It was the endgame of a depraved regime that would rather see the world burn to a cinder than lose its grip on power. From what was known of the weapons, they'd been designed as self-destruct buttons on a planetary scale. Their hair triggers would go off at the slightest threat to the regime. If Molotov ever went down, the world would go down with him. That was their goal, that was their purpose, to tie the fate of the world to the fate of one man.

And Roth had just allowed the one scientist who could give him the schematics of those weapons, all their specifications, the timeframes of their deployment, and most importantly, their vulnerabilities, to get his head blown off while in the care of a rookie agent who'd been riding a desk in Langley less than three months ago.

"Laurel, Tatyana, Ada, they're fighting with one arm tied behind their backs," Roth had said, "and they don't even know it."

"Because you won't warn them."

"That's what you don't understand. What you can't understand. If I tell them anything, if I interfere in any way, then all this," and he waved his hand as if it was the Hamlet Pub that he was referring to, "all these decades of work, untold sacrifices, will have been for nothing."

Lance didn't know what to say. How did you reason with a fanatic? How did you apply logic to absolutes? Lance accepted the fact that Roth knew things that he didn't. There were fears in Roth's heart, nightmares, that ordinary people could never bring themselves to imagine. Indeed, it was because of Roth that they didn't have to. He took on the fears that the rest of the world didn't want to face. Couldn't face.

That was Roth's role. He was a general. Lance was a soldier. He accepted that. But he also knew that all these plots, with their double agents and double-crosses, their moves and measures and countermeasures, were what had kept the Cold War going for decades longer than it needed to. And he knew that if left unchecked, those same plots and schemings would pull the world back into war.

"You took a big risk telling me all this," Lance said.

"Oh?" Roth said. "Why's that?"

"You know why."

Roth merely shook his head. "You're not half the monster you think you are, Lance Spector."

"You wait and see," Lance said.

"This job is in your DNA, Lance. You couldn't turn your back on it if your life depended on it. It's always the same."

"What are you talking about?"

"Laurel, Tatyana, Ada. It's no different than the girl in Montana you took in. Or..."

"This has nothing to do with them."

"You can't turn your back on the child. I've seen the profiling."

"Easy, Levi."

Roth raised his hands as if in surrender. "You can't save all of them, Lance. In fact, in the world we inhabit, I'd venture to say you can't save any of them."

Lance didn't know what to say. The CIA's psych profilers, if they really got their claws into a man, could read him like a book. They could predict a subject's future decision-making so accurately that they were developing theories incompatible with any concept of free will. They were reducing the human brain to a series of amoral, godless chemical reactions. Reactions that could be perfectly understood. Perfectly predicated. It was antithetical to what Lance believed, and yet, he couldn't deny their force.

There was someone he'd failed to protect once, someone who'd trusted him, someone who'd depended on him for her very life, and they knew how it haunted Lance. They knew what parts of his brain lit up when he thought of her. They knew what chemicals flowed, what electrical signals fired.

"So I should just stop trying?" he said.

Roth smiled sanguinely. "I'd say you should, but I know you won't."

Lance got back into the car and continued north into the highlands. As the mountains rose, the road grew progressively windier and less traveled. At stretches, snow lay on the ground inches thick.

He'd been getting updates on Ada's position, but at some point, the coordinates stopped moving. The car, at least, had stopped moving.

He drove on toward the location, and it was another hour before he finally approached the marker. A few miles beyond the town of Aviemore, high in the Cairngorms, was a turnoff. It was covered in snow, and there were tire tracks in it, a few hours old but still visible. He followed them until his car started to skid and then continued on foot.

A few hundred yards farther up the track, he found the Volvo. It was stuck in the snow, and two sets of footprints led on from it. He examined the car, which revealed little, then followed the footprints up the slope. When he reached the crest of the rise, he saw a small cabin ahead, woodsmoke rising from its chimney. He approached cautiously, silently, gun drawn.

Twenty yards from the cabin, the trees stopped, and he stopped with them. In the east, the first sign of dawn was beginning to redden the sky. He sat down on his haunches next to the tree and lit a cigarette.

Then he waited. He knew the training Ada would have received, had a fair idea of the state of mind she would be in, and he didn't want to approach the house before it grew light. It took about thirty minutes, and in that time, there was no movement or sound from the house whatsoever. The house, the trees, the surrounding country, everything was silent and still.

When it was bright enough, he put his gun on the ground next to the base of the tree and rose to his feet.

He began walking at an ordinary pace through the snow toward the door. He'd taken about ten strides and was just approaching the porch when the loud, clean crack of a gunshot rang out into the air.

53

Ada watched the man as he in turn watched the house. She'd been lying awake on the bed when she first heard him, and now she was on the floor, her back to the wall, watching his reflection in a mirror across the room. She could make out the red glow of his cigarette and, as the sun rose, his silhouette.

On her lap was her gun, ready to fire, and on the bed next to her, Natasha lay sleeping.

Ada waited for him to make the first move. He was patient, a professional, probably GRU. He didn't rush but watched and waited like a wolf hunting. He could wait as long as he wanted, she thought. Eventually, he would come into the clearing, and when he did, she would be ready.

As the sun rose, she thought it strange that he would wait for it to get bright. The increased visibility could only be to his disadvantage. She wondered what he was thinking, but before she could resolve the thought, he was on the move. He rose to his feet and stepped into the clearing. Without thinking, acting purely on adrenaline, Ada stood up and, in a single motion, spun around, leveled her gun at his head, and fired off a single shot.

The glass in the window shattered, dropping in its frame in a cascade, and the man, moving almost too quickly to see, dropped to the ground in the same instant that she pulled the trigger.

She remained absolutely still, paralyzed, staring at the body in the snow. Natasha looked at her from the bed, wide-eyed with terror.

Another kill. Her third in less than as many days. The count was racking up faster than she had yet come to terms with.

She kept her eyes on the body, motionless in the snow, and kept her gun trained on it.

"Stay down," she whispered to Natasha and listened for any sound that there might be other gunmen.

Natasha came across the bed like a frightened animal and gripped onto her. Ada took her eyes off the body for a moment, less than a second, then heard his voice.

"Ada Hudson?"

"Stay down," she shouted, swinging the gun back in his direction. But he was gone.

"Ada Hudson," he said again. "My name is Lance Spector. I'm with the CIA."

She spun wildly, then saw that he was on the front porch of the cabin, not ten feet from her window, with both hands in the air and a strangely bemused expression on his face.

"Stay back, or I'll blow your head off," she said.

"We don't want that."

She squinted her eyes at him. She had no way of knowing who he was or who'd sent him, but this didn't feel like a GRU assassination attempt.

"I'm with the CIA," he said again. "I'm here to bring you in."

"How do I know that?"

"You could trust me," he said.

The smug look on his face was almost enough reason on its own to shoot him. "I'm not in a very trusting mood."

"I could have approached the house in darkness," he said. "I waited for daylight."

She knew that much was true, for what it was worth. "The CIA's compromised," she said. "There's a rat in London that's been trying to kill me ever since I started this mission."

"I know," he said.

She shook her head. She wanted to believe him. She wanted to be brought in. But she couldn't bring herself to lower the gun.

"I'm unarmed," he said.

"Bullshit."

"I watched the house from over there," he said, indicating the tree he'd been at when she saw him. "My gun's at the foot of that tree."

"Why would you leave your gun there?"

"A show of good faith," he said.

She shook her head again. At every step, she'd been double-crossed by her own side or outmaneuvered by the Russians. How could she know this wasn't another trap?

"How did you find me?" she said.

"You used the CIA credit card at the car rental."

That was accurate. Indeed, it was the reason she'd used the card—to send a flag to Tatyana.

"Natasha," she said to the child, "put your shoes on."

Natasha did as she was told, and Ada went closer to the

window. The glass was gone, and icy air filled the room. She kept her gun on the man while speaking to Natasha.

"You see that tree over there?" she said.

"Yes," Natasha said.

"Will you do me a favor?"

"You want me to check if his gun is there?"

Ada glanced at her. She was more perceptive than she looked and understood more English than she'd let on. "Don't go anywhere near the man. If he moves, I'll shoot him."

Natasha looked back at her. So much had happened in the past twenty-four hours that she was past the point of trying to make sense of things.

She left the room and hurried through the cabin to the front door and then out to the porch. She was only a few yards from the man, but if he so much as flinched, Ada was ready to blow his head off.

Natasha cut the man a wide berth, and when she got to the tree, she bent down and cried out, "Found it."

When she got back to her feet, she was holding a pistol.

Ada glanced at her, then back at the man. "Okay, sweetie. Put it back on the ground and come inside."

The man said nothing. He let the gun speak for itself.

"You keep your hands in the air," Ada said to him as Natasha hurried back into the bedroom. Ada waited for her, thinking of what to do next. Natasha came in and climbed onto the bed to get a better look.

"Take off the jacket," Ada said to the man.

Moving very slowly, he let the jacket slide off his arms and fall to the ground.

"Pull up your shirt. I want to see your waistband."

He pulled up his shirt.

"Turn around," she said.

He turned three-sixty, then let go of his shirt. "Can I put my hands down?"

"You do exactly what I tell you," she said, but she didn't know what she wanted him to do. Her gut told her he was telling the truth. The CIA had sent him. That was what made the most sense. She looked at Natasha and raised her eyebrows questioningly.

Natasha shrugged.

The man cleared his throat. "There's a plane waiting for us back in Edinburgh," he said.

"Is there?"

He nodded.

"To take us back to London?"

He nodded again.

"Where multiple attacks have been made on our lives?"

"I can do something about that."

"You sound so confident."

He shrugged, then lowered his hands.

"Hey," she barked. "I didn't say you could do that."

"Look," he said, "either you come back with me, or you shoot me. Either way, I'm not standing out here any longer, freezing my nuts off."

Ada shook her head. "Don't tempt me."

54

Tito knew how to find people. He received a target, a name, a photo, and he tracked it down with the single-mindedness of a bloodhound. He did it for corporations, for litigants, sometimes for law enforcement, and he could usually go to bed at night, safe in the knowledge that the person he'd located wasn't about to die as a result of his work.

This time was different.

He knew Stan, knew what he was mixed up in. If the GRU wanted a target, it could be for only one reason—a bullet to the skull.

He still couldn't believe Stan had given his name to the Russians. Their friendship was over, as far as he was concerned. Once this job was done, he didn't want to see or hear from Stan Morel ever again. In fact, he highly doubted Stan would be around for very much longer. Things tended to go south fast when people started blackmailing their own friends.

But be that as it may, it didn't help Tito's current situation. Someone in the Kremlin had his name now. If he didn't deliver the goods, he would be in for a world of pain.

And so, he sat in front of his computer and scoured every network and data feed he had access to, searching for anything at all that looked like a match on one Ada Hudson, US Citizen, twenty-five years old, officially employed by the US Department of Agriculture and stationed at the Embassy in London.

There were tens of thousands of images of her online, and not just from her own social network feeds. There were corporations that specialized in gathering data on people and making it available for a fee. Tito knew that the ordinary citizen would have been horrified to know just how much information he could obtain on them, legally, on the open market, with nothing more than a name and a credit card.

Within minutes, Tito had enough images of Ada Hudson to construct a full three-dimensional model of her face. That information was then fed into a number of civilian-grade facial recognition algorithms he had access to. From what he had, he was confident that as soon as she was picked up by a camera, the system would make the match.

He finished setting up the search and then got up and made a pot of coffee. By the time he got back to his desk, his screen was filling up with dozens and dozens of possible matches. They were false positives, women that, to the computer, looked close enough to get passed up the chain. All the images had been captured in the past couple of hours by live cameras across the country, and Tito began the time-consuming task of sifting through them and comparing the captures to his reference images of Ada.

He'd never met her, never seen her in real life, and so

had to look at the references closely each time before discarding a match.

His system relied almost exclusively on cameras owned and operated by private security firms. There was nothing illegal at all about what he was doing. He hadn't hacked their systems.

People forgot it, but every time they walked into a bank, or a convenience store, or a gas station, or passed an intersection in their car, or used a crosswalk, or a bank ATM, or public transit, or in literally tens of thousands of other situations, they were being recorded.

And even when they did think of it, what did people assume happened to all that footage?

Surely it was too expensive to store. All those hard drives, all those data centers. They assumed it was deleted. Of course they did. Unless the police requested access to it very soon after it was recorded, unless there was some major incident, an armed robbery, or a car accident, or a terrorist attack, people assumed that data was all erased. Wiped clean. Recorded over.

But that wasn't what happened. Not at all. The world's everyday interactions, ordinary people going about their ordinary business, millions upon millions of them, being tracked by millions upon millions of cameras, located at millions upon millions of sites, was far too valuable simply to delete.

It was rented out, harvested, analyzed in near real time by data-mining firms all over the globe. Insurance companies, private investigators, credit reference agencies, university researchers, anyone who could afford to pay for it could have, for a monthly fee, access to a global surveillance network on par with those of even the most repressive governments.

And all completely legal.

Tito had set his search parameters as narrowly as he could, scanning feeds only within a fifty-mile radius of Edinburgh and only from the last thirty minutes. It reduced the number of false positives and also meant that if a match actually was made, it would be actionable. There was no point knowing where she'd been a day ago.

As he scrolled through image after image, all women in their mid-twenties, all blonde, all athletic, he began to feel like he was swiping through the feed on his own dating app profile.

And suddenly, he stopped.

He scrolled back and looked more closely.

He looked at his reference images.

It was her. He was sure of it.

She was walking through the executive terminal of Edinburgh Airport. She was holding the hand of a young girl, and next to her, looking like he meant business, was a well-built man in his thirties with a military look to him.

He looked at the time stamp on the feed. The footage had been captured scarcely five minutes earlier.

He almost knocked over his coffee in his haste to grab the phone.

55

Stan never signed up to be a killer. He wasn't an assassin. He was a drone operator. He was a technician. He was a computer guy. He'd made it clear to Chapman right from day one that he didn't want to get his hands bloody.

But Chapman was dead.

Hamish was dead.

And Viktor Lapin didn't care one jot what Stan had and hadn't signed up for.

Stan had no doubt that the British security services were already searching for him. They had Chapman's body. They had the drone and laptop he'd used in Edinburgh. It wouldn't be long before they found the warehouse in Lambeth and started closing in the net.

Unless he got his ass to Moscow in short order, he was fucked, and he knew it. He was at Saint Pancras station in London, sitting at a café in the main concourse. The loudspeaker announced another departure to Paris, leaving in fifteen minutes, and he pulled out his phone.

Viktor's voice came on the line almost immediately. "Give me good news, Stan."

"I found her," he said.

"Did you?" Viktor said, almost jovially. "That wasn't so difficult now, was it?"

"You don't know what it cost me," Stan said.

Stan regretted what he'd had to do. Lying to Tito. That had cost him a good friendship. He'd never actually given Tito's name to Viktor. He'd only said that so Tito would do what he needed.

"I don't care what it cost you," Viktor said.

"Ada Hudson is in Edinburgh. At the airport."

"Where is she going?"

"There's a US government jet fueling at the executive terminal. The log says it'll be flying to Farnborough."

"Is the child with her?"

Stan's waitress came over with his coffee, and he waited for her to leave. "The child's with her, and a man."

"So they'll be in London in about an hour?" Viktor said. "That doesn't give you much time, does it?"

"Time for what?" Stan said, his pulse quickening.

"To get a drone in the sky."

"A drone in the sky?" Stan said. "I don't have a drone, Viktor. I don't have anything. The whole operation here's been burned to the ground. I'm getting on a train. That's what we agreed."

"Listen up, *Stan*," Viktor said, his voice suddenly cold, a sinister emphasis on Stan's name. "You get me a proper surveillance drone over Farnborough Airport before that plane touches the ground, or it'll be your daughter I go after next."

Stan wanted to lash out. He wanted to swear up and

down at Viktor and tell him to go fuck himself. He wanted to kill him.

But instead, keeping his voice as calm as he could, he said, "The authorities here are already after me. You would be better served if you got someone else to handle this for you."

"I don't have anyone else, Stan."

"There's a train to Paris in ten minutes. I need to be on it."

Viktor was quiet for a moment, then said, "You're going to finish what you started, Stan. Are we clear?"

Stan swallowed. "We had a deal, Viktor."

"Are we clear, Stan?"

"If I don't get out of the country now, I never will."

"Think of your daughter, Stan. What's more important? Your safety or hers?"

Stan picked up his coffee and took a sip. There was nothing he could do. He had no leverage. "What do you want me to do?" he said, his voice thick with resignation.

"Nothing so very difficult. I just want you to do what you always do."

"I'm not a killer, Viktor."

"Don't worry, Stan. All I need from you is eyes on the target. I've got someone else who can take the shot."

56

Roth sat in the Old Hamlet with a cup of coffee in front of him and his phone on the bar.

Harry was looking at him from across the bar. "Who took the jam out of your doughnut?"

Roth shook his head. "I don't think I know anymore, Harry."

Harry refilled his cup, and Roth took a sip. He let out a long sigh, and Harry said, "If you're going to sit there and moan about it, you might as well say what it is that's bothering you."

Roth shook his head again. The coffee was awful, as acidic as vinegar, and he wondered how Harry managed to make it so bad. "This is godawful coffee, by the way."

"Sorry about that."

"You don't sound sorry."

Harry shrugged. "Maybe I don't want people ordering the coffee."

"Why not?"

"Coffee's two quid a cup. I want people to spend money."

Roth nodded. He took another sip and grimaced.

"Why don't you just put yourself out of your misery and order a drink?" Harry said. "You look like you could use it."

Roth nodded, and Harry began pulling him a pint. Roth watched him work. He wondered, more and more lately, what his life might have been like if he'd taken a different path. It wasn't written in stone that his life had to be the way it was. He'd foregone most of the things generally regarded as necessary to a happy life. Love. Family. The comforts of home. He'd dug himself into a pit that there was no climbing out of. And he was still digging.

"I have to deliver some bad news today," he said to Harry.

Harry nodded absently and put the pint on the bar.

"Some bad news to an old friend," Roth said, more to himself.

Harry put a shot glass on the bar and filled it.

"What's this?" Roth said.

"That's on me."

Roth raised the glass, then downed it in a single motion.

"You know," Harry said, "sometimes what seems like bad news to you isn't so bad to someone else."

Roth shrugged. "I think this is going to be pretty bad to the person receiving it."

Harry leaned forward and touched his nose as if about to impart some very valuable information and said, "Just tell them, who knows what worse news this bad news is saving them from."

Roth slid the shot glass in his direction and said, "How about another one of those?"

Alona would know by now, of course. Wives always knew. It wasn't official. Tenet wasn't AWOL yet. But Alona was no fool. She could read between the lines.

He finished up and put some money on the bar.

"That's not necessary," Harry said.

"If it wasn't necessary," Roth said, "you'd have given me better coffee."

He put his coat on and went outside to hail a cab. It was a short ride to Tenet and Alona's neighborhood, and Roth barely had time to collect his thoughts before the cab was pulling over.

"This is it," the driver announced.

Roth looked out at the building, an exquisite Edwardian terrace house, divided into six apartments and restored to full splendor. The other houses were occupied by government ministers, embassy officials, royal officeholders.

"You getting out?" the driver said briskly.

"Sorry," Roth said and paid the man.

He got out and walked toward the door, freshly painted in a glossy green, its brass fixtures gleaming from recent polish. Shrubs along the side of the path were pruned to such symmetrical perfection that he reached out and brushed his hand on them as he passed, just to see if they were real. He reached the door, where a small sign on the letterbox read, 'No Advertisements,' and pushed the buzzer.

He waited. Nothing happened. He took a deep breath, annoyed at how nervous he felt. He pushed the buzzer again and took a few steps back from the door. He hadn't been face to face with Alona for a very long time, and he didn't want to startle her.

He was about to pull out his phone and call the office when the door opened.

He'd prepared his words in advance, knew down to the last detail what it was he wanted to say, but when he tried to speak, his mind went blank. His voice caught in his throat.

There she was, Alona. It was hard to believe it was really her.

She was standing in the doorway, looking down at him, and for a split second, he saw that she didn't even recognize his face. He'd changed in forty years. But she hadn't. Not a bit. Every detail of her face was exactly as he remembered. Every hair on her head, every glint of light against her eyes, every eyelash, was exactly as it had been, untouched, perfect.

"Levi," she said, as she realized it was him, there, after all those years. And then, as suddenly as it had appeared, the flash of recognition gave way to a look of utter despair.

Because it was at that moment that she realized why he was there.

She knew what he did. She knew he and Tenet worked together closely. She hadn't seen him face to face, Roth had assiduously avoided social engagements and embassy events that might have seen their paths cross, but she'd always been aware of his presence in Tenet's life, if not her own.

"Alona," Roth said, but the word turned to ash in his mouth.

She couldn't have been more horrified if she was looking at a ghost. Tears began streaming down her face, and it was only then that he realized what she was thinking—what his sudden appearance would suggest to her mind.

To her, his being there could only mean one thing.

"He's dead, isn't he?"

57

Stan left the train station in the first cab he could find, and as he gave the driver his home address in Clapham, he prayed there wasn't an anti-terrorism police squad waiting for him when he got there.

He asked the cab driver to wait for him when they arrived at the house.

"Sure I'll wait," the driver said sarcastically, before pulling off.

Stan watched him leave, then looked up and down the street, checking for anything out of the ordinary. The street was lined with elegant Victorian townhouses and a row of cherry trees that blossomed extravagantly every spring. It all looked as it always did, not a milk bottle out of place.

He walked up to the front door, unlocked it slowly, and listened before going inside. In the kitchen, his half-empty bowl of cereal was still on the counter where he'd left it a few days earlier, the milk beginning to turn. He picked it up and rinsed it in the sink before putting it in the dishwasher. It was a strange act, he thought, given that he would soon be leaving the house, and the country, for good.

He shouldn't even have been there. The police could have pulled up at any moment. For all he knew, a SWAT team was already watching him. But he was so ensnarled in Viktor's plot now that he thought it was better to keep going than to cut and run.

He took a laptop and cellphone from his bag and set them up on the kitchen counter. Then he went upstairs and unlocked the door of one of the bedrooms. It was a door he always kept locked. The house backed onto Clapham Common, one of the largest parks in Central London, and the window in the room looked out directly over it.

There was no furniture of any kind in the room. Instead, facing the window was a large mechanical contraption about the size of a small car. It was painted khaki green and had two small wheels at the base for towing. It was too big to have been brought into the room intact and had been disassembled first and then reassembled personally by Stan once in place.

It looked like a large catapult, which was essentially what it was. Officially described as a pneumatic launcher, it was designed and built by a wholly-owned subsidiary of Boeing called Insitu. The patents were filed publicly by Boeing in the late-nineties but later classified by the US government for security reasons and removed from the register.

The launcher, which the company internally called the SuperWedge, was marketed to a number of NATO militaries and was part of a package that included its sister product, the ScanEagle long-endurance, low-altitude drone.

Neither the launcher nor the ScanEagle drone were commercially available. Stan had purchased his anonymously through an illicit Dark Web arms marketplace. The drone had been launched from the USS Mahan, stationed in the Mediterranean during Operation Unified Protector in 2011, and was shot down over the capital by a military group loyal to Colonel Gaddafi before finding its way onto the open market.

It was a formidable piece of equipment, far more powerful than anything Stan could have purchased legally, with stabilized electro-optical cameras and an integrated communications system with a broadcasting range of over sixty miles. It was four-and-a-half feet long, with a wingspan of over ten feet, weighed forty-four pounds, had a flight endurance was almost twenty-four hours, and could fly at speeds of over ninety miles per hour. Stan's particular model had additionally been equipped by the US military with ImSAR, the smallest and lightest synthetic aperture radar system then in existence, capable of providing high-resolution, real-time ground imaging under all environmental and weather conditions.

It was military-grade hardware, and it looked like it. Stan had initially intended to use it for his more demanding jobs with Chapman, but when it arrived, he immediately realized it would attract the attention of British military radar stations if he ever used it.

And so, it sat in the spare room of his house, until now.

Stan had previously gone to the trouble of modifying the window of the bedroom, widening it by four feet, and replacing the multiple small panes of glass with a single, large untempered piece.

He also knew that the instant he flung it out over one of Central London's busiest public parks at over a hundred miles-per-hour, the authorities would take note.

As soon as he launched it, the clock would begin ticking. If he didn't get out of the country very soon after, he wouldn't be able to do so without getting false identification papers.

He checked that the launcher was powered up, pressurized, and connected to the laptop downstairs. Then he opened the curtains of the window and made sure the drone was aimed directly at the center of the glass. He had less than twelve inches of clearance on each side.

He disconnected the drone from its charging supply and hardline network connection, then went back downstairs to the laptop, where he ran through the pre-flight diagnostics on custom software he'd written himself.

When everything was ready to go, he clicked on the button that began the launch sequence. He half-expected it not to work, for there to at least be some last-minute bugs to iron out, but less than a second after he clicked the button, the entire house was filled with an extremely loud whooshing sound, followed by a crash of glass as the window shattered. A pulse of air shot through the house, blowing out windows in every room, and his ears popped painfully from the sudden change in air pressure. This was immediately followed by the sound of falling rubble.

"Fuck me," he whispered.

He ran upstairs to the room. The drone was gone. The window was gone. The launcher had fired with such force that it had been flung backward about six feet, like a howitzer, crashing into the wall behind it and breaking through to the next room.

He walked over to the window and looked out over the park. Far in the distance, he could just about make out the rapidly disappearing silhouette of the drone as it gained altitude northward over the city.

58

Roth was the grim reaper incarnate. All he had to do was look at Alona's face to see it.

His presence meant despair, destruction, death.

She'd almost married him. She'd wanted to have his baby. She'd loved him so completely that when he left her, it broke her heart utterly. But now, when she looked at him, it was as if she was looking at a monster.

And, he supposed, she was right. That was what he'd become. That was what a job like his did to a man.

"Alona," he said, taking a step forward.

She backed away, raising her hands as if afraid he was about to strike her. He came closer and tried to put his arms around her. She resisted, pushed him back, and then surrendered, sobbing into his chest as he held her tightly in his arms for the first time in forty years.

It was a terrible moment, heart-rending, and yet there was a part of his soul that savored it. As he breathed in the scent of her hair, the very same as he remembered, as he held the delicate form of her shoulders against his chest, it was as if the passage of decades, the revolution of the planet around its star over and over and over, had been undone in an instant.

For a brief moment, all the world was new. His life was different. He'd taken another path, made the opposite choice. He'd chosen love. He'd chosen Alona over the Agency.

"He's not dead," he whispered. "He's not dead."

In an instant, everything changed. Her body stiffened. She recoiled from him so suddenly it was a shock to him.

She narrowed her eyes, wiped her tears, and with a voice as harsh as an angle grinder cutting sheet metal, said, "Then what the hell are you doing here?"

The question was fair—expected even. What *was* he doing there? There were half a dozen officials in London who could have delivered the message.

The truth was, he was holding out hope. It was futile, his mind knew it, but his heart held on anyway. Tenet wasn't dead, but what Roth was there to say wasn't so different as if he was. And with him out of the way, with his rival gone, there was a part of Levi Roth's heart that couldn't let go of the chance that things might be different.

"He's unhurt," Roth said, and that much was true. Tenet was unhurt. He was alive and well at the Russian embassy in Paris. In fact, he was probably being taken very good care of —vodka, caviar, the finest cigars.

But that didn't mean everything was okay. It certainly didn't mean Alona would ever see him again. The truth was, his being alive would probably cause her more pain than his death ever could. To know he was alive, a traitor, a defector, living in luxury in Moscow while she suffered all the consequences, surely his death would have been easier to bear.

"If he's unhurt," she said, "then where is he?"

"He's in Paris."

"On a mission?"

Roth nodded. That was true too.

"He didn't tell me he was going anywhere," she said cagily.

"He couldn't tell you."

"He told me everything."

Roth shook his head. "Not this, Alona."

She bit her lip. She still didn't know why he was there, but she didn't like it. "He's in danger, isn't he?" she said grimly.

Roth nodded.

She looked at him more closely now—suspicious. Something didn't add up. This wasn't the first time her husband had gone on a dangerous mission. He worked for the CIA. Danger came with the territory. It lurked behind every closed door, in every hotel room closet, in every darkened parking lot and foreign city.

No, danger was nothing new. What was new was Tenet's keeping it secret from her. And Levi Roth, standing there on her front stoop as if forty years didn't mean a thing.

"Why are you here, Levi?"

"Alona...."

She raised her hand as if she didn't want to hear her name on his lips.

"He's in Paris," Roth said for the second time, but she was already shaking her head.

"No," she said quietly. "You're not here to tell me where he is. You're here to tell me that you're the one who sent him."

Roth said nothing. There was nothing he could say.

"Where in Paris?"

"The embassy," Roth said, reverting again to half-truths. It was a useless deception, though—cowardly.

It wouldn't be long before the whole world knew Richmond Tenet's name. His defection would make front-page headlines globally. Both ends of the media spectrum would have a field day. The news networks would have their biggest advertising quarter since the Clinton impeachment.

Tenet would go down as the highest-profile US defector since the blistering fever pitch of the Cold War. Both sides of the political aisle, as well as the very deepest, darkest recesses of the nation's intelligence apparatus, would make sure of it.

In Washington, hands would be wrung, legislation would be rushed through, committees would be convened, senators would grandstand, and the subpoenas would flow like grocery store flyers.

It would be a whirlwind, a firestorm, a vortex, and Alona would be at the very center of it. People she regarded as her closest friends, her most intimate allies, would abandon her in an instant. On their resumes, on their public websites and profiles, every mention of Richmond Tenet would be erased. And so too would Alona, in their social calendars, in their cellphone address books.

Anyone she'd had dinner with in the last five years, anyone she'd emailed or called or been seen with in public, anyone she'd worked with at the Palestinian Rights Organization she headed, would immediately create distance, withdraw, turn their back. No one wanted a call from the CIA, or the FBI, or worst of all, a Washington journalist.

Even Alona would come to curse Tenet's name. She would come to see her marriage as a forty-year sham. She would believe that he'd betrayed far more than his country, far more than his oaths and duties of office. He'd betrayed her, his wife, the life they'd shared. It would all be reduced to nothing more than a ruse, a sleight of hand, a con.

And she would hate him for it. To his grave, she would curse him.

And Roth knew that she would never know the truth. Even on her death bed, even after Tenet was dead, he wouldn't tell her of the sacrifice he'd made, the true nature of his mission.

There were operational reasons for such secrecy, of course. There were intelligence risks that couldn't be predicted, vulnerabilities that might be exposed by her knowing the truth of her husband's life.

Of course there were.

But only to a point.

On her death bed?

Surely he could tell her then. If he was there. If circumstances permitted. For her to die knowing her husband wasn't a traitor, surely that was something the voracious beast of national security could tolerate.

But could Roth?

And wasn't that what it all boiled down to? Armies, nations, wars. To the contents of the heart of a single man? The heart of a general. The heart of a President. The heart of a king, or kaiser, or tsar, or führer.

Roth still loved this woman. He saw that now, recognized it in himself at last, even if it was forty years too late. She'd loved him too, once. Loved him more than she loved Richmond Tenet, and told him as much. But would she still? And would she if she knew he wasn't a traitor?

As it stood, no one knew but Roth. And he was going to bury that knowledge so deeply within himself that it might as well not have existed.

He would do so for the security of the mission.

And he would do so from the jealousy of his own heart.

It was a mission from which there would be no return. There would be no victory. And for Alona, it would bring only shame, humiliation, and the constant threat of death from both sides.

Roth had it in his power to lessen that burden. To tell her what her husband truly was.

He looked at her. He knew what she was thinking. Her mind was running desperately over the permutations, the memories of an entire marriage, processing the millions of interactions, the careless moments, the throwaway words, going back all the way to the days when she and Tenet and Roth all drank together in the Old Hamlet and thought they were building the world anew.

Roth was wise enough not to underestimate her. She'd have seen things, even when there was nothing to see. She slept next to Tenet every night. Heard him speak in his dreams. She was a wife. She would know things that should be unknowable.

"You're not here to tell me something, are you?" she said slowly. "You're here to apologize for something. That's it, isn't it, Levi? You're here to atone."

"I'm here to tell you...."

"You sent him to Paris," she said. "That's why you're here. To confess."

He couldn't lie to her.

"You're here to lessen your own guilt."

"I'm here to tell you he's gone off-script, Alona."

"What does that mean?"

"He went of his own volition."

"His *own* volition?"

"He defected, Alona. He betrayed us."

Her face went pale. She looked at Roth as if looking at a

ghost, her head slowly shaking. "That's a lie," she whispered.

"It's not a lie."

"It's a lie, Levi Roth. It's a lie, it's a lie, it's a goddamned lie."

He shook his head. "It's not."

He could scarcely believe what he was doing. It was as the plan dictated, it was as had been agreed and discussed, and yet, it was an outright betrayal. He was poisoning her memory of Tenet while at the same time harboring a hope of his own.

It was false. He was false.

"He wouldn't do that," she said.

"We've been watching him, Alona. Tracking him. The evidence has been growing for some time, and he knew we were closing in."

"You were watching him?"

"We're watching everyone," Roth said.

"It's just not possible."

"Everything under the sun is possible."

"I lay next to that man every night for forty years. I know what's possible."

"Didn't he ever leave you with questions?" Roth said. "Unexplained absences? Late night walks with the dog? Secrets?"

"He works for the CIA," she said. "Or have you forgotten?"

"I haven't forgotten."

"His work is secretive."

"Not all his secrets were part of his work," Roth said, planting the poison, inserting the knife, and turning it.

She was crying now, silently, tears falling down her face to the floor. Roth knew he didn't have to spell things out. All men had their secrets, and all wives had their suspicions, their fears, stolen glances, interrupted phone calls. Roth knew her imagination would fill his words with more meaning than he ever could if he kept talking.

"Maybe you didn't know your husband as well as you thought you did," he said.

Roth despised himself for this. There were other ways he could have gone. This was only one option, and perhaps not even the best one. He could have shown her the evidence. She was trained in the craft. She'd have known what she was looking at. Phone records, transcripts, intercepted emails, secret meetings with Russian associates caught on camera.

It had been Roth's choice to go down this path, to insinuate infidelity, to poison every memory she had of the man who'd loved her his entire life.

"He wasn't what you thought he was," Roth said, inserting finality in his tone. "He never was."

She looked at him then. He thought she was going to say something, but she stopped. Then she stepped forward, drew back her hand, and slapped him across the face.

She hit him hard, as hard as she could, with such force he was knocked back a step. Then, in a voice that was caustic and harsh and dry, she said, "Get away from this house, Levi Roth. Get away from me."

"Alona," he gasped.

"No," she said, shaking her head. "Oh, no. I never want to set eyes on you for as long as I live."

59

A da did her best to keep Natasha's spirits up during the flight. The child seemed to slip into despondency from one moment to the next, and Ada talked to her, asked her questions, pointed things out, just to keep her distracted.

"Do you like planes?" she said, and the instant the words escaped her lips, she realized her mistake. Just a few short days had passed since Natasha had been on a plane with her father.

The child said nothing.

"We're going to get you somewhere so nice," Ada said, changing the subject. "Somewhere safe."

"We're going back to London, aren't we?"

Ada nodded. She put her arm around her, and Natasha rested her head on her shoulder. A few minutes later, she was asleep.

Lance was sitting facing them, and Ada looked up at him. "I'm worried about her."

He nodded. She looked at him, waiting for him to say something, but he remained silent.

She let out a sigh. She found him difficult to read. Elusive. Distant.

Not that she wasn't glad to have him. His presence was a comfort, of course. Even when she'd had her gun on him, she sensed that he'd come to help her, to bring her and Natasha to safety. She sensed that her ordeal was coming to an end.

Still, a little small talk would have been nice. She and Natasha were both traumatized. They'd seen more death and bloodshed in the past forty-eight hours than at any other time in their lives. They were nearing the limit of their endurance, but Lance merely treated them like an extension of his mission, like they were a cargo to be delivered.

And what was worse, he treated them both equally, like there was no difference between them, like she was as helpless and in need of rescuing as Natasha was.

He was watching the child sleep, and Ada said, "What's going to happen in London?"

His mind had been far away, and her words brought him back to the present as if she'd woken him. "To the kid?" he said.

Ada nodded.

"Roth wants her brought in to the embassy."

"Is that safe?"

"I don't know."

"Did they catch the rat?"

"I don't know," he said again.

"You don't know, or you don't think it's worth the hassle to tell me?"

"I don't know."

She let out another sigh and turned to look out the window.

He seemed to sense that he'd annoyed her.

He moved in his seat and said, "Want some coffee?"

She kept her gaze fixed on the window, studiously avoiding eye contact with him.

"Suit yourself," he said.

"I'll tell you what I want," she snapped. "I want you to treat me like the agent who kept this child alive for the last few days."

He lowered himself back into his seat, and for the first time, she felt she had his full attention. "Sorry," he said. "You're right."

"I've had the Russians taking potshots at me. I've had my own agency double-crossing me at every turn...."

"I know," he said.

"I've had," and she lowered her voice even though there was no one on the plane but them, "I've had to *kill* people."

"I know," he said again. "You did good."

"It's just..." she said, letting her words trail off.

Lance nodded at Natasha. "She was lucky to have you."

"Thank you."

He got up and said, "Sure you don't want coffee?"

"Fine," she said.

He poured two cups and came back. He put one of them in front of her, black, and took a sip of his own. He said nothing, but she saw now that it wasn't that he didn't care about her, it was just that he didn't like to fill the air with words.

"I would have died before I let anything happen to her," she said.

He nodded, then sipped his coffee again.

"What's going to happen to her?"

"At the embassy?"

"Yes."

He shook his head. "I don't know."

"You don't know much, do you?"

"I know what I need."

She leaned down to her coffee cup and blew on it.

By the time they finished their coffee, the plane was landing on the tarmac at Farnborough. Lance got up as soon as the plane stopped moving and went to the door. He opened the latch and then looked out carefully, getting a lay of the land before letting Ada and Natasha come close.

"All clear?" Ada said from behind him.

"We'll wait here for the car," he said.

A few minutes later, a black Mercedes S-Class sedan with diplomatic plates and tinted windows pulled up next to the plane.

"All right," he said. "Straight to the car."

Ada took Natasha by the hand and helped her down the steps. The driver got the door for them. They climbed into the back, and Lance got in next to the driver.

"What's our destination?" Lance said as soon as they were moving.

"Instructions are the embassy. Nine Elms."

"Route?"

"The motorway."

"The M3?"

"It's the most direct route," the driver said.

Lance nodded. "All right."

The driver looked at him. "Is everything all right?"

"It's fine."

"Sounds like you're expecting trouble."

"I always expect trouble," Lance said.

Ada looked at Natasha and smiled. The back of the car was nice, tan leather with executive upgrades, including a small refrigerator in the armrest between the two seats containing drinks and snacks. "Can we eat these?" she said.

"Help yourselves, ladies," the driver said.

"Take anything you like," Ada said to Natasha.

Natasha took a Sprite and opened it.

They followed the ring road around Farnborough and got onto the motorway at Southwood. Ada watched Lance from her seat. She could see his face in the mirror. He was tense, his eyes darting in every direction, scanning for threats.

"Do you mind if I adjust this?" he said, pointing to his wing mirror.

The driver shrugged, and Lance angled it so that he could see behind the car.

On the motorway, they hit the early morning traffic entering the city, and their speed reduced to a standstill.

"This isn't good," Lance said to the driver.

"It's traffic," the driver said. "What do you want me to do?"

"How far to the M25?"

"Two more junctions."

"Take us off at the next exit," Lance said. "We need to keep moving."

"Aye, aye," the driver said.

They inched toward the next exit, bumper to bumper, and it was five minutes before they saw the sign for it.

"Here," Lance said. "Take this exit."

"You're the boss," the driver said, pulling into the exiting lane. It was moving better, and the car was able to pick up a little speed. There was a pedestrian overpass ahead, and they got up to about twenty miles-per-hour when Lance suddenly yelled, "Down. Everybody down."

The driver turned to look at him, and in the same instant, a bullet pierced the windshield, shattering the glass in concentric circles in front of his face. The car swerved violently, and Lance grabbed the wheel, steadying the vehicle before it veered off the road completely. Through the shattered glass, he could see nothing.

It was only then that Ada realized the bullet had passed clear through the driver and struck the back seat mere inches from Natasha's head. Ada grabbed Natasha and pulled her down to the floor.

The car veered off the road into the gravel shoulder, and another bullet flew through the windshield, this time right where Lance had been sitting. Lance was already crouched below the level of the dashboard, but the bullet shot clean through his seat. If Ada was still where she'd been, it would have hit her.

"Stay down," Lance yelled as more and more bullets hit the front of the car.

Then they hit something. Airbags filled the cabin, and the car came to a dead stop.

"Keep her down," Lance yelled again, and then he was gone.

———————

60

L ance pushed open the door and climbed out of the car, keeping low as two more bullets clanged against steel. He needed to get to the shooter before one of his shots hit Ada or the kid.

He drew his gun and fired once in the approximate direction of the shooter. There was a concrete barrier running along the grass divider between the exit lane and the motorway. The shooter was on the other side of it, meaning Lance could use it as cover if he could get to it. He fired two more covering shots, then made a dash for it, running out from behind the car and across the traffic lane. Bullets followed him, pelting into the ground and sending chips of stone and dust into the air as he ran and then slid behind the barrier.

As he caught his breath, more bullets struck the top lip of the barrier just inches above his head. Each shot was perfectly placed to hit as close to the corner of the concrete as possible, sending shards flying and the bullet itself ricocheting downward as if rounding the corner.

The shooter was clearly a pro, most likely GRU-trained, his aim as fast and true as any Lance had seen.

For an ambush, the position was perfect. The traffic brought the cars to a near standstill, and the pedestrian bridge provided a raised platform spanning all traffic lanes. Everything was in the attacker's favor. The only details that weren't perfect for the shooter were the position of the exit lane and the concrete barrier which ran along the side of it. It provided Lance with a line of cover leading all the way to the base of one of the bridge's supporting piers.

What Lance couldn't see was how the shooter had known exactly where they'd be or what exact vehicle to target. There must have been some other form of surveillance going on. Perhaps a drone overhead that had followed them from the airport, or even a tracker on the car.

As the bullets continued to hit the concrete, Lance crawled along the length of the barrier, keeping below the sniper's line of sight.

After a few shots, the sniper redirected his fire at the car. Lance reached over the barrier and took a blind shot in his direction. He had to draw his fire and prevent him from focusing on the car, which Ada and the child were still inside.

Lance crawled until he was a few yards from the bridge pier. It was a scaffold of rusty, crisscrossed steel girders and would be as easy to climb as a ladder. The danger was that if the shooter had a line of sight on it, Lance would be easy fodder as soon as he exposed himself.

He reached over the concrete and took another blind shot. A bullet was returned almost instantly, striking the concrete exactly where Lance's hand had been and sending chips of concrete in his face. The shot had definitely come from the bridge.

Lance crawled on until he was at the base of the pier, directly beneath the bridge, and fired again. His bullet hit the underside of the bridge, and this time, no shot was returned. The shooter didn't have an angle on him. However, he would by now have realized the danger and would relocate. If he got a new shooting position on the far bank of the road, he would be able to keep Lance pinned down indefinitely.

On the highway itself, people were in a state of complete panic. The cars had already been bumper to bumper, but now, some of the passengers had begun to abandon the vehicles, preferring to run for cover than sit and wait out the gunfight. Others were trying to pull their vehicles into the shoulder and use it as an extra traffic lane. Their engines revved and growled as the cars, reversing and jerking forward aggressively, struggled to free themselves from their boxed-in positions.

Above the ruckus of engines and car horns, high overhead, Lance noticed a military drone. It must have been following since the airport, and explained how the shooter knew which vehicle to target.

He looked back at the Mercedes. While the shooter had been distracted, Ada had managed to get Natasha out of the car. They were crouched behind it, using it as cover.

"Ada," Lance called out, struggling to get her attention over the noise.

She looked his way.

"I need you to cover me," he called.

Her eyes darted over the chaotic scene, and she called back, "There's too many civilians."

He didn't have time to argue. Any minute, the sniper would get to a new position and pin him down.

He stood up and grabbed hold of the steel pier. Immediately, Ada pulled her gun from her jacket and began firing up toward the shooter's position. She was shooting through the windows of the vehicle, and her bullets knocked out what was left of the shattered glass.

Lance began climbing and was just reaching the top as the sniper's shots began striking the car. Ada's covering fire had pinned him down and prevented him from repositioning. As Lance pulled himself up onto the bridge, bullets began pelting the steel around him. They were from a handgun, not the rifle, and Lance dropped to the ground as Ada continued to provide covering fire.

Lance could see down the length of the bridge to the sniper's position. He was at the far end of it, concealed under a Spyder mesh blanket, the rifle on its tripod aimed at the road.

He fired three more shots in Lance's direction, then got to his feet and ran.

Lance got up and chased after him. At the end of the bridge, the brush opened up into a clearing. A hundred yards ahead of him, Lance saw the man and stopped running. He stretched out his arm, took a breath, steadied his aim, and depressed the trigger.

The shooter stumbled like a felled deer and collapsed to the ground, dropping his pistol as he reached out with both arms to break his fall. As soon as he hit the ground, he immediately began scrambling toward his gun.

"Stop moving," Lance called. "It's not worth it."

The man reached out and put his hand on the gun.

"Don't do it," Lance said.

"Go to hell," the man cried and swung around with the pistol, letting off a shot that was so far wide Lance didn't even know where it went.

Lance aimed and fired again. This time, his shot struck the ground, a few inches from the man's leg.

"Next one hits," Lance said.

The man dropped the gun and began trying to get to his feet. Lance watched him struggle. He was still trying to run.

"If I wanted to kill you, you'd already be dead," Lance said, walking toward him.

The man was still on the ground. He gave up trying to stand and turned to face Lance. "I am already dead," he said.

From his accent, Lance could tell he was Russian. He was a hitman, a soldier following orders, nothing more.

"You're not dead yet," Lance said.

"I will be."

"You mean when the GRU finds out you talked?"

The man spat, not directly at Lance but at the ground, and said, "You're wasting your time. I'm not going to talk."

"We'll see," Lance said.

"Even if I wanted to, there's nothing I know."

"You don't know who your target is?"

"My target is the occupants of your car."

"How many occupants?"

"Three, plus driver. Man, woman, child."

"See," Lance said. "You know more than you think."

"Go fuck yourself," the man said.

"You're in a tight spot," Lance continued. "You didn't just fail your mission. You allowed yourself to be caught. That's the first rule of the GRU. Don't get captured."

The man looked up at the sky.

Lance nodded. "That's right. Your friends, they're watching."

The man tried to get to his feet again, a hopeless gesture, and Lance put his foot on his chest and pushed him back to the ground. "Just talking to me for this long will look suspicious," he said. "For all they know, you're telling me everything."

"Why don't you stop playing games and just finish me off?"

"Maybe I'm an asshole," Lance said. "Maybe I used to kill ants with a magnifying glass when I was a kid." He pointed his gun at the man's knee.

The man shook his head.

"Maybe I want you to make this difficult," Lance said.

The man reached for his pocket, and Lance pulled his hand away.

"I need cigarette," the man said.

Lance reached into the man's pocket for him and pulled out the smokes and a lighter. He gave one to the man, took one for himself, then lit them both.

The man sucked deeply on the cigarette, never taking his eye off Lance.

"What do you want to know?"

"Who gave you the job?"

"GRU gave me job."

"I need a name."

The man sucked the cigarette again. He blew out the smoke.

Lance could see he was going to need a bit more persuading. "Tell me," he said, "what kind of man takes on a contract to kill a nine-year-old girl?"

The man sucked again, hard enough that the ash at the end of the cigarette migrated visibly toward the filter. "I don't pick and choose," he said, tapping the ash to the ground.

"Yeah," Lance said, "well, neither do I." He pointed the gun at the man's knee and said, "What does a bullet cost me? Five cents?"

"If I talk, I'm dead," the man said again.

Lance shook his head. "That's what everyone says," he said, "but really, you're not dead until you're dead." He pulled the trigger.

The gun jerked in his hand at precisely the same time that the man's leg did. To Lance, it seemed like the two were connected, like they were parts of the same organism.

The man let out a long, terrible wail and grabbed his leg like it was an object that didn't belong to him.

Lance moved the gun to the other knee and said, "Ready to go again?"

The man screamed in pain and terror, and Lance grabbed him by the chin and forced him to look him in the eye. "You took a job to kill a little girl," he growled. "I'll do this all day if I have to."

The man began to sob. Finally, his mind accepted what his soul had known for a long time—the end was nigh.

"Lapin," he sobbed. "Viktor Lapin. Main Directorate."

61

Tatyana lay on her back, breathless, staring at the ceiling. It was the middle of the night, and Declan had just left the bed to take a shower. She shouldn't have been there, Laurel had told her as much, but Declan scratched an itch for her that needed scratching. She'd gone so far as to tell Laurel that if Roth wanted to start choosing her sexual partners, he was welcome to do so, but until he made up his mind, she would keep choosing her own.

She heard the shower stop and called out to him. "I should get going?"

"Stay the night," he said.

"I can't."

She'd told Declan nothing about her work, and he never asked. Not once. If anything, it was his lack of interest that was notable. But was it suspicious? Theirs was a very *particular* type of relationship. Declan Haines was a very *particular* type of man. What they did together didn't leave a lot of time for small talk.

Tatyana didn't ask about his life either.

That wasn't because she wasn't interested. She just didn't want him to return the favor. And also, she didn't need to ask. She had all the information on him she could ever want. She knew more about him than he knew about himself—his banking history, tax records, personal and business expenses. She knew where he ate when he traveled for work, where he ordered from when he was at home, what time of night he was most likely to cheat on his diet and call for a pizza. She could have prepared a meal plan for him, down to the last gram of protein and calorie of fat. He wore a smartwatch, which meant she knew where and when he slept, how many hours he got, how much he tossed and turned at night, what his resting heart rate was. She knew his Starbucks order—short americano, extra shot, almond milk. She knew his parents' blood types, what genetic conditions he was susceptible to, how far over the speed limit he drove, and that he didn't like to parallel park.

She knew that he watched far more porn than was normal and that his tastes in that department ran counter to what was generally considered acceptable. Some of his predilections were weird, some disgusting, some disturbing.

She didn't just know the text of his searches, she knew how long it took him to reach orgasm once he started a video. The heart rate and blood pressure data from his smartwatch confirmed the exact moment of climax.

It was startling how much data the NSA could gather on a person. The minutiae of it. The level of detail. People could be married fifty years and not know the things she knew about Declan.

And yet, she hardly knew him at all. He was a collection of data points, surveillance records, spreadsheet columns— nothing more.

She did know he was damaged psychologically. He had

issues, therapists, demons. And yet, as if drawn by some animal magnetism deep within her own psyche, she kept finding herself back in his bed.

She'd vetted every aspect of his life. Laurel and Roth had done the same. There were some skeletons in his closet, some financial irregularities, tax issues, he'd been to Moscow, but most notable was the deviant sexual tendencies. As far as Tatyana was concerned, what he did in his bedroom, and what she did in hers, was not a matter of national security that the CIA needed to concern itself with. She was getting something from the relationship, something she needed, and that was the end of it.

Declan emerged from the bathroom with a towel wrapped around his waist and said, "Is there really nothing I can do to entice you to stay?"

"I wish I could," she lied, throwing on a hotel robe.

She couldn't have stayed even if she'd wanted to. It would have left her too vulnerable. There were too many security considerations.

She went into the bathroom and looked at herself in the mirror.

"Will I see you tomorrow?" he said.

There were marks on her neck from his hands. She was ashamed of them, ashamed of what she was doing with Declan. She knew it said something about her psyche, something she had yet to come to terms with, an unresolved psychological trauma.

She took out a compact and began covering the marks with makeup.

"Tomorrow?" she said. "I'll have to check my calendar."

She watched him in the mirror, then shut the compact and went back into the room.

"I didn't hurt you...."

"I'm fine," she said, looking away.

She passed him without saying goodbye, without giving him a kiss or any sign of affection, and let herself out of the room.

She took the elevator from his floor to the lobby, then transferred to the private penthouse elevator and took it up to the suite.

She opened the door quietly and listened before entering. She went straight to her own room, glad not to see anyone, and took a very long, very hot shower. When she got out, she went back to the living room, where there was a bar fridge full of snacks, and almost bumped into Laurel in the dark.

"Oh, sorry," she said.

"That's okay," Laurel said, looking at her.

"I was just taking a shower."

"Is that what you call it?"

"Don't start."

Laurel raised her hands. "Hey, I didn't say a thing."

Tatyana turned on a lamp and went to the minibar, scanning its contents for something to eat. "You're up late," she said to Laurel.

"I was on the phone to Roth."

"Still in London?" Tatyana said, pulling out a half-bottle of white wine and a packet of candy-coated cashew nuts.

"Still in London," Laurel said.

Tatyana held up the wine. "Want a glass?"

Laurel shrugged. "Just a small one."

Tatyana poured two glasses and handed one to Laurel.

"What's the update from Roth?" she said.

"Well, Lance and Ada were attacked on their way back to the embassy."

"Are they okay?"

"The child's shaken up, but they have a medical team on hand. I think she's speaking to a therapist at the embassy now."

Tatyana nodded. She knew what it was like to lose a parent. So did Laurel. "No amount of therapy ever helped either of us," she said.

Laurel nodded. "No, it didn't."

"Maybe you should recruit her."

Laurel shook her head. "Very funny."

Tatyana sat on the sofa. A fire was still burning in the fireplace, and she stretched her feet toward it. "Did you speak to Lance?"

Laurel said nothing, and Tatyana looked up at her. She shook her head. Tatyana was going to say something but stopped herself.

"If he has anything to say," Laurel said, "he knows how to get hold of me."

Tatyana nodded. "He hasn't called me either," she said.

"You have a boyfriend," Laurel said.

Tatyana smiled flatly. "That's one name for it."

Laurel came over and stood by the fire. "There's something else," she said.

"Oh?"

"Richmond Tenet is at the Russian embassy in Paris."

"The London Station Chief?"

"The one and only."

Tatyana breathed out through her teeth. "Guess we found our rat then."

Laurel nodded.

"Do you know him?" Tatyana said.

"No, but Roth does."

"And?"

"They go back decades, Tatyana."

They both went quiet, then. A defector at this level, the sheer scale of the breach, the assets, the operations, as London Station Chief, Richmond Tenet would have had his fingers in so many pies it would take months just to fully assess the damage.

"They'll be patting themselves on the back in Moscow," Tatyana said. "This is the type of defection they've been seeking for decades."

"It will change everything."

"Will it mean house cleaning here in Washington?"

Laurel nodded. "I think it will have to."

A defector at Richmond Tenet's level was the CIA's worst nightmare. It wasn't just a matter of the raw intelligence he could betray, as damaging as that was, or the insights into US intelligence thinking he would pass on, it was the personal relationships. Every single person close to him would suddenly be under a cloud of suspicion. Aspersions would be cast everywhere. Who had known what? Who should have seen it coming? Whose operations and ways of thinking were most compromised by the breach?

Events like this were inevitably followed by a house cleaning, a purge, a period of bloodletting during which the CIA would inflict more harm on itself than the GRU ever could.

"What will it mean for Roth?"

"It won't be good."

"Will he be recalled?"

"I don't know," Laurel said, "but one thing's for certain. Roth has vouched for Tenet many times in the past."

"That doesn't necessarily mean...."

"He's also had numerous secret meetings with him, going back decades."

"Tenet's the London Station Chief. There are lots of reasons Roth would want to meet secretly with him."

"He hasn't done the same with other station chiefs."

Tatyana nodded.

"Plus, there's the fact that he pulled you off this case. You were the natural choice to bring in Sacha Gazinsky. You said so yourself."

"It should have been me over there," Tatyana agreed. She'd never seen Laurel's face so pale. She was ashen. Roth was her mentor. He was her everything. Losing faith in him would have felt like losing faith in a father.

"Ordinarily, I'd have given him the benefit of the doubt," Laurel said.

"But now?"

Laurel shook her head. "I don't know," she said quietly.

Tatyana picked up her glass of wine and downed the contents. She saw that Laurel had done the same and refilled both their glasses with what was left in the bottle. "So?" she said. "Where does this leave us?"

"I know I have no right to ask this of you," Laurel said.

"Consider it done."

"It will be dangerous, Tatyana."

"I know that."

"I'd go myself, but...."

"You don't want Roth to know," Tatyana said, finishing her sentence.

Laurel nodded, almost imperceptibly, and said, "I never thought it would come to this."

62

Declan Haines stood in front of the mirror, staring at his face, seeing nothing in the reflection but a monster. Increasingly, he fantasized about his own death. He imagined in excruciating detail the moment when the lights would go out. Would he feel it? Would he know it was happening? He imagined it as an emptiness, an obliteration, a void. And he craved it.

But he didn't do anything about it. Instead, he went about his business, made more and more money, and followed to the most precise detail the instructions that Viktor Lapin sent from Moscow.

There was something about this mission from Viktor, the targeting of a Russian defector, that Declan found immensely compelling. In fact, if it wasn't for the mission, he was quite sure he would have already ended his life.

He truly was a man with nothing to lose, and Tatyana Aleksandrova was like no one he'd ever met before. He had an uncanny ability to read people, to sense in them the weaknesses and frailties that existed in his own psyche, but she was something else. She was a black box. A mystery.

He knew very well that he was playing with fire. He knew exactly how dangerous a game it was. But he'd already decided that if his life was to end, she was as good an executioner as any.

Now, when he imagined the moment of his death, it wasn't his own finger that pulled the trigger, it was hers, and the last image to flash across the cells in his retinas would be her face.

He looked around the bathroom, searching for anything she might have left behind. Viktor had instructed him to do that. He checked the garbage can, the cabinet beneath the sink, the water tank behind the toilet. He checked around the shower, the faucet, the folds of each towel on the heated towel rack. He unscrewed the light figures, the light bulbs, and the other electrical fittings with a small screwdriver and checked that nothing had been left behind.

It was all clear, as it always was. In the time he'd known her, Tatyana hadn't left so much as a Q-tip behind.

He went to the bedroom and repeated the process, practically dismantling the bed, removing the sheets and covers, opening every drawer, flipping the mattress.

He did such a comprehensive job, and so consistently, that he'd had to bring the hotel's housekeeping staff in on it. By the time he was done, the room looked like it had been ransacked by burglars. He picked up the phone.

"This is Declan Haines in 403."

"Ah, yes, Mr. Haines," the concierge said knowingly.

The staff all thought he was some sort of freak—the man who overturned his entire room every night—but the alternative was to tidy it himself, an option he'd never seriously considered.

"Send housekeeping up."

"Sir, they're not on the premises until five in the morning."

"I spoke to your colleague about getting a special service."

"Ah, yes, sir, of course. There is a special fee for that."

"You'll get your fee," Declan said and hung up.

He took out his wallet and counted out two hundred-dollar bills, and left them on the bedside table for the ladies. Then he took out another five bills and put them in an envelope.

He put on some clothes, his hotel slippers, and left the room for the bar in the lobby. Viktor would be expecting his report.

The elevator dinged its arrival at the lobby, and he went to the concierge and handed the man the envelope.

"Ah, Mr. Haines, housekeeping is on its way."

"Good," Declan said. "I have a small bag in the hotel safe."

The man scanned the register and said, "Of course, Mr. Haines. Would you like me to get it for you?"

Declan nodded, and the man left and came back a moment later with a Louis Vuitton leather portfolio.

"Can you get someone to open the bar for me," he said, taking the bag.

"Right away," the concierge said, and Declan went into the empty bar and took his usual seat in the corner.

It was next to a fireplace, but at this time of night, it was never lit. There was no one there other than Declan, but a hotel of this level prided itself on catering to its guests every whim. That meant if you wanted a bartender in the middle of the night, you got one.

He sat down and exhaled slowly, steadying his breath. He didn't enjoy speaking to Viktor and needed to steel himself for it. The bartender arrived, and Declan raised a finger and made a little circular motion. The bartender nodded and a moment later arrived with a perfectly mixed old-fashioned. Declan charged it to the room and then leaned back in the chair and took a sip.

He opened the portfolio the concierge had given him from the safe and took a phone from it. He didn't own the phone. He didn't know who it was registered to. All he knew was that Viktor had sent it.

He dialed the number and waited.

"Declan," Viktor said, his voice sounding more distant than usual.

"The signal's bad," Declan said.

"It's my end. I'm not in Moscow."

"Where are you?"

"Nowhere that concerns you."

"Well," Declan said, "she was no different tonight than any of the others. It was straight to business. In and out with minimal conversation."

"She had nothing with her?"

"She didn't bring a purse. She didn't bring a phone. She brought nothing but a small makeup compact, and she didn't leave that behind. I searched the room from top to bottom."

"What about clothing?"

"Just lingerie and a hotel robe."

"Did you search the robe?"

"There was a room key in the pocket. Nothing else."

"She took it with her when she left?"

"Yes. She took everything."

"What about the soap and shampoo from the hotel."

"I check every bottle after she leaves."

"And they're normal?"

"They're normal."

"Did she sleep?"

"She never sleeps."

"So you just fuck, and she leaves?"

"You've seen the video."

"No small talk? No wine?"

"I tried," Declan said. "I left her alone in the bedroom during my shower. You have the video. You tell me if she did anything suspicious."

Viktor sighed. "She's a real fucking freak, isn't she?"

"She is what she is," Declan said.

"She likes it rough."

"A lot of people like it rough."

Viktor let out a hollow, mirthless laugh. "No, they don't, Declan. Not that rough. It's just the freaks like you that like it that way."

"Well, they're not hard to find."

"She takes it farther than most," Viktor said.

"Maybe."

"Sometimes, I think you're going to kill her."

Declan had thought the same thing, more than once. There was some trauma in her past, something she was intent in reliving, over and over, until she'd made sense of it. She always wanted it tighter and tighter, longer and longer, until he feared it might go too far.

"I'm not going to kill her."

"But you could."

"No."

"I've seen your tape, Declan. I know what you're capable of."

"That's not the man I am."

"People don't change, Declan. Once a monster, always a monster."

"That was a mistake."

"Was it?"

"Yes, it was," he said.

"Well, I think the time has come for you to return to your old tricks, Declan."

"What are you talking about?"

"When are you seeing her next?"

"I don't know."

"Well, make it soon, Declan. Make it very soon."

"I'll try, Viktor. She can be hard to get hold of."

"She'll be back, Declan. Like a fly on shit, she'll be back for more."

"And when she is...."

"When she is, I want you to take it all the way."

"What does that mean?"

"You know what it means."

"You want me to...."

"Yes."

"Kill her?"

"It's nothing you haven't done before."

"She's CIA, Viktor."

"You can make it look like an accident."

"An accident? A strangulation? Are you crazy?"

"Don't worry. I'll have a plane ready for your extraction as soon as its done."

"I don't want an extraction."

"What you want isn't a factor, Declan."

"Viktor, I can't do this. I swore to myself...."

"Listen very carefully, Declan. Not only will you do this for me, but you'll enjoy it, you sick, twisted...."

Declan was about to tell Viktor where he could go when the hotel's penthouse elevator dinged. The door opened, and out walked Tatyana.

Declan immediately ducked behind the seat in front of him and hissed into the phone, "Viktor, she's here. She's here."

"What?"

"Tatyana, she's here."

"Where?"

"I'm in the lobby."

"What?"

"I'm in the lobby. She hasn't seen me. She's walking over to the concierge."

"What is she saying?"

"I can't hear her."

"Don't let her see you."

Declan remained absolutely still. He was watching her through a gap between the armchair in front of him and the wall. On one shoulder, she was carrying a leather overnight bag. The concierge called for the bellhop. The bellhop took the bag from her and brought it outside to a waiting cab.

She was going somewhere.

The concierge handed her an envelope. She opened it and took out whatever it contained before passing it back to him. Then she followed the bellhop out to the cab.

"She's gone," Declan said.

"Gone where?"

"Into a cab."

Viktor was silent for a moment, then said, "Is there another cab?"

"No."

"Can you find one?"

"She's already gone, Viktor."

"Fuck."

"Can't you track the cab from above?" Declan said. "One of your drones?"

"She had luggage?"

"She had a bag, yes."

"She's going to one of the airports."

"The concierge gave her something."

"What did he give her?"

"Hang on," Declan said. "I'll call you back."

Declan's pulse raced as he got up and approached the concierge's desk. If Tatyana returned for any reason and saw him there, she'd think he was spying on her.

"Is my room ready?" he said to the concierge.

"I believe they're still working on it, sir."

Declan leaned on the counter and looked down at the concierge's desk. The envelope he'd given Tatyana was right there, and on the front, embossed in gold leaf, was written in an elegant script, "La Péninsule".

The concierge saw him look at it and quickly grabbed it, putting it inside his jacket pocket. "Is there something else, Mr. Haines?"

"No," Declan said. He went back to his seat in the bar and called Viktor immediately.

"Does La Péninsule mean anything to you?" he said when Viktor picked up.

"La Péninsule?" Viktor said, and from his tone of voice, Declan could tell that he knew exactly what it was. "It's just a few blocks from our Embassy in Paris," he said. "It's a hotel."

"Then I think you know where she's headed," Declan said.

63

Tatyana was the only passenger on a government jet from Andrews Air Force Base to Orly Airport south of Paris. She fell asleep soon after takeoff, but at some point during the flight, turbulence woke her.

She rubbed her eyes and got up to stretch her legs. There was a coffee urn on a servery behind her seat, and she poured herself a cup. Her mind went to the last time she'd been on a plane, the flight with Roth to London and the huge fight they'd had.

She'd known then that something wasn't right. Sacha Gazinsky was *so* valuable, *so* important, and Tatyana had such a strong existing relationship with him. He wasn't just an acquaintance, she'd slept with him. She knew what he wanted, who he was, what motivated him. But Roth ordered her back to Washington and got Laurel to find someone else to bring him in—a completely untested, inexperienced recruit from the London office.

Everything that followed, the shootings in London and Edinburgh, Sacha Gazinsky's death, Lance being called in to clean up the mess and bring Natasha in safely, was a direct result of that order.

Roth couldn't have orchestrated a bigger shitshow if he'd tried.

That was suspicious.

And now, one of his oldest colleagues at the Agency, a man he had secret meetings with, a man he'd gone to bat for multiple times, had just defected to the Russians.

That was suspicious.

Things like this didn't just come out of nowhere. Tatyana knew. She'd been through it. In the years leading up to Tenet's defection, there would have been signs, questionable decisions, unexplained intelligence leaks, lucky breaks for the Russians that couldn't just be coincidence. Roth must have been there to see them, and they should have set alarm bells ringing immediately.

But no bells were rung.

In fact, according to Laurel, Roth staunchly defended Tenet whenever someone tried to scrutinize his actions.

This whole thing was fishy.

She went back to her seat and flipped open the file Laurel had given her. Her mission wasn't complicated. Tenet, the London Station Chief, was a sixty-nine-year-old man with high blood pressure and a penchant for taking an umbrella with him whenever he left the house. He was American, had a wife of near forty years who was Israeli, and a Bedlington Terrier named Winston.

His location had been confirmed by Keyhole satellite at the Russian Embassy in Paris, a building Tatyana had the benefit of being personally familiar with.

She would have to be careful when she got there. She knew how the embassy's facial recognition system worked. If she walked through the door undisguised, the whole place would be on lockdown before she was halfway across the lobby. There were flaws in the software, however, serious limitations in its algorithm, that she knew exactly how to exploit.

She brought her hand to her neck and touched the bruises. They were sore, and it was getting to the point that she would need more than concealer to hide them.

Her relationship with Declan had reached a plateau. Either she did something now to end it, or she would end up going down a rabbit hole of deviant behavior that she might not reemerge from. She knew what she had to do. As soon as she got back to DC, she would tell him.

In any case, if she didn't end it soon, Laurel surely would. A one-night stand, even a brief fling, was one thing. That, within reason, would be tolerated. Everyone needed to blow off steam once in a while.

But an ongoing relationship, even one as transactional as what she had with Declan, was something else entirely. It raised a completely different set of security concerns, created a much wider array of vulnerabilities.

They said to keep your friends close and your enemies closer. For Tatyana, it was never that simple. For her, everyone, whether friend or foe, had to be kept at a distance. No one could get close. Least of all, someone like Declan. On paper, he had impeccable credentials. He even contracted for the DoD and had a government security clearance. But the more Tatyana got to know of his private life, the more worried she'd become. He was more than a deviant. She increasingly suspected that the pornography he watched, and perhaps some of the things that he'd done behind closed doors, weren't just questionable but actually crossed the line into the illegal. She hadn't seen proof yet, but her suspicions were growing.

.

Yes, there was no question. She had to end it. There were other ways for her to *let off steam,* so to speak.

The plane landed, and she stepped out into a misty Paris morning. The temperature was about the same as in Washington, and, for once, she was dressed appropriately in heels and a waist-length black Burberry coat. There was a BMW sedan waiting for her on the runway, and she descended the steps and got into the back seat.

"Madame?" the driver said.

"La Péninsule," she said.

Driving through the streets of Paris brought back a lot of memories for her. When she was with the GRU, she'd spent more than her share of time there. The city was a perennial haunt of the Russian oligarchy, and very often, Igor Aralov sent her there to catch a target with his guard, and pants, down.

The cab pulled up outside the hotel, and she got out. She didn't need to check-in, she'd had the concierge at the Saint Royal do that for her before leaving Washington. The two hotels were sisters, and he'd even been able to program a room key for her.

Because of its proximity to the embassy, it was perfect for conducting her operation, but it also meant there was a small chance of her running into someone who might recognize her.

She hurried through the lobby, past the white marble concierge desk with its enormous vases of fresh flowers, straight to the elevators. She'd always liked this hotel, its sense of style, its classic Parisian elegance. A maid in a black and white dress was dusting the crystal wall sconces by the elevator with a feather duster. There wasn't a thing about her that was out of place, from her uniform, to the way her hair was tied back, to the way she moved discreetly from one sconce to the next. To Tatyana, it felt as if the entire place, including the maid, had been transported wholesale from the palace at Versailles.

In her room, a wide set of glass doors ran the entire width of the balcony. They were draped in sheer lace that swayed like water when she opened the doors. She went out to the balcony and lit a cigarette.

The view was stunning, looking out at Montmartre in the distance, the Basilica of the Sacré-Cœur commanding the hilltop. She stood out there in the cold, smoking until the bellhop arrived with her bag.

Then she went inside and put the bag on the bed. Its contents were simple—a pair of black yoga pants, a black spandex bodysuit, black sneakers, and a hairband. She laid out the clothes, which would make her look like a jogger, and made sure nothing was missing. When she was satisfied, she checked the time, then set an alarm for two hours and lay down on the bed.

When she woke up, it was just beginning to get dark. She picked up the phone and ordered room service. She ate on the bed, looking out over the balcony at the lights of the city, and when she was done, she went into the bathroom and used ordinary cosmetics to adjust her appearance in ways that she knew the Russian facial recognition system had trouble processing. Then she put on the black clothing, a pair of black leather gloves and her coat, and left the room.

64

Tatyana walked purposefully down Avenue Foch toward Porte Dauphine. She passed a park, some public tennis courts, and an outdoor swimming pool that was closed for the season before rounding onto Boulevard Lannes. On her right, a high iron fence marked the outer boundary of the expansive grounds around the Embassy of the Russian Federation.

She didn't have a gun with her. She planned to walk right into the consular section of the embassy through the front door. A gun would have been more liability than asset.

The compound had been built in the seventies by Leonid Brezhnev's government and was far more modern and open than other Soviet buildings of the era. There had been an impression inside the Kremlin at the time that France might prove friendlier to Soviet overtures than other NATO states. When designs were being drawn up for the new embassy, the selection was made with an explicit eye on impressing the French public and improving relations with Paris.

It was designed by one of the most respected architects in Moscow and was to be a showcase of the benefits of modern socialism and its superiority as an economic model. As a result, a number of uncharacteristic concessions were made to aesthetics rather than the Kremlin's usual obsession with security and intimidation.

Brezhnev himself attended the dedication ceremony in 1977 and even conducted a tour of the complex. Playing the role of tour guide personally, he took journalists, photographers, and a number of French dignitaries through the secure diplomatic quarters, the consular office, an art gallery containing many of the Soviet Union's most in-vogue artists, four public event spaces, a concert hall, and even a model elementary school for the children of embassy staff.

For that reason, even if Tatyana hadn't been acquainted with the layout of the compound already, she would have been able to get everything she needed for the operation from public sources.

Immediately behind the consular section was a residential compound containing three apartment blocks. They'd been built to rival, in terms of comfort and design, anything then available to ordinary citizens in the West. They were square buildings, four stories high, with open courtyards at the center for a communal garden and children's play area.

The apartments embodied a strange mix of traditional, almost tsarist decorative elements, such as wall tapestries and marble columns, with what the Soviet Industrial Design Institute of the day regarded as the very cutting edge of modern luxury. They were an act of architectural propaganda, a showcase of luxury and quality that never actually existed inside the Soviet Union.

But they also served a more practical purpose.

The Kremlin quickly realized that staff housing was a powerful tool for maintaining control over embassy staff stationed abroad. Defections were at an all-time high, and they were more than just a source of embarrassment and threat to morale. They challenged the very credibility of the Soviet system as a viable alternative to capitalism. If Russians jumped ship every time they got the chance, what did that say about the system they lived under?

The government saw that by providing embassy employees with housing, and their children with schooling, defection became significantly more difficult to pull off.

All things considered, the Paris Embassy had been a success for the Kremlin. It improved French perceptions of Russia significantly, at a key juncture in the Cold War, while simultaneously increasing Kremlin control over its diplomats.

But it came at a cost.

The entire embassy compound was significantly less secure than it would otherwise have been, and Tatyana knew exactly where the weaknesses were and how to exploit them.

The perimeter of the compound was officially protected by Russian soldiers, but for political reasons, they were rarely on display. Instead, the bulk of the security was provided by the Russian Federal Security Service, known as the FSB, with guards who wore civilian-style uniforms.

From across the street, Tatyana watched two FSB guards as they loosely supervised foot traffic in and out of the main consulate entrance. It was just after dark, and the office workers were clocking off for the evening while nighttime staff showed up for their shifts. Tatyana joined them and passed through the metal detectors and initial security check by flashing a false employee identity card.

The lobby of the consular section was open to the public and served as a sort of cultural center, promoting life and business in modern Russia. There was a reception desk for directing visitors, a coffee stand, and a gift shop selling books, gifts, and other kitschy Russian paraphernalia.

The gift shop had closed for the night, but the coffee stand was still open. Behind the reception desk, a set of glass doors led to a central courtyard, where access to the secure portions of the compound was controlled. Two guards manned a more robust security check there, complete with airport-style x-ray scanners and metal detectors. In the other direction, a corridor led to public washrooms and a number of event spaces.

Tatyana went to the coffee stand and bought herself a coffee. There was a black leather bench near the stand, and she sat on it and sipped the coffee, getting her bearings. A number of security cameras scanned the lobby, and she counted four guards in their toned-down FSB uniforms. They were highly trained and fully prepared to use lethal force, but they looked like the private security guards at a shopping mall.

Behind the scenes, she knew there was also a substantial GRU presence in the compound. They oversaw active operations in France and beyond but also provided additional security for the embassy.

Tatyana, of course, had worked for the GRU, and there was a chance of her running into someone she'd worked with. She'd already killed every man in Moscow she'd been personally answerable to, but there was a handful of other officers and agents who might still have recognized her. Laurel had sent her a list of GRU personnel currently stationed in Paris, and none of the names were familiar, but she was acutely aware of the risk she was running.

The GRU did not look fondly on defectors, to put it mildly, and she'd just walked right into their lair.

She finished her coffee and threw the cup in the trash, then went down the corridor to the public washroom, where she entered a stall and shut the door behind her. She didn't lock it. She had to wait a minute for someone else to leave, then climbed up onto the seat of the toilet, then the water tank, and pushed one of the ceiling panels up off its frame. The panel was made of a textured, manufactured product that was both fire-retardant and sound-attenuating. It was a thick, cardboard-like substrate that would not be able to hold her weight.

Each panel was held in place on a steel frame that was suspended with steel cables from a concrete ceiling about two feet higher up. The cables were capable of holding a weight of one-hundred-twenty kilos each. As long as she kept her weight on the frame and not on the actual panels, she would be able to move around without falling through the ceiling.

She pulled herself up onto the frame and replaced the open panel behind her. She wasn't a moment too soon. The second she replaced the panel, someone entered the bathroom.

Tatyana remained completely still while she waited for whoever it was to leave, then she took off her coat and left it on the panel she'd just climbed through.

The crawlspace was dark, with no light other than what came through cracks between some of the panels. From the cracks of light, she could just about make out where she was going. She could also tell if the room immediately below her was occupied or not.

Moving extremely carefully, she began climbing along the steel frame, inching forward, avoiding putting weight on the panels. It took her fifteen minutes to progress as many yards, at which point she came up against the cinderblock wall that marked the edge of the women's washroom. She knew from the schematics that it was a structural wall that stretched from the outer perimeter of the building all the way to the central courtyard. Along it, the steel ceiling frame was supported by a large steel beam bolted to the wall. The beam was a foot wide at the top, and she crawled along it for a hundred yards without reaching a cross wall.

She passed over offices, storage rooms, and other private staff areas, some empty, some occupied. At one point, she was just a few feet above the heads of a group of FSB guards who were taking a break. The slightest sound would have alerted them to her presence. The slightest slip would have sent her crashing through the ceiling to the ground below.

She proceeded extremely carefully, in absolute silence, until a brick wall barred her way. She put the back of her hand against it. As expected, it was cold. That meant it was the exterior wall to the courtyard. She stopped moving and held her breath, listening. She knew there were ventilation outlets along that wall. They were covered on the outside by a steel grate and on the inside by a wire mesh and air filter that made them difficult to see. She shut her eyes, remained still, and listened. On her skin, she felt the faint trace of a cool breeze and concentrated on where it was coming from. She followed it until she was face to face with an opening in the wall that was two feet by two feet.

There was no light coming through, but the cool air left her in no doubt that it led outside. She pulled the mesh and air filter away, revealing the grate, and then pushed against that to see if it budged. It did not. She felt around the edges of it to see how it was fastened, but it was held in place from the outside. She leaned back and put her feet against it, and pushed as hard as she could. It still didn't move. She put both feet against a single slat of the grate, a three-inch wide sheet of medium-grade steel plate, and exerted all her pressure on that. It began to bend. She pushed harder until it bent enough to slip out of its housing, falling to the ground outside.

She held her breath as it hit the ground with a dull thud. It left in its place an opening in the grate two inches wide, and she held her face up to it and peered out.

She was looking at the central courtyard. There were small lights along the pathways that lead through a landscaped garden, and more light spilled from the windows of the surrounding offices and rooms.

There were no guards.

She broke five more of the slats, one at a time, then squeezed through the opening and dropped to the ground. She lay flat against the ground, face down in the snow, and remained completely still. Much of the embassy looked out on the courtyard, and Tatyana, in her black clothes, would show against the white snow even in dim light if anyone was looking out.

When she was certain she hadn't been seen, she very slowly began to crawl toward a large bed of shrubs. The plants were bare and had been trimmed back for winter but still provided some cover. She moved along the side of the shrub bed until she was close to the center of the courtyard. From there, the plants ended, and it was open ground to the other side of the courtyard. Directly across from her, there was an opening in the ground floor. The upper floors continued overhead, creating a sort of tunnel. Through that tunnel, she could reach the section of the compound that contained the staff residences.

It was there that she knew the GRU reserved a number

of apartments for their own purposes. That was where she would find Tenet.

She watched the opening. She was about to make a run for it when suddenly, bright floodlights came on, washing the entire courtyard in light.

65

Tenet sat at the counter and looked into his cup of tea. This was it, his new life.

He was in a Soviet-built apartment. It felt like the set of a seventies spy movie but was comfortable enough. Serviceable. Mid-century modern, they would have called it in the magazines.

The armchairs had stainless steel ashtrays built into the arms of the seat that could be revealed and retracted at the touch of a button. The shower had a built-in radio. There were many features like that, the height of luxury for the day, he supposed, though they felt to Tenet more like artifacts from another planet.

He'd crossed a threshold to a new world.

He could still see through the window, out over the fence of the embassy complex, the skyline of one of the world's greatest cities. Paris, with all its culture and history, its restaurants and bars, its thousands of cafés serving cognac and foie gras until the early hours of the morning, were right there.

And yet, they were forever out of reach.

He could see that world, but he would never touch it again for as long as he lived.

He was on the other side now, and there would be no crossing back.

He would have luxuries. Cuban tobacco, caviar, fine wine, champagne, all he had to do was tell his handler, and it would be brought right to him. Even women would be brought if he asked. That much had already been made clear by the handler. The stern GRU officer in a prim black suit delivered a briefing on his arrival that reassured him that his every desire, his every whim, was in her power to grant.

"We look after our own," she'd said. "Like the devil."

He'd done well, she said. He'd served the Motherland. And now, he would receive his reward.

He might know a measure of freedom someday, when he was in Moscow and the fear of reprisal by the CIA had faded, but for now, he couldn't leave the compound. He couldn't even leave the apartment. The CIA was aware of his defection, and it would not be long before they tracked him to Paris.

"We can't guarantee your safety until we get you back to Moscow," the handler had said.

"What about inside this compound?" he asked.

"The embassy is hallowed ground," she said without a hint of irony. "It is protected by every law and custom of diplomacy. Coming after you here would start a war."

Tenet doubted very much that anyone would go to war over him, traitor that he was. He also doubted that the GRU could guarantee his safety anywhere, law and custom notwithstanding.

"In fact," the woman said, "because of the diplomatic

status of this compound, you are probably safer here than you will ever be in Moscow."

She said it as if she expected the words to be a comfort to him. He'd merely smiled. "You're saying I'll be fair game in Moscow," he said.

"You're a traitor, Mr. Tenet," she said then. "What did you expect?"

And that was it, that was the hero's welcome he'd been promised. That was the fruit of his decades of risk.

Although he supposed he should have expected it. He knew how it all worked, how defectors were treated on both sides of the fence, and he knew what their survival rate was. He'd personally handled over a dozen high-profile Russians who'd sought to cross the line. He knew survival depended on two things. How good they were at staying off the radar, and how much personal insult the GRU had taken as a result of their defection. Both were hard things to predict. He'd seen extremely valuable scientific and cultural defections that had barely raised an eyebrow inside the Kremlin. And then he'd seen relatively low-value business and intelligence defectors who'd been hunted so viciously that they never stood a chance.

Tenet was well aware of the risks. He'd taken on this mission a very long time ago, in full knowledge of what he was getting himself into. And while he knew that the CIA would treat his defection very seriously, he also knew that Roth would do his utmost to keep him out of harm's way. There were limits to what Roth could do without raising suspicions, but, combined with the Kremlin's protection, it should be enough to keep him breathing.

What scared Tenet wasn't the CIA. The danger was, as it had always been, squarely from the direction of the Kremlin. If Viktor or one of his bosses so much as suspected the slightest whiff of what Roth and Tenet were really up to, it would be a very gristly end for him indeed.

He sipped his tea and wondered what the future held. How long would he last in this new world? How much value would he be able to siphon back to Roth? How much of a difference would his sacrifice make, when all was said and done?

The hardest part was leaving Alona behind. It wasn't just that he would never see her again, he could almost have accepted that, if only he could have told her the truth. The way it stood, she would think he was a traitor and a liar as much as anyone else. She would think that he'd kept this from her all these decades. She would think he'd chosen to abandon her and that their marriage had been nothing more than cover, a sham, a lie.

He'd even toyed, at times, with the idea of bringing her with him.

But he knew it wouldn't have worked. She loved him, in her own way, but not enough to follow him to Moscow.

He pictured her receiving the news that he was gone. Surely she'd heard by now. Had she received an envelope? A phone call? Had she seen it in the news?

No, he thought.

The news would be delivered in person, and it would be delivered by Levi Roth. Tenet had always known there was something between them. A history. A broken heart. He'd never been as blind to their relationship as he'd let on.

But he'd accepted it. He'd come to terms with it. It was a price he was willing to pay to be the man who lay next to Alona every night.

For Roth, though, this was a second chance. His only rival for Alona's heart, his only obstacle back to her, would be suddenly gone. Roth had let her slip through his fingers all those years ago, but now, by some strange bend in the arc of fate, a twist in the karma of the world, it would be Tenet's sacrifice that gave Roth a chance to win her back.

It was a byproduct of the plan, an unintended consequence, but not for the first time, Tenet wondered how unintentional it really was. He pushed the thought from his mind. He knew Roth better than that, he told himself. Levi Roth was a better man than that.

But then, was any man really better than any other?

Was any of them above the lowest of them?

He sipped his tea and was just thinking of turning in for the night when the bright floodlights overlooking the consular section came on. He went to the balcony and pulled aside the lace curtain. There didn't seem to be any activity outside, and after about a minute, the lights went back out. But then a knock came on his door.

The door opened without waiting for him, and his handler stepped inside.

"It's them, isn't it?" Tenet said.

She nodded.

He was surprised. This was a very swift response. The CIA wasn't in the habit of making knee-jerk reactions. They preferred to let the dust settle, to understand the situation, before moving in for the kill. The thought crossed his mind again that this was all some sort of twisted plan of Roth's. Surely he should have been able to hold off this attack.

Tenet looked at his handler. "You don't seem surprised," he said.

It was then that he noticed movement outside. The handler had come over to the balcony and stood next to him. She made a hand signal out the window, and Tenet saw that there were guards out there, waiting.

She had a transmitter on her wrist, and she spoke into it. "Package secure."

Tenet listened as the replies came back to her.

"Corridor secure."

"Building secure."

"Perimeter secure."

"We should leave," he said, but from the look on her face, he realized that wasn't what was going to happen.

"We'll be fine right here," she said.

He looked out the window again. There were dozens of men out there, waiting. "You're setting a trap," he said.

She nodded. "We're setting a trap, and you're the bait."

66

Lance was in a conference room in the embassy. He stood by the window. Outside, a mist rose off the Thames, making the MI6 building across the river look farther away than it was.

The door opened, and Ada came in with two cups of coffee.

"How is she?" Lance said.

"She's sleeping now."

"What did the therapist say?"

"That it will take time."

Lance nodded. "That's all they ever say."

"Are you speaking from experience?"

He looked away, out the window again, and Ada cleared her throat. She handed him his coffee and sat at the table. "Roth will be here in a few minutes," she said.

Lance nodded absently and sipped his coffee. Ada did the same. A silence filled the room until she broke it by saying, "Nice view."

He nodded again, then said, "I never could get into the Bond movies, though."

"I'm shocked," she said. "I thought those movies were a prerequisite for CIA recruitment."

Lance shrugged. "He's always so pleased with himself. He's too slick. Too glamorous."

"You have something against glamor?"

He looked at her. "Depends."

"I'm thinking," she said, and she eyed him up and down, "that you're more of a Jason Bourne man."

He took a long sip of his coffee. "Now you're talking my language."

The conference room was separated from the rest of the office by glass walls, and Lance looked out at the people working. There were desks and cubicles for twenty CIA analysts. By the elevator, there was a reception desk, and next to that were some offices for senior staff and the Station Chief.

The whole floor was abuzz with activity. First, the news had come in that Tenet was missing, and then the rumor began to spread that he was at the Russian embassy in Paris. If it was what it looked like, it was the biggest CIA defection in decades, and this small office was ground zero.

Roth was there, of course, and a phalanx of officials was already *en route* from Washington. In a couple of hours, the place would have the look and feel of a battle station under fire.

At that moment, Roth was in the Station Chief's office, speaking to the new man, Tenet's replacement, bringing him up to speed on as many open loops as possible.

"Your boss chose a fine moment to disappear," Lance said.

Ada looked at him, then down at her coffee. "He didn't disappear. He defected."

"He almost got you killed, didn't he?"

"More than once," she said. "And he's the reason Sacha Gazinsky's dead."

"He'll get what's coming to him," Lance said. "Mark my words."

"He better," she said.

Lance wasn't sure what Richmond Tenet deserved. All he knew was that things were definitely not as they appeared to be.

He sipped his coffee. There was something he wanted to say to Ada, he'd been wanting to say it for some time, but there never seemed to be a good moment. He decided now was as good a time as any.

"I was at the embassy in Moscow," he said.

She looked up at him and didn't immediately realize what he was saying. "When?" she said.

"When it was attacked."

"Oh," she said, and a sudden look of pain crossed her face.

"I thought you should know."

She shook her head. "It's got nothing to do with me."

Lance nodded, but he knew it did have something to do with her. According to the State Department, her mother had been killed in the blast.

"I just wanted to say I'm sorry."

"Why would you be sorry?" she said, and he could see that it had been a mistake to bring it up. It was too raw—too recent.

"I shouldn't have said anything," he said.

She took a sip of her coffee and said, "I'm sorry."

"It's okay."

"I guess I haven't quite...."

"Processed it?"

She nodded.

"I shouldn't have brought it up. I just thought you should know I was there."

"I did know," she said. "I saw the Keyhole surveillance."

He nodded.

"There was nothing you could have done."

"I could have...."

"What? Saved everyone?" She shook her head.

It wasn't the first time someone had said that to him in recent days. "Well, for the record," he said, "there's nothing more you could have done for Sacha Gazinsky either."

She shrugged, looked at her watch. "He's taking his sweet time in there," she said.

Lance finished his coffee and said, "You want a refill?"

She nodded, and he took both of their cups out to the reception. The receptionist told him she'd make a fresh pot and bring it into the conference room when it was ready. He went back into the conference room and sat at the table across from Ada.

She looked at him with a vacant gaze in her eyes, practically staring, her mind a million miles away. "What is it?" he said.

She shook her head, bringing herself back to the present. "Natasha," she said. "She's not safe here, is she?"

Lance shook his head. "The GRU's going to keep coming after her."

"They won't ever let it drop."

"It's against their religion to let something drop. Sacha humiliated them. They made him head of a hugely important program, and he threw it back in their face."

"He did it for his daughter."

"And that is precisely why they won't let her live. She's the reason for his betrayal. She symbolizes the insult.

SAUL HERZOG

They're going to come at her again and again until someone gets through."

"And we can't be there to protect her forever," Ada said.

"No," Lance said. "Not forever."

She nodded. The receptionist entered with a fresh pot of coffee and poured them each a cup. "He's on his way," she said, putting the pot in the center of the table.

"Thanks," Lance said.

They waited for her to leave, and Ada said, "I made Sacha a promise."

Lance nodded.

"He didn't care what happened to himself. The only thing he wanted was to save Natasha. Her protection was the only condition of the deal he was making with the government."

"If that's the case," Lance said, "we might still be able to get it for him."

"She was all that mattered," Ada said. "He must have said it a hundred times."

They could see Roth approaching from across the office. He was alone, and Ada stood up as he entered the room.

"Don't get up," Roth said, motioning for her to sit back down. He looked at Lance. "What would it take for you to show respect like that?"

"You want me to stand?" Lance said.

Roth ignored him and took his seat.

"If you want me to stand, just say the word, boss."

Roth leaned forward and shook Ada's hand.

"This is your first time meeting?" Lance said.

Roth nodded. "I'm sorry it couldn't be under better circumstances."

Lance turned to Ada. "The circumstances don't ever get better."

Ada cleared her throat. "Mr. Director," she said. "I'm sorry for what happened."

Roth shook his head. "Nonsense," he said. "I'm the one who should be apologizing. It wasn't your fault. It was ours."

"I was the one there."

"You were being sabotaged by your own side. It's a miracle you made it this far."

"I wish I could say the same for Sacha Gazinsky."

"Sacha Gazinsky knew the risk he was taking when he decided to defect," Roth said. "He knew what would happen if they caught up to him."

Ada nodded. "It wasn't for himself that he did it."

"No," Roth said. "I read your report."

"The child, Natasha, needs an experimental therapy," Ada said.

"For a rare genetic condition," Roth said, scanning through the report which he had in front of him.

"The only hospital that can treat her is in Boston," Ada said.

Roth nodded. "Hannson, right? The State Department is reaching out to him."

"Without that treatment, she'll suffer a lot."

"There are a lot of sick children in the world," Roth said.

Lance spoke up for the first time. "What does that mean?"

Roth sighed. "Come on, Lance. Don't give me a hard time over this."

"Over what? A child's life?"

"You know this is out of my hands."

"You were all over it when there were weapons blueprints to be had."

"Lance, we're not Child Services. I don't make the rules."

"So we're just going to throw her to the wolves? Let the GRU get her and make an example of her?"

"If she still had something to bargain with," Roth said.

"Sacha gave me the blueprints," Ada said. "He fulfilled his end."

"No," Roth said. "Those drawings were of the Petrel system only. He promised the schematics for all five prototypes. That was the deal."

Ada threw her hands up. "He was killed."

"And the Petrel schematics were lost," Roth said. "I still don't know what happened to them."

"That wasn't Sacha's fault," Ada said, her voice rising. "It was mine."

"It was Richmond Tenet's fault," Lance said quietly, eyeing Roth. "And Richmond Tenet was whose responsibility?"

Lance knew there was more to the Tenet situation than Roth had said. Roth was acting way too complacently. Ordinarily, he'd have bent over backward to get to a source like Gazinsky. And he'd be downright apoplectic if a Station Chief defected without warning.

When he'd first come to Lance, he'd already known Laurel and Tatyana were walking into a trap. He'd known Ada wasn't going to make it back to the embassy alive without help.

Roth was up to something. He was scheming, spinning out one of his plots, like a spider spinning a web. Lance was sure of it.

That was Roth's job, of course. The President hadn't named him CIA Director, and given him control over billions of dollars of taxpayer money, just to tell people what he was up to. He was supposed to be secretive. He was supposed to be duplicitous, even to his own people. And he was good at it. Perhaps the best.

And Lance knew he wasn't in the habit of making errors of judgment either. He and Tenet had been thick as thieves for decades. If Tenet was on his way to Moscow, Lance was almost certain it was Levi Roth who'd sent him.

"Listen to me," Ada said, trying to sound calmer than she was. "Isn't it in the CIA's interest to keep Natasha alive, even if it's just to stop the Kremlin making an example of her? Wouldn't that signal to others inside Russia that defection is something they should be willing to risk?"

Roth sighed. "Look," he said. "I can only do what I can do. I'm not running a kindergarten. I'm not authorized to adopt children and look after them just because it's the nice thing to do. My only power, my only legitimacy, is in combating real and present threats to the national security of the United States."

"Protecting Natasha promotes further Russian defections."

"It's a goodwill gesture," Roth snapped, losing his cool for the first time. "It's hearts and minds, Ada. It's not security. Not anymore."

"The CIA doesn't care about hearts and minds?"

"No," Roth barked. "We don't. That's the State Department's role. If Natasha Gazinsky is coming to the US, it will be their decision, under their supervision, and on their dime. That's how it works."

"But with your recommendation...." Ada said.

"My recommendation?" Roth said. "What do you think it's going to say, Ada? I won't lie to them."

"So you'll tell them...."

"I'll tell them there was a chance to get something of value from her father, but that that chance was lost. And her treatment will cost millions of dollars. Dollars that could be spent helping other people. It's their decision at that point."

Lance watched them argue, watched Roth, the expression on his face, the tone of his voice, the movements of his eyes.

Ada was shaking her head. She couldn't believe what she was hearing. She was still innocent, still naive. She hadn't been in the system long enough to learn how things really were. She was still operating under the assumption that America was one big Santa Clause, prancing around the globe sprinkling fairy dust and helping poor people grow crops and cure malaria.

Lance had seen it more than a few times. People, good people, smart people with the best of intentions, but who needed to know better. She worked for the CIA. She'd seen what the government was capable of. She hadn't been assigned to help a kid get a doctor. That wasn't her job. The suits in Washington, the politicians and bureaucrats and lobbyists, they let worse than this happen every day of the week. They wouldn't just let Natasha die, they would stand by and let the children of an entire nation die. They would sell weapons to warmongers. They would develop chemicals to destroy crops and poison water. They would douse the world in petroleum and light the match. And they would watch it burn, all of it, if they thought for a second it was in their interest.

Ada didn't know that yet. Not really. Perhaps she never would. Lance had seen that too—people who just couldn't come to terms with the brutal, inhuman, savage calculations that the world really operated under.

One Russian child?

Natasha Gazinsky was an ant to the men who really

pulled the strings. She was less than an ant. She was dust. She was nothing.

"She's not safe here in London," Ada said, her voice taut, growing quieter as it dawned on her that she had no power, that her words weren't going to sway the outcome, that Roth was merely irritated by the argument.

Lance said nothing.

He felt for her. He agreed with her. But he knew that if he wanted to help Natasha, he had to calibrate every word.

He cleared his throat. "She's not safe in Boston either," he said.

Ada turned to him, and he saw the look on her face. She'd trusted him, and now he too was turning on her.

"Lance, what are you talking about? She needs that doctor."

"They'll find her in Boston, Ada. They know as well as we do about her medical condition. If we send her there, they'll find her, and they'll kill her."

Ada shook her head. She couldn't believe it, the betrayal, the callousness. Her eyes filled with tears. "If we don't get her to that doctor," she stammered.

"The only way Natasha is safe," Lance said, "is if the Kremlin no longer wants her dead."

"And that's never going to happen," Roth said as if that brought the argument to a close.

Lance watched Roth closely then. He'd said the words as a probe. He knew Roth, had known him a long time. He knew his tells.

"Now is not the time to go kicking a hornet's nest," Lance said.

Roth nodded. "Our job is not to protect the life of one Russian child. Our job is to protect our entire country."

Ada still couldn't believe what she was hearing. All she could do was shake her head.

Lance regretted hurting her, breaking her, but there was no other way. He looked at her, and for a second, he thought she was about to slap him in the face, but they were interrupted by a sharp rap on the door.

"What is it?" Roth said.

It was the new Station Chief, breathless. "Sir, there's something you need to see."

"What now?"

"An incident at the Russian Embassy, sir."

"In Paris?" Roth gasped.

The Station Chief nodded. "Someone went after Richmond Tenet."

The blood drained from Roth's face. He almost knocked over his chair in his haste to get out of the room. When he was gone, Lance and Ada were left in silence, staring at each other.

She was about to lay into him, but Lance raised a finger to his mouth. "The only way Natasha's safe," he said, his voice barely above a whisper, "is if everyone in Moscow involved in this case, everyone who knows her name or cares whose daughter she is, is dead."

atyana remained completely still. She wasn't sure what had triggered the floodlights, but there was no alarm. Inside the building, she could still see people going about their business as if it was nothing unusual. Even the guards seemed unperturbed.

After about a minute, the lights went back off, and as soon as they did, she dashed across the courtyard to the tunnel. There, she stopped to make sure the coast was clear in the lawn beyond. She could already see the three residential apartment blocks. It was the third that contained the GRU units. The entire second floor of that block was reserved for their use, and she was sure it was there that they would have stashed Tenet. She scanned the line of balconies and saw that only one of the six apartments overlooking the lawn had its lights on.

She made her way silently through the lawn, keeping low and using the trees and shrubs for cover. When she reached the building, she crept along the back of it until she was directly beneath the apartment with the light on, then leaped up and grabbed the floor of the balcony. She pulled

herself up and then crouched on the ground, waiting, listening. Everything was silent. There was a lace curtain inside
the balcony's sliding door, and through it, she could make
out the silhouette of a single person sitting at a counter.

She readied herself to strike. Once she moved, there
would be no further time to think. If the person sitting at
that counter matched Tenet's description, she had to know
now what she was going to do. She was a trained assassin,
but most of her work had been as a honeytrap, not a killer.
She could still recall the face of every person she'd ever
killed, and would for the rest of her life. It was not something she took lightly.

This wasn't an officially authorized mission. She and
Laurel were acting on partial information, extremely imper-
fect intel, and they'd purposefully kept it secret from Roth.
There could well be more going on than met the eye. Things
were rarely as they appeared.

Tatyana went over in her mind, one last time, what had
brought her to this point. There was a leak in London.
Everything that had happened to Ada Hudson in the past
seventy-two hours was more than enough proof of that. And
there was no earthly reason for Richmond Tenet to be in the
Russian embassy in Paris, a guest of the GRU, other than if
he was the rat.

Whatever about Roth and his decisions over the past
few days, Richmond Tenet was the cause of Sacha Gazinsky's death, and might still be the cause of Ada's and
Natasha's.

He deserved to die.

And Tatyana was the only one there to do it. She wasn't
carrying a gun, which meant it had to be done by hand, but
it was what it was.

She took a deep breath and rose to her feet. Putting her

hand flat against the glass pane of the door, she tried to move it. It was unlocked, well-oiled, and slid open silently. She slipped in through the lace curtain and shut it behind her.

The man at the counter didn't look up at her. He felt the breeze of the door opening, he knew she was there, but he remained motionless.

"Richmond Tenet?" she said.

He looked up at her slowly, calmly, as if he'd been expecting her, and the look on his face was not fear, it was sadness.

"You poor girl," he said quietly.

"What?" she said.

"Run," he mouthed silently, and in the same instant, a door in the corridor to her left burst open, and a guard opened fire with a submachine gun. She leaped across the floor in Tenet's direction, still intent on killing him. A hail of bullets followed her across the room, inches behind her. In a single motion, she knocked over a table, flung a chair at the soldier, and was about to grab Tenet and use him as a shield when the front door of the apartment flew open, and two more guards burst in.

There was no time to react. Bullets flew at her from two directions. The glass on the balcony door shattered. Feathers filled the room from the pillows on the sofa. Pictures fell from the walls. Outside, dozens of flashlight beams danced on the balcony and shone at the windows as more soldiers approached.

She slid across the ground, bullets flying mere inches above her, so close she felt their jet stream, then leaped toward the guard who'd opened fire from the corridor. He'd been knocked off balance by the chair she'd flung, and she shoved his gun upward just in time for his burst of fire to spray the ceiling above her. Before he could react, she grabbed his arm and bent it at the elbow, breaking it with an audible snap. He dropped the gun, and she swung him around between her and the other guards. She felt his body tense and spasm as their bullets pelted his back, then shoved him in their direction and rounded the corner into the bedroom. Crouching to one knee, she scanned the room. It was dark, empty, and a second set of glass doors led out to the balcony.

A split second passed, flashlight beams moved over the lace curtain, and then the glass doors shattered. She shut her eyes and covered her ears just in time to avoid the blast of a flash grenade. Then she rolled forward and, as the first guard stepped into the room from the balcony, swung out her legs and wrapped herself around him. As he hit the ground, she grabbed the pistol in his holster and jammed it into his ribs, pulling the trigger. Then she swung around and fired at the two guards entering from the corridor.

She turned back toward the balcony just as another flash grenade exploded. It caught her by surprise and blinded her for a moment. Her ears rang painfully, a single steady tone that blocked out everything else, and in her confusion, she managed to register metal tear gas canisters coming in through the window and rolling across the floor toward her.

She made it to her feet, and half running, half staggering, reached the balcony doors just as another guard was entering. With a loud grunt, and using all the strength she could muster, she shoved him back outside, past three other guards who didn't have time to react, and knocked him over the far wall of the balcony. She held onto the shoulder straps of his body armor and let his weight pull her over the edge with him. In the second it took to fall, she kept him below her. He hit the ground with a thud, breaking her fall, and wheezed like a pierced tire as the air was knocked from his lungs. She pulled a tactical knife from his belt and jammed it into his rib cage and rolled over, pulling him with her so that his body shielded her from another burst of gunfire on the balcony. His submachine gun, a Russian-made PP-2000, lay next to her, and she grabbed it and returned fire. She sprayed bullets along the length of the balcony, then swung the gun in a wide arc, firing out over the lawn in the direction she was about to run.

She was still firing when she shoved the man off her and began sprinting blindly through the darkness, ducking and dodging, using shrubs and plants for cover as bullets pelted the snow around her. As she descended the slope toward the back of the compound, she triggered floodlight sensors every twenty yards or so that came on with a pop and bathed her in white light. Behind her, she could already hear the barking of attack dogs being set loose.

When she saw the perimeter fence, she leaped, grabbed the steel poles at a height of eight feet, and flipped herself over the top. She landed on the other side on a concrete sidewalk. In front of her, a single-lane street separated her from the enormous Bois De Boulogne park.

She crossed the street into the park and took cover among the trees as police sirens closed in on the embassy from every direction.

Amidst the chaos in the office, Lance slipped out of the conference room and made his way to the service stairwell by the reception. He was on the sixth floor, and there were elevators, but the stairs attracted less attention.

He ran down the stairs and entered the lobby on the ground floor through the service door. He was at the staff exit, passing the Marines who guarded it, when he heard Ada's voice behind him.

"Lance."

He wanted to ignore her and keep going, he needed to get out of there before Roth noticed he was missing, but against his better judgment, he stopped.

He turned to see her hurrying toward him.

"Take me with you," she said.

"Keep your voice down."

"I'm coming to Moscow."

He looked up at the security camera over his head.

"You can't," he said.

"Why can't I?"

He shook his head, exasperated by the question. "A million reasons."

He turned to leave, but she grabbed his arm. "I don't care about the danger."

"You say that now."

"Lance," she said desperately. "I gave Sacha Gazinsky my word. I told him I'd protect her."

"Then stay here."

She followed him out of the building. He hurried down the steps and raised his hand to one of the waiting cabs. It pulled up in front of him, and as he opened the door, Ada grabbed him again.

"Please, Lance. I have to do this."

He knew it was a mistake even as he said the words, but there was a Marine up by the entrance watching them. "Get in," he said, making room for her to squeeze into the cab.

"Thank you," she said as he climbed in after her.

"Let's go," Lance said to the driver, patting the back of the passenger seat headrest. "Come on."

The cab pulled out of the embassy compound, and Lance let out a sigh of relief.

"I'll do everything exactly as you tell me," Ada said, but Lance wasn't listening.

He looked at his watch and said, "Where was Roth when you left?"

"Still in the situation room."

"Did you hear anything else about Paris?"

She shook her head. "Just what you heard. Someone made a move on Tenet, and it wasn't Roth."

Lance nodded. "All right," he said. "That's going to tie him up for a while." He looked at Ada. "What do you know about Viktor Lapin?"

She shook her head. "Nothing."

"Can you get access to his file?"

"I should be able. Unless they've been restricted."

"Okay, I need you to pull as much information as you can about him."

"Is that who we're going after?"

Lance didn't answer. He tapped the driver on the shoulder and said, "Take us to Saint Pancras."

"Saint Pancras?" Ada said. "Lance, it's a hell of a train ride from here to Moscow."

"You go in," he said. "Get us two tickets to Brussels. Then wait for me."

"What? Where are you going?"

"I won't be long."

"Where are you going, Lance?"

"We need passports, documents, disguise materials."

"And you want me to go in there alone and buy two tickets to Brussels?"

"There'll be less attention on flights to Moscow from there. After you get the tickets, log on and get us everything you can about Viktor Lapin. Once Roth realizes you're missing, your remote access to the database will be cut."

"You want me to wait for you?"

"Pull everything you can on Igor Aralov, too," Lance said. "He was Viktor's predecessor at the Main Directorate. Viktor will have taken over his asset list. You should be writing this down."

"Viktor Lapin, Igor Aralov, Main Directorate. I got it. What I want to know is where you're going?"

"I've got an apartment on Brick Lane. It's got the things we need."

"How long will you be?"

"I'll meet you by the payphones in the central concourse in thirty minutes."

The cab pulled up outside the train station, and Ada put her hand on the door. She hesitated before opening it.

"Go in, do what I said, and then wait," Lance said. "And don't attract attention. I'll meet you in thirty minutes."

She opened the door and got out. The minute she shut it behind her, Lance leaned forward and said to the driver, "Brick Lane. And step on it."

The driver decidedly did not step on it, but traffic was light on the Embankment, and he was out of the taxi and riding the elevator up to the apartment ten minutes later.

In the apartment, he went to the kitchen and opened the top drawer next to the sink. Behind the drawer, he'd cut a panel from the back of the cupboard, and he reached in and pulled out a metal box. It was about the size of a shoebox and contained passports, other identity documents, and cash. He took what he needed, including a Russian passport and a French one. The photo in the Russian passport was of a man in his sixties. The photo in the French one was of a woman. Lance then went into the bedroom. On the floor inside the closet was another metal box, and this one contained a number of ziplock bags. Each bag was labeled, and he went through them, reading the labels until he found the ones that matched the names on the passports.

He put the bags in his pocket with the documents and then took the elevator back down to the street. Outside, he hailed a cab and told the driver to take him to Saint Pancras.

Lance looked out the window, thinking, tapping a hand on his knee nervously. He reached into his coat and took out a cell phone.

"You know what?" he said to the driver. "Forget the station. Take me to Heathrow."

The driver nodded, and Lance leaned back in his seat, shut his eyes, and let out a long sigh. It was for the best. He didn't know what he was walking into in Moscow, and someone needed to be in London with Natasha. It was clear no one else at the embassy was going to have her back.

He looked at the phone and let out another sigh, then dialed.

"Hello?"

It was Laurel's voice.

Lance suddenly needed to clear his throat.

"Hello?" she said again.

"Laurel?"

"Who is this?"

"It's me, Lance."

A long silence followed, five seconds, ten seconds, until Lance said, "Are you there?"

"Oh, I'm here," she said, and he could tell from her voice that she wasn't going to let him off the hook lightly.

"I need you to do something," he said.

"Oh?" she said.

"It's important."

"Lots of things are important."

"Laurel, please. I'm sorry."

"I thought you were dead, Lance," she said, the emotion in her voice rising. "I was at your funeral."

"I know," he said quietly.

"I mean, you could have at least sent a message, a call, something so that I knew you were alive."

"I know."

"Unless I'm the reason you left."

He said nothing, and another silence filled the air.

"I figured as much," she said.

Lance sighed. He could still get what he needed from Ada. "I shouldn't have called," he said. "I'm sorry."

He was about to hang up when she stopped him.

"Lance, wait. Why did you call?"

"I've got a name I need you to run."

"Russian?"

"Yes. Viktor Lapin."

"Isn't he Aralov's replacement?"

"Yes," Lance said. "And he's orchestrating the attacks on Gazinsky's kid."

"So you're going after him."

"I'll be in Moscow in eight hours."

Laurel typed into a keyboard and said, "Does Roth know?"

Lance didn't answer, which, he supposed, was answer enough.

"He's not in Moscow."

"What? Where is he?"

"Arkhangelsk."

69

A da sat at a café in the central concourse, choosing a table that gave her a clear view of the payphones. She sat down and ordered a coffee, then took out her phone and began downloading every file she could find relating to Viktor Lapin.

It seemed that, until this most recent operation, he'd succeeded in keeping his hands relatively clean. His career was initially unremarkable—just one more paper-pusher in an organization that had turned bureaucratic formality into an art form. But slowly, patiently, he'd managed to climb the GRU's internal recruitment ladder far higher than his resumé would have suggested. He was unassuming in every way, the son of a Moscow city cop, modest in dress and personal style, lacking any of the ostentatious habits and vices common to Kremlin elites. If he stood out for anything, Ada would have said it was an apparent lack of ambition.

And yet, not only was he now a director in the Main Directorate, with his own office, staff, and portfolio, but he had been named the successor of Igor Aralov, one of the most formidable officers the GRU had seen in a generation. As Aralov's successor, Viktor would have inherited some of the most high-profile operations in the entire organization.

If it was power he was after, and it was hard to imagine he'd risen to his present position for any other reason, then he was certainly putting himself within striking distance of Molotov's inner circle.

Lance had been right. As long as Viktor Lapin was alive, there was no chance of Natasha finding safety. Sooner or later, a hitman would find her and put a bullet in her.

Ada looked out at the payphones. Above them, an enormous Victorian clock showed that Lance was late. She sipped her coffee for five more minutes, then ten, and began to wonder if she wasn't in the right place for the meet.

She called over the waitress and asked if there were any other payphones in the central concourse. The waitress said there were not, and Ada put some money on the table and left the café. She walked over to the phones and looked around. There were sightlines clear across the concourse. Maybe Lance was watching from one of the surrounding areas. She stood still, removed her shades, and shook out her hair as if trying to attract the attention of a man at a bar.

The clock above the concourse showed he was now twenty minutes late. She waited, and waited, and when he was forty-five minutes late, and each additional minute felt like a fresh insult, she accepted the truth.

He wasn't coming.

She went outside and caught a cab back to the embassy, unsure if Roth or anyone else would have taken note of her absence. She arrived and passed through security, expecting at any moment to be stopped and arrested. Everything was perfectly normal. She passed the Marines, walked through the lobby, and waited for an elevator without anyone saying so much as a word to her.

The elevator opened, and she glanced around. The office was still in turmoil, the atmosphere more like a Wall Street trading floor than CIA London Station. She went to the receptionist and asked where Roth was.

"Still in the Station Chief's office. Someone tried to assassinate Tenet."

"Someone?"

The receptionist shook her head. "It wasn't us."

"I see," Ada said.

It seemed no one had noticed her absence, or even, for the time being at least, Lance's. She walked toward her desk, she needed to see if there was anything she could do to conceal the fact she'd accessed Viktor's file, but when she got there, she found Natasha. She was sitting on Ada's chair, slowly swiveling back and forth in half-arcs, her legs swinging.

"How long have you been sitting here?" Ada said in Russian, trying and failing to conceal her surprise.

The child shrugged.

"Didn't the doctors want to look at you?"

"They did."

"And the therapist?"

The child nodded.

Ada looked at her. She'd expected, without really thinking through the details, that once they got to the embassy, everything would be taken care of. She'd expected the professionals, a child welfare team that knew what it was doing, people who understood what a child needed and how best to help her through the mountain of trauma she'd just been through, to step in and take over.

"They didn't have more things they wanted to do with you?" Ada said.

Natasha shrugged.

"They didn't tell you where you were going to sleep?"

Natasha just looked at her.

Ada sighed. This was a curveball. She looked around the office. Everywhere, people were barking into phones or pounding away at keyboards. The analysts were in the midst of what might well turn out to be the biggest intelligence disaster of their careers. The station chief, their boss, had just defected to the Russians, and not a few of them were going to lose their jobs in the resulting fallout.

They hadn't even noticed the nine-year-old sitting at Ada's desk.

"Come on," Ada said to Natasha, leading her over to the vending machine in the corner and telling her to pick out whatever she wanted. Natasha picked some items, and they went through the process of loading in the coins and watching candy bars and chips falling to the receptacle like prizes. Then Ada brought her back to the desk and said, "Wait here. I'll be back in a minute."

Natasha leaned back in the chair and opened a candy bar, her left leg swinging back and forth, kicking the leg of the desk in a way that was going to irritate the guy in the next cubicle.

He'd have to deal with it himself, Ada thought as she walked over to the receptionist. "Who brought up the child?" she said.

"A State Department case officer."

"Did he say anything?"

"*She*," the receptionist said, "didn't say anything. I assumed you were expecting her."

"I was not," Ada said.

The receptionist shrugged slightly, and Ada gave her an exasperated look. "What am I supposed to do with her?" she said, dropping her voice a tone.

"Don't ask me."

"Do you have kids?"

The receptionist shook her head. "I can try to get the case officer on the line, if she's still in the building."

Ada sighed. There was a constant, unacknowledged tension between the CIA and the State Department. Ostensibly, they pursued the same objective, but to Ada, it seemed more like they were permanently at each other's throats. They saw eye to eye on nothing, and frequently, it seemed that State went out of its way to obstruct the CIA, as if it was the CIA, and not foreign actors, that were the real enemy.

"She wasn't that bad," the receptionist said, sensing Ada's hesitance.

"Fine," Ada said.

The receptionist dialed an internal number and waited. "Ms. Dorman? Yes. I've got Ada Hudson here for you." She handed the receiver to Ada.

"This is Ada Hudson."

"Ms. Hudson, yes. I wanted to speak to you."

"What's she doing back here? You were supposed to look after her."

"She's had her full medical, Ms. Hudson, as well as an initial psyche assessment."

"You only had her a few hours."

"She's not in need of any immediate medical attention."

"She just witnessed her father's head get blown off. People have been chasing her across the country trying to kill her."

"She's clearly going to need counseling, but that's a process that takes time."

"Time for you guys to clear your busy schedule?"

"I can't just throw doctors at her and get her all fixed up. She's gone through a significant trauma. Our assessment is that she's going to need months of counseling. Probably years."

"Did you read my report?"

"Of course I did."

"Her life's in danger. How can you just bring her back here and leave her at my desk? We're not equipped to look after a child up here. *I'm* not equipped...."

"I understand that, Ms. Hudson."

"It's no place for a child."

"Ms. Hudson, I'm a case officer. I can only take this so far."

"What am I supposed to do with her?"

"Your report was authorized by Director Roth. Perhaps he can...."

"She's only nine years old. She needs to be taken in. She needs a home. A bed. A hot meal."

"Listen, Ms. Hudson. I want to help you."

"Then help."

"You need to get in touch directly with the Under Secretary of State for Political Affairs."

"The Under Secretary of what?"

"In Washington. This is in his hands."

"I don't even know what that is."

"Write this down—the Harry S Truman Building in Washington. Ask for the Assistant Secretary for Europe. His name is Don Greenspan."

"He's in charge of this?"

"He's in charge. Or his boss is."

"Who's his boss?"

"The Secretary of State, and above him, the President."

"So it's political?"

"Of course it's political. And if you can't get some bigwigs at the CIA to back you up on what's needed, you're going to have a very hard time getting them to take on this kid."

Ada sighed. "Okay," she said. "Thank you." She hung up and looked across the office at Natasha. She was still sitting in the chair, eating her candy bar.

"How did that go?" the receptionist asked.

Ada handed her the piece of paper with Don Greenspan's details. "Can you get this guy on the line?"

The receptionist looked at a clock on the wall that showed the current time in Washington. "I can try," she said. "But are you sure you want me to?"

Ada thought for a second, wondered if she shouldn't hold back, try going through Roth again. Contacting political appointees in Washington was way above her pay grade, not to mention a serious breach of protocol. She didn't even know what she would say if she managed to get through to someone important enough to make a decision.

But then she thought about what would happen to Natasha if she didn't find a way to cut her a deal.

"Place the call," she said.

The receptionist went through the process, asked for Don Greenspan, and said she was calling on behalf of Ada Hudson at the CIA. There was a brief wait, and then she handed the phone to Ada.

"Mr Greenspan?" Ada said.

"This is Ada Hudson?" Greenspan said.

"Yes."

"I read your report."

"Then you know why I'm calling."

"The minor."

"Her name is Natasha."

"Gazinsky, right?"

"That's correct. I sent her down to State, but they sent her right back."

"I understand she was given medical attention."

"As you can see in my report," Ada said, "she's going to need a hell of a lot more medical attention than that."

"Ms. Hudson, I'm afraid that won't be happening."

"But her father cut a deal. Her protection in exchange for classified weapons research."

"That deal was with the CIA."

"With all due respect, sir, it was with the US Government."

"Well," Greenspan said, "if that's the case, then where is the research? Langley already confirmed with my office that there's nothing of value to be had from Sacha Gazinsky's offer."

"That's because he died trying to get it to us."

"Be that as it may."

"He's dead because of us, sir. Someone in our office sold him out."

"Look, Ms. Hudson, I don't make the rules. All I can tell you is that the deal Sacha Gazinsky was trying to make is no longer on the table."

"But how is that possible?"

"I don't think it's complicated," Greenspan said. "He didn't live up to his end of the bargain. We don't live up to ours."

"And that's it? Simple as that?"

"Yes, it is."

"Like buying a used Honda?"

"I don't know what to tell you."

"This is a little girl's life we're talking about. You're telling me you want me to kick her to the curb?"

"That's not how I'd put it."

"How would you put it, Mr. Greenspan?"

"I don't appreciate your tone."

"My *tone*? Are you fucking kidding me? I've got a nine-year-old child sitting at my desk right now, eating Reese's Peanut Butter Cups. You tell me what I'm supposed to do with her now. When I hang up this phone, what is the government's position on what happens to her next?"

"Ms. Hudson, I don't...."

"You don't what?"

"I don't think this conversation...."

"No, Greenspan. I'm really asking. A little girl, right across the room, tell me what you want me to do? Call security? Have her removed forcibly? Call her a cab and send her across town to the Russians?"

"She's their citizen."

"They're going to put a bullet in her head."

"I don't know what you want me to say."

"I want you on the record. I want it in your words, for the transcript, the official word from the White House. Tell me what to do with her?"

"You're not being fair."

"Do I call security? Do I put her in a cab? Hell, I can kill her for you if you want. Save a cab fare."

"I'm hanging up."

"If you hang up, this conversation is front page of the *Washington Post* tomorrow morning."

It was then that the tone of his voice changed, telling her finally that the gloves had come off. "Let me be frank with you, *Ada,* before you say something you're going to regret."

"I'm not going to regret...."

"The only way this whole clusterfuck plays out is with

that child dead. You know it. Levi Roth knows it. The President knows it. The only difference is, they've accepted it."

"She's not dead yet."

"But she's going to be. It's a guaranteed outcome."

"You're telling me we can't protect one child?"

"Not if she needs to be at that one specific hospital in Boston all the time. How are we going to hide her there? She'll be a sitting duck no matter what we do."

"So we're not even going to try?"

"You're not listening. That child is a ticking time bomb. It's only a matter of time until she goes off. The Russians are going to find her, and they're going to kill her, and when that happens, no one in this administration wants to be the chump holding the fucking ball. Do you understand?"

Ada was taken aback. She couldn't believe this was the official stance of the State Department, the US Government, even the President. "You're all a bunch of cowards," she stammered. "You'd rather keep your own hands clean than do what needs to be done."

"And you're flushing your career down the fucking toilet," Greenspan said.

Ada's heart was pounding. She wanted to rip the phone from the desk and fling it out the window. "I gave her father my word," she said.

"Honestly, Ada," Greenspan said, "no one here gives a fuck about your word."

70

The journey to Arkhangelsk was more complicated than a flight to Moscow would have been. The city's military sensitivity, combined with its remoteness, meant the Kremlin kept close tabs on movement in and out of the region. That was especially true of the airport, where the name of every passenger was sent immediately to the FSB data center in Yaroslavl for cross-referencing.

It meant flying direct was out of the question, even under false papers. Instead, Lance bought a ticket on the next British Airways flight to Saint Petersburg. From there, he could get a local connection to Vologda, a city about three hundred miles north of Moscow.

Before checking in, he went into a washroom and locked himself in a stall. He took one of the ziplock bags from his pocket and opened it. Inside was a hyper-realistic silicone mask that matched the photograph in the Russian passport he'd taken from the apartment. He put on the mask and went to the mirror to check himself. There was no one else in the washroom, and he leaned close to the mirror, examining carefully the seam where the silicone met his skin. He made a few adjustments until he was satisfied, then took out the cell phone he'd been given at the embassy. He removed the battery and SIM and threw them in separate trash cans, along with the additional mask and passport he'd brought for Ada.

He checked in, passed security, boarded his flight, and three hours later, was in Saint Petersburg. From there, he transferred to his Aeroflot flight, which took another hour. That plane was at half-capacity, and when the hostess offered him vodka in a plastic shot glass, he took it. He cleared border control in Saint Petersburg without incident and passed the police check at Vologda Airport equally smoothly.

From Vologda, he could have taken the train to Arkhangelsk, but the bus was safer. It was also significantly slower. A cab dropped him at the bus station, which looked like a rundown, red-brick warehouse. High narrow windows, opaque with dirt, stretched up toward the roof like the windows of a church.

It was very cold, and his breath billowed around him as he watched the cab drive off into the mist.

Around the station, kiosks were selling food and snacks. He bought something from an older woman in a headscarf, and she handed him a paper bag containing eight pierogies, piping hot. He picked one out with his fingers and blew on it. He dipped it in a small bowl of sour cream and put it in his mouth. The dough had been hand-rolled, and inside was a filling of ground beef, tomato, peppers, and dill.

He ate the pierogies, one after the other, and made his way to the ticket booth. He was traveling without luggage or weapons, so he had nothing to carry. The next bus to Arkhangelsk was in a few hours, so he left the station to kill time, making his way toward the city center. The area around the bus station was decrepit, the concrete apartment blocks that towered over it dismal even by Soviet standards. He walked a few blocks and arrived at an enormous intersection. He watched the chaotic traffic before attempting to cross. The intersection was little more than a circular expanse of concrete, a few hundred yards in diameter, with a large bronze statue at its center of the poet, Nikolay Rubtsov.

Lance made his way through the slush, the cars more or less directing themselves around the intersection without the guidance of lanes, signs, or painted lines on the road.

On the other side of the intersection was an enormous Soviet-era post office, a few poorly stocked stores, and his destination, the Hotel Vologda. It was an old building, neoclassical in style, that had once passed as grand. No longer.

He went to the front desk, where a bespectacled woman in a stern dress watched him over her wire rims. He got a room for about twenty dollars and then went to the restaurant across the lobby, which looked more like the cafeteria of a school or hospital than anything belonging in a hotel. Large communal tables were arranged in rows, and he took a seat at one. Two men at the far end of the same table were eating steaming piles of white-colored food from white porcelain plates, accompanied by a sort of compote. They were the only other customers.

Lance sat there, leaning back on his chair and watching the clock mark time. He was in no hurry, which his waitress must have sensed, as fifteen minutes passed without her giving him any service. He wasn't sure if smoking was allowed, there was no sign, no ashtray on the table, so he lit a cigarette anyway and no one objected.

The floor of the cafeteria reminded him of something from his childhood—concrete, polished as smooth as marble from years of use, with pieces of blue and green glass baked into it for decorative effect.

He'd finished his cigarette and stubbed it out beneath his foot by the time the waitress finally approached.

"What can I get you?" she said in the heavily accented Russian of the region.

She was about fifty, with stocky legs that rose up into her stiff, starched skirt like rods entering a piston.

"I'll have whatever's good."

"Are you a hotel guest?"

"Yes."

She sighed and left. He lit another cigarette, and a few minutes later, she came back with a pot of tea, some cubed sugar in a bowl, and a glass. He sipped the tea for thirty more minutes until she returned with the same white food the men at the other end of the table had been eating. It was steamed dumplings with a thick, creamy mushroom sauce poured over it. Small pieces of fatty pork floated in the sauce.

Lance ate it and, when he was done, drank more tea with another cigarette.

Up in his room, he took a shower and, afterward, lay on the bed and stared at the ceiling. There was a phone next to the bed, and he called the receptionist for a wake-up call. Then he slept.

When the phone woke him, it took a moment for him to remember where he was.

"This is your wake-up call," the receptionist said.

He went downstairs, checked out of the hotel, and walked back to the bus station. As he passed the statue of the poet, he thought of a line he'd once read in one of his poems.

'Bread carries itself.'

He looked up at the statue and said the words to himself as if testing them. It was a distinctly Russian sentiment, an analog to Marie Antoinette's statement about cake. Indeed, when the Russian Army was mobilized in 1914, Grand Duke Nicholas Nikolaevich refused to make allowance for a single ounce of the bread and other rations the soldiers had to carry to the front. When the choice was extra weight or starvation, bread carried itself.

Lance's bus was coming in from Moscow and had another eleven hours to go before its arrival in Arkhangelsk. He boarded and found a seat near the back. The bus was crowded, thick with body odor, and the people who'd been on since Moscow had set themselves up with pillows, blankets, and other items to make themselves comfortable.

Lance made his way to the back, where he squeezed into a seat next to a woman in her sixties who was none too pleased to have to make room for him.

Someone opened a window while they were in the station, but once they got back on the road, it was shut again because of the cold.

He tried to sleep. After a few hours, they stopped at a remote village, and a woman came on board selling snacks and drinks. Lance bought tea from her and sipped it as they pulled out of the village.

He looked out the window. The landscape was as desolate as any he'd ever seen. At some point, they crossed the treeline, where forest gave way to tundra, and the snow whipped across the barren land and onto the road in fierce eddies, causing impenetrable whiteouts so regularly the driver had no choice but to ignore them. Each time it happened, in an act of pure will, he kept his foot on the gas and maintained speed, pushing forward blind.

71

Ada booked two rooms at the Belgrave Hotel close
to the embassy, one for herself and Natasha, the
other for a security detail of two armed agents
that she'd persuaded Roth to authorize. They left the
embassy in an unmarked Mercedes sedan, its windows
tinted so they wouldn't be seen by any GRU asset that might
be watching the embassy. At the hotel, one of the agents
went ahead to check in. The other escorted them up to the
rooms.

"You two going to be okay?" he said as she opened her
door.

"We'll be fine. I'll let you know if we need anything."
The two rooms were directly across the hall from each
other, and she was about to enter when she said, "Oh, one
thing. I guess I need to feed her."

"Call for room service," he said. "Have it sent up to our
room. We'll bring it across."

Ada took Natasha into the room and, while Natasha got
settled, Ada unpacked the bag they'd been given at the
embassy. There wasn't much in it, a few basic toiletries and

some fresh clothes for Natasha.

The room had two beds, but they both sat on the same one. "Let's get you something to eat," Ada said.

She ordered hamburgers and fries for both of them, and then they sat back and watched TV. After a while, one of the agents arrived with their food. They ate on the bed, and soon after, Natasha fell asleep watching a reality TV show she seemed to be familiar with.

It was then that Ada got to work. Laurel Everlane had updated Gazinsky's file from Washington, and Ada spent the next few hours reading it and speaking to as many of the doctors on Charles Hannson's team as possible. If she was going to be of any use to Natasha, she needed to know about her condition, what was in store for her, and what sort of treatments were available, both in Boston and elsewhere.

It didn't take long for her to realize that Sacha Gazinsky's assessment of the situation had been correct. Natasha's only hope of survival was with Charles Hannson's team at the Children's Research Hospital in Boston.

Her condition, if left untreated, had a one hundred percent mortality rate. There would be periods, such as was the case currently, when the illness went into remission, and Natasha could live quite normally. But the pain would always come back, and each time it returned, it would be orders of magnitude worse. Very soon, certainly by the time she was twelve, it would be unbearable.

The case notes for other patients around the world documented in vivid detail the particularly cruel nature of the condition and its effect on the body. In every case, the children eventually begged their parents and medical teams to end their pain, end their suffering, end their lives. Pain killers, even the strongest opiates, had no effect. The condition, it seemed, was related to the brain's ability to interpret and process pain, and, in fact, it wasn't the condition itself that killed the subjects, but the fact that their pain reached a level so unbearable that they begged for release.

In one of the documented cases from Sweden, a ten-year-old patient was in so much agony she'd tried to bash her own head open against a wall.

Laurel's report said Sacha had accessed the journals. He'd read the articles. He'd known what was coming for his child if he didn't act.

And he also knew how it would play out. He wasn't in Sweden. He was in Russia. The doctors weren't going to do whatever he and Natasha asked, not once the government got involved. And the government would get involved. According to Laurel's file, the Scientific Research Institute of Hygiene, a Russian military facility in Sverdlovsk that specialized in pain research, had already requested blood samples and other clinical data relating to Natasha's case.

It was an open secret among government scientists that at the Sverdlovsk facility, the word 'hygiene' was a blatant euphemism. Sacha was all too aware of the kind of work they did there—the development of interrogation and torture techniques, psychological weapons testing, experimentation into the limits of human endurance and pain. That Natasha's case would be of interest to them was inevitable. It provided entirely new ways of studying the experience of pain and its interaction with the central nervous system. The Russian military had long ago come up with theories as to the upper limits of human pain and what happened to a person when those limits were reached. Natasha presented an opportunity to test those theories. That they would come for her was an inevitability.

Indeed, just weeks before his defection, Sacha learned of Sverdlovsk's request for Natasha's case file. If he'd been scared before, this terrified him. It was the step that pushed him over the edge—that convinced him to sabotage his own test launch.

Ada had spoken to a number of Hannson's doctors, gathering as much general information as she could, but if she wanted to talk about Natasha's case specifically, she needed to speak to Hannson himself. He'd been sent a file by Laurel and knew the basics of the situation. He was performing surgery, but she'd been told he would be out soon and would return her call as soon as possible.

She looked at Natasha, asleep on the bed next to her, and thought of what would happen to her if the Russians ever got hold of her. A shiver ran up her spine. It was no wonder Sacha had done what he'd done. He had no choice.

Her phone rang, and she answered immediately.

"Yes?"

"Ms. Hudson, this is Charles Hannson returning your call."

"Thank you for getting back to me," Ada said.

"No," Hannson said, "I'm the one who's grateful. You people put your lives on the line every single day. I've read the report sent by the director's office, and if there's anything I can do to be of service, I'd be proud to do it."

"Well," Ada said, surprised to be finally speaking to someone who wanted to help her, "from what I've been told, Natasha Gazinsky is a viable candidate for your treatment."

"If these records are accurate, then I would say she's an ideal candidate."

"You think you'll be able to save her?"

"I can't make any promises, but the prognosis is good."

"And when could you begin treatment?"

"It would need to be as soon as possible. She's already

nine and will soon be entering a phase of rapid deterioration if we don't get started."

"Did the report outline any of the non-medical factors that are complicating the case?"

"No," Hannson said. "The report was strictly limited to the medical situation, but I could read between the lines."

"Meaning?"

"Well, it was classified. It was drafted by the CIA. The medical records are Russian."

"So you understand that it's related to an ongoing CIA operation?"

"Yes, I do."

"So let me ask you this, doctor. How possible would it be for you to administer your treatment from a location other than the Boston Children's Hospital?"

"Could you bring her to the Harvard Medical School? We have a research partnership there."

"Right now, I can't even bring her into the country."

"That certainly complicates things," Hannson said.

"There are also significant security considerations you should be aware of."

"I assumed there would be."

"The CIA will take steps to ensure your safety, but we can't always be there, and there are people inside the Russian government that are actively searching for Natasha Gazinsky."

"I see."

"Any treatment you offer her will have to take place under conditions of extreme secrecy."

"Would my team be in danger?"

"I won't lie to you. In a situation like this, anyone close enough to be hit by a stray bullet is in danger of becoming collateral damage."

Hannson went quiet, and Ada waited a moment before saying, "Are you still there?"

"I'm here," he said. "I was just thinking...."

"You can be frank with me, doctor."

"It's not just my patients that I'm responsible for. It's also the safety of my team."

"Of course," Ada said, preparing herself to counter his arguments for backing out.

But he didn't argue. He said, "I want to administer her treatment personally. If I'm her only doctor, then I'm the only one at risk."

"Doctor Hannson," Ada said. "Are you sure you want to do this?"

"I'm sure."

"You're under no obligation...."

"I know that."

"Well, thank you."

"My son," he blurted, "I was opposed. I mean, no one would ever accuse me of being overly patriotic. I was against the wars in Iraq and Afghanistan."

"You don't have to explain yourself to me," Ada said, unsure what it was he was trying to say.

"He died," Hannson said. "He knew the risk he was taking when he signed up. And he knew I was against it. But he went anyway. And he paid the price."

"I had no idea," Ada said.

"He was willing to pay the price."

"I'm very sorry, Doctor."

"I don't know, maybe it doesn't make sense to you, but if you're telling me there's a benefit to our country in this, to our security, then I'm willing to do my part."

"There was a benefit," Ada said. "I don't know if it's still there. That's why the State Department withdrew its support."

"This is related to the explosion over the Arctic, isn't it?" Ada said nothing for a moment, and Hannson said, "I'm sorry. I shouldn't have said that."

"If you're putting your life on the line," Ada said, "then you might as well know, Natasha's father was a scientist for the Kremlin. He was going to give us valuable information in exchange for her treatment."

"But now?"

"Now, he's dead."

"I see."

"So the government is saying there's no longer a national security benefit to helping her."

"But he died trying to live up to his end of the bargain?"

"He did," Ada said.

"All right."

"All right?"

"That's enough."

"You're still in?"

"Just tell me what you need."

"Okay," Ada said. "Can your treatment be administered outside the United States?"

"Well," Hannson said, "the method involves highly advanced genetic treatments. The sequencing is the complicated part, it has to be done here, but Natasha doesn't have to be present for it to happen."

"So you could do that work in Boston while Natasha stayed here?"

"Yes. And once the sequencing is complete, I could come to her."

"Could you come to London? Could you administer the treatment at the embassy here if I got clearance?"

"Not at the embassy, no. There are complex technical requirements. I have a contact at the Great Ormand Street Hospital in London. I believe it's just a few miles from the embassy. It has one of the most advanced pediatric units in the world."

"That's a very big hospital," Ada said.

"Yes, it is."

"Security would be difficult."

"I see."

"Secrecy would be even more difficult."

"What about a private clinic?" Hannson said.

"Would they have the equipment you need?"

"You'd be surprised what private clinics in London have access to," Hannson said. "There's a specialist on Harley Street I've worked with in the past. We're quite close. She's the director of the Belvedere Clinic. One of the most prestigious private clinics in the world."

"Do you think she'd help us?"

"They're used to complicated situations there. They treat the British Royal Family, foreign heads of state, African dictators. They provide top-notch security, world-class treatment, and absolute discretion."

"Can you send her name to the CIA so they can vet her?"

"I can."

"They'll call her and explain what we need."

"You should know," Hannson said, "this isn't going to be cheap. The price will be eye-watering."

"I'll have to figure that out."

"If the State Department withdrew its support? That means the money is gone too. Not to mention the British government."

"You leave all that to me. Just get on the phone with your contact. Tell her to expect a call from Langley."

72

Viktor fidgeted with his phone. Things were a mess, and he needed to report back to Suvorov. It was a call that was not going to go smoothly.

He was sitting in a leather chair in the lobby of his hotel, and through the window, could see the desolate central square of Arkhangelsk's modest commercial district. A single street lamp bathed the gusting snow in a cold, blue light.

He beckoned the bartender. "Scotch. No ice."

"Very good," the bartender said.

He lit a cigarette and inhaled deeply. As he blew out the smoke, the phone in his hand began to vibrate. Even before looking, he knew it was Suvorov. He let it ring once, staring at the lamppost outside, and wondered how bad it would be.

"It's me," he said, raising the phone to his ear.

"Gazinsky's daughter is still alive."

"Sir, I can explain...."

"I think I've heard enough of your explanations, Viktor."

"The assassin failed, but the moment I get back to Moscow...."

"Oh, no, Viktor. You're done. You're through."

"What?"

"If killing a nine-year-old child is too much for you, I'll just do it myself."

"But, sir...."

"Don't, Viktor. Natasha Gazinsky is the least of your worries."

"What are you talking about?"

"You know exactly what I'm talking about."

"I absolutely do not."

"You sly fucking piece of shit. You tried to pull a fast one on all of us, didn't you?"

"Sir, what are you talking about?"

Suvorov laughed hollowly. "What am I talking about?" he taunted.

"The attack in Paris," Viktor said weakly.

"Did you honestly think you could reel in a fish like Richmond Tenet without the rest of us noticing?"

"I was going to tell you."

"You weren't going to tell anyone. You were going to bring him all the way to Moscow like a dog and leave him at the President's feet. And then you were going to wait for your pat on the head."

"Honestly, sir...."

"You thought this was your ticket to the big leagues, you dumb fuck."

"I found him in Aralov's book. He called him Gray Coat."

"I know exactly where you found him, you mutt."

"Aralov kept him secret for decades. I thought the sensitivity justified...."

"You're not listening," Suvorov said. "There is nothing, literally nothing, you can illuminate for me."

"If I show you the files. This guy was a goldmine. The source of all Aralov's breakthroughs."

"Viktor, for your own sake, stop talking."

"I can be on a plane in an hour," Viktor said desperately. "I'll show you the whole thing."

"Viktor, Viktor, Viktor," Suvorov said as if admonishing a child. "The penny still hasn't dropped."

"What penny, sir?"

"If you can't read the writing on the wall, I'm not going to spell it out for you."

"Do you mean?"

"Just sit tight in Arkhangelsk, Viktor. When I want you, I'll send for you."

"Sir," Viktor protested, but the line went dead.

Viktor looked at the phone, then slammed it hard against the table, shattering the screen.

He sucked hard on his cigarette and blew the smoke at the bartender who was delivering his drink. "Bring me another," he said before he'd even touched it.

This was what failure tasted like—truly bitter. He'd rolled the dice, taken a stab at the big prize, and come up short.

Suvorov was going to make him pay. He was going to make this hurt. That much was clear.

The bartender brought the second drink, and Viktor picked it up and offered it to him. "Don't make me drink alone," he said. The bartender took the drink, and Viktor said, "To the Motherland."

The bartender drank dutifully, and Viktor told him to have his driver sent around. He finished his cigarette, then went to the front of the hotel, watching for his car from inside the lobby. There wasn't a soul outside on the square.

When the car arrived, he hurried down to it and got in the back seat.

"Where to, boss?" the driver said.

"You tell me."

"Sir?"

Viktor lit a cigarette. He thought for a second. It crossed his mind that perhaps the time had come to end his life. Suvorov was going to make him pay dearly for what he'd done. There was no question of that.

He looked the driver in the eye and said, "I want, maybe, to *ruin* something."

"I'm sorry, sir, I don't take your meaning."

"I want to dirty something."

"You want to *dirty* something?"

"Yes. And hurt it."

The driver gave no sign that he understood, but he did turn back to the wheel and start the engine. They sat there for a minute, idling, until Viktor said, "For heaven's sake, take me somewhere."

"Of course, sir," the driver said nervously and pulled into the street.

He didn't take them far, just a few blocks north toward the port. If the streets had been desolate before, they were positively abandoned now. Long disused railway tracks were inlaid into the cobbles, and the commercial buildings gave way to boarded and shuttered storage sheds.

The car rounded a corner and came to a halt in a narrow alley between two brick warehouses. To their left, a single street lamp flickered above a steel door.

"What is this place?" Viktor said.

"You'll see."

"You're mad if you think I'm getting out alone here."

"You're safe here, sir. I think it's what you asked for."

"If this is some sort of trick of Suvorov's."

"I don't know who that is, sir, but this is no trick. If you go to that door and press the buzzer, you can...."

"*Hurt* something?"

"Precisely, sir."

"I press the buzzer. Then what?"

The driver leaned back and looked at him solemnly. "And then the door will open."

Viktor didn't know what he'd been expecting. He didn't know what he wanted. What he did know was that whatever was behind that door wasn't going to be worse than what was waiting for him in Moscow. He got out of the car and lit a cigarette. He was wearing his good shoes, he thought, as he trudged through the slush.

He pressed the buzzer, and a man's voice answered. "Yes?"

"My driver said there was... *something* here."

"Did he?"

A light came on in a grubby window on the second floor. A man was standing there, looking down. Viktor stared up at him, then raised a hand. A moment later, the door buzzed.

Viktor wondered if he should call it a night now, quit before something very bad happened. But instead, he pushed open the door and entered the building. Inside, old incandescent light bulbs in wire cages hung over a large workshop. Mechanics' pits had been set into the ground. Around them, engine grease stained the concrete.

To his right was a metal stair. He climbed it to a steel landing with another steel door at the top. He waited. Nothing happened. He finished his cigarette and threw the butt off the platform, watching it fall to the shop floor below.

There was a clang of metal on metal from the door before it swung open. A burly man with dark stubble and a grimy shirt stood there, blocking his path.

Viktor looked at him. He looked back, sizing him up.

"Hand's up," he said.

"This is ridiculous," Viktor said but raised his hands and let the man pat him down.

The man found Viktor's gun holstered beneath his left arm but didn't remove it. "What's this?" he said.

"I work for the government," Viktor said.

The man looked at him uncertainly, then said, "What are you doing here?"

"Same thing as anyone else."

The man sighed and stepped aside, letting him keep his weapon.

Viktor squeezed past into a room that had once been a foreman's office. Now, it was decorated like a gaudy, down-at-heel brothel from a prior decade. A red carpet had been laid on the floor, and matching curtains hung on the windows. There were fluorescent bulbs on the ceiling, but they weren't on. Instead, light came from a number of ordinary house lamps draped in pink cloth lined with tassels. The combination of industrial fixtures and outdated, bourgeois décor was disorienting.

Across the room, sitting on a stool next to a high wooden table, was an unattractive older woman in a silk robe that only partially concealed her breasts. On the table, she had a glass of red wine and a small, metal cashbox. On the floor next to her, a gas heater glowed red.

The burly man was standing behind Viktor, quite close, and he stepped forward to make space.

"How are you, honey?" the woman said.

Viktor glanced past her, trying to see into the other rooms further down the catwalk. They all had large windows overlooking the shop floor, but lace and cloth had been draped over them for privacy. Inside, he could see the movements of people silhouetted against more lamplight.

Viktor was no stranger to brothels, but there was something different about this place. It made him uneasy.

The man walked past him to the woman and told her in a hushed tone what Viktor had said outside. The woman listened intently, then looked up at Viktor.

"I trust you're not here to cause trouble."

"No trouble," Viktor said. "I'm here for the same reason as any man."

She looked at him curiously. "Not all men come for the same thing."

There was a coat rack by the door, and Viktor took off his coat and put it on a hook. "So," he said, "what now?"

"You tell me," the woman said, letting the front of her robe fall open to reveal a voluptuous bosom.

"I'm looking for something..." Viktor began, not sure what it was he wanted to say.

"Younger?" the woman said.

"Yes," Viktor said, a little too quickly.

She shrugged. "You can sit down. Nadia won't be long."

There was a sofa against the wall with a TV across from it. The burly man was already sitting on it, watching a soccer match, and on the arm of the sofa next to him was a remote control and an overflowing ashtray.

Viktor would have liked to get a look at Nadia before committing, but it didn't seem like that was an option. "How about something to drink?" he said to the woman.

She bent down to a cabinet beneath the table and pulled

out a shot glass and a bottle of local vodka. She poured a shot without asking him what he preferred.

"Whatever you have is fine," he muttered.

He lit a cigarette and nursed his drink. After about ten minutes, a bearded man came out of one of the rooms on the catwalk. He entered the office, closing his fly as he walked, and seemed in a hurry to leave. Neither the woman nor the burly man said a word to him as he took his coat from the rack and put it on. Then he opened the door and was gone.

Viktor looked at the man and woman, then at the door of the room that the bearded man had just come from. It was slightly ajar, and a warm glow came from the lamps inside. Inside the room, he heard crying.

He looked back to the man and woman. They could hear the crying too but said nothing. The man let out a long sigh and hoisted himself up from the sofa. Viktor expected him to check on the girl, but he was merely going for a pack of cigarettes on the woman's table. He opened the pack, put a cigarette in his mouth, and sank back into the sofa.

Viktor waited, hesitant, uncertain what was supposed to happen. He looked at the woman. She looked back at him as if expecting him to make the first move.

He got up and went over to her, pulling his wallet from his pocket.

How much?" he said.

73

By the time the bus pulled into the station in Arkhangelsk, Lance was cold, stiff, and tired. It had been a long journey, but he at least knew he hadn't been picked up by GRU monitors at the train station and airport.

Outside the station, he got in a cab and told the driver to take him to the Moscow Industrial Bank, which had a large branch close to the center of the city. When they got there, he asked the driver if he would wait for him.

"How long will you be?" the driver said.

"Ten minutes. I'll make it worth your while."

The driver shrugged, and Lance left, unsure whether he would wait or not. It was late, and the bank was closed, but there was a phone by the door to reach the night-duty manager.

"I need access to my box," he said when she picked up.

"Now?"

"Yes, now. I'm at the door."

She sighed and typed something on a computer keyboard. "Client access?"

"Vanguard eighty-three."

The line went dead, and he put the receiver back on its holder. A moment later, a guard in a brown uniform opened the door and led him down a corridor to a brightly lit room filled with safety deposit boxes.

Lance found his box, then looked over his shoulder at the guard. "How about a little privacy?"

"Of course," the guard said, shuffling back out to the corridor.

Lance opened the box using the same combination he used for dozens of such boxes around the world. He hadn't packed the box himself but knew what it would contain. Inside, as well as cash and documents, was a Beretta Model 71 pistol chambered in a .22. It was a single-action, semi-automatic, light-weight gun with an aluminum frame and a three-and-a-half-inch barrel. The ammo was easy to get virtually anywhere on earth. As well as the gun, there was a supply of ammo and a suppressor.

He loaded the gun, attached the suppressor, and put it in his coat pocket.

Then he went back outside. The cab was still there, and Lance said to take him to the Azimut Hotel, which was only a few hundred yards away.

He knew the hotel. He'd been there a few years earlier. It was a straightforward hundred-room building on six floors. It was built in the Soviet era and in the Soviet style. Over the entrance was an enormous tiered chandelier, and in the lobby, faux-marble pillars gave the place a discordant Mediterranean feel.

He went into the lobby and checked in. The hotel hadn't yet upgraded to keycards, and the concierge gave him a regular, metal key for his room. It was attached to a large wooden fob to prevent it from being lost or stolen. Guests were supposed to leave their key at the front desk when leaving the premises. There were rows of numbered cubbies behind the reception for them. Lance saw that he could tell whether a room was occupied or not by whether a key was in its cubby.

"Is there a payphone?" he said to the receptionist.

He could have made the call from his room, but because it was international, it would have gone through reception, which he didn't want.

"By the bar, sir."

The bar was empty. Lance went to the payphone and dialed for an operator. He asked to place a reverse charge call to Laurel's number in Washington. It took a minute to connect, and then Laurel's voice came on.

"Where have you been?"

"Were you worried?"

"Don't push me, Lance."

"I was on a bus. I couldn't fly in."

"So you're in Arkhangelsk?"

"I'm at the Azimut. Do you know what room Viktor's in?"

"Six hundred."

"On the sixth floor, I presume?"

"I'm sure you'll find it."

Lance wanted to keep the conversation going, but Laurel said, "Is that it?"

He hesitated a second, then said, "That's it."

He took the elevator to the sixth floor without stopping at his own room first. The sixth floor was reserved for suites, and Viktor's was at the far end of the corridor, the last door on the left. Lance knocked lightly and stepped aside, keeping his back to the wall. There was no answer. No light was coming from the crack beneath the door.

He knocked again.

Still no answer.

He picked the lock and let himself into the room, locking the door quietly behind him. Moving silently, he swept through each room of the suite. When he was satisfied that no one was there, and after checking that the curtains were drawn, he turned on a lamp.

The room contained a number of ashtrays, one on a side table by the bed, another on the coffee table in the sitting room, and another on the windowsill overlooking the square outside. All of them were full of cigarette butts. The room itself reeked of smoke.

In the bathroom, he saw the toiletries one would expect of a man traveling alone for work. There was a towel on the floor next to the shower.

In the closet, two out-of-style blazers hung from hangers, and in the trash, a number of small liquor bottles from the minibar.

There was no doubt he was at the right place.

He took a coke from the minibar and opened it. It was a waiting game now.

Almost too easy.

If he'd wanted, he could have killed Viktor, then gone down to his own room three floors below for a good night's sleep. In all likelihood, no one would find Viktor's body before morning.

On the desk next to the minibar was a leather briefcase. Inside it was a manilla envelope containing a number of eight-by-fourteen-inch surveillance photographs of Natasha Gazinsky. They had been digitally enhanced, zoomed in to a high magnification. Handwritten on the back of the envelope was a draft distribution list, two columns of names, one headed 'London', the other 'Boston'.

There were six names in each column—the hitmen Viktor was planning to send after Natasha.

On the lower-left corner of each image was a watermark showing the coordinates and altitude of the drone that had taken them. The drone itself was identified as an Aeryon SkyRanger quadcopter.

Lance put the pictures in his coat pocket and turned off the lamp. Then he sat on a leather armchair near the window and lit a cigarette.

It was over an hour before he heard Viktor fumbling with his key at the door. The door opened, and Viktor flicked on the lights. Lance watched him calmly. Even with the light on, Viktor still didn't notice him. He shut the door and removed his shoes, and only then did he see Lance sitting there with a wry smile on his face and a silenced Beretta pistol on his lap.

"Don't," Lance said in Russian when Viktor made to reach for his gun.

Viktor stopped. He moved his hand slowly from his coat and, as if he'd been expecting this, said, "Suvorov sent you."

Lance shook his head. "Wrong."

He said it in English, and Viktor realized his mistake. "I was just doing my job," he said, but there was no force in his words.

Lance shrugged. "You were doing your job. Now I'm doing mine."

Viktor let out a long sigh, and Lance gave him a moment to let the reality of his situation sink in. Then he reached into his coat pocket and pulled out the envelope containing Natasha's pictures. "Why are you still going after her?"

"Why do you think?" Viktor said.

"She's nine years old."

"The Kremlin wants to send a message."

"That they kill little girls?"

"That defecting is never worth it."

"And what do you make of that, Viktor?"

"It doesn't matter what I make of it."

"Right," Lance said. "You're just doing your job." He looked at Viktor closely, trying to get a read on him. There was a lot to be gained in the final minutes of a man's life, and Lance knew not to squander it. "You sent a hitman after a nine-year-old girl. A Russian girl."

"I told you, I was following orders."

"Well, Viktor, that's what got you."

"What do you mean?"

"It was the hitman on the motorway who gave me your name. If you hadn't sent him, I wouldn't be here now."

Viktor's face remained motionless, betraying nothing. "I did what I had to do," he said quietly.

"There was someone else there," Lance said. "Someone helping the gunman. A drone operator."

"A contractor," Viktor said. "What of it?"

Lance opened the envelope and took out one of the surveillance photos. "He made these."

"Yes."

"I'm going to need his name."

"And why would I give you that?"

"Because we're going to be friends, you and me."

"You're going to kill me."

"True," Lance said, taking out a cigarette, "but the question is, how am I going to do it?" he put the cigarette in his mouth and lit it. "I could throw you out this window. Let you smash on the ground like a watermelon."

Viktor said nothing.

Lance got up and walked over to him. He put the

cigarette in Viktor's mouth, then went back to his seat. "See," he said. "Isn't it nicer when we're friends?"

Viktor shut his eyes as he inhaled, then said, "I want to die like a man. Like an officer. I deserve that much."

"It remains to be seen what you deserve."

"I tell you who took the photos," Viktor said, "and you let me die at my desk, by my own hand."

"I can live with that," Lance said, then a thin smile crossed his lips, and he added, "if you can."

Viktor wasn't impressed. "You're a funny guy."

"I try," Lance said. "Now, tell me the name of the drone operator."

Viktor shrugged. "Go after him if you like. What do I care?"

"Then give me his name."

"He has a daughter of his own, though," Viktor said. "You should know."

"Why should I know?"

"Isn't that what all this is about? Daughters?"

"Who said that?"

There was a strange look on Viktor's face, and Lance wondered for a second if he knew more than he was letting on. It was impossible, there was no way he could, but he was making Lance uncomfortable.

"Sacha Gazinsky got into this whole mess," Viktor said, "because of his daughter."

"And?"

"And so did my drone operator. He's a contractor. British ex-military. He didn't take this job by choice."

"Everything's a choice."

"I threatened his daughter," Viktor said. "That's no choice."

Lance shook his head. He didn't like this kind of talk. If

this British ex-military drone operator was taking pictures of Natasha so they could be sent to hitmen, that was a problem. "Just give me his name, Viktor."

"You think you're doing something so noble, saving an innocent little girl."

"I never said that."

"Captain America, here to save the day."

Lance lit a cigarette. "What are you trying to say?"

"It's a contradiction," Viktor said. "That's all."

"Well, there. You've said it."

"You're here to kill me for making Natasha Gazinsky an orphan."

Lance moved his hand to the gun. He wasn't in the mood for too much more of this.

"But you're doing the same thing."

"I'm not going after children."

"No," Viktor said, "but Sacha Gazinsky was no angel. The research he was doing would have killed millions of people. And he would be doing it still if it weren't for his daughter."

"I'm not here because you killed Sacha Gazinsky," Lance said. "Now, give me the drone operator's name before I lose patience."

"Fine," Viktor said. "Like I said, it's all the same to me."

"The name, Viktor," Lance said, picking up the gun.

"Stan Morel. His name is Stan Morel."

"Good," Lance said, holding up the list of hitmen. "Now, these guys? Do I have to go after all of them too?"

"You say that like it's even an option."

"It's an option."

Viktor shook his head. "No," he said. "It's not an option. They'd tear you to shreds."

"Be that as it may," Lance said, "did you send any of them the pictures of Natasha?"

"Not yet."

"You're sure of that?"

"I was going to," Viktor said, "but I was removed from my post at the Main Directorate before I could."

"You were removed? By who?"

Viktor pointed upward at the ceiling.

Lance looked up. "The Prime Directorate?"

Viktor nodded.

"Who at the Prime Directorate?"

Viktor smiled thinly. "I'm not telling you that."

"Suvorov," Lance said. "That's what you said when you saw me."

Viktor's jaw clenched.

"You thought he'd come for you."

Viktor sucked hard on his cigarette, then took a long time to exhale.

"Why protect him? He wouldn't do the same for you."

"André Suvorov," Viktor said at last. "He's taking over the Gazinsky file personally."

Lance nodded. He let Viktor finish his cigarette, but when it was done, Viktor seemed reluctant to let it go. He kept the butt firmly between his lips, as if he knew it was the last thing delaying the inevitable.

"You're really here because of the girl?" he said, as if he couldn't believe anyone would go to so much trouble for such a small thing.

Lance knew he was just buying time now, clutching at straws. "Where's your service weapon?" he said.

"All this way for one little girl?" Viktor said. "It doesn't make any sense."

"Why doesn't it?"

"All this trouble. What is she to you?"

"Time's up, Viktor. Enough talk."

Viktor shook his head. "You're not here for Natasha."

"Then what am I here for?"

Viktor let out a hollow laugh. "I know why you're here."

Lance raised an eyebrow. "Okay?"

"Richmond Tenet."

Lance shook his head.

"A defection like that," Viktor said. "Your top man in London. That's something worth traveling for."

"I'm going to be honest with you, Viktor. I could give a fuck about Richmond Tenet."

"How can you say that? He's going to compromise every operation this side of the Atlantic."

Lance shrugged. "You got any final words to get off your chest?"

Viktor moved slowly toward the window. Lance let him. He removed his jacket and threw it lightly to Lance. "My pistol is in the pocket," he said.

Lance took it out and examined it. It was a Makarov, the gun that had served as the Soviet standard military and police sidearm from its introduction in 1951 until its replacement almost fifty years later. It was a nice gun, worn from decades of use.

Viktor was at the window and reached up to the curtain, pulling it aside to give himself a view to the square. It could have been a signal to someone, there could have been a team out there, but Lance didn't think so.

Lance removed all but one of the bullets from Viktor's gun. "You ready to do this?"

"Can I have a drink first?"

There was a limit to how much slack Lance was willing

to cut this guy in exchange for information. "Do I look like a bartender?"

Viktor sighed. He was looking out the window intently at something. He turned to Lance and said, "I'm actually glad you're here."

"Sure you are.."

"No, really."

"Well, that's just as well, isn't it?" Lance said. He handed Viktor his gun and kept his own at the ready. He'd just armed his opponent. One wrong move and he would blow Viktor's head off.

Viktor looked at the gun in his hand. "It was my father's," he said.

Lance said nothing.

He wouldn't have understood all this," Viktor continued, waving his hand around the room. "He wouldn't have approved."

"All men think that," Lance said. "There's not a son alive that doesn't feel he disappointed the old man."

"No," Viktor said, shaking his head. "In my case, it's true. My father was a Moscow city cop for fifty years. He'd seen it all. Or thought he had. He thought he knew what evil looked like."

"You think otherwise?"

"If my father knew me now," Viktor said, "if he knew the man I'd become, it would be his worst nightmare."

Lance nodded. He was no stranger to such thoughts.

"Do you know where I was before I came here tonight?" Viktor went on.

"I do not."

"A brothel."

"I'm not a priest," Lance said. "Save your confessing."

He kept his eye on Viktor's hand. He was holding a

loaded gun now. Viktor put the gun on the table, almost absentmindedly, and let out a long sigh. "I'm actually not a good man," he said.

Lance exhaled smoke.

"I didn't want to go after the girl," Viktor continued.

"If I get Suvorov," Lance said, "will Natasha Gazinsky be safe?"

"As safe as she can be," Viktor said. "She'll be on a list, but there are thousands of names on such lists. If you get Suvorov, there will be no one at the Prime Directorate overseeing her case. Natasha will go to the bottom of some pencil-pusher's pile."

Lance nodded. "In that case," he said, "we've got nothing left to discuss."

Viktor sucked on his cigarette and blew the smoke against the glass. He was still looking at something out there. "I was with a girl tonight," he said. "A prostitute. I shouldn't have...."

"Was it worth it?" Lance said.

Viktor turned and looked at him. "She was crying."

"Crying?"

Viktor nodded, almost imperceptibly.

"The girl was crying?" Lance said again.

"I couldn't stop myself."

Lance raised his gun, pointed at Viktor's head, and pulled the trigger. The gun recoiled and the sound of a suppressed bullet pulsed through the room. Viktor's head jerked, and his body flew backward, knocking over the desk on its way to the floor. Blood and brains spattered on the wall.

Lance stubbed his cigarette in the ashtray and looked down at Viktor. On the floor next to him was his father's gun.

It was only a gesture, letting him die by his own hand with his father's gun, but Lance felt good about depriving him of it. He got up and went to the window. Outside, the wind whipped the snow in ferocious eddies. By the lamp post, Lance saw what Viktor had been looking at—a lone dog, skulking around the square, shivering.

74

Tatyana was back in her hotel room. She couldn't stay long. She'd failed her mission, there had been GRU agents everywhere, and somewhere in her mind, still percolating through layers of confusion and anger, was the realization that she'd just been sent right into a trap.

She was standing in front of the mirror in the bathroom, holding the sink in both hands as if she was about the rip it from the wall. The cold tap was running, and when the sink was full, she bent down and plunged her face in the water.

She held herself there, face submerged, for thirty seconds, forty-five, sixty, then rose back up suddenly, spilling water, gasping for air.

Her mind darted. Images, uncorrelated, disparate, flashed through her mind. She had to unravel it, make sense, connect the dots before she got herself killed.

Something had gone very wrong. The GRU had been waiting. Even Richmond Tenet seemed unsurprised.

She'd been set up.

The image of Tenet's face flashed before her. He'd

looked up and, as calmly as if she was there to change his towels, said, "You poor girl."

What did that mean?

And the expression on his face?

Her mind darted from Tenet to Laurel. "I have no right to ask you this," Laurel had said. Tatyana had taken the mission without so much as a second thought. She'd wanted to do it. "I'd go myself," Laurel said.

But Laurel hadn't gone herself.

She'd sent Tatyana.

And Roth. What was it he'd said to her? "You've been letting your guard down. You're getting sloppy. I don't want you in London." Something was off. Roth and Tenet's relationship went back decades. All those secret meetings, unrecorded phone calls, off-the-record conversations.

Tatyana hadn't parsed it yet. She didn't know how the pieces fit together. And she didn't have time to figure it out. All she knew was that when she'd entered Tenet's room, the GRU was waiting for her.

She'd already been back in the hotel room for ten minutes. She had to get out of there. She looked at the bed. Laid out on it were the items she'd brought with her—documentation, credit cards, two passports, all given to her by Laurel.

Could she trust them?

She was about to leave empty-handed when the phone on the nightstand began to ring.

Her jaw clenched. She glared at the phone like it was a rattlesnake. It could be another trap.

She walked over and picked it up. "Who is this?"

"Tatyana! It's me."

"Laurel?"

"You're okay?"

"You sold me out," Tatyana blurted, emotion getting the better of her. "You sent me right into a trap."

"No," Laurel said.

"They were waiting for me, Laurel. They knew I was coming."

"I know they did."

"What are you talking about?"

"You were sold out."

"By Roth?"

"Not Roth."

"Who then?"

"Tatyana, it was Declan."

"Declan? How?"

"He's reporting to Moscow."

"How is that even...."

"And he knows where you're staying. You need to get out of that hotel. Now."

"Where can I go?"

"Don't go to the embassy. Roth never sanctioned this. He's going to be furious."

"I'll find somewhere to lay low and report back," Tatyana said, and as she said the words, she noticed out of the corner of her eye a shadow pass the window on the balcony.

Instinct took over. The glass at the window shattered, and in the same instant, she picked up the receiver and flung it. A man dressed entirely in black, his hands gloved and his face covered by a black balaclava, came through the door and in the same instant was hit in the face by the phone.

Tatyana ran toward him and knocked the gun from his hand as three more men came through the shattering glass doors. She pulled the man in front of her and used him to absorb a spray of gunfire, then she pushed him forward and followed him. He stumbled toward the other men, bullets pelting his body, and as he reached the first of them, Tatyana leaped over him and grabbed the next man by the neck. Using the weight of her body as she fell, she yanked his head backward and to the right in a sharp jerk. He fell to the ground on top of her, shielding her from more bullets. She grabbed his gun, the same submachine gun the GRU guards at the embassy had, and rolled through the shattered door out to the balcony. Shards of glass bit into her flesh and the two remaining men followed her. She fired and caught both of them in the face and chest as they emerged through the lace curtain.

She watched them fall, but before they'd even hit the ground, she realized there was a helicopter in the night sky above the hotel. She looked up as a sharpshooter let off a hail of gunfire in her direction.

She leaped to her feet and began running. In a second, she'd spanned the width of the balcony as a stream of bullets hit the ground behind her, sending chips of stone and dust into the air. The balcony had a two-foot decorative stone wall around it, and she jumped over it and dropped to the other side, grabbing hold of it to stop herself from falling to her death.

The building now shielded her from the helicopter, which would take a moment to reposition around the corner and get a new line of sight.

She was seven floors up and looked down at the street below. The height was dizzying. Her grip faltered, and she almost lost hold of the ledge. The balcony overhung the floor below by about half a foot, and she scrambled with her feet trying to get some sort of purchase. The helicopter passed overhead, and the shooter got his line of sight. He took two shots, missing by mere inches.

Tatyana swung her legs under the overhang and felt the glass of a window. The helicopter was steadying its position, which would give the shooter better aim, and she knew she was running out of time. She swung her legs again under the ledge, kicking the pane of glass, which refused to break. The shooter let off another shot. It struck so close that she felt the chips of stone hitting her hand.

She let go of the ledge with a single hand to give her feet extra reach, then kicked the window again. Her feet bounced off it.

In desperation, she flung all her weight outward, then, as her momentum returned, kicked herself in the direction of the window and let go of the ledge.

She was certain she was about to plummet to her death, but she had no other choice. Bullets flew by her so close she felt the air around them.

Her momentum carried her inward toward the window, the glass shattering before her from the shooter's bullets, and she flew through the window, landing on the floor inside, ducking for cover as more bullets flew overhead.

The room was dark, unoccupied, and she ran forward, jumped over the bed, and kicked open the door. From there, she ran down the service stairwell, taking entire flights with a single leap. When she reached the ground floor, she opened the door a crack and scanned the lobby. It was clear. She hurried through it, out the front door, and into one of the cabs in front of the hotel.

The chopper was above her somewhere. She could hear it but couldn't see it. Police cars were arriving in droves, lights flashing, sirens blaring. A crowd was gathering, straining to see what was going on.

"Take me to the Metro," Tatyana said to the driver frantically. "Go, go, go."

He pulled away from the curb and made his way through the police and crowd. No one paid them any mind. When they'd gone a few blocks, Tatyana began to breathe. She had to get her bearings, collect her thoughts.

There was a TV screen on the back of the seat in front of her. It was showing news footage of her attack on the Russian embassy. News crews in helicopters were hovering above the scene, their spotlights scanning the grounds, while dozens of police cars lined up in the streets around the embassy.

"Crazy night," the driver said, eyeing her in his mirror.

Tatyana looked back at him, pointedly holding his gaze. "Drive," she said.

75

The guards escorted Ada and Natasha to the car. They got in the back, and the two guards sat up front.

"We're going to a medical clinic on Harley Street," Ada said.

She was nervous as the car made its way out of the hotel parking lot. When they stopped at traffic lights, she found herself reaching into her jacket for her gun. Everything went smoothly, and the car made easy progress through the morning traffic. They went north over the Thames and followed Grosvenor Place past Buckingham Palace. On Park Lane, they passed the glamorous five-star hotels and restaurants and from there went up Marylebone Road before turning onto Harley Street.

Harley Street was an area that specialized in medicine, with many of the world's most expensive consultants and specialists maintaining exclusive facilities inside its quaint houses.

The car stopped outside an Edwardian townhouse

where a discreet bronze plaque announced the Belvedere Clinic.

"Wait here," Ada said as she got out. "If you see anything suspicious, call it in immediately."

The driver nodded. His partner looked at his watch and said, "How long do you think you'll be?"

"I'm not sure."

"We're coming up on fourteen hours. If you're going to be a while, this is a good place for a shift change."

"Okay," Ada said. She brought Natasha up to the front of the clinic, with its large wooden door painted a glossy black. There was a buzzer, and beneath it, a small sign read, 'By Appointment.'

She pressed the buzzer.

The door was opened by a young woman in a white suit that was reminiscent of, but not quite identical to, a nurse's uniform.

"Ms. Hudson?" she said.

Ada nodded, and the woman made way for them to enter.

If the building's exterior was reminiscent of Edwardian elegance, the interior was more like a glitzy club. Ultra-modern crystal shards hung from the ceiling, and mini-malist white furniture was arranged in front of a slick receptionist's desk.

"If you'd like to take a seat," the woman said, "the doctor will be right with you."

They sat, and Ada put a hand on Natasha's back. The child glanced around the clinic, her eyes wide with anticipation. She was no stranger to doctors' offices, and Ada had explained to her what to expect, but she was still scared.

After a few minutes, a nurse in an actual nurse's uniform appeared and asked them to come with her. They followed her down a hallway with plush, emerald green carpets and up a wide staircase that doubled back on itself at each floor. On the third floor, there was another waiting area, and they sat down again.

"Can I get you anything while you wait?" the nurse said.

"Some water," Ada said.

Across the room was a large window. Beyond the surrounding rooftops, the enormous spire of the BT Tower rose up toward the sky.

The nurse brought them two bottles of water on a tray with glasses and ice. A few minutes later, a woman in an expensive gray suit and Valentino high heels appeared. She was in her mid-fifties, and when she reached to shake Ada's hand, Ada noticed a Cartier watch on her wrist.

"My name is Dr. Julienne Blackwell," the woman said. "You must be Ada and Natasha."

"We are," Ada said.

"Natasha," the doctor said, "do you understand me when I speak English?"

Natasha looked at Ada, then back to the doctor.

"She speaks a little English, don't you, Natasha?"

"Yes," Natasha said timidly.

"Well," Julienne said, "my colleagues in Boston filled me in on your condition, and I can tell you that I'm very happy to be able to help you in any way I can."

Natasha nodded.

Blackwell went to the reception desk and picked up some documents. "Now," she said, "I understand that you're nine years old, Natasha."

"Yes," Natasha said quietly.

"And as for a legal guardian," Blackwell said, turning back to Ada.

"I've got some paperwork from the Director's office," Ada said.

Blackwell took the papers from Ada and looked them over. "It says here that you're authorized to act on behalf of the Government of the United States in this matter," Blackwell said.

"Yes," Ada said.

"I see," Blackwell said.

"We just want you to do a checkup for her," Ada said. "So that the doctors in Boston can be prepared."

"Dr. Hannson did tell me what he needed," Blackwell said. "We're all set to do the assessment and take the samples." She paused. "It's just...."

"Yes?" Ada said.

"Perhaps we could go into my office," Blackwell said. She turned to the nurse and asked her to wait with Natasha, then led Ada up the hall to her office. "Ms. Hudson," she said as soon as she'd shut the door, "I'm going to need a little more background on why this child, who I understand is a Russian citizen, is being brought into my office by a foreign government."

"Yes," Ada said, "I wasn't sure how much Hannson had told you."

"He didn't tell me that Natasha would be brought in without a legal guardian."

"Her parents are dead."

"Then the legal authority would revert to her own government, wouldn't it?"

"You're talking about the government that's trying to kill her," Ada said.

"Be that as it may...."

"Look," Ada said, cutting her off, "if you want me to go to the Russian embassy to get some piece of paper granting me guardianship, it's not going to happen. The Russians are trying to kill her. What you need to decide is whether or not, given that fact, you're willing to give her the treatment she needs."

Blackwell thought for a moment, then said, "Both her parents are dead?"

"Her father died trying to defect to our side. Before he died, I gave him my word that Natasha would get the treatment she needed."

"And there's no chance of getting the British government to step in? If what you say is true, surely she would qualify for some sort of protection."

"Not within the timescale we need," Ada said, "and not with the degree of discretion we need. If I go to your government, they'll take over Natasha's case, and I won't be able to protect her."

Blackwell listened intently to every word, then said, "Ms. Hudson, can I be frank?"

"Of course," Ada said.

"This raises issues. Legally, ethically, it's complicated."

"No," Ada said. "It's not complicated. This is as black and white as it gets. The Russian government wants this child dead. They want to use her death to send a message to anyone else in Russia thinking of defecting. Natasha needs our help, and if we don't take care of this, you and I, right here, right now, I can promise you that no one else will. My government, your government, they see this child as a liability, and if they can wash their hands of her, they will. Believe me."

"Surely there are official channels...."

"There are," Ada said, "but they're not going to be used. No one in the State Department, or the CIA Director's office, or the British Home Office, wants this file on their desk. Either we do this now, you and I, or it doesn't happen at all."

Blackwell went quiet. Ada was beginning to lose hope in her when she sighed and said, "Fine."

"You'll do it?"

"Send her in."

"Of course," Ada said.

"Alone," Blackwell added.

Ada looked at her.

"If I'm going to treat her, then I want to speak to her in private first."

Ada went back to the waiting area and took Natasha by the hand. "I'm going to bring you to the doctor's office, all right?"

Natasha went along with her, and when they got to the door, Ada said, "I'll be right outside."

Natasha nodded, then went into the office alone.

Ada waited with bated breath, fidgeting nervously for what felt like a very long time, and when the door finally opened, she jumped to her feet.

"Everything's fine," Blackwell said.

"And?"

"And Natasha is a very brave young woman. I'm going to take her into the examination room now."

"Should I come?" Ada said.

"If you're needed, someone will come for you."

Ada sat back down. The nurse offered her coffee, and she accepted. She sipped it for the next thirty minutes until Blackwell emerged from the examination room. "There's something you need to see."

Ada followed her into the examination room. Natasha was lying on a table with a surgical gown covering her body. She was awake and seemed comfortable.

"Natasha, are you okay?" Ada said in Russian.

Natasha nodded. Next to her, some sort of machine, it looked like a refrigerator, was hooked up to a display. Blackwell brought Ada to the screen, which showed a scan of Natasha's arm.

"There," Blackwell said, pointing to something on the screen.

"What am I looking at?" Ada said.

Blackwell looked at her pointedly. "You tell me."

"I assure you, doctor, I have no idea."

"If this is some sort of CIA...."

"Doctor, believe me, whatever's been done to this child...."

"Someone's inserted something into her arm."

"*Inserted* something?"

Blackwell took Ada by the arm and pulled her back out to the corridor. "I need you to tell me right now. Did you know that was in her arm?"

"I swear to God," Ada said, "I had no idea. I brought her here because I promised her father she'd get treatment. That's it."

"Because if this is some sort of CIA scheme to get me to...."

"To what?"

"I don't know," Blackwell said, "*harvest* something."

"It's not," Ada said. "We didn't know this child existed until a few days ago, and whatever's happened to her, it wasn't on our watch. You have to believe me."

Blackwell shook her head. She was spooked. She took a few paces away from Ada then turned back to face her. She wanted to say something but didn't seem sure what it was.

"Tell me," Ada said. "Whatever it is."

"It's a chip," she said.

"What do you mean, it's a chip?"

"It's a computer chip."

"In her arm?"

"Like something from a movie?" Blackwell said.

"A movie?"

"A CIA spy movie."

"It's not ours."

"Then it's theirs."

"Could it be a tracking chip?"

"I don't have the slightest clue what it could be."

"Can you take it out of her?"

"This is an examination," Blackwell said. "That would require a surgical procedure."

"Doctor, if that thing was planted by the Russian government, it could be a matter of life and death."

76

Tatyana checked in to a cheap hotel on the *Rive Gauche* and stripped naked. She'd stopped at a drug store on her way and bought hydrogen peroxide, hair dye, scissors, and a sewing kit. In her room, she cleaned her wounds, patched up her clothing, and put in the hair dye.

Then she sat on the bed, took a deep breath, and waited for the dye to take effect. The room was basic. She'd paid in cash and wouldn't be there long. There was a phone by the bed, and she picked it up. As she dialed Laurel's number, she realized her hand was shaking.

"Tatyana! Are you okay?"

"They came after me, Laurel."

"I know."

"A team of them, with a chopper."

"Are you hurt?"

There was a sound from the corridor outside Tatyana's door. "Hold on," she said. She moved silently to the door and peered out the peephole. A maid with a cart was going into one of the other rooms. She went back to the phone. "Sorry."

"What's going on?"

"Nothing. I'm at a hotel."

"You're sure you're okay?"

"I'm pissed off is what I am."

"Because I sent you into that shit show?"

"It's not your fault, Laurel. It's mine."

"You're human."

"I can't believe I was so stupid. I mean, *I'm* supposed to be the honey-trap. I fell for my own trick."

"I've been thinking about that," Laurel said.

"And?"

"Well, how did he find you?"

"I met him at the hotel."

"How did they know to go to the Saint Royal?"

"What are you saying, Laurel?"

"You know what I'm saying. Who, other than you and me, knows about the hotel?"

Tatyana bit her lip. "Do you really think...."

"I don't know," Laurel said. "But I smell a whole lot of shit, and it's coming from Roth's direction."

"I smell it too," Tatyana said, "but the thing is, even if the Russians had help, it never should have been so easy for them to get inside my head."

"What do you mean?"

"Declan knew exactly what he was doing. It was like he had an instruction manual to my brain."

"Don't be too hard on yourself, Tatyana. They have your psyche profile. Of course they know what buttons to push."

"I thought I'd at least have made it a challenge for them."

"Well, it's about to get a lot more challenging. I'm going to take care of him for you."

"I can take care of him myself."

"Well, that's the thing."

"What's the thing?"

"You can't come home yet."

"Why not?"

"I'm sorry, Tatyana, but there's one more target."

"You're kidding me."

"He's on a train from London to Paris as we speak. If you don't get him, we may lose him for good."

"Who is he?" Tatyana said, sighing. There was a mirror over the desk in the room, and she looked at herself in it.

"His name is Stan Morel. He's been photographing Natasha Gazinsky for the Main Directorate."

"That's not a Russian name."

"He's British. Ex-military."

"He's a contractor?"

"Yes."

"If they want pictures of Natasha Gazinsky, they'll just hire someone else."

"That's what I said to Lance."

"You spoke to him?"

"Briefly."

"This is his target?"

"It's our target."

"Honestly, Laurel, going after a contractor, it's...."

"I know."

"It's vindictive, Laurel."

"I know, Tatyana."

"Lance doesn't know when to rein it in, does he? He finds out this little girl needs his help and just starts tearing the world apart."

"I know he does. It's just, he knows that Natasha Gazinsky will be safer with this guy dead."

"I mean," Tatyana said, "if you want me to go after him, I'll go after him. It's just...."

"Just what?"

"I don't know. I thought things would be different, you know?"

"On our side of the fence?"

"Yes, on your side of the fence."

"I'm sorry."

"This Stan Morel, he works for whoever pays him. He's just some guy who took the wrong job."

"If you don't want to do it...."

"It's not that, Laurel. I mean, is he even political?"

"Not as far as I know."

Tatyana shook her head. "How long have we been talking?" she said, changing the subject.

"Do you think you're being traced?"

"I've got hair dye in."

"Oh."

"Yeah."

"Well, this guy will be arriving on the Eurostar from London in less than an hour."

"*Gare du Nord*?"

"Yes."

"Laurel, if you tell me to go, I'll go, but for the record, this is overkill. This guy isn't a threat to Natasha Gazinsky any longer. He isn't even in the same country as her. He's on the run, near as I can tell."

"What would the GRU tell you to do in this situation?"

"They'd tell me to kill him."

"Well then."

"But we're supposed to be better than them."

"I don't know, Tatyana. They kill our guys. We kill their guys. We're not better than them. We're the same as them."

"This isn't even a CIA order, though, is it? It's Lance Spector going rogue because he's trying to save this one girl. I've seen it before, Laurel. It's a pattern."

"It's the same pattern that got you out, Tatyana."

Tatyana sighed. "He's sucking us all into his world."

"I know."

"Send me the package. I've still got the cell."

She hung up the phone and got into the shower. She washed out the dye and examined the result in the mirror. It wasn't perfect, but with every cop in the city looking for a dark-haired femme fatale, it would do.

By the time she was dressed, the data package had arrived. It contained some images of the target and his train itinerary. Nothing else. She had thirty minutes to get to the station, barely enough time in the morning traffic, but instead of leaving immediately, she sat down on the bed. She was tired, not just from the events of the last twelve hours, but from everything, all of it.

She was no longer sure she could trust Roth. Every new fact made her more suspicious of him.

But worse than that, she wasn't sure she could trust herself. She'd let her guard down, and the first man she let in her bed was a spy. And not just that, but she'd let him get right under her skin. What did that say about her judgment? Her mental state?

She'd known the things she was doing with Declan weren't normal. They weren't healthy. They were triggered by a specific trauma in her past, and she was looking for release from the memory of it. In her own messed-up way, she was looking for resolution. She still woke up at night, clutching her neck, gasping for air, and she knew she needed to do something to exorcise that demon.

But to let it become a vulnerability, a flaw open to exploitation, to let the GRU back into her bed after she'd fought so hard to break free of them, that was too much.

And it had almost gotten her killed.

She stood up and took a breath. Looked in the mirror. If there was one thing she knew, she told herself, it was how to survive.

She left the room and got a cab from the Pont Neuf. The data package included access instructions for a drop box at the Zürich Berenberg Bank of Commerce, located across from the Église Saint-Eustache near the train station.

The cab made good time, and she got out a block before the bank. Approaching on foot gave her a chance to scope it out before walking in. Two men entered before her, both in suits, and she kept an eye on them while also checking to see if anyone entered behind her. No one did. She asked the guard to direct her to the safe deposit boxes, and he pointed down a short corridor with a stone floor. She hurried down the corridor and found the boxes, which were accessed by a code she'd been sent by Laurel. She opened her box, brought it to one of the wooden stalls for privacy, and looked inside. It contained the usual items—cash, documents, a US military 9mm SIG Sauer M17. Not her first choice of weapon, but with the train arriving in less than ten minutes, she didn't have time to be picky.

She slipped the gun in the waist of her pants, left the bank, and hurried the couple of blocks to the station. The Gare du Nord was one of the city's main stations, and it was already busy with commuters. She walked into the international concourse and checked the arrival times. The target's train was right on schedule. She couldn't access the platform without a ticket, so she bought a bouquet of roses and a cup of coffee and brought them to a bench. The flowers would attract attention, but who would think the girl holding them was his killer?

A minute later, a modern, high-speed train pulled into the station and came smoothly to a stop. Tatyana sipped her coffee and watched the passengers disembark. About a hundred people got off the train and began making their way along the platform toward her. They passed a security guard and continued right by her. She watched them, one hand holding the flowers and the other at her waist, ready to grab the gun beneath her shirt.

She scanned the faces for her target. He was near the back, carrying a briefcase, and she waited for him to pass her before getting up. She left the flowers behind and followed him, keeping a distance of about forty feet.

He broke off from the group to take an escalator, and she knew he would become suspicious when she did the same. At the top of the escalator was an executive lounge. She wondered if he was meeting someone there, perhaps there was some intelligence to be gleaned, but she knew that option was off the table as soon as he looked back over his shoulder. She looked away, tried to look casual, but she saw the expression on his face change.

He was near the top of the escalator, she was near the bottom, and she thought he was going to run for it, but he didn't. He reached into his coat and drew a gun.

Tatyana flinched. The bullet flew wide, and she was about to return fire when a woman and child appeared at the top of the escalator. She hesitated, and the target broke into a run.

Tatyana sprinted up the rest of the steps. Below her in the concourse, people began to flee in panic. She reached the top of the escalator and saw that the target hadn't dropped his briefcase. It slowed him down as she chased, and as soon as he was within range, she stopped, steadied one hand in the other, aimed, and pulled the trigger.

The man's legs continued even as the top half of his body collapsed. She'd hit him at the center of his back, and he took a few final staggering steps, then hit the ground, sliding forward over the smooth surface, the briefcase still firmly clutched in his hand.

His gun was on the ground a few feet away from him, and she approached calmly, like a tennis player crossing the court to pick up a ball.

He squirmed, struggling to get up. She bent down and took the briefcase. He looked up at her but offered no resistance.

"Stan Morel?" she said, pointing the gun at his face.

"Please," he said, raising his hand.

She turned her head, as if spattered blood might get in her eyes if she didn't, and fired.

77

R ichmond Tenet was sitting in the luxurious passenger cabin of a Challenger 605 jet as it taxied along the runway at Le Bourget. He'd expected to be debriefed in Paris, but after the attack, the GRU had expedited his transfer to Moscow. Nothing convinced the Kremlin of an asset's value faster than a CIA assassination attempt.

When the hostess offered him a glass of Louis XIII cognac shortly after takeoff, he knew he'd made it to the top of someone's priority list. Perhaps even President Molotov's himself.

He tried to relax on the flight, which was difficult even with the booze, and when the plane landed at the Khodynka Aerodrome in Moscow, he felt his pulse pounding. When the plane came to a halt, a black Mercedes pulled up next to it. Tenet descended the steps of the plane and got into the back of the car. It had been upgraded for high-value passengers with a reinforced undercarriage, bullet-proof glass, and its own emergency air supply.

Someone was pulling out all the stops.

The Khodynka Aerodrome was located within sight of the GRU headquarters, which was a building so gargantuan it supposedly contained more concrete than the 1980 Moscow Olympic stadium.

The car pulled up to a secure entryway beneath the east wing of the headquarters and came to a halt. Waiting at the door were four armed guards flanking an extremely attractive blonde woman in a tight-fitting blue dress.

"Mr. Tenet," the woman said in Russian when he got out of the car, "Welcome to Moscow."

"Thank you," Tenet said, following her into a cavernous concrete corridor that had been built to the same specifications as a Moscow city subway tunnel. The walls of the tunnel were painted an institutional green, and the distinct smell of chlorine lingered in the air. They passed through a guardhouse lit by bright fluorescent lights. On either side, tall stacks of paper sat on wooden desks.

At the end of the guardhouse was an elevator large enough to drive a car into. Tenet, the woman, and two soldiers entered the elevator, which brought them to the ground floor. From there, they transferred to another elevator, and this one gave a glimpse of the luxury that was to come. The elevator looked more like it belonged in an old European hotel than a Soviet-era office building. The walls were inlaid with oak paneling, and crystal light sconces were set into them that clinked and chimed as the elevator ascended.

When the doors opened, they stepped out onto the top floor. This was another world entirely, with plush carpeting, floor-to-ceiling mahogany bookshelves, and large windows lined with sixteen-foot high curtains of gold-trimmed red velvet.

"I feel like I'm back in the Savile Club," Tenet said.

The woman in the blue dress nodded politely and led him to a set of heavy oak doors. Stepping aside, she held out an arm. "This is as far as I go."

"Thank you," Tenet said.

He wasn't quite sure what awaited him beyond the doors, other than that a series of very intense debriefings were likely in his future. He'd rehearsed for it with Roth, over and over, for years, but still, it was daunting.

He pushed open the door expecting to find people inside, but the room was empty. There was a large window with a wide vista over the Khodynka, and in the center of the room was a round wooden table with eight chairs set around it. On the table was an ominous-looking tape recorder, an anachronistic reel-to-reel machine like something the FBI would have used in the eighties. Next to it was a small wooden box. There was also a crystal decanter containing vodka and a single crystal glass, as well as an ashtray, a packet of Russian cigarettes, and a steel lighter.

"Just the one glass?" he said to the woman.

She gave him the thinnest of smiles, and when he entered the room, she shut the door behind him. He heard it lock.

Something wasn't right.

He sat at the table and waited. No one came. He looked at the tape recorder, the glass, the cigarettes, the vodka. Everything was set up for one man.

For him.

With a sigh, he picked up the cigarettes and lit one.

The tape recorder was a Polish model, Unitra. He hadn't seen one in years but knew why it was here now. It used a unique type of quarter-inch magnetic tape that was known for its sensitivity. The tape was thin as a cost-saving measure during Communism, but this also had the side effect of making it extremely difficult, even impossible, to tamper with without leaving signs of interference.

It became the tape of choice for anyone wishing to show that a recording was unaltered.

He was about to press play but stopped himself. Instead, he reached for the decanter and smelled the vodka. It was very good. He poured himself a generous measure, drank it, then lit another cigarette, inhaling deeply.

His attention turned to the wooden box. He knew all too well what it contained.

78

Suvorov stood at the open door of his office. Down the hallway, Richmond Tenet was being escorted to the conference room by his secretary. Suvorov was tempted to go in, to gloat, but that would destroy the poeticism of the scene he'd set up.

The phone on his secretary's desk was ringing, and she hurried to answer it.

"Who is it, Katrina?" he growled.

"Sir," she said, looking up at him from the phone. "It's the Navy Testing Facility in Nyonoksa."

"It's Viktor. Put him through."

"I'm sorry, sir. It's not Viktor."

Suvorov looked at her curiously, then went to his desk and picked up the phone. He waited for the click of the connection, and then a nervous voice came on the line.

"Sir, this is Commander Zhirkov. I have replaced Anpilov here at the Nyonoksa facility."

"And?" Suvorov said impatiently.

"Well, sir," he said hesitantly.

"What do you want, Zhirkov?"

"I have some bad news, sir. Your man from the Main Directorate...."

"Viktor Lapin," Suvorov said. "What of him?"

"He was just found in his hotel room."

"Found?"

"Dead, sir. Military police are in possession of the scene."

"Suicide?" Suvorov said.

"I'm afraid not, sir. He was shot from across the room."

"And the killer?"

"Sir, we've shut the airport."

"I want the passenger manifest of every plane that entered the city in the past four days. Do you hear me, Zhirkov?"

"Yes, sir."

"Flag any name that's not active-duty military personnel. And the trains too."

"We'll send it over right away, sir."

"Anyone, Zhirkov, and I mean anyone you can't account for, I want flagged."

79

Laurel was in the suite at the Saint Royal, sitting at her desk. On the computer screen, a terminal window updated constantly with streams of raw data—Keyhole satellite feeds, CCTV systems, financial transactions, live police dispatch information.

When Stan Morel's train pulled into the *Gare du Nord,* she was watching. She'd tapped into the station's camera system and watched as Tatyana followed Stan, as he fled, as he fired at her and she gave chase, and as she pulled the trigger.

Tatyana left the scene, but Laurel kept watching. She watched onlookers timidly approach the body, then police, then paramedics. A detective arrived and cordoned off the scene. That could be dealt with. A phone call to the DGSI in Paris would do the job.

Laurel watched it all with the fascination of someone watching a soap opera, and when the body was finally taken away, she stood up from the desk and checked her watch.

"An eye for an eye," she said to herself, picking up a pair

of black leather gloves and pulling them on over her mani-
cured fingers.

She opened a drawer in the desk and took out a stainless
steel box magazine, then went about loading it carefully
with ten .22 Long Rifle cartridges, polishing each as she
went to remove any trace of fingerprints. They were small
bullets and would be considered inadequate to the task by
many, but Laurel had chosen them deliberately. They were
quiet, left no mess, and the Ruger Standard Model that fired
them was easy to conceal. Laurel's particular model had
been equipped by the US Navy with two layers of suppres-
sion, one of stainless steel and the other of an aluminum
alloy. Together, they made for an extremely quiet gun.
When she'd loaded the gun, she went to the sink and carefully added a few tablespoons of water to the suppressor.

Then she went to the bedroom, where she'd laid out a
maid's uniform that she'd purchased earlier from one of the
hotel housekeepers.

She put on the dress, old fashioned with a short skirt
and white apron, and then had to find somewhere to hide
the gun, which, with the added length of the suppressor,
was thirteen inches long. She'd intended to strap it to her
inner thigh, but the skirt was too short to conceal it. She
settled for a pocket at the front of the dress beneath the
apron.

Her agreement with the hotel management, which had
given her the entire top floor of the hotel to carry out her
operation, and included the installation of communications
infrastructure on the roof and the use of a private elevator,
was conditional on one thing—that absolutely no bloodshed take place within the four walls of the Saint Royal
Hotel.

What she was about to do would breach that agreement.

She left her room and took the elevator to the basement level, where the housekeeper she'd purchased the uniform from was waiting for her with a cleaning cart. She took the cart back into the elevator and pushed the button for Declan's floor. When the door opened, she wheeled the cart to his door and knocked lightly. "Housekeeping," she called gently, giving herself a vaguely foreign accent.

The door opened, and a man in a hotel robe stood there looking at her. Laurel had seen him in pictures, but his physical presence was more impressive in person. He was over six feet tall and had a muscular, athletic build that was partially visible through the loosely draped robe. Through the robe, she could see thick, black hair on his chest. She had to admit, she could see the attraction.

"I can come back," she said meekly, but she already knew he'd let her in. She'd adjusted the uniform in all the right ways, opening a few buttons on the blouse, taking a few inches off the hem of the skirt. She'd also omitted the thick black tights that were part of the uniform, and replaced them with a more suggestive pair of her own, with a seam running up the back from the heel.

"No need," he said. "Come in."

He stood in the doorway, making just enough room for her to pass if she was willing to brush against him.

When she was inside, he shut the door and then, perhaps even unconsciously, moved in front of it.

Laurel looked at him, sizing him up. What was it about this man that had allowed him to infiltrate her team so easily? What had he known about Tatyana that made her so vulnerable? And who, apart from the GRU, had helped him?

"Are you going to let me get to my cart?" Laurel said, making her voice softer and sweeter than usual.

He stepped aside and made a sweeping gesture toward

the door, like an usher showing the way to a king, but again, only leaving enough room for her to pass if she brushed against him.

She took a step back, luring him away from the door, but he didn't take the bait. Instead, the expression on his face changed, and he said. "What is this? What's going on?"

"Why is something going on?"

"You," he said, almost confused at the thought, "you're not afraid of me."

"Should I be?"

"No," he said, "but you're... *pretending*...."

He reached for the door, but he was too late.

"Don't," Laurel said, drawing the pistol.

He took one look at it and knew what it meant. "Tatyana," he said.

"That's right."

He nodded slowly.

"You don't seem surprised," Laurel said.

"I'm not surprised."

"Oh really?"

"You don't go after a woman like that and expect to get away with it," he said. "I told them as much."

"Told who?"

He shrugged. "*Them.* The Russians. The GRU."

"Who specifically?"

"Is that what you're here to find out?"

"I'm not here to find out anything. I'm here to keep a promise."

Declan nodded again. He was very calm. He seemed almost in agreement with her as to what was happening, what needed to be done.

"Why did you get into this position?" Laurel said. "You're an American. Successful. Rich."

"I've got my issues," he said.

"And Igor Aralov captured them on tape?" Laurel said.

He nodded. "You know about it?"

"I know Aralov. I know his methods."

"You haven't seen the tape then?"

Laurel shook her head. "You seem almost more worried about that than the fact you're about to be shot."

"Is that what's going to happen?"

"You know it is."

Declan sighed. "I promise you, if you knew what was on that tape, you'd feel the same way."

Laurel was being careful. She knew this man was a skilled manipulator. He had a US government security clearance, was called on regularly by Congress to give expert testimony, and had even gotten the better of Tatyana Aleksandrova. And yet, knowing all that, she still couldn't help feeling drawn to something in him.

"How did you find Tatyana?"

He shrugged. "I got the signal to make contact."

"With Aralov?"

"Yeah, but when I called, it wasn't Aralov who picked up."

"Aralov's dead," Laurel said.

"So his replacement, Viktor...."

"Viktor's dead too," Laurel said, then added, "now." She was taunting him, which was unnecessary, but for some reason, she couldn't help it.

"Viktor told me to come to the Saint Royal. When I got here, some surveillance photos were sent to my room."

"Of Tatyana?"

"Yes."

"And you made contact?"

"I made contact."

Laurel pursed her lips. She wasn't sure what to make of this. "How did Viktor know where to find Tatyana?"

Declan smiled. "Would a guy like me know a thing like that?"

"I suppose not," Laurel said, "but answer me this. How did a creep like you worm your way into Tatyana's bed so quickly?"

Declan looked very smug, which suited Laurel. It made him more inclined to brag. "I guess I was offering something she was interested in."

"And what could that be?" Laurel said.

"I'd venture to say you know *exactly* what it is."

"Don't," Laurel said, aiming the gun at his crotch.

"Hey," Declan said, "you're the one asking the questions."

"I'm trying to find out what could possibly have made a trained GRU assassin let a stranger like you into my house."

"It's not complicated," Declan said.

"Then please enlighten me."

"It wasn't sex."

"I saw her coming back from your room," Laurel said. "Don't tell me it wasn't sex."

"We fucked, sure, but that's not what it was about."

"Well, it seems to me like you met her in the bar and spent all of five minutes getting to know her."

"That's the thing...." Declan said, searching for the right words. "Some *connections* are *deeper* than words."

"*Connections*?" Laurel said, doing her best not to roll her eyes.

"Go ahead," Declan said. "You mock her as much as you mock me."

"I'm not mocking her."

"I know you know what I'm talking about."

"I assure you," Laurel said, "not a word you say makes a bit of sense to me."

"Come on," he said, and he gave her a strange smile. "It's written all over your face. You didn't have to dress like that to come here."

"What's that supposed to mean?"

"I get it," he said. "You're doing your job. You're asking these questions for *professional* reasons."

"I am."

"*Please*," he said.

Laurel clenched her jaw. "Well, whatever you two were doing, I hope it was worth it."

"Why don't you let me show you?" he said, and then, for some reason known only to himself, he pulled open the belt of his robe.

Laurel glanced down, then back at his face. "I sincerely hope that's not supposed to impress me."

"Tell me you're not tempted."

"Put it away."

"You wanted to know what kept your friend coming back for more."

"Put it away before I shoot it off."

He didn't put it away. In fact, the situation was arousing him, so much so that Laurel had to force herself not to look at it.

"Someone hurt her," he said.

"Hurt Tatyana?"

"Hurt her badly. A man."

"You don't need a psychology degree to know that."

"No," he said, "you don't."

Laurel raised the gun. "I think I've heard enough of your bullshit."

"Have you?" he said, raising an eyebrow as he let his robe fall to the ground.

"This is ridiculous."

"The same thing happened to you," he said. "I can smell it on you. You've been hurt too."

"Fuck off."

"Was it daddy?"

"I mean it," Laurel said. "Shut up now, or I'll blow it off, I swear to God."

"*Blow* it off?" he said, grinning.

She fired a shot, shattering the mirror behind him, missing him by mere inches. "Next one hits," she said.

He didn't seem to care. "Girls like you and your friend," he said. "need men like me."

"You don't know what you're talking about."

"Then why did she keep coming back for more? And what are you doing here, dressed like a...."

"You shut your mouth."

"I know you," he said, nodding his head. "I know you, and I know what you want."

"You know nothing about me."

"You keep waving that gun around," he said, "but you still can't pull the trigger."

"You want to bet?"

"Do it then," he said. "I should have done it myself a long time ago."

Laurel still hesitated.

"Look at you," he said, his eyes widening. "You poor girl. Admit it. You want a taste."

She raised the gun to his face.

He was stoic, unflinching. "What happened to you?" he said. "Why don't you sit on my knee and tell me all about it? Let's see if I can't make you feel better."

She pulled the trigger. His body fell back against the door and slumped to the ground heavily in front of it. She took a deep breath, then went over to him. The .22 was as tidy as intended. It made no exit wound. Instead, it created a small hole in the center of his forehead about the size of a quarter. A thin line of blood ran from the wound over his forehead and pooled in the gap between his lips.

"Fuck you," she said, then pulled open the door, yanking it and shoving him with it to make enough room to get past.

80

Ada hovered around Blackwell as she conducted further examinations. The chip was small enough to be removed. It would require a local anesthetic, a small incision, and then removal with forceps.

"It could be done here," Blackwell said.

"Now?"

"Yes."

"Would it be painful?"

"There will be discomfort. She'd need a few hours to recover."

Ada looked at the child. Sacha had said over and over that she was the only thing that mattered. Had he done this? Had he put the chip in her arm? If he had, and if it contained the data, then he might have just given her the one form of leverage that could save her life. He'd foreseen the difficulties that might arise, the reluctance of foreign governments to step in on behalf of a child in her situation, and he'd made her worth the risk.

"I need to call the embassy," Ada said.

Blackwell nodded.

"Print everything," Ada said. "The scans, the test results, whatever you can. They're going to want to see it."

Blackwell printed everything and put it in a sealed envelope. Ada called down to her bodyguards and asked for one of them to come up. When he arrived, she saw that the shift change had already happened.

"I'm Smith," he said.

Ada handed him the envelope. "I need you to go to the embassy and put this in Levi Roth's hand personally. Is that clear?"

"Crystal."

"What's your partner's name?"

"Rodney."

"Tell him to wait with the car."

Smith left, and Ada immediately called Roth. If she played this right, she might be able to get Natasha the deal she needed.

"Hudson," Roth said when he picked up, "what's going on?"

"I'm at the clinic with Natasha. We found something."

"What do you mean, found something?"

"A computer chip. In her arm."

"You mean embedded?"

"Beneath the skin, yes."

"It could be a trap, Ada. A toxin. Don't touch it."

"The doctor has taken scans. They're on their way to the embassy as we speak."

"I'll get the analysts looking at them immediately."

"It could contain the blueprints," Ada said, almost hesitantly.

"It could," Roth said, "or it could be some Russian booby trap."

"She's all that matters," Ada said.

"What's that?"

"That's what Sacha kept saying to me. He said it a hundred times. Natasha is the *only* thing that matters."

"Well, if those are more than a father's doting words," Roth said, "we'll know very soon."

"Yes, sir."

"And Ada?"

"Yes, sir?"

"Good work."

"Thank you, sir." He was about to hang up, and she said, "Mr. Roth."

"What is it?"

"You could use this as leverage."

"You mean with the State Department?"

"The chip. It could contain all the data Gazinsky promised."

"We'll cross that bridge when we get to it."

"I think this is a bridge we should cross now."

He hesitated a moment, and when he spoke, his tone had changed. "I see," he said.

"Before we know what's on the chip. Before anyone knows," she said, her heart pounding in her chest.

"I understand, Ada."

"Would they go for it? They'd have to, wouldn't they? The chip could be anything."

"Or it could be nothing."

"Tell them that's her condition. If they want to find out, they need to sign the deal they were going to sign with her father."

"*Her* condition, or yours?"

"Ours," Ada said, scarcely able to believe she was speaking like this to the Director of the CIA.

"What's required?" Roth said. "I can get something drafted."

"I've arranged for the doctor from Boston to treat her here in London," Ada said, "but that's going to require a release of funds."

"Doctors are expensive," Roth said.

"She's also going to need legal status here in the UK. A new name. A new passport. Someplace to stay."

"I'll see what I can do, Ada."

"The chip is inside her body," Ada said. "Some paperwork in exchange for finding out what's on it? I think that's a fair trade."

"You've got balls, Hudson. I'll give you that."

"So we have a deal?"

"I think they'll go for it," Roth said.

"Thank God," Ada said, more to herself than to him.

Then he said, "Well done, Ada. You did good by her. You pulled the threads together."

"Thank you, sir."

"You made this happen. Whatever promise you made to the father, you kept."

She hung up the phone and immediately sat down. She couldn't believe it. She just traded with the Director for Natasha's life, and it worked.

She went back into Natasha's room. Natasha seemed happy enough. If anything, her spirits were higher than they had been before. Blackwell checked in on them and said that they were free to go. She also told Ada that the tests for Hannson would be complete in a few days and that everything would be ready for Natasha to begin treatment soon after.

Ada helped Natasha dress, then they thanked Blackwell and the nurses and went back down to the ground floor. In the lobby, Ada asked the receptionist if she wouldn't mind going outside to check that their car was there.

"Black Mercedes?" the receptionist said.

"That's it."

"Right outside."

Ada took Natasha's hand and led her to the car. They climbed into the backseat.

The guard was a big guy. He looked at Ada in the mirror and nodded.

"Rodney?" she said.

"Yes, ma'am."

"Take us to the embassy."

The car pulled into the street, and Ada asked Natasha in Russian how she was feeling.

Natasha looked at the bandage on her arm and nodded. "Good," she said.

"You did so well," Ada said. "Your father would be very proud."

Natasha nodded again, then said, "You don't have to worry so much about me."

Ada was surprised. "Why do you say that?" she said.

"Everything's going to be all right."

"You're a very brave girl," Ada said.

"My father told me to be brave. He said he might have to leave me but that everything would be all right in the end."

"He told you that?"

"Yes."

"What else did he tell you?"

"He told me to be good."

Ada nodded. She wondered if Natasha had processed yet the fact that she was never going to see her father again.

She looked out the window. They were passing the

Elephant and Castle tube station, and Ada turned at the driver.

"This isn't the way to the embassy," she said, and she suddenly felt a chill run down her spine. She'd made a mistake.

In that same moment, the driver reached back, pointed a gun at her face, and pulled the trigger.

81

T enet stubbed out his cigarette and immediately lit another. There was no point delaying the inevitable, he thought, as he pressed play on the tape recorder. The reels of the cassette began to turn, the tape unspooling from one side and re-spooling on the other.

Roth: The time's come.

A shiver ran down his spine. The Russians had been listening. They knew everything. He remembered the conversation from the Hamlet pub just a few days earlier. All was lost. Everything they'd been working on had been for naught.

Tenet: I suppose we're not getting any younger.

Roth. No, we're not.

Tenet: And Igor Aralov is dead.

He sucked his cigarette, tapping the ash on the floor. He remembered where the conversation was going, and it was painful to listen to it.

Tenet: It's now or never then.

Roth: You're sure you're ready. I won't judge...

Tenet: I'm ready, Levi.

Roth: You don't have to...

Tenet: I know what I'm agreeing to, Levi.

It was a slap in the face to have it brought back to him now, like this. It was like watching the final moments before a car crash and not being able to change anything.

Roth: You'll never see her again.

Tenet's pulse pounded, and a thought entered his mind. It appeared that he and Roth had been defeated, outmaneuvered, outplayed. But what if Roth hadn't been outmaneuvered at all? What if this was his doing?

There had been times before when Tenet's mind had dared wander over this territory. Why, he'd wondered, did the entire trajectory of the CIA's plan against the Kremlin depend on removing the one man that stood between Roth and Alona? Was that purely coincidence? And how convenient if it was.

Roth: She'll hate you. She'll curse your name.

Tenet: I know that, Levi.

Roth: And that's a price you're willing to pay?

_____

He stopped the tape, rewound, replayed.

_____

Roth: She'll hate you.

_____

It made no sense, and at the same time, it made all the sense in the world. It was a tale as old as man. How could it be otherwise?

He almost couldn't bear to keep listening. He'd heard enough. He knew where it led, and already, his mind was rushing through the years of his life, decades of interactions, meetings, successes, failures, painting them with this new brush, re-examining them in this new light.

Nothing was as he'd thought. Nothing was as it had seemed.

Half his life was being redrawn, reinterpreted. It was all a lie.

He was a fool.

The one man who'd been there all along, right from the beginning, the confidant of presidents, the man he'd trusted more than any other, had betrayed him.

It was Roth. It had always been Roth. The man Alona thought about in the deepest recesses of her mind, when she thought no one else was watching, had sent him to his death.

For years, things had been happening in London that didn't make sense. Agents were lost. Unexplained accidents occurred. Sources turned up dead.

The recording was just days old, but already, it felt like it had been forty years in the making.

Tenet: We're slipping toward war, aren't we?

Roth: Yes, we are.

Tenet: And there's nothing we can do to forestall it?

Roth: Maybe if Aralov was still alive. But even then.... This is a clock that's been ticking a long time. It's got to run out eventually.

Tenet: That's what I thought.

Tenet poured himself more vodka. This was too much. The scale of the deception. It was hard to take in, even for him.

What was behind it? What drove a man like Roth?

Had he been in the pocket of the Russians all along? Forty years? Or was this a recent betrayal?

And how much had he recorded? The Hamlet Pub had always been Roth's idea, Roth's place. And always the same spot, that one booth at the back. Was that all it took?

And what of Alona? He wasn't so blind that he hadn't noticed.

Forty years ago, the heady final days of the Cold War, Roth and Alona had been in love. He knew that was true. A man didn't lie next to a woman for four decades and not learn at least some of her secrets.

She'd loved Levi Roth. He knew that. And Roth had broken her heart.

Was all this some mad scheme to get her back? Men had done more—fought wars, sacrificed lives—for the same objective.

Roth: You'll be fleeing to Moscow as a fugitive. You'll be on the run.

Tenet: I understand.

Roth: But when you get there, they're going to welcome you with open arms.

Tenet had actually believed it. He'd swallowed the whole plot, hook, line, and sinker. He'd pictured Igor's old files being opened and all the groundwork he'd laid over the years paying off. He'd actually believed he'd get inside the Kremlin, get all the way to Molotov, and sway him to Roth's bidding.

His eyes filled with tears as he listened to the rest of the recording. There it was, laid plain before his eyes, the product of forty years of his life. Listening now, it all sounded so transactional, so cold. But at the time, it was laid out so masterfully that he'd never seen it for what it was.

He stood up. The cigarette in his hand was unfinished, but he flicked it away. It hit the window, and the ash scattered and fell. Outside, the cold, gray Moscow sky hung over the city like mud after a flood.

He looked at the wooden box. There was only one thing it could contain. Roth had sent him here for one reason, and one reason only—to find his death.

He opened the lid to reveal a very old Russian Imperial service revolver. He picked it up and checked that it was loaded. Then he crossed himself, put the barrel in his mouth, shut his eyes, and pulled the trigger.

nnabel's was one of the most exclusive private members' clubs in all of London. It was stylish and flamboyant to the extent that some found garish and others found irresistible. Where other clubs opted for centuries-old oak-paneling and shelves of leather-bound tomes, Annabel's went for a ritzier, more upbeat tone. Its décor was anything but staid, with almost dazzlingly bright, crystal chandeliers hanging from the ceilings and extravagantly ornate hand-drawn wallpapers in every room. The marble staircase wound through a series of bars and restaurants, each with its own unique character, some serving expensive whiskies and cognacs and cigars, others specializing in the finest *haute cuisine*, intricate cocktails, and an extensive list of old world wines and champagnes.

People were always surprised when Roth told them he was a member. They imagined that the more staid, traditional clubs, such as the nearby Savile, to be more to his taste. The truth was, the security at Annabel's was second to none. He'd carried out an audit some years back and the privacy afforded there, the discretion of the staff, and the difficulty of concealing surveillance equipment in the walls made it the perfect meeting place. He went there when he wanted the Russians to know who he was meeting but did not want them to be able to eavesdrop on the actual conversation.

For truly secret rendevous, of course, the Hamlet Pub remained unmatched. Which was where he'd just come from.

He was sitting in the Jungle Room, a third-floor bar decorated with intricately hand-painted tropical birds. Tall palms swayed in the breeze created by the bamboo ceiling fans. He was alone, waiting for his lunch in the largely empty room, trying to calm himself before calling Laurel.

He'd expected this. He'd known his actions would create suspicion. It was bound to happen. What he hadn't factored in was Laurel and Tatyana going behind his back to kill Tenet. Thankfully they'd failed. In fact, their attempt would only serve to make the plan appear more real to the Russians, but that didn't change the fact that it was a flagrant disregard of his authority. He needed to contact Laurel, he needed to calm her and Tatyana down, and he needed to choose his words carefully.

The waiter arrived with his Chardonnay, and he took a sip—fresh-cut grass, stone fruit, butter.

He took his phone from his pocket and was about to dial Laurel's number when it began ringing. She was calling him.

"Roth, it's me."

"You have some nerve going around my back...."

She interrupted him. "Roth, she's dead."

"What?"

"She's dead, Roth. She's gone." Her voice was frantic.

His blood ran cold as his mind went immediately to Tatyana. "Oh God," he gasped, his voice almost giving way.

"They got her, Roth. She was in the car, and they just...."

"How?" He could hardly breathe. This was his fault—his doing.

"I don't know. It just came through my feed. I'm pulling up satellite surveillance, Keyhole surveillance, MI5 is on the scene...."

"Laurel, slow down. You're not making sense."

"I'm sorry, it's just, this just came through now and...."

"I need you to calm down. What's MI5 doing in Paris?"

"Paris? No, Roth, London."

"London?"

"I'm talking about Ada. Ada Hudson."

"Ada?" He glanced out the window as if he might still see it happening—as if he might yet stop it.

"Ada was killed. Someone got to her driver while he was waiting."

"That means...."

"The child, Roth. They have the child."

His head was spinning. The Russians had the girl. That meant they had the chip.

"Laurel, listen to me...."

"I'm looking at the surveillance footage. One of her guards left the clinic early."

"On Harley Street?"

"Yes, Roth."

"But no one knew she was going there except...."

"You. You knew."

"Laurel, listen to me very carefully. I need you to narrow down who else could have known where she was. If there's a mole in my house...."

"I thought Tenet was your mole."

"I'll explain everything, Laurel. I promise. But not now."

"I'm looking at her call record. Oh my God."

"What?"

"She spoke to you ten minutes before she was killed."

"Laurel, you need to slow the fuck down."

"Jesus, you were both pinging the same cell tower."

"Laurel, we need to focus."

"Where were you?"

"I spoke to her from a safe place."

"I need to know what's going on, right now."

"Laurel, please, I'll tell you everything."

"I don't know what to think anymore."

"You don't have the full picture."

"*You're* telling *me* that?"

"What's that supposed to mean?"

"Something's wrong, Levi. Something's very wrong, and whatever it is, you're in the middle of it."

Roth's jaw clenched. He needed her to trust him for just a little longer, he needed her to follow his orders, and he was getting close to losing his temper. "You need to get your head in the game, Laurel, or I'll order you to stand down."

"Is that a threat?"

"Just... just watch your step."

The line went dead. She'd hung up on him. He looked at the screen to confirm it.

This was bad.

The waiter came over with his lunch, and Roth gave him a withering look. "Charge my account," he said, rising to his feet.

Outside, rain was falling on Berkeley Square. Something wasn't right. Ada had taken every precaution. The Russians shouldn't have been able to find her.

He'd spent so many years trying to convince the

Russians that they had a double agent in London that he'd neglected the signs of an actual leak. He'd noticed, of course. He'd taken steps to find it. He'd fed false information through the network and waited for it to filter back. He'd set up traces on every source, every asset, every agent in the city, including Tenet.

It hadn't been enough. Whoever was leaking information in London had just graduated to the level of existential threat.

And Roth had no idea where to look to find him.

83

André Suvorov heard the gunshot from the conference room, and the expression that crossed his face was more a snarl than anything. He got up and went to the door. His secretary was at her desk.

"Katrina," he said.

She looked at him. "It's done."

He strode down the corridor to the room Tenet was in and told her to unlock it. She looked at him and hesitated.

"Go on," he said.

She took the key from her pocket, inserted it in the keyhole, and turned it. Then she stopped.

"Open it," he said.

She pushed open the door and immediately stepped back.

"So skittish," he said.

"Sorry, sir."

He brushed past her into the office. When he saw the mess, he felt almost giddy. Tenet's body was slumped backward in the chair like an exhausted man sleeping, arms dangling at his sides, legs sprawled beneath the table. His head hung over the back of the chair, facing the ceiling.

Behind him, a red spatter, as if someone had sprayed red paint from a can for just a second, stained the wall. On the floor was a pool of blood, pieces of skull, some brain.

"What a mess," he said, looking back to the door.

The secretary wasn't there.

He went to the body and looked down at it. No mistake, no room for error, here was Richmond Tenet, arch-confidant of Levi Roth, dead as a carp in a fish market. Tenet and Roth had been closer than close, at the very pinnacle of American espionage, and they had been there since the very beginning. They'd plotted not just the downfall of President Molotov but the subordination of the entire Russian nation to the whim and whimsy of American interest. If they'd had their way, Russia would have become little more than a vassal state, a Chechnya, a Dagestan, an Ingushetia.

Suvorov wet his lips with his tongue. He leaned over Tenet's head and looked down into the lifeless, reptilian eyes of his slain enemy. They stared unflinchingly back.

"Katrina," he barked. He went out to the corridor and found her, standing by her desk, staring at the wall. "Place a call," he said. "Get me Levi Roth. I want to rub his nose in this shit."

She looked at him, surprised by the order. It wasn't every day that a member of the Dead Hand asked to speak to the Director of the CIA.

"Do it," he said.

She pulled out the phone directory. It wasn't a call that could be made directly, and she needed to consult the procedure. As he waited, Suvorov found himself licking his lips again.

Would Roth remember him, he wondered.

How would he? It was too much to ask. So much time had passed, forty years, and Suvorov had been such an insignificant player. He'd been a very different man back then, an insect occupying the very bottom rung of the KGB ladder—a driver, a gopher, a bodyguard. He'd once wiped his boss's ass for him when the man was too drunk to do it himself. He'd taken a used condom in his hand from the same boss to put in the trash. At that time, Roth and Tenet were both full-blown agents, handling operations, running sources, getting people killed. They didn't have time for a cockroach like Suvorov.

"Well?" he said impatiently to Katrina.

"The call has to be placed by Operator Service. I'm putting in the request now."

Suvorov reached into his breast pocket and took out a very long, very fat, Cuban cigar.

"How long will that take?"

"I don't know, sir. Not long."

"I've waited forty years," Suvorov said. "I suppose I can wait a little longer."

He made for his office, lighting the cigar as he did. When he reached the door, he stopped and turned back to Katrina.

"Oh, and sweetheart, clean up that mess, would you?"

Her face went pale, she looked like she might cry at the thought of it, and he let another sneer pass his face as he shut the door. It was true what they said, he thought, sinking into his seat and puffing on the cigar lustily. There really was nothing quite so sweet as the taste of revenge.

He smoked and was half done with the cigar when the phone began to ring. He leaned back in his seat and picked up the receiver.

It was an American voice, speaking English. "Please hold for Director Roth."

He waited. There was a pause, then a click, and he wasn't sure if the connection had been made. "Hello?" he said.

When the voice answered, it was exactly as he remembered it. "This is Roth."

"Levi Roth," Suvorov said, almost in awe at having gotten his attention.

"Who is this?"

"No one you remember, I'm sure."

"If this is some game."

"It's no game, Levi. You know it's not a game."

Roth said nothing.

Suvorov sucked his cigar, the sneer glued to his lips. "You know," he said, "we're actually very old friends, you and I."

"I highly doubt that."

"You don't remember, of course. Why would you? You were a busy man."

"I don't know what you're talking about."

"Of course you don't, although, I don't know, maybe you have some recollection."

"Recollection of what?"

"Such an important period in your life. I'd venture to call it... *pivotal*."

"You better start making sense, or I'm hanging up this phone."

"There was a driver. You must remember that."

"That's it. I'm hanging up."

"All those surreptitious liaisons in dingy pubs. All those midnight dropbox pickups. Someone had to get Gregor Gorky from point A to point B."

"Gregor Gorky?"

"Don't tell me you've forgotten him too."

"No," Roth said, and for the first time, Suvorov sensed that he had the man's full attention, "I haven't forgotten Gorky."

"I'm glad to hear that, Levi. I mean, as his driver, his valet, I was closer to him than anyone."

"Wait a minute," Roth said.

"That's it," Suvorov said, nodding his head for no one but himself.

"The driver. The one who couldn't talk."

"I could talk."

"You needed a machine."

"I got over that."

"You had a hole in your throat."

"All healed now, I assure you."

"Fuck me," Roth said. "I think I can hear it in your voice now. They said it was self-inflicted."

"They said a lot of things, Levi. I assure you."

"Gorky said you shot yourself in a bet."

"It was more like a dare, actually."

"Russian roulette."

"A terrible game. I really don't recommend it to anyone."

"So here you are, back from the dead."

"I was never dead, though I came close a few times."

"Calling me to gloat about Ada Hudson and Natasha Gazinsky, you cretin."

Suvorov laughed.

"Did I say something funny?"

"The penny really hasn't dropped, has it, Levi?"

"What penny."

"Oh, you disappoint me. I expected more from the man they call the spymaster."

"What are you talking about?"

"I'm talking about your old friend. The one you brought with you when you met with Gorky."

Roth sounded like he was going to say something but stopped himself.

"What's the matter? Cat got your tongue?"

"You son of a bitch."

"No witty retort?"

"I'm going to skin you alive."

"Skin me alive? Is that supposed to scare me?"

"Oh, you should be scared."

"I'm done being scared, Levi Roth. There was a time when I was afraid, but that time has passed."

"Afraid of me?"

"Let me ask you this, Levi. What do you think happens to a man like me, like the man I was forty years ago, when his principal defects? What do you think is waiting for that poor schmuck when he gets back to Moscow?"

"Don't tell me you've been nursing that grudge this whole time."

"The basement of the Lubyanka is no small thing, Levi. I don't know if you can even imagine what they do to someone like me in a situation like that."

"Oh, I know exactly what they did down there."

"Of course you do, Levi. I've seen your file. I've seen your ledger."

"Then you know."

"I know I have to wear dentures because of what they did to me, Levi. I ache when it's damp. I have to sit down to piss."

"Tenet and I didn't do that to you."

"Of course you didn't. Americans don't believe in torturing people."

"The Kremlin did that."

"My own compatriots, my brothers in arms in defense of the Motherland. Can you believe it?"

"What have you done with him?"

"With who?"

"You said you had my friend."

"Say his name, Levi."

"You say his name."

Suvorov laughed. "Still holding out hope," he said, the glee in his voice bubbling over.

"He's dead, isn't he?"

"My secretary's cleaning up his brains as we speak." There was another pause on the other end of the line. Suvorov tried to picture Roth's face—wished he could have seen it. "A sad day for the dynamic duo."

"How did it end?"

"Do you mean, did I send him to our old friends in the basement?"

"If you did...."

"Relax, Levi. I gave him Gorky's old gun, although I doubt he knew it."

"He pulled the trigger himself?"

"I'm not petty, Levi. I didn't do this to humiliate him." Roth said nothing. He knew enough to know there was more to come. "Do you know the Russian word for nostalgia, Levi?"

"Enough games," Roth said. "If you wanted to put yourself on my radar, you've succeeded. I hope you've got your family in a safe place."

"Levi, there's no need to be crass."

"That's no idle threat, André Suvorov. I'm going to come for you in force."

"No, you're not."

"And why's that?"

"Because you need to do business with me."

"I decide who I need to do business with."

"I'm headed for the top, Levi."

"I could give a shit where you're headed."

"The Dead Hand, as they call it on your end."

"If that was true...."

"It's true."

"It will only make me go after you all the harder."

"But I haven't told you the worst part yet."

"What's that?"

"When your friend killed himself, do you know what he was thinking?"

"He was thinking he'd been betrayed."

"Betrayed, yes. How interesting your mind went there."

"We both knew there was a rat in London."

"He didn't die thinking about your rat, Levi. He died thinking about you."

"What's that supposed to mean?"

"Come, Levi. A man as cunning as you? Surely you know."

Levi said nothing.

Suvorov sucked hard on the cigar, allowing himself to inhale the heavy smoke. This was it. His moment of revenge. "Nothing to say, Levi?"

"What did you do?"

"I merely made a suggestion."

"What suggestion?"

"I won't insult your intelligence by spelling it out."

"Alona?"

"Of course, Alona. What else would cause a man of your stature to purposefully send a friend as old and as loyal as Richmond Tenet to certain death?"

More silence. Suvorov knew he'd hit his mark.

"I always had an eye for the details, Levi. Even then. All the things another man might miss. Like the fact that you and Alona never arrived at the pub together. Even when you were coming from the same place."

Roth still said nothing.

"And just so you know, Levi, in case you're getting any ideas, let there be no misunderstanding between us. If anything happens to me, if I feel so much as a hint that I'm being targeted, Alona Almagor dies. Are we clear?"

84

R oth sat in the back of his car, mute, staring out the window.

He'd been outplayed utterly. This man in the Prime Directorate, André Suvorov, had planned his moves for decades. He'd waited patiently, watched untiringly, and now, finally, out of nowhere, like a viper, he'd struck.

And Roth hadn't seen it coming. He'd known, of course, that something would come for him eventually. In this game, that wasn't a risk—it was a certainty. One moved from operation to operation, from country to country, leaving an utterly scorched earth. Sooner or later, something was going to come.

But this had blindsided him completely. Perhaps he was losing his touch.

Suvorov had help from the inside. That much certain. Some mole, some sleeper agent deep inside the CIA's London operation, was leaking information, and Roth didn't have the slightest inkling where to look.

All he knew was that he'd just lost a crucial battle. The plot to put Tenet in the Kremlin would have been the very pinnacle of Roth's career, his crowning achievement, the *coup de grâce* against Molotov's insidious regime.

But Suvorov hadn't just known Tenet was a trap, he'd known the intimate details of their lives too. He knew what was at the heart of the two men's relationship. Perhaps he knew it better than they did themselves.

Roth loved Tenet's wife.

And Roth wanted her.

She wouldn't be able to forgive this, though. And Roth wouldn't be able to forgive himself. Having a rival for a woman's heart was one thing, but being the man who'd sent him to his death, that was something else.

If there'd been any chance, it was dead now, poisoned.

"Sir?" the driver said.

They were in front of Annabel's, and Roth hadn't said where he wanted to go. "Sorry," he said, pulling his mind back to the present. He needed to get to the embassy, but there was something he wanted to take care of first.

The car pulled into the traffic, and Roth felt a heavy lump in his throat as they wound their way through the gray streets. When they arrived at the address, he remained seated, staring out the window.

"Everything all right, sir?"

"Yes," Roth said, but he made no movement.

He was staring at the door, thinking, remembering. There'd been moments in his life like this before—forks in the road that forced him to decide what kind of man he was, to find out what he was truly made of, to measure the timbre of his own soul.

Tenet had died thinking Roth betrayed him.

What Roth was trying to determine now was whether or not it was true.

He let out a long sigh and got out of the car. It seemed to

take an enormous effort to walk the distance to the door, like he was wading through mud. Every step was a labor.

He knocked and waited.

He didn't feel himself. Time seemed to be passing slowly. Sound seemed dull. Everything outside his immediate field of view blurred.

Alona approached, and the moment she saw Roth, her expression turned to abject grief. She knew why he was there, and it was all she could do to keep standing.

"Alona, open the door," he said, the words thick and gooey in his mouth.

She shook her head.

"Please," he said.

She stood there, unmoving, looking out at him through the window as if the thin pane of glass separating them could somehow protect her from what he'd come to say.

He could see the tears on her face. He would have held her, consoled her if she would let him. Even now, he could imagine a future with her, a life spent making up for all that lost time.

But there were two sides to a man, two natures. Suvorov had calculated that threatening Alona was enough to keep him safe from Roth. But maybe that was a miscalculation. Roth had given up Alona before, after all. Why wouldn't he do it a second time?

Roth wasn't one of those men who pretended he was so different from the monsters he spent his life fighting. After all, to fight them, one had to act like them, think like them, do the things they did. A man, whether born in Moscow or Vienna or New York, had to survive the same bloodthirsty struggle, tooth and nail, using the same tools, the same tactics. The laws of nature did not change depending on what side you were on.

He thought of Lance, the man who'd killed the woman carrying his child. That was a man who understood the cost of the fight, the rules of engagement, the scale of the struggle.

"Open the door," he said again. "Alona, please."

She reached for the latch and clicked it open. He stepped forward, entering slowly, and she immediately stepped back.

"You're a messenger of death, Levi," she said, her voice cracking with emotion. "You bring only one type of news."

She was correct, but it didn't change what he had to do. "Alona," he said helplessly.

"He's dead, isn't he?"

He nodded.

There was something about the look on her face then that scared him. He felt suddenly small before her, insignificant, like she was qualified to pass judgment on him, not just for herself but for the world at large.

"I knew it the moment I saw you," she said. "You're cursed, Levi. Death follows you like a plague."

He didn't know what to say—there was nothing he could say. And yet, he couldn't bring himself to turn his back on her. He stepped forward again.

"Get back," she hissed, rearing like a cat.

"Please," he stammered.

"One more step and, so help me, I'll kill you myself."

"I can help..." he stammered.

"Help?" she spat. "You'd love that, wouldn't you? Step in now and save the day. Well, it's too late, Levi. It's too goddamn late."

"Alona."

"Get out of here. Get out of my sight."

She came toward him. He backed away onto the porch, and she slammed the door.

But still, he couldn't leave. He looked at his hands. They were shaking. He felt uncertain on his feet, as if he might at any moment collapse.

He stood there for a minute, still as a statue, waiting for he knew not what until he saw movement at the curtain by the window. She was checking to see if he was gone.

Slowly then, he turned and went back to the car.

85

Lance was in a hotel room in Kapotnya, an industrial district in the far southeast of Moscow. He'd spent time there before and knew the area. He stood by the window, looking out at the smokestacks of the oil refinery and state factories in the distance. The chimney of the Tets-22 power plant billowed smoke into the sky in such quantities one could believe that was its purpose.

His room was on the third floor with a good view of the approaching streets. Outside, old-style lampposts cast an orange hue on the cobbles every hundred yards or so.

If anyone was coming, he'd know.

He lit a cigarette and went to the laptop on the desk. He'd picked it up from a CIA dropbox and had it running a financial systems trace on Suvorov's credit cards. It had found something—a transaction at the Ritz-Carlton in Central Moscow. The transaction had been processed less than a minute earlier, and the amount, a hold of over a thousand dollars, suggested a room deposit.

He left his room and had the concierge call him a cab.

He took it to the nearest Metro station and from there caught a train to Teatralnaya. He exited the station by the Vitali Fountain, right in front of the Bolshoi theater, and from there, walked to the Ritz-Carlton on Tverskaya.

He watched the hotel from across the street, leaning against a lamp post and smoking a cigarette. Tverskaya was a wide boulevard with eight full traffic lanes running toward the State Museum and the Memorial to the Unkown Soldier. When he was done with the cigarette, he threw away the butt and crossed the street.

A doorman in tails and top hat held the door for him, and a bellhop asked if he wanted to check-in.

"I'm meeting someone at the bar," Lance said in English.

The bellhop nodded, and Lance went into the bar. There were a few other customers there, business people, young women in expensive dresses, three men in black leather jackets smoking cigars.

"What can I get you?" the bartender asked.

"What's your finest vodka?"

"I have an Imperial Collection," the bartender said. "Super Premium."

"Sounds good."

"It's very good," the bartender said, reaching for the top shelf. He brought down what looked like a gold pineapple on carriage wheels. "Fabergé," he said, opening the carriage. Inside it was a crystal bottle. "Two hundred dollars an ounce."

"Charge it to my room."

"And what room is that, sir?"

Lance shrugged. "I don't remember."

"The name then?"

"Name is Suvorov."

The bartender poured the drink, and Lance knocked it

back like a three-dollar Jägermeister at the Eureka bar back in Deweyville.

"Another?" the bartender said.

"No thanks," Lance said, taking out his wallet. "Just the check."

The bartender printed the bill and handed it to him. Without looking at it, Lance counted out ten crisp hundred dollar bills from his wallet. He made sure the bartender saw the count, then leaned over and handed it to him. The bartender looked him in the eye, then looked around to see if anyone was watching. He tried to take the money, but Lance held on to it.

"You're going to have to remind me of my room number," Lance said, then, enunciating each syllable very clearly, said, "Suvorov."

"I'm sorry, sir," the bartender said hesitantly.

"Don't be sorry," Lance said, pulling back the money. "The concierge will help me, I'm sure."

The bartender swallowed, then, speaking very quickly, said, "Suite three. Ninth floor."

Lance gave him the money and went over to the elevators. There was a special elevator for the penthouse suites, and Lance stepped inside. It had its own operator, dressed like the doorman in a suit and top hat. Lance handed him a hundred-dollar bill and said, "Up, please."

The operator looked at Lance, then at the money, and held his key card up to a sensor. He pressed the button for the penthouse, entered a security code on a keypad, and the elevator began its ascent. It arrived on the ninth floor with a ding, and Lance turned to the operator. He was young, mid-twenties, and seemed smart enough to know what was in his own best interest.

"Is this the only elevator with access to the top floor?" he said in Russian.

"The only one for guests."

"Can you put it out of action?"

"Sir?"

"That button," Lance said, pointing to a button with a picture of an alarm bell on it. "If you press that, how long will the elevator be disabled?"

"Ten minutes," the operator said.

Lance pushed the button, then said, "Give me your hat and coat."

"I'll lose my job."

"Don't worry about that," Lance said, counting out five bills.

The man gave him the uniform, and Lance handed him the money. "Put it somewhere safe."

The operator bent down to put it in his sock, and as he rose back up, Lance hit him, not too hard, in the face. He stumbled backward, blood flowing from his nose.

"Get on the ground," Lance said, putting on the uniform. "Tell them I knocked you out."

"But...."

Lance raised his fist, ready to hit him again.

"Okay, okay," the guy said, getting on the floor.

Lance looked at him, then counted out five more bills and said, "Keep the elevator here as long as possible."

The man took the money, and Lance stepped out into the top floor corridor. It was decorated in the gaudy, over-the-top style typical of high-end Moscow hotels, with a surfeit of red velvet, cut crystal, and gold tassels.

There were four penthouse suites. Suvorov occupied the third. Lance went to the door and rapped lightly. He took a step back so as to be clearly visible through the peephole.

"What is it?" a voice bellowed from inside.

Lance waited for the light at the bottom of the door to darken, then kicked it in. It flew inward, smacking the person behind it. Lance pulled out his gun, the same suppressed Beretta 71 he'd used to kill Viktor Lapin, and entered the room, shutting the door behind him with his foot.

"What is this?" Suvorov stammered.

"You know what this is."

"How did you...."

Suvorov was crawling backward on the floor, creating as much distance as possible between himself and Lance. He was completely naked, blood flowing from his face. He had his hand on his nose, trying to stem the blood. Lance walked toward him slowly, scanning the room as he followed Suvorov all the way to the bedroom. In the bed, an attractive brunette in her twenties was on the hotel phone, trying furiously to reach the front desk.

"Put it down," Lance said.

She put down the phone and pulled the bed sheets up over her chest. She looked at Suvorov, the blood on his face, then at the gun in Lance's hand, and started to cry.

"Don't do that," Lance said.

She tried to stop but was beginning to panic.

"You're going to be fine," Lance said. "It's this guy who's got to worry."

Suvorov had backed all the way to the bed. His jacket was on the floor next to him, and Lance could see that was what he was going for.

"Get over there," he said, waving his gun toward the bathroom.

Suvorov looked one last time at the jacket.

Lance picked it up and searched it. In an inside pocket, he found Suvorov's gun. He put it in the waist of his pants.

"You're making a big mistake," Suvorov snarled. "Roth and I, we have an understanding."

"Do you?" Lance said, hardly listening. He rounded the bed and picked up Suvorov's phone from the bedside table. Then he yanked the hotel phone line from the wall. "Where's your phone?" he said to the girl.

She started crying again, and Lance took her purse and looked inside. He found her phone and put it in his pocket.

"Now," he said, turning his attention back to Suvorov. "Let's get you into the bathtub."

Suvorov knew what that meant, and his eyes widened in horror. The girl began crying again, and again Lance told her to stop.

"I have a deal with Roth," Suvorov said, more frantically than before. "He would never order this."

"You're right," Lance said. "He didn't."

That was when Suvorov realized he had nothing, no leverage, no ace up his sleeve. Whatever deal he'd cut with Roth wasn't going to help him now.

"If you kill me, the Jewess dies," he stammered.

"The Jewess?" Lance said.

"Roth's lady friend. I've made arrangements. If anything happens to me, she dies."

"That's not why I'm here," Lance said.

"Of course that's why you're here."

"I'm here because of the girl," Lance said.

"What girl?"

"Don't pretend you don't know," Lance said. "Now get in the bathtub."

"You're making a mistake," Suvorov said again.

"Get in the tub, or I'll shoot you where you sit, I swear to God."

"You're really here for the girl?" Suvorov said, his voice frail with terror. "Natasha Gazinsky?"

"You see," Lance said, "call me sentimental, but I can't sleep at night knowing the likes of you are out there looking for little girls."

"I'm not looking for her."

"I know how you work. You're not going to let her slip away. It sends the wrong message."

"I'm not looking for her because I already have her, you fool."

"What?" Lance said.

"That's right," Suvorov said triumphantly. "My man took her. He's preparing to bring her back to Moscow as we speak."

"You're lying."

"Call Roth," Suvorov said. "Call him before you pull the trigger. If I'm lying, kill me."

86

Roth got out of his car, back into the interminable rain, and hurried into the Old Hamlet. He was expecting to see Harry behind the bar, but there was another guy there, someone Roth didn't recognize. The bar was fairly lively with an afternoon crowd of office workers.

Roth went up to the bar and asked for a pint. When the bartender gave it to him, Roth said, "No Harry tonight?"

"It's his night off."

Roth nodded. His usual booth was occupied, so he took another table and sipped his drink. He was slightly irritated by the crowd. He'd been hoping to drink in solitude, to drown his sorrows with some light conversation from Harry. This wasn't what he'd had in mind.

His phone began vibrating, and he took it from his jacket with a sigh. He was surprised to see that it was a Russian number.

"Roth, this is Lance."

"Lance! Where the hell...."

"I've got someone here claiming to have kidnapped Natasha Gazinsky."

"What the hell is going on?"

"I'm in Moscow, Roth."

"You were never ordered...."

"Is it true?"

"Is what true?"

"Was Natasha Gazinsky taken?"

"Yes, and we desperately need...."

"Hold your horses. I'm here with André Suvorov, and he's going to tell you where she is."

"You're with Suvorov?" Roth said, his heart pounding as he thought of what that meant for Alona. "What have you done?"

"Nothing yet, but unless someone starts making sense very soon...."

"You can't kill him, Lance."

"Why not? He's made of flesh, isn't he?"

"If you kill him, Alona dies too."

"Then you better find out where he's holding Natasha Gazinsky because if someone hurts so much as a hair on her head, so help me...."

"Put him on the phone, Lance. For God's sake, put him on the phone."

There was a pause, then Lance's voice again. "He's on speaker, Roth. He can hear you, and I can."

"Suvorov? Is that you?"

There was coughing, then, "It's me. This animal barged into my room...."

"You heard him," Roth said. "Unless you give him Natasha Gazinsky, he's going to kill you."

"And if he kills me, your little lady friend dies too, Levi."

"It's not going to come to that," Roth said, "is it, Lance?"

"That's up to him."

"If I give you what you want," Suvorov said, speaking to Lance now, "what guarantee do I have that you'll leave nicely?"

"I'll vouch for him," Roth said. "He'll do as I say."

"No, I won't," Lance said to Suvorov. "I'll do what *I* say and if that child is hurt...."

"Levi," Suvorov said, "you get this hound out of my bedroom right now, or we've got nothing to talk about."

"I'm not going anywhere," Lance said.

"And I'm not negotiating with a gun to my head."

"You don't have a choice."

"I have a choice," Suvorov said. "Go ahead, pull the trigger. See what happens."

"Lance," Roth said. Some people at the bar glanced his way, and he dropped his voice. "I need you to trust me. Get out of there and leave it to me. I want Natasha Gazinsky back as much as you do."

"I wish I could believe that, Levi."

"Lance, you have my word."

"Your *word*?"

Suvorov interrupted, "This is the man who killed Viktor Lapin, isn't it? I'm not negotiating with this animal."

Roth's hand was shaking. This was going to go sideways fast if he didn't defuse the situation. "Operating on no one's orders but his own," he said.

"Get him out of my room, Roth. Get him the hell out before he does something we all regret."

"Lance," Roth said. "I need you to listen to me. He's got agents in London with instructions on what to do if he dies. It's not going to be pretty, not for Natasha."

"Or for Alona."

"Or for her," Roth said, "but he's ready to make a deal. Just give me a chance to negotiate with him."

There was silence on the line, then Roth heard Lance speaking to Suvorov. "You tell him where to find that child right now, or I swear to God I'll put so many bullets in your skull...."

"I want him out, Levi," Suvorov cried. "I'll tell you where to find the girl. God knows she's not worth my life."

"If I get him to leave...."

"If you get him out, I'll give you the girl. You have my word. She's in London as we speak, awaiting transportation."

"She better be," Lance said.

"You hear me, Levi? Call off this hound."

"Lance?" Roth said.

"If that girl isn't in your custody in an hour, I'm coming after this piece of shit," Lance said. Then to Suvorov, "I don't care what deals you've cut, and I don't care how many threats you've made. If Natasha dies, you die. Simple as that."

Some sounds followed, the shutting of a door, Suvorov's voice speaking in Russian to somebody else, then he was on another phone line, ordering his security detail up to his room.

"Suvorov?" Roth said. "Are you there?" There was no answer. "Hello?" he said, louder.

"I'm still here," Suvorov said. "I'm waiting for confirmation that your dog is out of the building."

"If he said he'll go, he'll go."

"All the same," Suvorov said.

Roth heard more sounds in the background. Suvorov's security detail had arrived and wanted to get him out of the hotel. They gave him clothes, left the room, someone told someone else to hold an elevator, and then they told Suvorov a car was waiting.

Roth waited as Suvorov made his way through the hotel. He heard the elevator, a car door shutting, and then an engine starting. Then Suvorov said, "I thought we had an understanding, Levi."

"We did. We do."

"I told you what would happen if you came after me."

"I didn't come after you."

"That hound of yours is a problem."

"I can control him. You don't need to worry."

"I am worried, Levi. I'm very worried."

"I'll get him out of Moscow."

"You didn't even know he was here."

"All you have to do is give us the girl...."

"I can't give you the girl. The President has involved himself personally."

They must know about the chip, Roth thought. He could see no other reason why the President would care about the fate of one young girl. "What do you care what happens to her?" he said. "What does the President care?"

"I could ask the same of you, Levi."

"I don't," Roth said. "It's Lance that cares, and his reasons are... well...."

"*Personal*?"

"Yes."

Suvorov sighed. "Well, that's going to cost him, Levi."

"What are you talking about?"

"I mean, my hands are tied. The Institute of Hygiene in Sverdlovsk has flagged that child. It's something to do with her medical condition. There's some experimentation the President has taken a personal interest in."

"Experimentation?"

"And I think your hound is going to have a problem with that."

"You're damn right he's going to have a problem with that."

"So take care of it."

"What?"

"You heard me."

"Who do you think you're talking to?"

"The question is, who do *you* think you're talking to, Levi?"

"I'm talking to Gregor Gorky's driver."

Suvorov laughed. "We all begin somewhere, Roth. You know that better than anyone."

"Why don't you just cut to the chase, Suvorov? Save us both a whole lot of time."

"I was Gorky's driver, then I was tortured in the Lubyanka, and now, if everything goes according to plan, I'm about to become the head of the Dead Hand."

"You're mad."

"Oh ye of little faith," Suvorov said.

"I'll believe that when I see it," Roth said.

"And see it, you will, Levi. See it, you will."

Roth leaned back in his seat. "If that's true...."

"It's true," Suvorov said, and something about the way he said it, about everything he'd said up to that point, made Roth believe it. This upstart, Gregor Gorky's valet, was angling to become the most powerful man in Russia, other than the President. And he was also angling for a deal with his CIA counterpart.

"Well," Levi said, "that...."

"Changes things?"

"I want Alona Almagor off the table. Whatever threat you've arranged...."

"Why, of course," Suvorov said, sounding very pleased with himself. "I would hate for something like that to get in the way of our relationship."

"*We* don't have a relationship."

"Come now, Levi. We can't pretend that. There's far too much at stake."

Roth sighed. He knew what this was. It wasn't the first time he'd traded with the Devil, or at least *a* devil, and God knew it wouldn't be the last. It was part of the game, part of the territory, and pretending otherwise was futile.

"Tell me what you want."

"Such a hurry," Suvorov said. "Don't they do foreplay in America?"

"You're testing my patience, Suvorov."

"You and I...."

"There is no you and I."

"Oh, but there will be, Levi. You know it as well as I do. And just like you can't have a threat hanging over Alona's head, I can't have one hanging over mine."

"You mean Lance."

"He's a hound that's tasted too much blood, Levi. You're not going to be able to control him, and you know it."

"So you want...."

"Him eliminated. When that happens, I'll rescind my contract on your girlfriend."

Roth picked up his glass and drained it, then raised his hand to the bartender for a refill. Secret understandings, surreptitious side deals, were a fact of life in their business, the grease that kept the wheels turning. That didn't mean he liked it, but he was prepared to live with it.

It was deals like this that kept bloodshed at bay, kept nations off each other's throats, but at a price. They were an opiate, they lessened immediate pain, but the ultimate cost could end up being life-threatening.

"If threats are our only aligned interest," Roth said.

"Oh, Levi, we have so much more than threats to bind us."

"Such as."

"Such as the *status quo,* Levi. What greater interest could there be?"

"The *status quo*?"

"Everything I want from you, Levi, you're going to give gladly."

"And why would I do that?"

"Because that's what allows us to go on as we always have, what keeps our nations in balance—in harmony."

"Harmony?"

"What would you call it?"

"Only someone like you would describe the Cold War as harmony."

"You know as well as I do what the alternative is."

"Peace?"

"Bloodshed, Levi. Bloodshed."

"That's one possibility."

"And I think we'd both prefer the *status quo* to that possibility, wouldn't we?"

The bartender arrived with Roth's beer. He waited for him to leave before saying, "For more than half a century, your nation and my nation have been so close to nuclear war that the fate of the entire planet rests on nothing more than a hair-trigger."

"A trigger that has not been pulled."

"Yet."

"What's the alternative, Levi?"

"I'll tell you what the alternative is. Disarmament. De-escalation."

"How about a little *Glasnost* in there for good measure?" Suvorov said, laughing hollowly. "How about some *Perestroika*?"

"It's been tried before," Roth said.

"Come now, Levi. Let's be grown-ups. Neither of us is so naive as to believe in a world of lambs and doves, and, how you say in America, *cotton candy*?"

"What would you prefer, Suvorov?"

"Human nature, Levi. Struggle. Endless struggle."

"How very Russian."

"Let's not pretend it can be otherwise. As you said yourself, the world rests on a hair-trigger. The weapons have been built. The power exists to erase nations, lay continents to waste."

"Wipe out civilization," Roth said.

"A power like that?" Suvorov said. "Once out, it cannot simply be put back in its box, Levi. Not now. Not ever."

"So, what are you saying?"

"I'm saying, if there has to be a hair-trigger if we are forced to live in the endless shadow of annihilation, wouldn't you rather it be your finger on the trigger and not someone else's?"

87

Roth drained his pint. What Suvorov was suggesting changed everything, realigned the planetary axis, altered the very ether of the world Roth inhabited.

Levi Roth, at his core, was a simple man, a man of loyalties, of tribalisms, of *us* and *them*.

The elixir Suvorov was holding before him was a one-way path. Once embarked on, there would be no turning back. A single taste, and he would be hooked.

There was a name for it, of course—a name as old as kingship, as old as loyalty itself.

That name was treason.

Plain and simple.

Punishable by death.

And yet, Roth could see the logic of it. He could feel the irresistible pull of its gravity. Secrecy begat secrecy. Power begat power.

After all, who's side really was he on? And who was on his? Had he not more similarities with Suvorov, more common cause, than he did with practically anyone else?

Did they not understand each other as no one else could? Did they not feel each other's pain?

And was not the world a safer place, less likely to suffer catastrophe, if he and Suvorov saw eye to eye?

Who, he thought, truly kept the world on course? Who held the wolf at bay? The petty, self-interested governments of a hundred warring nations? The presidents and prime ministers? The kings and sultans?

Nixon? Reagan? Khrushchev? Brezhnev?

Priests?

Who kept humanity from slipping into the abyss?

It was the agencies, the apparatus, the deep state. It was the CIA, the NSA, the KGB, the GRU. They were the real watchers on the tower, the puppetmasters pulling the strings.

Or, at least, that was the vision Suvorov was selling.

Roth got the check and left cash on the table. He went outside. It had stopped raining. For once, the sky looked like it might clear. His driver was down the street, and he was about to beckon him over when his phone started to ring.

It was Laurel.

Her voice was high-pitched, shrill, frantic, the words spilling in an incoherent mass. "You're at the Old Hamlet Pub," she said. "You're there. You're there."

"Slow down, Laurel. What's the matter?"

"I see you. I'm looking right at you, you son of a bitch."

"What are you talking about?" he said, glancing skyward.

"Don't try to lie to me. I can see you standing there."

"I'm not lying. I am where you say I am. What's going on?"

"What are you doing there, Levi?"

"Laurel, you're not making any sense."

"What the hell are you doing there, Levi? Tell me right now or so help me God...."

Roth's mind was running at a hundred miles an hour, flitting through the myriad scenarios she could be upset about. There was no shortage of them, but he had no idea which she'd latched onto.

"I'm at a bar, Laurel. A place I know."

"Tell me what you're doing there."

"A beer. Alone. Nothing more."

"You're lying."

"I just told an old friend her husband was dead. I needed a drink. Why don't you tell me what this is about?"

"Oh, please don't pretend you don't know, you goddamn son of a...."

"Laurel, really, you need to tell me what the hell is going on right now."

"It's about Ada Hudson. Natasha Gazinsky. You selling all of us out for whatever goddamn plot you're cooking."

"Natasha Gazinsky? What have you found?"

"The Keyhole footage. Ada's shooter."

"What about him?"

"He brought her there."

"Brought who where?"

"There, the Old Hamlet. Where you are."

"What on earth are you talking about?"

"The shooter, Roth. He brought Natasha to that bar. The very bar you're at."

"That doesn't make sense," he said.

His driver was just pulling up, and he was about to open the door when Laurel said, "I'm looking at the footage right now. I put a trace on him. He brought her to that pub after taking her from the car."

Roth turned around and looked back at the pub, its

medieval façade, its lead-framed windows. "I don't understand," he said.

"*You* don't understand?"

"Laurel...."

"Don't *Laurel* me. Something's very wrong, Levi."

"What did he look like?"

"Who?"

"The man who took Natasha. What's his build?"

"Bulky. Very bulky. Lumbered about like an ogre. I didn't
get a look at the face."

"I'm going back inside," Roth said, hanging up.

He felt dizzy entering the pub. The ground seemed to
shift beneath his feet like he was walking on a boat.

"Where's Harry?" he said, stumbling past the bar.

"Not in," the other bartender said.

"Where the fuck is he?"

The bartender altered his bearing, straightened up,
crossed his arms. "Like I said...."

Roth moved on, pushing through the crowd toward the
back of the room.

"Hey," the bartender called after him.

"Out of the way," Roth said to the other drinkers,
pushing them aside, passing his old booth, the place he'd
hatched a thousand plots. He went through the swing doors
to the washrooms and was only just in time, dropping to his
knees in front of a toilet in the men's room and retching
violently.

"Fuck me," the bartender said from the doorway when
he caught up.

"Give me two minutes," Roth said between bouts.

"One minute," the bartender said, "then you're out."

Roth finished what he was doing, then spat in the
toilet. He went to the sink and washed out his mouth,

eyeing the mirror. "What are you looking at?" he said to his reflection.

He reached into his coat pocket, looking for the cold, steel reassurance of his gun. Without taking it from his coat, he flicked the safety.

Then he went back out to the narrow hallway and looked at the two heavy wooden doors there. He'd walked past them a thousand times before. One went upstairs to an apartment that was sometimes used by the pub for staff housing. The other went to the basement. Both were covered in tattered posters and advertisements.

He tried the door to the basement. It opened, leading to a dark staircase. There was a light switch on the wall, but he didn't use it. He went down the stairs in darkness. At the bottom was another door, this time locked. He pressed the barrel of his gun against the keyhole and fired. The shot rang out like a crack of thunder, and the door swung open.

It led to a dimly lit cellar. Roth saw movement, sudden, violent. Without knowing what was before him, he pulled the trigger. In the enclosed space of the cellar, the bullet compressed the air. He felt it in his ear.

Six feet in front of him, lying on the ground, clutching his gut in agony, was the hulking mass of Harry Staples.

Here it was at last. His mole. The reason Richmond Tenet was dead, and Ada Hudson, and dozens of other agents. So many, in fact, that since the end of the Cold War, London Station had suffered a higher mortality rate than even Beirut, or Kabul, or Baghdad.

"Levi," Harry cried, gasping for breath.

"Harry," Roth said quietly.

Harry's hand was on his stomach, blood gushing through his fingers in the steady rhythm of his pulse. He didn't have long.

"I expected to see a lot of things in my life," Roth said, "but never this."

Harry looked up at him, struggling to speak. "Spare me the lecture."

"Never this," Roth said again.

"You only ever saw what you wanted to see."

"I thought I saw *you*, Harry."

"The world isn't as you see it, Levi. You're blind. All of you are."

"All of us?"

"If you're going to kill me, do it. Pull the trigger."

"All right," Roth said, raising the gun. But he didn't pull the trigger. For some reason, he couldn't. "Was it money, Harry?"

"You're so blind you can't see the truth, even when it hits you right in the face."

"They had dirt. They blackmailed you."

Harry spat. "I did it because I'm a believer, Levi."

"A believer? A believer in what?"

Harry shook his head. He would have laughed if it didn't hurt so much. "In what?" he said, shaking his head. "In the future."

"Russia?" Roth said.

"The resistance, Levi. Freedom. Choice."

"What choice?"

"A world that isn't run by the one percent of the one percent."

"The one percent?"

"The vested interests, the mega-corporations, the entire military-industrial complex."

"Harry, what are you talking about?"

"I don't expect you to see things my way, Levi. Not now. Not after all the years you've spent serving them."

"You're not making any sense."

"You work for them, Roth. You do their bidding. They pull the strings, send you on your varied errands, and you can't even see it for what it is."

"Harry, what is this?"

"There's no man so completely enslaved as the one who can't see his own chains," Harry said.

Roth just shook his head. What was this nonsense? Harry was British. He'd thought they didn't fall for this shit.

Harry looked down at his hand. He seemed genuinely shocked by the amount of blood, as if he hadn't known a human body could contain so much.

His defiance began to crack. "I broke the code, though, didn't I?" he said. "In the end, I broke the only code we had."

"What code?"

"He was a friend, of sorts."

"Who was?"

"Your mate. Tweedle Dee."

"Tweedle Dee?"

"That's what Suvorov called him, back in the day. Guess what he called you?"

"You and Suvorov?"

"Even then," Harry said, nodding. "Even then."

Roth shook his head. It was too much to take in—the scale of the deception. It was too much.

"Where's the girl?" he said.

Harry motioned to a small door in the corner. "She's scared," he said, "but I didn't hurt her. I swear."

"It's not me you need to swear to."

Harry tapped his breast pocket. "Key's in here," he said. "Now do what you came to do, Levi."

Roth pulled the trigger, the simplest thing in the world, and Harry jerked once and slumped forward. Roth went to him, checked his shirt—the key was where he'd said it would be—then went to the door. It was steel, reinforced with a deadbolt, but the lock slid open smoothly. There was a room beyond, concrete, windowless, possibly a bomb shelter, possibly it had always been a cell.

Light came from a single bulb. Against the far wall was an old-fashioned television, and facing it, a steel bedframe. Natasha was sitting on the bedframe, hugging her legs, her eyes vacant. The TV was on, but she wasn't watching it.

Roth went to her and picked her up in his arms. "You're all right now," he said. "You're all right now."

88

Roth brought Natasha up the stairs, through the bar, and out to the waiting car. The people in the pub didn't know what to think, and he didn't explain.

He put her into the backseat and got in next to her.

"You're going to be all right, Natasha. Everything's going to be all right."

She said nothing. He could see she was in shock. He took off his coat and put it over her.

"Get us to the embassy," he said to the driver, then called Laurel. "I have her."

"Thank God."

"We're *en route* to the embassy. I want a medical team there as quickly as possible."

"Ada Hudson made arrangements with a private clinic. A Doctor Blackwell. She was recommended by the doctor in Boston."

"No. I want our own people on this. At least until we have the chip."

He heard Laurel type on her keyboard. "The 48th

Fighter Wing is at RAF Lakenheath," she said. "They have full medical facilities. We could send her there."

"Have them come to the embassy," Roth said. "Tell them to bring what they need to perform a surgery."

He hung up, and it wasn't long before the car was passing the security gates at the embassy. The driver was directed to a secure loading bay where four Marines and the Station Chief awaited them. The Marines put Natasha on a stretcher, which only added to her confusion. Roth stayed with her, holding her hand, as they made their way down the corridor to the elevators.

As the elevator rose to the sixth floor, the Station Chief said, "The British doctor is coming in."

"Blackwell?"

"Yes."

"I never asked for that."

"Laurel sent for her. She said the kid would need a familiar face."

"They barely met," Roth said, but looking at the child, he could tell it was probably the right call.

The elevator arrived, and they brought Natasha straight to a conference room. When the Marines cleared the room, Roth helped Natasha off the stretcher and onto a small sofa.

"I'll get some water," the Station Chief said, leaving the two of them alone in the room.

Roth looked at her. He wasn't sure if she understood what was going on. Through the glass wall of the conference room, they could see the people outside hurrying about their business.

When the Station Chief returned, he'd forgotten the water but had Blackwell with him.

"Doctor," Roth said, rising to his feet, "thank you for coming on such short notice."

The doctor took a look at Natasha, then bent down to be at her eye level. "Natasha. Are you all right? Remember me?"

Natasha wasn't responsive. The doctor turned to Roth. "They just said she was kidnapped?"

Roth nodded, glancing at the child.

"Where are the police? The authorities? This isn't some lawless warzone you're operating in."

Roth put a hand on her arm and led her out of the conference room. "Doctor," he said, "I assure you, we're not acting unlawfully."

"Well, it sure looks that way."

"We have our own way of doing things."

She shook her head. She was frustrated. He could see that. It would have been easier for him if she wasn't there, but he could see that the child needed her. The CIA simply wasn't equipped to give her what she needed.

"I shouldn't have been pulled into this situation," Blackwell said.

"You're right," Roth said. "Believe me, I understand the concerns...."

"I need to know this child is safe. I need to know that the decisions being made for her are in her interest. I need the legal framework around child protection...."

"Doctor," Roth said, "this is a *particular* situation. It's difficult."

"I understand that, but...."

"On their way back from your clinic, the agent who was accompanying Natasha...."

"Ada Hudson?"

"Yes, Ada Hudson. Doctor, I'm sorry to have to tell you this...."

"Tell me what?"

"Ada Hudson's dead."

The doctor's face went pale. "Dead?"

"I'm sorry."

"I was with her... *hours* ago."

"The Russians...."

Blackwell raised her hand. "Don't tell me," she said.

"So you see," he said, "when I say this is a particular set of circumstances...."

"The child needs counseling," Blackwell said, cutting him off. "She needs someone to talk to, immediately."

"I think a familiar face would do her good."

She nodded. Roth could tell she was a competent professional, used to being in control of the situation, but right now, she looked like a deer caught in headlights.

"The legal situation is going to be formalized," he said. "I assure you."

"I'm going to need paperwork very soon."

He nodded. "My office is already talking to the Home Office. An agreement is going to be made."

"The agreement Ada Hudson was trying to make?"

"Yes," Roth said. "It's going to be honored. You have my word."

She took a few deep breaths, calming herself.

"Can I get you anything? Water?"

"Was Natasha present when...."

"When Ada was shot?" Roth said. "Yes, she was."

"And you have your own team coming in to remove the chip?"

"They're in the air," Roth said. "They'll be here in minutes."

Blackwell nodded. "All right," she said. "I'm going to talk to Natasha. Try to get a read on her state of mind. There's a risk here of permanent psychological...."

"Thank you," Roth said.

Blackwell went back into the conference room, and Roth shut the door. He went to the receptionist's desk and leaned on it heavily.

"Are you all right, sir?"

"Can you get me some coffee?" he said.

The receptionist left and came back with a glass of water and some coffee. He took the coffee to a seat by the elevators and sank into it. The events of the day were taking their toll.

He sipped the coffee, watching Blackwell and Natasha through the glass door of the conference room. Shortly after, the medical team from Lakenheath was arriving. He brought them to the conference room, and Blackwell came back out.

"How is she?" Roth said.

"As you'd expect."

"Will she be okay?"

"You need to get her into a stable environment," Blackwell said. "Not an embassy. Not a CIA safe house."

"Something normal," Roth said.

"Yes, something normal."

He invited Blackwell to wait with him while the operation was performed, but she didn't want to stay. He saw her to the elevator, then went back to the receptionist for more coffee. It wasn't long before a medic in a surgical gown came over to him, removing some disposable surgical gloves. Roth noticed there was blood on them.

The medic was followed by a nurse carrying a small metal surgical dish.

"Did you get it?" Roth said.

The nurse handed him the dish. Inside was a small cube, about the size of a small set of dice. It had been rinsed of blood.

"What is it?" he said.

"It appears to be a bundle of SDUC cards, sir. Not yet commercially available, but not impossible to access."

"Her father was a scientist."

The medic nodded.

"So," Roth said, "what are they exactly?"

"They're memory cards, sir."

"Like what I have at home in my camera?"

"Similar."

"But different?"

"These are new, sir. There are a few corporations bringing them to market. SanDisk, Panasonic, Toshiba."

"Where are these ones from?"

"They're unbranded, sir, but I'm sure your analysts could figure that out."

"And they'll be able to read the information on them?"

"I'd imagine so, sir. Each card could contain up to eight terabytes of information. In total, you could be looking at a package of sixty-four terabytes."

"A lot of data."

"Correct, sir."

Roth held the little cube up to the light.

"I see."

The medic looked at the nurse, then back at Roth. "Your patient, by the way, is stable."

89

I t was dark when Roth finally left the embassy. Natasha was asleep in the conference room, a nurse from the Air Force watching over her, and the Station Chief had left for the night. The chip had been copied, and the original was on its way to Langley for analysis.

He went down to the lobby, called his driver, and let out a sigh of relief as he got into the back of his car.

"Where to, boss?"

Roth was too tired to think. "I don't have a hotel."

The driver nodded. "There's the embassy account at the Dorchester."

"Is it available?"

"I can call and find out."

Roth put his head back and shut his eyes. The car started moving, and when he opened his eyes, they were on Park Lane. A few minutes later, he was outside the Dorchester.

He went inside, where the concierge was already expecting him, and said, "Have the bar send up a single malt."

"A bottle, sir?"

"A bottle."

He found his room and collapsed into the leather chair by the fire. He was getting old. He could feel it in his bones. Around him, his friends were dying. The walls of his castle were crumbling. His enemies were closing in.

Another city, another hotel room, another lonely night.

There was a knock on the door, and he straightened up. "Come in".

No one entered. Instead, the knock came again. With a sigh, he pulled himself from the chair and went to the door. He was about to open it when he paused. He checked the peephole. He'd been expecting the bartender, but that wasn't who was standing there.

It was Tatyana.

She couldn't see him but knew he was there, looking at her.

"Aren't you going to invite me in?" she said.

He opened the door without saying anything. They looked at each other. She had reason to want him dead, but he didn't know if that was why she was there now. He stepped aside, making room for her to enter, then shut the door.

They each took a chair by the fire and then sat there, facing each other, the fire crackling in the hearth.

"I've ordered up scotch," he said.

She nodded. He was nervous but tried not to show it.

"I thought you were in Paris."

"I was," she said.

"Laurel said you were still there."

She shrugged. "Sometimes, people lie."

He swallowed. A silence rose between them and

stretched out. It was broken only by another knock on the door.

"Are you expecting anyone?" he said.

She smiled thinly. Shook her head.

"Come," Roth said, and a bartender came in with a crystal decanter of scotch, a small ice bucket, and a jug of water.

"I didn't realize you had company, sir?"

"Neither did I," Roth said curtly.

The bartender went to the cabinet and took out two rocks glasses. He sensed the tension in the room and poured them each a measure without asking if they wanted it. Then he was gone.

Roth picked up one of the glasses and raised it. Tatyana did the same, then they drank.

He looked at her. She was breathtaking, truly, and she was angry. He felt like he was in a cage with a tiger.

He wanted her to speak first.

She took another sip of her drink and put it on the table. Then she slowly took a pack of cigarettes from her jacket.

"Well," she said at last, "aren't you going to tell me?"

"Tell you what?"

"Come on."

He let out a hollow laugh. She was setting him up to implicate himself.

"I'm sure you can appreciate," he said, "that I have a lot of open loops at any given moment."

"Oh, of course," she said. "A big, important man like you."

He took out a cigar to buy time.

"Look at me," she said.

He looked at her. "If there's something you want to ask."

"You know what I'm asking."

"I assure you…" he began, but she cut him off.

"They knew exactly where to find me."

"They must have been scouring every CCTV camera…."

"No," Tatyana said. "They knew. They were told."

He looked at her, then at the fire.

"You're going to make me say it, aren't you?" she said.

"I'm sorry if…."

"Did you do it, Levi? Did you sell me out?"

The words hit him like a slap in the face. He lit the cigar, trying not to show his discomfort.

"I knew it," she spat.

"Tatyana."

"You coward."

"It's not that simple."

"Sure it isn't."

"I have fewer options than you'd imagine."

"It's not too few options that's your problem."

"I'm trying to avoid a war."

"Because God knows the world would instantly fall apart without your intervention."

He puffed on the cigar, creating a cloud of smoke.

"Look at me," she said.

He couldn't. He couldn't bring himself to meet her gaze.

"*Why*, Roth?"

"I needed to offer them something," he said at last.

"Me?"

"Something valuable. Something to make them believe Tenet was what he appeared to be."

"And you chose me?"

He let out a long sigh.

She leaned forward, and for a second, he thought she was going to kill him. Instead, she picked up the bottle and poured herself another drink.

She knocked it back, then stood.

"Tatyana," he said.

"There's nothing more to say, Levi."

"Tatyana, please. You know I see you as...."

"As expendable."

"As a...."

"As a what, Levi?"

He shook his head.

"What?"

He couldn't say it. She went to the door, opened it, and was gone. He stared at the door long after she was gone.

90

When Tatyana left, Roth was so tired he didn't even get up from the seat. He poured another drink, closed his eyes, and when he woke in the morning, there was a pile of ash and a burn in the carpet where he'd dropped his cigar.

He'd been woken by his phone. It was Laurel.

"I've got a breakdown on this data if you're interested," she said.

"What data?"

"*What data?* The chip from Natasha's arm. *That* data."

"Of course," Roth said, looking at his watch. He'd slept in.

"Tatyana and I have been analyzing it all night."

"Tatyana helped you?"

"Of course she did," Laurel said, and it was clear from her tone she was aware of the tension.

"Okay," Roth said, starting the coffee machine. "What have you got for me? Let's see what all this fuss has been about."

"It's big, Roth."

"Big enough to justify...."

"It's the keys to the kingdom. Every schematic. Every design decision. Every technical innovation. It even includes the designs of failed prototypes that were scrapped."

"So Gazinsky...."

"Kept his promise. The entirety of Project Oppenheimer is here, spelled out in exquisite detail."

"The Pentagon guys will cream their pants."

"It's nasty, though. A real Satan's shopping list."

"And what's on that list?"

"There's Petrel."

"The missile that leaks radiation wherever it flies."

"Yes, and there's also a Petrel variant. It doesn't have the same loiter capability, but according to the schematics, can reach a top speed of Mach Twelve."

"Did you say Mach Twelve?"

"That's not all. There's also a hypersonic boost-glide vehicle. The schematics call it *Poshlost*."

"*Poshlost*?"

"It means something in Russian."

"I know what it means, but I haven't heard of it in reference to a weapon."

"This one's capable of Mach Twenty."

"Fuck me."

"Exactly."

"Our missile defense systems...."

"Useless. Nothing we have can counter anything remotely that fast."

"And I don't suppose they're planning to use these new rockets with conventional payloads."

"I don't think so, boss. Their accuracy, even under ideal conditions, will be abysmal. In some cases, they don't even attempt a target radius of less than three miles."

"So they're not precision systems."

"No, they're old-fashioned clusterfuck systems, designed to hit cities, not specific targets."

"And we can't stop them."

"In terms of missile defense, these things will bring us back to the Stone Age."

"What about the underwater system?"

"Poseidon."

"Is it included in the cache?"

"Yes, and it's every bit as nasty as we thought. Another weapon of last resort, capable of delivering a hundred-megaton payload laced with cobalt-60."

"How lovely."

"Then there's the directed-energy prototype they're calling *Pogrom*."

"A laser?"

"It looks like an attempted rip-off of our own navy's AN/SEQ-3 Laser."

"Did Gazinsky include anything that might help pinpoint a leak?"

"Not directly, but once the Pentagon gets a look, they'll know if it's based on our system."

"If someone on our side's been opening the kimono."

"We'll find them."

"Okay, so according to my count, that's...."

"Five prototypes. The Five P's mentioned in intercepted communications. *Poshlost, Poseidon, Pogrom*."

"And the two *Petrel* variants."

"The schematics aren't limited to delivery systems, though," Laurel said. "There's also a horde of classified documents relating to other things."

"What sort of other things?"

"Internal emails, memos, secret executive orders, military directives. Thousands and thousands of them."

"What do they say?"

"Tatyana will need to get a team together. There's too many for one person to go through alone."

"She's willing to do that?"

"Willing? Roth, what happened between you two last night?"

"I'm sure you can imagine."

"I'm sure that I can't."

"Well," Roth said, changing the subject, "from what you've read of the documents so far...."

"It's incredible. They were looping Gazinsky in on all sorts of chatter. Top-level shit."

"Dead Hand level?"

"Some of it, possibly. There's discussion on how to go about breaching international weapons conventions, what human viruses are suitable for weaponizing, what pathogens could be used to destroy crops and livestock in various climates, what parts of the globe are most susceptible to various kinds of dirty bomb."

"Sounds like Molotov's speech from the Mausoleum last year," Roth said.

"Exactly."

"No one listens to us, isn't that what he said?"

"No one listens to us. You'll listen to us now."

"Everyone listens to the man holding a hand grenade," Roth said.

"Yes, they do."

Roth sighed. He'd known it would be bad. Now he knew how bad. "Well," he said, "at least it will help convince our critics in the White House of the urgency."

"Oh, it's going to do a lot more than that."

"What do you mean?"

"Gazinsky marked up these documents in a way that makes one thing very clear."

"And what's that?"

"Every one of these weapons has a flaw."

"A critical flaw?"

"Probably, if we start working on countermeasures."

"For all five systems?"

"I think Gazinsky believed it was possible to counter all five. And I think he was giving us a roadmap to do it. Thousands of pages, drawings, graphs, charts, numbers. He was obsessed. It goes back years."

"How many years?"

"Since before he knew his daughter needed our help, if that's what you're asking."

"So maybe he wasn't...."

"Maybe he wasn't as politically disinterested as he let on."

"If he was planning all this."

"Well, put yourself in his position. A scientist, working on weapons designed to render large portions of the planet uninhabitable. He knew if he quit, they'd simply put someone else in his place."

"So he sabotaged all of it?"

"He'd been gathering the data for a long time. If you ask me, he never wanted to see these weapons become a reality. Natasha's illness just gave him the final push he needed to pull the plug."

"I see."

"And there's something else."

"What else could there be?"

"Gazinsky kept copious notes."

"Okay."

"The information he received, it was supposed to be sanitized. They wanted him looped in on technical matters only."

"Of course."

"GRU command lines, meeting attendance lists, party distribution lists, anything identifying specific Kremlin leaders, all of that was supposed to be redacted."

"But it wasn't?"

"Over the course of years, millions of documents, electronic messages, mistakes were made."

"And he kept track of the mistakes?"

"He didn't just keep track. He made charts. He drew lines connecting different names, different places, specific events."

Roth felt his pulse quicken. He had a feeling he already knew where this was leading, and also what it was going to cost. "Where did all those lines lead, Laurel?"

"To one man."

"And what man is that?"

"Gazinsky didn't know his name, but he had a Dead Hand connection."

"I see."

"He's referred to on the chart as The Sleeper."

"The Sleeper?"

"That's right, and if we can find out who that is...."

"We end the entire program."

Yes," Laurel said.

Roth's tone had been steadily dropping, enough that Laurel noticed it. "Is something the matter?"

"Nothing's the matter."

"I thought this would be good news."

"It is."

"You don't sound pleased."

Roth sighed. He knew what the outcome of this was going to be. He knew where this road led. Alona's face flashed across his mind. When he pictured her, she was already dead.

"Suvorov," he said quietly.

"What's that?"

"The Sleeper, Laurel. His name is André Suvorov."

91

L ance sat alone in a dingy bar in Kapotnya. It was late, and a group of men at the bar had been getting progressively drunker for some time. Lance was at a table in the corner, minding his own business, drinking black coffee and smoking cigarettes. No one paid him any attention until one of the men from the bar stumbled over and slammed a shot glass on his table.

"Drink," he bellowed.

Lance looked up at him. He was wearing the insulated blue overalls of the nearby Tets-22 power plant and an ushanka fur hat.

"No, thank you," Lance said.

He knew how to pass for a local in that part of the city. He'd practiced the accent. It was a useful skill. The GRU monitored Central Moscow very closely, but here in the outskirts, if one could fit in, it was possible to fly under the radar.

The man wasn't leaving the table. He'd taken offense at Lance's refusal to drink, and looked back to his friends to check that they were still watching. There were six of them there, all in the same overalls, the same hats on their heads, ear flaps flipped up, and they were all watching.

Lance was tired. He hadn't been looking for trouble, or, for that matter, much of anything. Across the bar, the door opened, letting in a gust of icy wind. Four women came in, dressed to the nines in heels, skirts, earrings, lipstick. That wasn't good. There would definitely be trouble now. The man would be emboldened. He would show off. He would pick a fight.

The women found a table, and the man went over to his friends and picked up a bottle of vodka from the bar. He came back over to Lance's table and slammed the bottle on the table.

"I said drink."

Everyone in the bar was watching now—the women, the bartender, the man's friends, the other scattered customers. Lance didn't move. He kept his eyes fixed on the cup of coffee in front of him.

The man picked up the bottle and tried to shove it into Lance's mouth. "Drink," he boomed. "Drink!"

Lance grabbed his wrist. Vodka got all over his clothes. He glanced around the bar. People looked away. The bartender pretended not to notice. The man's friends were enjoying it, making eyes at the women, checking to see if they were impressed.

"Who drinks coffee in a bar?" the man announced to the entire bar. "Who the hell drinks coffee in a bar?"

He swiped Lance's cup off the table, shattering it on the floor.

Lance rose to his feet slowly. He sized up the man, sized up his six friends. They were big guys, and their blue overalls were heavily padded.

"Now, why did you go and do a thing like that?" Lance said.

The man took a step toward him. Their faces were just inches apart. He said, "Cops drink coffee in bars. That's who."

Lance locked eyes with him, thought about ending the discussion right there and then, but instead, he turned to the guys at the bar. "If he gets hurt," he said, "it's your fault."

"The fuck did you say?" the man said, bearing down on him.

Lance pushed him back.

One of the other guys came over. He was smoking a cigarette, and he held the butt between his thumb and forefinger before flicking it at Lance. It hit his shoulder, scattering ash on his jacket.

Lance brushed the ash away deliberately. Another man came over. Three of them, now. These were the men, Lance thought, that the US Government had spent trillions of dollars defending itself against. With their grease-stained overalls, their car payments and sore backs, their calloused hands and bottled domestic beers, they weren't so different from the men in a thousand towns back home. They showed up for work, punched in, cashed their check, paid their bills.

It was on their backs that Russia was built.

And America.

He didn't begrudge them blowing off a little steam. If they wanted a fight, he supposed he'd give them one. They were drunk. They'd be slow. Their movements had all the liveliness of a freight ship pulling into port. No one would be seriously hurt.

They closed in.

Lance took off his jacket and put it on the back of a chair.

"Maybe he's looking for a boyfriend," one of the men said. Laughter erupted.

Lance was about to ask him if that was an offer when his phone began to vibrate. It was one of Roth's burner phones. He'd picked it up, along with some identification documents, two handguns, and cash, from a dropbox after he'd left Suvorov's hotel. It could only be Roth calling.

He raised a finger, as if to tell the men to hang on a second, then pulled the phone from his pocket and answered.

"Levi, can I call you back? I was about to get into something."

The men looked on awkwardly, uncertain how to react to this interruption. Lance looked like a guy who could hold his own in a fight, and that, combined with the sudden switch to English, was putting them off. They looked at each other.

"I want you to go after Suvorov," Roth said.

Lance looked apologetically at the men, as if to say he'd only be another second, but already they'd begun backing away. He put his hand over the receiver and said, "Wait up, fellas. I'll be right with you." Then, to Roth, "You know, I had Suvorov by the balls earlier. That would have been the perfect time to take him out."

"I know," Roth said.

"But you made me cut him loose."

"I needed to talk to him."

"Oh, I bet you did."

"What does that mean?"

"You know what it means."

"I needed him to tell me where Natasha Gazinsky was."

"Bullshit. Laurel gave you Natasha Gazinsky. Not Suvorov."

Roth hesitated, then said, "He threatened someone close to me."

Lance already knew that. Suvorov had told him as much. What Lance didn't know was what else they'd talked about.

"When you go after Suvorov," Roth said, "someone goes after my friend."

"Alona, right? Tenet's wife?"

"That's right."

"And that's a risk you're willing to take?"

Roth hesitated before saying, "Yes, it is."

"If something happens to her, Roth."

"I'll get her protection."

"I know what regret feels like."

Roth was quiet again, then said, "I know you do, Lance."

The men in overalls were all back at the bar now, acting like nothing had ever happened. Lance got the bartender's attention. "A bottle of vodka," he said. "And seven, no, eight glasses." Then to Roth, he said, "Do we have a location for Suvorov?"

"Laurel's tracking him on satellite. Looks like he's headed for an old Soviet skunkworks north of Moscow. You're going to need a car."

The bartender put the bottle on the bar, and Lance began pouring a round of shots.

"Do we have schematics for the facility?"

"No, we do not," Roth said. "It might be better to hit him on the road."

"All right," Lance said. "Anything else?"

"That's all."

Lance hung up, then beckoned the guys in overalls. "Shots, fellas?"

92

Roth made one final call before leaving the hotel room.

"Don't hang up," he said as soon as she picked up. "Please. It's important."

He heard her breathing, smoking a cigarette. She said nothing. He could picture her every movement, every gesture, the angle of her wrist, the way she held a cigarette and tapped it against the side of an ashtray.

He cleared his throat. "Alona, you're not safe," he said, his voice as dry as sand.

More silence. He heard her exhale.

"The man who killed Richmond...."

"You're the man who killed Richmond."

He didn't argue with her. The time for that had passed. Now, it was about keeping her alive, nothing more. "They're coming for you."

There was another long pause, then she said, "Is that all you wanted to say?"

It wasn't, but he didn't dare bring up the things he

wanted to. Instead, he said, "Did you hear what I said? The Russians. They're coming."

"I'm hanging up."

"Alona, don't. Let me bring you in. It's the only way to keep you safe."

"I'd rather die than let you bring me in," she said, the anger in her voice like grit.

"This is no time to take a stand, Alona. Your life is in danger."

"My *life*," she spat, "is no concern of yours."

"Please let me protect you. If not for yourself, then for...."

"There's nothing left for you here, Levi. You need to stop contacting me. You need to forget about me."

He couldn't accept that. "Hate me if you want to," he stammered, "curse me all the way to hell, but let me bring you in. You won't be safe outside the embassy."

"It's never going to happen, Levi."

"This isn't just a threat. They're coming, and when they do, it's going to be ugly."

"A lot of things in this world are ugly."

"I'm not leaving you out there in the cold."

"Oh, that's rich. *You* not leaving *me*."

"I just want you to be protected."

"Protected? You're the reason they're coming, Levi. If you'd only left me alone. If you'd just let me be...."

"I was trying to do my job."

"Your job? Really? Your job required you to kill my husband?"

"He wasn't supposed to die."

"They're coming for me because of you, Levi. You killed Richmond, and when I die, you'll have killed me too."

"I never meant for any of this...."

"Don't start groveling now, Levi," she said. "Spare us both that indignity, please."

"Alona. Listen to me."

"Listen? Let me ask you something."

"Okay."

"How do you know they're coming?"

"What do you mean? It's my job to know…."

"But for me, now? How do you know they're coming?"

"What are you saying?"

"They told you, didn't they?"

"They threatened you."

"They gave you an ultimatum—a threat."

"Alona. No."

"They told you they'd come for me if you didn't do what they wanted."

"That's not how it happened."

"It's true, Levi. I know it is. They gave you a choice, and this is the outcome."

Roth made to speak, but no words came out of his mouth.

"You chose this. You chose all of it, as surely as if you were pulling the trigger yourself."

"Alona, please."

"You did this, Levi. No one else."

"Alona, I thought…."

"I know exactly what you *thought*. You forget, Levi, I've known you since the beginning. I knew the man you were before any of this happened, before you were Director, before you rubbed shoulders with the President."

"I'm still the man I was then."

"That's the problem, Levi. You're still that man, and I never loved him. Not then, and not now."

"Alona. What we had…."

"You were a schoolboy, Levi. A boy scout. Always so eager to please."

"You're just...."

"You were obsequious, Levi. You carried your past around with you like a wound."

"My past? I never told anyone but you about that."

"You couldn't have been more ashamed if they told you to wear the Yellow Star."

"What are you saying?"

"You were so..." and she paused, searching for the word, "so *servile,* Levi. I couldn't love you. I detested you."

Roth's chest constricted. It was a struggle to breathe. He found himself gasping for air and had to sit down.

"I never loved you, Levi. I never loved you."

"Alona, I know what we had...."

"I was with you because they ordered me to be there."

"What are you talking about?"

"They told me to get close. They targeted you."

"Who targeted me?"

"Mossad, you fool. They thought you were their way in. They thought you'd flip."

"I don't believe you."

"Why not? Because we fucked a few times."

"Because we were in love, Alona."

She laughed. "If you think that, you're a bigger fool even than I thought."

"You're saying this...."

"Because it's true."

The line went dead.

93

Lance walked along the dimly-lit, cobbled street, looking carefully at each parked car as he passed. The street was lit by old-style lamps, and the bulbs quivered slightly, like candles. He came to an old, black Mercedes and crouched down between it and the car next to it. It was exactly what he needed, something with enough power under the hood but old enough that it could be hot-wired without triggering a remote alarm.

In the sleeve of his jacket, he had a long, steel file. He pressed it against the window of the driver's door, slid it down between the glass and door, and, after a few tries, unhinged the lock mechanism.

The door opened. He got into the driver's seat and jammed the same file into the plastic panel beneath the steering column. It came loose to reveal three sets of wires. One led to the column-mounted controls, another to the dashboard indicators, and the third to the ignition and starter. He followed each set with his fingers until he found the one he was looking for. Then he connected the battery. The dashboard electrics came to life. He touched the same wire to the ignition. It sparked, and the engine turned once. He touched it again, and the engine fired up. He revved it, pressing the gas pedal with his hand, then got up into the seat and drove off.

As soon as he was on the highway, he called Laurel. "I'm on the road."

"Clean?"

"I think so."

"Okay," she said, "you're going north. There's a military research facility near the town of Dmitrov. The target arrived there in a convoy of four armored SUVs."

"Armored?"

"Modified G-Class wagons. They arrived about thirty minutes ago and haven't emerged since."

"Any escort?"

"Police motorcycles. Four of them."

Lance changed lanes and overtook some trucks. He was on the main Moscow ring road following directions for Reutov and Mytishchi. "Roth said we don't have schematics for the site."

"It was a proving ground. It's on a CIA watch list, along with thousands of other old Soviet sites. Past scans have shown near-zero surface activity, no unusual emissions readings or heat signatures. We thought it was abandoned."

"Apparently not."

"There is an army barracks about thirteen miles away. Large enough for about four hundred men."

"A Dead Hand unit?"

"The surface buildings are from the fifties. None have power. There's a chain-link fence around the perimeter. Unguarded."

"There must be an underground compound of some kind."

"And given Suvorov's status, I wouldn't be surprised if the perimeter is a lot more secure than it looks."

"Mines?"

"Mines, sensors, you name it."

"Okay," Lance said. "I'll call you when I'm closer."

He merged with the northbound traffic out of the city. The moon was so bright he could have driven by it. He was on an ugly stretch of road, two lanes in each direction separated by a rusty metal fence. A snowbank, black with filth, ran along the shoulder. Ramshackle gas stations, truck stops, and strip clubs marked the last of the city as he crossed the Klyazma. Beneath the bridge, the rigid symmetry of the Moscow Canal gave way to a meandering river course.

It was thirty minutes from there to the outskirts of Dmitrov, where enormous concrete high-rises lined both sides of the highway. He got off at a new German supermarket and passed the city on a regional road in dire need of repair. He had to slow down a number of times because of the potholes. At places, they were so deep that traffic cones had been placed around them.

He passed a hydroelectric dam, the lake beyond it enclosed in high levees. High-tension transmission lines on rusted scaffolds ran by the road as he passed through progressively smaller, more decrepit villages. When he was about a mile from the southern entrance of the compound, he pulled into a gas station.

A neon light in the window said it was shut for the night. He stepped out of the car, keeping the engine running, and lit a cigarette. It was very cold, very still, and he looked up at the sky. Somewhere above, Laurel was looking back down.

He took out his phone and called her.

"Do you have me?"

"I have you."

"If he leaves for Moscow, he has to pass my location, correct?"

"Yes, but how are you armed?"

"Two Glocks."

"That's it?"

"That's all I had time for."

"He'll be traveling with at least twelve men, all armed heavily."

"I'll have to be careful then," Lance said.

He walked over to the road and checked the approach. The speed limit was eighty kilometers per hour, and the asphalt was cracked badly. Suvorov would approach from the north, coming over a slight rise about a hundred yards from where he stood. If they drove at the speed limit, they wouldn't see him until it was too late to react.

He walked over to the rise and scanned the approaching country. No buildings, no vehicles, nothing. He finished his cigarette and flicked it into the ditch, then walked back to his car and lit another.

94

Lance moved the car to the edge of the road. It was a stick shift, and he put it in neutral and pulled the handbrake. There was just enough of an incline that if he released the brake, the car would roll forward into the road. He opened the fuel tank, tore a strip of cloth from his shirt, and stuffed it into the opening of the tank. It soaked up gasoline like the wick of a candle.

He got out and paced back and forth, smoking another cigarette. After a few minutes, he climbed onto the hood of the car to get a better view. He couldn't see over the rise in the road, but there was a mist in the air that would catch the light of any approaching high beams.

It was from the opposite direction that he saw the first light. A car was approaching. He looked at his watch. It was an hour until sunrise. He got down from the hood and waited. The car slowed as it approached, then pulled up next to him. The driver rolled down his window. He was about seventy and had the tan, leathery skin of someone accustomed to working outdoors.

"Is this your place?" Lance said to him.

He nodded. He looked at Lance's car, the engine running, the rag hanging from the gas tank, then he looked back at Lance. He was at a point in his life when the things he saw no longer had the power to surprise him, and with a look of supreme resignation, he said to Lance, "I just made a mistake stopping, didn't I?"

Lance shrugged. "Doesn't have to be."

The man's lips moved as if he was going to say something, but he didn't.

"You're right in what you're thinking," Lance said.

"And what am I thinking?"

"That trouble's coming."

"When I was born, Stalin was in the Kremlin. If trouble's coming, I know what to do."

"And what's that?"

"Look the other way."

"You're sure of that?"

The man reached into his pocket, took out a very old cell phone, and handed it to Lance.

Lance took it. "When the police come," he said, "tell them what you want. You won't see me again."

"I'll tell them nothing."

Lance nodded. "There'll be GRU men too."

"Then the less I saw, the better."

Lance nodded. They understood each other. He handed the man back his phone. "Come back when it's light. The less you know...."

The man nodded. He drove off in the direction he'd come from, and Lance got back onto the hood and watched the road to the north.

His phone vibrated, and he answered.

"We've got movement," Laurel said.

"Coming my way?"

"Yup, and moving fast. Target is in the fourth SUV. There are two police motorcycles at the front of the convoy. Two at the rear."

"How far out?"

"At current speed, two minutes."

Lance looked north. He saw no sign of them yet. He kept Laurel on the line and got down from the hood. He checked his guns.

"Sixty seconds," Laurel said.

He put another cigarette in his mouth and lit it.

"Thirty seconds."

He inhaled deeply and blew out smoke. In the moonlight, it looked blue.

"Twenty seconds."

He heard the engines before he saw the glow of their lights. Then he went over to the fuel tank and held his cigarette to the rag. It caught fire.

He went to the driver's door, leaned inside the car, and put his hand on the brake. A single police motorcycle sped by, blue and red lights flashing, followed by a second, then the first of the SUVs. He released the brake, leaned his weight into the car, and shoved it forward.

As it began to move, he backed away.

The next SUV sped by, veering slightly at the last second to avoid hitting it.

The third SUV clipped it, shattering a light and careening right, then left. There was a deafening screech of rubber as the driver jammed the brakes, then it veered off the road and into a ditch.

The fourth SUV slammed headlong into it.

Lance was thirty feet back and felt the impact of the concussion in the air. The sound of the impact would have been heard half a mile away. The car exploded in an enormous fireball that billowed into the sky in a plume fifty feet high. Lance raised a hand to shield himself from the heat.

The two rear motorcycles jammed on their brakes, desperately trying to avoid the explosion. The drivers hit the ground hard, their bodies sliding and rolling on the asphalt like rag dolls.

Lance drew his guns. Neither motorcycle driver got up. He turned to Suvorov's vehicle, its windows shattered, fire billowing from the hood. Airbags had deployed but had already been incinerated in the blaze. Inside, the bodies of four men, their skin black and crusted like burned barbecue, sat strapped to the seats.

He raised his gun. He was about to put a bullet in each corpse, just to make certain, but the fuel tank of the SUV caught fire, and the entire thing exploded in a second fireball, even larger than the first.

Ahead on the road, the other vehicles had stopped and were desperately trying to turn around. Someone fired a bullet. Lance ducked, then strode over to the nearest police motorcycle. The driver was unconscious, maybe dead. The engine was running.

He got on the bike, revved the engine, and sped off northward in the direction the convoy had come from.

He rode hard through open farmland, making a beeline for some trees in the distance. There wasn't much time before dawn, and he needed as much cover as he could get.

He reached the trees and turned eastward onto a badly paved road. After a mile, it led out from the trees into more farmland. It was poor land, mostly grass, and would provide no cover from overhead surveillance. There were few buildings, and those he passed were rusted-out, metal shacks.

He slowed down for what appeared to be a village, but as he neared, he saw it was just a collection of storage sheds.

He drove on and turned south onto another road, paved with concrete slabs laid out in five-yard stretches.

Ahead was another wooded area, and as he entered the tree cover, he saw the lights of a chopper in the sky to the north. It wouldn't be long before there were more.

He got off the bike and, using his elbow, broke the bike's taillight and running lights.

Then he turned off the other lights and called Laurel.

"You got eyes on me?"

"Yes. Remember that barracks I told you about? Troops are pouring out of it."

"I saw a chopper."

"There are seven more taking off as we speak. They're going to have that entire area locked down real soon."

"Tell me where to go."

"Keep going the direction you're going. Five miles east is the town of Sergiyev. You'll have to cross open country to get there, but there are no choppers that way yet."

"And from there?"

"The M8 will give you a straight shot back to the city."

"Any roadblocks?"

"Not yet, but there will be."

"Okay."

"And get rid of the phone."

He hung up, turned off the phone, and flung it into the trees. Then, with no lights, he drove on eastward until he reached the edge of the woods. He stopped there and killed the engine. He couldn't see any choppers, but he could hear them. The moonlight was enough to drive by, but it would also mean he'd be visible if a chopper got close enough.

He checked the sky one last time, then fired up the engine and went for it. He drove fast, east toward the dawn. When the road forked, he kept left. He came to a small river and kept to its south bank. On the other side was a train track.

It wasn't long before he could see the lights of the town. There were houses on his right, facing the river, their doors opening directly onto the road. He went on until he saw a large, brick warehouse. Behind it was a small lot with some parked vehicles. He drove into the lot and hid the bike beneath a lean-to.

Across the yard was a beat-up old pickup truck. He checked the door. It was unlocked. It took him a minute to hotwire it, then he revved the engine and listened to it. It sounded okay. The gas gauge said he had just over a quarter tank.

He pulled out of the lot and drove through the village, keeping to the speed limit. He followed the road to the M8 highway and joined the southbound lanes.

The highway was newer than the one he'd taken north, and the traffic was slightly heavier. The sun was beginning to lighten the sky. It wouldn't be long before he was joining commuter traffic.

He scanned the sky for choppers and saw none. He drove on, then opened his window and let the cool air hit his face. He lit a cigarette. He was just beginning to breathe easy when he saw the flashing blue lights of a police road-block up ahead.

95

Lance slid his guns under his seat as he approached the checkpoint. There were two police cars, their lights flashing, one parked on either side of the slower traffic lane. It looked like just two cops. The nearer one stood by his car, waving a flashlight. Lance slowed down and opened his window. The first cop waved him past and continued waving his flashlight. The second cop told him to stop. He came up to the window and shone a flashlight in Lance's face.

"Where from?" he said.

"Sergiyev."

"Heading into the city?"

"A trade show in Vidnoye," Lance said.

"What trade?"

"Welding."

The officer nodded. He looked into the bed of the truck. Lance had noticed earlier that it contained an industrial gas canister. He looked like he was going to wave Lance through, but he said, "License and registration."

The car behind had come to a halt, and the other cop was speaking to the driver.

Lance reached into his jacket and pulled out the ID he'd taken from Roth's drop box in Moscow. There'd been a Russian passport and driver's license for a man about Lance's age, and Lance had inserted his own photo into them when he was at the hotel in Kapotnya. He handed the license to the cop, then leaned over to the glove box and opened it. He didn't know what it would contain but saw that there was an old owner's manual with a clasp holding it shut. He opened it and found the proof of ownership inside. It was expired, but better than nothing.

The cop looked at the documents, then passed them to the other cop who brought them to his car.

Lance knew the address on the license was in Moscow, not Sergiyev. Also, the name didn't match the name in the vehicle ownership. It might be a problem. It might not.

He kept his hands on the steering wheel and waited while they ran the license. The cop at the car beckoned the other one over to him. They spoke at the car, then both came back to Lance.

Lance watched them in his wing mirror. One of them had a hand on his holster.

"Sir, step out of the vehicle."

Lance knew then how it would play out. Two local boys, neither of them yet thirty, and for what? He regretted it.

"Is there a problem?"

"Step out of the vehicle," he said again.

Lance sighed, opened the door, and got out of the cab.

"Hands on the hood."

He put his hands on the hood.

"Who is Yakov Yakovlev?" the cop said.

It must have been the name in the ownership. "My boss," he said.

"Does he know you're driving his truck?"

"I have his number on my phone. I can call him for you."

Cars were beginning to line up behind Lance's truck. The cops looked at each other uncertainly.

"Let me call him," Lance said. "He'll tell you."

"Keep your hands where they are," the cop said.

Lance could feel the engine running beneath the hood. He had his back to the cops and shut his eyes. He heard one of them approach. "Hands behind your back," he said, and at the same moment, Lance turned and grabbed him, bent back his arm, and spun him around to use him as a shield between himself and the other cop.

"Freeze," the other cop yelled, drawing his weapon.

Lance pulled the gun from the cop's belt and held it to his head.

"Don't shoot," the cop stammered. "Don't shoot."

"Drop your weapon," Lance said to the other cop.

The other cop hesitated.

"Drop it," Lance said again. "Drop it, and no one gets hurt."

The cop's eyes darted from Lance to his partner, desperately trying to decide what to do. Time compressed, so that each second that passed felt like an eternity.

"Go on," Lance said, "put it down, and we all go home in one piece."

The cop fired. The bullet hit the other cop in the shoulder, a few inches from Lance's face. Lance pushed the cop forward and ducked. He fired twice, hitting both cops in the legs. As they fell to the ground, he looked at the cars lined up behind the roadblock.

He leaped over the hood of the truck, then, using the

vehicles for cover, went to the second car in the line. It was a Volkswagen Golf, new, with a turbo engine. The cops were writhing on the ground where they'd fallen. With so many civilians in the way, they wouldn't fire now.

He tapped on the window of the Volkswagen with his pistol and motioned for the man to get out of the car.

"Please," the man begged, his hands in the air.

"Give me the key," Lance said.

The man got out, and Lance got in. The car was somewhat boxed in, but he was able to back up a little, then drive into the shoulder left of one of the cop cars and get around.

Then he gunned the engine, tearing down the highway as fast as he could. He got off at the very next exit—a Moscow suburb called Pushkino. There were more cars on the roads than there had been on the highway. He crossed the river and drove into the commercial hub, pulling into the first multistory parking lot he saw. He parked in a spot that was somewhat shielded from view by a pillar and left the Volkswagen there.

There were a few other cars in the lot, and he walked among them until he found an unassuming Lada sedan. He broke in, fired it up, and left the lot. He took surface streets through Korolyov and Mytishchi, making his way slowly through morning traffic all the way back to Central Moscow.

At Sokolniki Park, he pulled over and parked legally. He even put money in the meter. Then he walked the ten blocks to Leningradskiy Station.

96

In an experiment carried out at the Delaware Valley College in Doylestown, Pennsylvania, entomologists cut the heads off a number of *Periplaneta Americana*, more commonly known as the American cockroach, and sealed the wounds with dental wax.

The prevailing theory, based on casual observation, was that the cockroaches would be able to survive without their heads. Ganglia in their distributed central nervous system meant reflexes and motor functions should be able to continue in each body segment independent of the brain. Breathing could take place through spiracles, or small holes, throughout the body. And because they were poikilotherms, they wouldn't need to eat for an extended period.

The experiment successfully confirmed all hypotheses. Without a head, the cockroach body survived for weeks, sometimes months, doing almost all of the things it normally did—respiring, reacting to temperature variations and touch, moving around, releasing hormones.

And, as is all too often the case, as it was with cockroaches, so it was with men.

Dead Hand protocols were everywhere in the Kremlin, designed to do exactly what a cockroach's body did—continue living without the brain.

From the top down, when a GRU officer died, all debts were called, all grievances settled. Nothing, good or bad, went unpunished.

If the leadership in the Kremlin was ever taken out, every missile silo in the country would retaliate automatically against pre-programmed targets, the launch codes transmitted by sentinel satellites orbiting at geostationary positions twenty-two-thousand miles overhead. If God Himself smote every man in Moscow, the codes would still be transmitted.

In the event of a successful attack on the President's person, Dead Hand units all over the country would unleash an orgy of violence so terrible it would draw comparison to the purges of Stalin. There were so many names on Molotov's kill list, which grew with every passing year, that the Kremlin had very real fears for the country's continuity of government.

André Suvorov was no different. Like all mere mortals, he had not foreseen the time and manner of his death. But he had prepared for it. His list was not so extensive as the President's, there were rules about such things, but it was nevertheless formidable. And its successful execution was provided for under the terms of his appointment to the Dead Hand.

Within minutes of his being declared dead at the hospital in Dmitrov, a dusty analog phone in a basement section of GRU headquarters began to ring. The phone was on an old desk, surrounded by moth-eaten files in rusted cabinets, in a large area that had once been home to a whole team of secretaries and administrators. As their jobs were gradually digitized and replaced, the staff had been whittled down to its current state—a single, overweight bureaucrat in a gray suit and white shirt who smoked so many cigarettes in a day that he'd more than once set off the main smoke alarm for the entire building. He sat at an enormous desk on a raised platform that had originally served as the security station. It afforded him a view over the hundred desks on the floor below, and more importantly, the hundred black analog phones that sat on those desks. As well as a phone, each desk had its own filing cabinet and table lamp. The lamps weren't on. Instead, the light came from overhead bulbs in green metal shades that hung on eight-foot chains from the ceiling. They were the same lights, he'd learned, that were used in cattle barns.

When he heard the phone, he cocked his head like a farmyard hen listening for a fox. He initially thought it was the radio, which was droning from its home in the top drawer of his desk, but when he turned it off, the ringing continued.

He stubbed out his cigarette and rose to his feet. Each phone had a small red light, and he peered over the desks, looking for one that was flashing. Among the stacks of paper, photocopiers, old computers, and telex and fax machines, it wasn't easy to spot.

He squinted and searched, finally finding the red light, barely visible through the dust and murk. He hurried down the steps to the phone—it was rattling so hard it threatened to knock itself off the desk—and picked up the receiver.

On the other end was an automated female voice.

Event.

Event.

Event.

Protocol. Gamma. Four. Six. Active.

Event.

Event.

Event.

Protocol. Gamma. Four. Six. Active.

He hung up and looked up at the formidable filing cabinet next to the desk. Each drawer was labeled. He opened the one marked Gamma and flicked through it to file forty-six.

It contained a single sheet of paper with a list of names and four-digit internal GRU phone numbers. The numbers were to be dialed consecutively from the phone in front of him, and when they picked up, he was to confirm the name of the recipient and repeat the protocol—nothing more. If any failed to answer, he was to go on down the list and loop back at the end.

When he'd spoken to everyone, he was to disconnect the phone, destroy the files, then have building services come take away the desk, the phone, the lamp, and the filing cabinet.

He dialed the first number on the list and waited. It was Suvorov's secretary. When she didn't pick up, the system forwarded him to her out-of-hours number.

"Hello?" she said, her voice groggy with sleep.

"Confirm identity," he said.

"What? Who is this?"

"Confirm..." he began robotically, and she cut him off.

"Lina Kovalenko," she said. "What's going on?"

"Protocol Gamma forty-six. Confirm receipt."

"Protocol?"

"Confirm receipt."

"What's happened?"

"You know I have no idea," he said, breaking protocol.

She rubbed her eyes.

"Confirm...."

"Confirmed," she said and hung up.

97

A ndré Suvorov's secretary, Lina Kovalenko, was lying in her bed, in her apartment, next to her husband. She glanced at the clock next to the bed and sat up.

"What was it?" her husband said.

"Go back to sleep. I have to go in."

Twenty minutes later, she was in the back of a cab on her way to headquarters, and soon after, she was in the restricted elevator that led to the top floor. She passed the night receptionist without acknowledging her and went straight to her desk. She sat down in front of her computer and logged in. Then she opened her database terminal and ran a search.

Identifier: P_G_46
  Originator: André Suvorov
  Agency: Prime Directorate
  Event: Death
  Instruction: Await package

Restricted Database

So that was it. It had happened. Suvorov was dead.

She'd been his secretary for twenty years and didn't feel the slightest tinge of sentimentality. She was four years shy of full retirement. Her only thought now was what this would mean for that. If she was forced out early, it would cost her on her pension.

She sat at her desk, tapping her foot, and almost leaped when the elevator dinged. The doors opened, and a GRU courier emerged. He went up to the receptionist and gave her a slip of paper. She signed it, and he handed her a small sealed envelope.

"Who's it for?" Lina said when he was gone.

"You," the receptionist said.

Lina took the envelope, then asked for the delivery slip too. She read that first. It said the envelope had come from a private apartment not far from the Patriarshiye Ponds. She didn't recognize the address.

In drills, the envelopes that arrived were always crisp and new, straight from the stationary department on the third floor. This one was creased down the middle, top to bottom, the way Suvorov had a habit of doing. On one corner was a red wine stain.

She opened it carefully and found a note, written hastily in Suvorov's unmistakable hand. He'd used the Montblanc pen his wife gave him.

The note contained a set of instructions for accessing an ordinary commercial freight forwarding account.

She logged into the account and scrolled through the items. They were packages that were being held at various freight facilities around the world. Some had been consigned years ago and were held in storage for a small monthly fee. Others had been consigned more recently. The most recent had been in the forwarder's possession less than a day. They were spread out around the globe—eight packages in Moscow itself, three in London, two in Paris, one in New York, two in Washington, one in Berlin. The list went on.

She was under no illusion as to what they contained. She didn't know for certain, of course, but these packages represented the final orders of André Suvorov, only to be given after his death. They were unlikely to be anything other than kill orders.

She scanned the package details. Most were sealed envelopes, never more than a few hundred grams in weight, all marked for immediate hand delivery.

She went through the list, marking each package for immediate dispatch, then authorized payment and deleted the account.

It crossed her mind, though she tried to banish the thought, that her own name might be on his housecleaning list.

98

Fifteen hundred miles from Lina Kovalenko's desk in Moscow, at an utterly nondescript shipping facility in a drab industrial park in Croydon, South London, a mail sorting machine came to life with a loud clank. It picked up a padded envelope and dropped it onto a steel ramp, where it fell into a wire basket that was then picked up by an employee and placed in a steel delivery box.

The box was on the back of a Honda motorcycle, one of thirty parked in a row, that would depart the depot before dawn.

The driver rode from Croydon to Bloomsbury in Central London via Crystal Palace and Brixton. Traffic was light, and he was at the delivery address, a dilapidated hotel on Russell Square called The Imperial, in less than thirty minutes. The building looked more like an office block from the sixties—all concrete and symmetry—than anything people would choose to stay at for leisure. It had, in fact, once been the top choice for tourists planning a visit to the nearby British Museum. Those days were long gone.

He parked out front, turned on his hazard lights, and went inside.

"This has to be hand-delivered," he said.

The concierge was more interested in the fingernails she was painting than anything a delivery driver might have to say. She answered without looking up at him.

"What's the name?"

He looked at the envelope. "Marton Garas."

Reluctantly, she put the brush into the nail polish bottle and screwed it on. Then, careful not to ruin her work, she made a few dainty clicks on her computer. She picked up a phone and dialed, looking at the driver for the first time as she waited for an answer. "Yes, this is front desk. There's a package for you." She rolled her eyes. "It needs signing. Yeah." She put her hand on the receiver and said to the driver, "Can I sign?"

He shook his head.

"Yeah, no. He said no. Has to be you." Her hand went back on the receiver. "Has to be him, yeah?"

"Yes," the driver said.

"Yeah, has to be you."

She hung up and nodded at the elevators across the lobby. "All right. Room two-fourteen. Lift's behind you."

The driver walked through the empty lobby to the elevator and pushed the button for the second floor. It creaked as it rose, and when he got out, he saw that the hotel was so down-at-heel that some of the rooms had been rented out as offices. He passed an accountant, an immigration law specialist, and, at room two-fourteen, a small sign announced that he was at a business called Budapest Human Services.

He knocked on the door.

99

M arton Garas, the sole owner and employee of Budapest Human Services, was a large, muscular Hungarian with dark hair and stubble as coarse as a wire brush. He was forty-two years old, unmarried, drove a red 1994 Bentley Continental, and had caviar with champagne daily for lunch. He both lived and worked out of room two-fourteen at The Imperial Hotel. He could have afforded something nicer but preferred the hotel. It suited his purposes, was unassuming, anonymous.

He signed for the package, shut the door, and watched through the peephole until the delivery man was gone. Then he emptied the contents onto his desk.

It held a small, plastic thumb drive. Garas knew who it was from. He also knew the access key.

The thumb drive contained a cryptocurrency wallet—fifty thousand dollars in bitcoin and ethereum. It also contained files—surveillance photos, instructions, a name, an address at St James's Park.

He looked at the photos closely. They were of an elegant

older woman with dark features. The watermarks showed they were recent, all taken near the address in the last twenty-four hours. There was also some basic biographical information—she was a former Mossad agent, widow of the CIA's former London Station Chief, likely protected by a security detail.

When the job was complete, he would receive a second payment of two hundred thousand dollars.

He read the target's name.

Alona Almagor

He said it aloud, as was his habit, then deleted the files.

Marton Garas was a patient man. He had no shortage of other skills, but his ability to wait was the greatest of them. He was willing to spend months on a job. Not everyone could do that. He'd once watched a compound outside Madrid every day for eight months just to confirm the presence of a target.

And he would do the same for this job if he had to.

His preference, however, was to get it done immediately.

And so, he got to work. Using a virtual private network to mask his IP address and the Tor browser to hide his search traffic, he researched the neighborhood around the target's address. He memorized the street layout, the important buildings in the vicinity, the locations of CCTV cameras and known security systems.

Then he called down to the lobby and had them get him a cab. In the cab, he gave the driver an address on the target's street. It was, in fact, an address that did not exist, and as the driver searched for it, pissing and swearing and impatiently pulling u-turns before finally losing his temper, Garas was able to scope out the target's building, as well as what appeared to be her CIA security detail.

"You're having a laugh, mate," the driver said, once he'd confirmed for certain the address wasn't there.

"Calm down," Garas said. "I'll give you fifty quid to drop me at the Cavendish."

The driver brought him to the corner of Jermyn and Duke, where a nice little restaurant served Siberian Salmon roe. While not technically caviar, Garas had a fondness for it. He entered the restaurant, which had not quite opened for the day, and insisted on being seated.

"Do you have the foggiest idea who you're speaking to?" he bellowed at the host when she tried to send him away. "I have the owner on speed dial. Want me to call him?"

An intimidated waitress took his order—just fifty grams of the roe, just the one glass of champagne—he was on the clock, after all. The roe was served with some very English toast, crusts neatly removed as if for a picky child, and crème fraîche.

When he was done, he ordered coffee with cognac and thought about what he'd seen from the cab.

He was certain the black Audi was the security detail. Two men dressed in suits, sitting next to each other like a pair of imbeciles. They'd parked a hundred yards from the door—not the best view—and he wondered if the target knew she was being watched.

He paid his bill, then went for a gentle stroll the few blocks back to the address. He walked right by the Audi, studiously refraining from looking at it. When he was close to the front door, he dropped a small object on the ground and shoved it deftly with his foot into a flower bed.

The object was discreet, no larger than a coin, flat on the

bottom and slightly convex on top, like someone had sliced the top off a golf ball and painted it black.

No one would notice it, and its fisheye lens would give him an oblique visual on the target's front door until the battery died in forty-eight hours or a heavy rain washed it away.

He rounded the corner and sat down on a bench to check the feed. It was transmitting, giving him a view not only of the front of the building but also the narrow alley that ran next to it. The alley was hardly noticeable, a two-foot-wide pathway between two blocks that otherwise formed a continuous terrace for the length of the street.

He stopped a cab and told the driver to take him to a Hertz car rental office in Pimlico. There, he rented a gray Vauxhall Corsa and drove back to the address, parking behind the Audi so he could watch them as well as the building.

He wasn't expecting much to happen. This was the start of a marathon, not a sprint. It was the first day of a process that could end up taking months, and his purpose was merely to get a feel for things—the neighborhood, the target's habits, her routine, the way she walked, her body language. He also wanted to get a read on the security detail, find out how seriously they took their assignment, how diligent they were likely to be, whether they were round-the-clock or periodic, whether there was one team or many.

The details mattered. Having a security team was significant, but what really determined the outcome of a job like this was the little details, the personalities of the agents, the habits of the subject, whether she knew she was a target, whether she lived on the ground floor or not. Those details, and a million others, would determine how things played out.

He leaned back in the seat and lit a cigarette. Hertz would charge him a cleaning fee for the smoke, but he didn't care.

He could see the wing mirror of the Audi, which meant they could see him too. He leaned in away from the window. He wasn't too worried about the CIA. From what he'd seen, they weren't exactly a crack team. It was day one, and they'd already shit the bed—the two of them, sitting in the front seat of the car like Tango and Cash. They couldn't have been more obvious if they'd worn CIA ballcaps.

He sat there for about thirty minutes, watching, then went back to the Hertz office and returned the car. From there, he took a cab to his hotel and pulled up the video feed on his laptop. He needed more eyes on the street and began a scan for any hardwired cameras he might hack. If there were none, he'd look into setting up his own.

He planned to go back that night, so he ordered room service and then caught a few hours' sleep. When he woke, he rewound the footage taken during the afternoon and scrubbed through it at high speed. A few people entered and exited the building. None looked like his target. At five PM on the dot, the Audi drove away and was replaced by a Mercedes sedan, also black. He'd seen enough shift changes to know it for what it was.

He lit a cigarette and was beginning to think about dinner when something happened. It was five minutes after the shift change—about three hours ago. A side door in the alley opened, and someone slipped out of the building. It was a woman. He couldn't make out the face, she was wearing a headscarf, but her movements matched what he'd expect from his target. She took a few steps in the direction of the street, then, thinking better of it, stopped and went the other way.

A smile spread across his face. There was no way the timing was a coincidence. She knew she was being watched, and she didn't like it. Or at least, she didn't want the CIA knowing her comings and goings. Either way, she wasn't cooperating with her security detail, and that just made his job a whole lot easier.

He sped through more footage. She'd returned an hour later, again using the side door to avoid being seen.

He pulled up a map to see where the alley led. A quiet, cobbled street near Carlton Gardens with a park on one end. It was a short walk through the park to the tube station.

This was good. It was very good.

He looked at his watch, probably too late to get a car. He called Hertz anyway. They were closed. He had his own car brought up, not the Bentley, but a black Volvo SUV with stolen plates that he could afford to be reckless with if necessary.

He made his way back to St James's Park, stopping at a kebab shop on the way to pick up a Sultan's feast—two different styles of beef kebab with rice, saffron, butter, and grilled tomatoes. Then he drove to the street near Carlton Gardens and parked with his back to the alley. He didn't know if his target would show, but if she did, he'd see her in his rearview mirror.

He opened the window a crack, pulled up the camera feed on his phone, then propped it up on the dashboard while he ate the kebab. When he was done eating, he got out of the car and threw his garbage in a trash can. Then he got back in the car and lit a cigarette. He turned on the radio, a local station with pop music interspersed with inane talk, and kept the volume on low. It was three in the morning when he saw movement.

The same woman, the same headscarf, sneaking out the

side door of the building like a teenage girl with an overprotective father. He turned off the radio, stubbed out his cigarette, and leaned his seat back so he wouldn't be visible in the car. He adjusted the mirror to get a view of the alley.

It took a few minutes, but as surely as a pig to a trough, she arrived as expected. She came out of the alley at a brisk walk, cigarette in hand, and passed by him on the sidewalk. He could have opened the door and grabbed her.

But he was in no hurry.

He let her walk on another hundred yards, predicting she would cross the street to enter the park. When she got near the park gates, he fired up the engine. The street was very quiet, and he wasn't far enough away that she wouldn't register the sound of the starting car, even if only subconsciously.

He pulled out of the spot and made his way slowly along the cobbles. There was a certain sound the tires made on the stones. She glanced over her shoulder, and he thought she'd noticed him. That was fine. He didn't want to spook her. There would be plenty more opportunities. This was reconnaissance, nothing more.

A line of cars by the curb separated him from the sidewalk. He'd drive right by her. That was the plan. But then, suddenly, not thirty yards in front of him, she emerged from between two cars and stepped right into the street.

He couldn't believe it. He just looked at her. She reached the middle of the street and stopped, turned to face him.

He reacted without thinking, gunning the engine and bringing the car to life like a spurred horse. It lurched forward, accelerating from near zero to sixty in a matter of seconds.

She just stood there, staring, frozen in place like a deer in headlights.

When he hit her, she rolled up onto the hood and over the roof. He jammed the brakes with a screech of rubber and stared at her in the mirror. He waited for movement, a sign of life, anything. There was none. She was sprawled on the asphalt, her limbs at impossible angles, still as a sack of coal.

He put the car into reverse and went back over her, slowly, making sure to crush her. Then he drove forward again, making doubly sure.

100

W hen Roth got to the café in the embassy lobby, Tatyana was already sitting there, a paper coffee cup in her hand and a pastry on the table in front of her.

"Am I late?"

"I was early," she said curtly.

He nodded, ordered a coffee at the counter, and brought it to the table. As soon as he sat down, he felt awkward. It must have been obvious because Tatyana said, "You can quit acting like that."

"Sorry," he said.

"What's done is done."

"Water under the bridge," he said, eager to agree with her.

Outside, the Thames was moving under a morning mist with all the vigor of a mudflow.

"For what it's worth...."

"Please," she said, raising a hand. "Let's not."

He nodded, took a sip of his coffee. "Of course," he said. He was holding an envelope and let the contents slide onto the table. They were satellite images of Lance's attack on Suvorov.

She looked at them—the exploded vehicle, the bodies being removed from the wreckage by paramedics.

"Suvorov was pronounced dead at the hospital in Dmitrov an hour ago," Roth said.

"So it's done," she said, gathering up the photos and putting them back in the envelope.

"It's done."

"And Lance?"

Roth shrugged. "Looks like he got clear. Laurel lost him at some point."

Tatyana nodded, chewed her lip. Something was on her mind. He watched, waited for her to say it, but she didn't. She only sipped her coffee.

He cleared his throat. "Well, I guess that's it, then. This is how it ends. Suvorov's dead. Gazinsky's data is in our hands. Oppenheimer has been critically compromised."

"We got what we wanted," she said quietly.

He nodded.

"But it cost us," she added. "Didn't it, Levi?" She looked up at him, and there it was, that fire in the eyes like a predator before the strike.

"Everything has a price," he said.

She pulled her coat off the back of her seat and put it on her shoulders. She hadn't touched the pastry. "Are you going to throw that out?" he said.

She looked at it and then let out a long sigh. She'd been ready to leave but sank back into her seat. She pushed the pastry toward him. "I'm tired, Roth."

"I know," he said, and he did know. She was right. It had cost them.

He'd just received word that Tenet's body had been

incinerated in the furnace behind GRU headquarters. Sacha Gazinsky was scheduled for cremation by the Procurator Fiscal of the City of Edinburgh, at public expense, his body unclaimed. Ada Hudson was being airlifted back to Washington in a pine box. Harry Staples. Viktor Lapin. André Suvorov. Declan Haines. The contractors hired by the Russians. The list went on and on and on without end. It was enough to exhaust anyone.

Not to mention the fact he would never speak to Alona Almagor again. That was over. He knew it. The only connection he would have to her was the CIA security detail he'd assigned, and, without her cooperation, even that would end in tragedy eventually. He did not doubt that Suvorov would collect his debts. Even from the grave, they always did.

"Natasha Gazinsky?" Tatyana said.

He pulled his mind from its thoughts. "What?"

"Natasha?"

"Of course."

"What's going to happen to her?"

He shook his head. "You know as well as I do what her chances are."

"You son of a...."

He raised his hand to stop her. He didn't have the energy to be laid into for this. He'd done what he could. "I've approved the funds," he said. "The State Department and the British Home Office accepted my offer. It's a done deal."

"She has a chance then," Tatyana said.

Roth shrugged. "Sure," he said. "Suvorov's dead. Lapin's dead. Maybe she has a chance."

"You act like it makes no difference."

He shook his head. "It makes a difference, Tatyana. Believe me."

"You're just not holding your breath."

He took a bite of the pastry. It was almond with a sugar dusting and vanilla cream filling. "The President wants to meet us."

"Us?"

"You, me, Laurel. There's a plane fueling at Farnborough as we speak."

"What about Lance?"

Roth sipped some coffee to wash down the pastry. He didn't have an answer for that one. "He didn't mention Lance."

Tatyana was looking out the window, the MI6 building rising up from the riverbank like a cathedral.

"They'd take you in a heartbeat," he said.

"What?"

"MI6."

She looked at him. "It's not them I'm looking at," she said. "It's the river."

"Ah."

"It looks just like the Neva."

He nodded, took another bite of the pastry. She was still holding back. He could tell by the tension in her jaw. There was something she needed to get off her chest. "You might as well go ahead and say it."

She shook her head.

"Please," he said. "I threw you to the wolves. I traded your life for a chance at Molotov. I know you hate me for it."

She looked at him, absolute fire in her eyes, and said, "You really want to know what I'm thinking?"

"I do," he said.

"I'm thinking, I'd have done the same thing."

He let out a sigh, more relief than anything. She was

holding her cup, and for some reason, some moment of madness, he reached across the table to touch her hands.

She recoiled instantly, almost spilling the coffee. She couldn't have moved faster if a snake jumped at her.

She looked at him, and he, mortified, looked away. He didn't know what he'd been thinking. "We should get moving," he stammered. "Plane's fueling. Don't want to be late."

He began to rise to his feet when she said, "It doesn't change, does it?"

He looked at her. He didn't know exactly what she was referring to, but he understood the sentiment. "Things change," he said, "and things remain the same."

"My parents..." she said, and her words trailed off.

He waited for her to go on, but instead she said, "It just keeps going on and on, doesn't it? No end. No resolution."

"It's best not to think about it."

"One fight just bleeds into the next, and the only thing that changes is the men on the ground, the soldiers, because the last batch is dead."

"Tatyana...."

"It all just so...."

"Inevitable?"

"I was going to say futile," she said, "but yes, *inevitable*. Like there was no other way for it to be. Like this was what was ordained from the outset."

"Life is a struggle," Roth said.

"You don't need to tell me that," she said. "I know what struggle is."

He looked at her. He knew her story, the outline of her life. Her father's submarine accident. Her mother's death when she was four. He knew she'd been left alone in the apartment in Saint Petersburg with the corpse. He knew she'd grown up hard.

"But this," she said, waving her hand at the lobby. "We're in the US Embassy in London. The two greatest empires of the last three centuries. You'd be hard-pressed to find more power, more empire, at any other point in history."

"And yet it goes on," Roth said.

"And on, and on."

"The Great Game."

She nodded.

He looked at her. She'd seen a lot in her life, but she was also young. And there were things in the world he felt one had to be old to understand. "The Game will never end, Tatyana."

She nodded. She knew it was true. What she didn't know was why. "Eventually..." she said.

Roth shook his head, and she let the sentence die.

"There is no eventually."

"But if the conflict were to end...."

"We won't let it end."

"But why wouldn't we?"

"Have you heard of the scorpion and the frog?"

She leaned back and sighed. She was Russian, after all. She looked out the window again, then back at him. "At least in the fable, only one of them is a scorpion."

Roth shrugged. "Maybe that's why we tell it to children."

She'd finished her coffee and got up. She took both of their cups to the trash, and Roth finished the pastry. He said, "The Dead Hand, Tatyana. Have you ever seen their seal?"

"They don't have a seal," she said.

He raised an eyebrow and began walking toward the elevator.

"Wait," she said, following him. "Do they?"

"They don't use it much," he said, "but it exists. It's embossed in gold at the center of the table where they meet."

"How would you know that?"

He touched his nose conspiratorially and nodded. She rolled her eyes. They made it to the elevator, and he pushed the button.

"Go on then," she said while they waited. "You're dying to tell me. I can see it on your face."

"Their motto is *Bellum Internecinum!*"

"I see."

"Do you know what that means?"

"War something."

"War of annihilation," Roth said.

"Why am I not surprised?"

The elevator arrived, and they stepped inside. Roth pressed the button for the basement parking lot. The doors closed, and Roth said, "There's a matching seal on the underside of President Molotov's desk."

She looked at him. "The underside?"

"That's right."

"There's no way you could know that."

"Isn't there?" he said.

The elevator stopped, and the doors opened. They signed out of the embassy, and Roth said to the security guard, "We're leaving the country."

He nodded and updated his list. "Your car will be right down." Roth looked at his watch impatiently, and the guard added, "They were washing it, sir."

"Well," Roth said, "I suppose that's something."

They sat on a bench while they waited, and Tatyana looked at him. "I guess I'll never know if you're telling the truth, will I?"

"Truth about what?"

She rolled her eyes.

"This isn't a joke," he said. "It's real."

"Sure it is."

"Perhaps more real than you and I sitting here right now."

She shook her head.

"Really, Tatyana. I'm not exaggerating. This is the thing that hangs over all of us, from the day we're born until the day we die. Over all the billions of us. The one thing every man, woman, and child on this planet shares. The thing that could wipe us all out in an instant."

"Levi."

"The weapons they have, the keys they hold," he said, "could undo Creation itself."

"I get it, Levi. They fight. We fight. We all fight."

"There's a difference in the mottos on the two seals," Roth said.

"Is that so?"

"The one embossed on the Dead Hand's table says *Bellum Internecinum!*"

"War of annihilation."

"Right. And the one beneath the President's desk says *Bellum omnium contra omnes.*"

She looked at him blankly.

"Not a big reader of the classics, are you?" he said.

"Sorry, I didn't take Latin."

"It's Hobbes. I thought you'd have heard it."

"Well, I'm sorry to disappoint you."

"It means, The war of all, against all."

"Total war," she said.

"Essentially."

"Against everyone."

"It's a Hobbesian view of the human condition."

"How pessimistic."

"Written five hundred years ago."

"As if he saw us coming."

Roth nodded. "He did see us coming."

101

The car arrived, and Tatyana got in next to Roth. It drove out of the embassy and into the early London traffic, headed for Farnborough. A selection of morning papers had been set out on the seat, and she picked up a copy of *The Guardian*. The detonation over the Arctic was still the lead on every front page. Marine life was washing up on beaches all over Europe. The Russians were botching the cover-up, as usual. They were now claiming, though no one was buying it, that it had been a natural seismic event.

None of it was new. The world was at war, and the public knew it. It had been that way when they were born, it would be that way when they went to their graves. No one needed a newspaper to spell it out.

Roth cleared his throat. "You're quiet," he said.

"I'm thinking."

He nodded, picking up the *Financial Times*. "Oil is through the roof."

Tatyana shrugged.

"Molotov will be happy," Roth said. "Even shitting the bed, he comes out smelling like roses."

They were just passing the power station at Battersea when Roth's phone began ringing.

"It's Laurel," he said, looking at the screen. He answered and said, "I'm in the car with Tatyana. I'll put you on speaker."

When Laurel's voice came through, Tatyana could hear the strain immediately. "Are you still in London?" she said.

"We're on our way to the airport," Roth said, looking at Tatyana. He heard it too. They waited for Laurel to speak. "Did we lose you?" Roth said.

"No," she said, then another pause. "You haven't heard, have you?"

"Heard what?"

"Something's happened, Levi."

"I take it from your tone it's not good."

"It's not good."

"Well, are you going to make us guess what it is?"

"It's Alona Almagor."

Roth's face went pale. "Oh," he said.

Instinctively, Tatyana put her hand on his arm. He looked at her then, just for a second, and there was so much pain in his eyes that it broke her heart.

"Are you still there?" Laurel said.

Tatyana answered. "We're here."

"I sent a security detail to her house," Roth said weakly.

"She slipped out unnoticed," Laurel said. "It looks like she was evading the security detail."

"She didn't want my protection," Roth said.

Tatyana looked at him, his face ashen with grief. It was as if he'd just aged ten years.

"It was a hit and run," Laurel said. "A street near her home. Unlikely it was an accident."

"It just happened?"

"Just before dawn, sir. Local police are on the scene."

Roth looked out the window. "I'm so close."

"You couldn't have stopped it, sir."

"Of course I could have," he said. "Of course I could." He tapped the driver on the shoulder and indicated for him to turn around. "Who did it?"

"Black Volvo SUV," Laurel said. "Stolen plates."

"A professional," Roth said.

"I'll get you a name, Levi."

"Make sure that you do."

"Yes, sir."

"I want you to find this man, Laurel. You hear me?"

"I hear you, sir."

He hung up the phone, his face a portrait of sorrow. Tatyana could hardly bear to look at him. Here he was at last, she thought—Levi Roth, the man without the mask.

"Levi," she said, her hand still on his arm.

He cleared his throat, then looked at her and smiled thinly. "I loved her, you know."

"I know, Levi."

"I killed her."

"You didn't."

"Lance knew," Roth said. "When I told him to go after Suvorov, he knew it would mean this. He tried to warn me."

"Warn you of what?"

"I know what regret feels like."

"Sorry?"

"That's what he said."

Tatyana nodded. "You did what needed to be done," she said.

He reached into his coat for his cigarettes. He handed one to Tatyana and put one in his mouth. When he tried to light them, his hand shook so badly he couldn't do it. She took the lighter from him and got them lit. "I'll open a window," she said.

The morning air came in, cool and damp.

Tatyana looked at Roth. This was what defeat looked like. He'd lost all his roar, like a lion with his mane shaved off.

He caught her looking and straightened himself up. Cleared his throat. "*Bellum Internecinum*," he said.

She nodded. "*Bellum omnium contra omnes.*"

102

Roth sat in the lobby of the embassy, drinking coffee and rapping his fingers on the Formica table, staring blankly at the ground, waiting. He could think of only one thing, and could do nothing until it was taken care of.

Tatyana had waited with him, had tried to get him talking, tried to get a read on where his head was at. After six hours, he told her to go to the hotel. She'd tried to bring him with her, but he refused.

"Fly back to Washington if you like," he said as she stood up.

"I'll wait for you at the hotel," she said.

He nodded. "Take the driver, then. I don't need him."

She crossed the lobby to the elevator, and while waiting for it, looked back at him. He knew what she was thinking. That she might not see him again.

"You know I have to do this," he called out to her.

The elevator arrived, and she stepped inside. Then she was gone. He got up for more coffee, then went back to the table. At some point, the security guards went through a shift change, and someone asked if he wanted something to eat. He shook his head—ordered more coffee. It grew dark. There was another shift change. The fluorescent lights came on. The night staff came in.

The lobby was quiet by night, and Roth lit a cigarette. The guards said nothing. He chain-smoked and drank coffee and stared. He lost track of the hours. It was almost dawn when his phone rang.

He answered immediately and tried to speak. His throat was so dry that no sound came out.

"I have him, boss," Laurel said.

"Send the package."

"I spoke to Tatyana. She thinks...."

"Just send me the package," he said and hung up.

He lit another cigarette and looked at his phone. His screen lit up with a file transfer notification.

He opened it and read the information—a name, pictures, an address.

He took the elevator down to the basement and told the guard he needed an unmarked vehicle.

"I'll call you a driver, sir."

"No driver," Roth said. "I'm driving."

The guard logged the request and handed him a key. He went out to the lot and pressed the button on the key. A white Range Rover beeped and lit up.

Roth didn't like driving at the best of times. In Britain, he despised it. He put the vehicle in reverse, gears grinding, and lurched out of the spot. Then he made his way out of the lot, his front tires screeching against the curbs painfully on the narrow ramps. On the street, he drove fast enough that he was at risk of being pulled over. Thankfully, traffic was light, and in fifteen minutes, he was outside the address

Laurel had given him. It was a hotel on Russell Square called The Imperial.

He pulled up in front of it and turned off the engine. He took out his gun and checked it. He had no plan. This wasn't his area of expertise. If he died, it was a price he was willing to pay.

He called Laurel.

"This is a hotel."

"If you hadn't hung up," she said. "I'd have told you."

"Is he inside?"

"The camera across the street hasn't picked him up since I tapped into it."

"Which was when?"

"About thirty minutes ago."

"You also didn't give me a room number."

Laurel hesitated.

"Laurel, I need the room number."

"Roth, you have people who can handle this for you."

"I don't want them to handle it. I want to handle it."

"You're going to get yourself...."

"Are you giving me the room number or not?"

"Two-fourteen," she said, "but you might be better off staying put."

"Why?"

"If the last few days are a pattern, he'll be coming down those steps in front of you very soon."

"Alone?"

"Always alone, always in a long coat and hat."

Roth put down the phone. He lit a cigarette. The sun rose slowly, its light muted by the low cloud. The street began to fill—a street sweeper went by, a postman entered the hotel, a few early commuters walked by. Roth watched the doors of the hotel like a hawk, his gun between his legs as if he was trying to keep it from getting cold.

When he saw movement, his heart leaped in his chest. Through the door, he could see a large man in a long black coat and proletarian-looking cap. When the doors opened, he saw his face.

He stubbed out his cigarette hurriedly, spilling ash. Adrenaline coursed through his veins like oil in an engine. He checked the gun again, then rolled down his window.

"Excuse me, sir," he said.

The man had just reached the bottom of the steps, and he stopped dead when he saw Roth. He had the instincts of a professional. One look, and he knew what this meant. He was going to reach for a gun, Roth saw the thought cross his face.

"No one's that fast," Roth said.

The man slowly moved his hands from his sides.

Roth had his finger on the trigger, ready to fire.

"I knew it," the man said.

"Knew what?"

"That last job. Something wasn't right."

Roth knew the man was stalling now, borrowing time. Every second that the gun didn't fire was a second longer to live, a second that might turn the tables, however unlikely that might be.

"What wasn't right?"

"She snuck out of the building."

Roth nodded. Laurel had told him as much. She hadn't wanted his security detail.

"But it wasn't just that," the man said.

Roth looked at him. "What wasn't?"

"It was like...."

"Like what?"

"It was like she knew I was there."

"Knew?"

"Like she was trying to make it easy for me."

"You can't know that."

"Suicide by assassin," the man said.

Roth's jaw clenched. Every word was like a shard of glass. "I see," he said.

He'd heard enough. He felt the weight of the gun in his hand and inhaled deeply, pulling the trigger as he did.

The man sensed it coming. Before the shot even left the barrel, he was reaching for his own gun.

He never stood a chance. The bullet hit him in the chest, and he stumbled backward, reaching for the wound with both hands as if checking it was really there. His hat fell to the ground, and his gaze followed it as if worried he'd lose it.

The next bullet hit his forehead and exited his skull at the crown.

His body crumpled on the concrete like a sack of sand.

Roth felt exultant. He was breathing through gritted teeth, inhaling and exhaling so quickly it was almost a pant. There was an obscene quality to the breathing, like a man climaxing.

He opened the door of the car and stepped out. Then he went over to the corpse and emptied his gun into it.

"There," he said when the gun clicked empty, as if he'd just been vindicated in a bet. "You don't like that, do you?"

103

Lance stepped out of the cab and looked at the sky. It felt strange to be back. The apartment building soared above him as it had when he first saw it, its top lost in the low cloud. Around it, the mosques and liquor stores and bookies were as they'd been. Even the weather was the same.

The only thing that had changed was that he'd been alone that day, and now, he was holding the hand of a nine-year-old girl. He looked down at her. She looked back. He gave her a hand a squeeze. "Ready?"

She nodded.

As soon as they entered the lobby, the stench of urine hit them.

"Don't worry about that," Lance said.

She looked determined to overcome whatever he threw at her. He led her into the elevator, where the smell was even worse, and she made no sign even of having noticed.

"It gets better," he said. "You get used to it."

She looked like a soldier about to charge the front.

"The people are nice," he added.

The elevator creaked and jerked as it rose.

"I don't know," she said quietly.

They were speaking English. It turned out she was better at it than she'd let on, and for her safety, the CIA handlers were eager that she lose her accent as quickly as possible. They'd also given her a new look—hair cropped short, bangs in front of her eyes, a few simple makeup tricks to alter her appearance. At her age, tricking the facial recognition systems was less difficult than for an adult.

That, combined with the out-of-the-way neighborhood, and a few simple tips for avoiding cameras, made the handlers confident she'd be able to stay off the radar.

Roth had coordinated personally between the doctor in Boston and the Great Ormand Street Hospital in London to administer the medical treatment. After what had happened at the clinic, it was decided a large, busy hospital would offer more cover.

All in all, the prognosis was good. Sacha Gazinsky couldn't have hoped for more. He'd given his life to get his daughter this far, and Levi Roth, in a series of uncharacteristically charitable acts, had personally seen to it that everything in the CIA's power was done to ensure his sacrifice had not been in vain.

Roth had even arranged language lessons for Natasha, and trauma counseling with one of the best child psychologists in the country. It was like he was doing penance, as if by helping Natasha, he could undo some of the bad that had happened.

The elevator arrived, and Natasha looked at Lance uncertainly.

"Don't worry," he said, leading her into the corridor. "Everything's going to be all right."

He brought her to the door of his apartment and had to

search for the key. Only when he opened the door did he realize how inhospitable it all looked. Through Natasha's eyes it would have been even worse. Nothing about it was warm, or cozy, or the least bit welcoming. On the counter, an ashtray overflowed with used cigarette butts. In the sink, takeout containers had been left to fester. A wine bottle on the coffee table had spawned a small cloud of flies.

"I'll let some air in," Lance said, going over to the balcony to open the doors. Cool air filled the room.

"This is it," he said, turning back to face her.

She gave him a long, strangely mature look, then said curtly, "I see."

He felt guilty but reminded himself that these were the things—the urine, the graffitied walls, the apartment's chronic lack of comfort—that made it safe. The GRU wouldn't be caught within a million miles of a place like this. They had no eyes and ears here. And no one but Roth and Lance knew the details of the arrangement.

If Natasha's childhood was to have any semblance of normalcy, this was the place for that to happen.

Natasha had taken it on herself to explore the rest of the apartment—bathroom, bedroom, corridor, balcony. It took all of two minutes, and then she was back in the living room, standing by the doorway, looking at Lance.

"There's no bed for me," she said.

Lance wasn't sure what to say to that. He went into the kitchen. "How about some tea?"

She sighed and slumped into the sofa. He watched her as he filled the kettle.

She was staring at the wall. He followed her gaze to the square-shaped stain where a television set had once been. It was a depressing sight.

His confidence was slipping away. This had been his

idea. He'd fought Roth hard for it, sworn it was the right thing to do.

"She needs a family," he'd said.

"No one's contesting that, Lance."

"Well then, you tell me a better place."

"I'll tell you a thousand better places. From what I've been able to gather, this woman is one step away from being a prostitute."

"She's not a prostitute."

"And a drug addict."

"She's not a drug addict either."

"She's trouble, Lance."

"She'll get her act together."

"You don't know that."

"You're right. I don't know it."

"Then how can you, in good conscience, put a child into that situation?"

"Just trust me," Lance said.

"It's not a question of trust."

"You're right. It's a question of fate."

"Fate?"

"Yes."

"You can't be...."

"Serious? I'm deadly serious."

"This is a child's life we're talking about."

"And that's why I'm fighting for it, Levi. This is where she'll have a childhood. It won't be perfect, it won't be a fairy tale, but it will be real, and it will be a damn sight better than any of the alternatives."

"If something goes wrong," Roth said, and he raised a finger to emphasize his point, "one single thing...."

"And Tatyana and Laurel will have your head."

"Both our heads."

"It won't go wrong, Levi."

"You can't promise that."

"Fate, Levi. Blind fate. Not logic. Not reason. Tell me you don't feel it?"

"You're losing your marbles."

"These are the times, Levi."

"Times for what?"

"Times when you either do the thing you know must be done, or you turn your back."

Roth shook his head.

"You know it, Levi. You know I'm right."

"I know you're crazy."

"I'm giving you my word here, Levi."

"What does that mean?"

"I'll make sure it works out."

"You won't be there."

"I'll be there."

Roth paused then. "You'll be there?"

"Yes."

"Personally?"

"If I'm needed."

Lance wasn't quite sure what did it then, but Roth stopped arguing. Something that was said changed his mind.

Lance finished making the tea and brought it over to the sofa.

They drank it together, and Natasha said, "Am I sleeping on the couch?"

"No," Lance said. He looked at her, her eyes so wide, so scared. She'd lost everything, everyone. She was alone in the world now, and she knew it.

They finished their tea, and he got up. "Ready to go?" he said.

Natasha clutched his arm. "Go where?"

"Natasha," he said, "I'm not leaving you. Don't be afraid."

They walked across the apartment, her so close he almost tripped over her, and he opened the door.

"Where are we going?"

"Trust me," he said, stepping into the hallway.

She remained in the apartment, looking out at him.

"Come on," he said, holding out his hand. She put her hand in his, and they turned around to face the door across the hall from theirs.

Natasha looked at him, confused.

He knocked.

The door opened. It was the little girl.

"Hello," Lance said.

"Hello," she said.

Lance looked at Natasha. She was absolutely silent. She hadn't seen this coming.

"Is your mother home?" Lance said to the girl.

She nodded.

Lance put his head inside the door. The woman was just coming out of the bedroom, a pile of clean laundry in her arms.

"Oh," she said, surprised.

"We're early," Lance said.

"Come in. Come in."

They entered, standing by the door awkwardly, Natasha's grip on his hand as fierce as any he'd ever felt. Her nails were so deep he thought she might draw blood.

She was scanning the apartment. It was a different world from the one she'd just been in, with blankets, lampshades, curtains, upholstery. It was warm and cozy and welcoming.

But he could tell she was scared. She held his hand in

both of hers, motionless, her wide eyes darting from the woman to the little girl and back.

"I made soup," the woman said hesitantly.

Lance bent down to Natasha's level. "Do you want soup? We haven't eaten." He wasn't sure she'd even heard him.

"Maybe another time," the woman said.

Lance looked at her apologetically.

"That's okay," the woman said. "Tomorrow's another day. Let's have soup tomorrow. The four of us."

Lance led Natasha back to the other apartment and sat her down on the sofa. She glared back at him with the ferociousness of a lioness.

"You want to get rid of me," she stammered.

He let out a deep breath. He wanted a cigarette but didn't know if that was still allowed.

"You want to leave me there."

He shook his head.

She began crying. It wasn't a tantrum, which he would have known how to handle, but quiet, private tears that she tried to hide by burying her face in a cushion.

He sat with her, his hand on her back, and pulled a blanket over her. After about thirty minutes, she quietened down, and he picked her up and brought her to the bedroom. He lay her on the bed and was going to leave when she gripped his hand.

"Don't go."

He got down on the bed next to her, facing the ceiling, and her hand gripped his as if her life depended on it.

And perhaps it did.

He lay there for an hour, and another, and another. Each time he tried to get up, she clung to him so tightly that he surrendered to her. The day turned to evening, and he wondered if she would ever tire. She seemed determined not to sleep.

In the end, it was he who dozed off first. He woke up, and it was night. Natasha was no longer lying next to him. She was on the floor, blocking the door so that it couldn't be opened without waking her.

He watched her sleep for a few minutes, then walked over, picked her up, and put her in the bed. She didn't wake.

He looked down at her. They were the same. They both knew what it was to be alone.

Then he lay back down on the bed next to her and shut his eyes.

AUTHOR'S NOTE

First off, I want to thank you for reading my book. As a reader, you might not realize how important a person like you is to a person like me.

I've been a writer for fifty years, and despite the upheavals my industry has faced, the ups and downs, the highs and lows, one thing remains constant.

You.

The reader.

And at the end of each book, I like to take a moment to acknowledge that fact.

To thank you.

Not just on my own behalf, but on behalf of all fiction writers.

Because without you, these books simply would not exist.

You're the reason they're written. Your support is what makes them possible. And your reviews and recommendations are what spreads the word.

So, thanks for that. I really do mean it.

While I have your attention, I'd like to give you a little bit of background into my opinion on the events portrayed in this book.

Writing about politics is not easy, and I hope none of my personal thoughts and opinions managed to find their way into this story. I never intend to raise political points in my writing, and I never intend to take a stand. I'm one of those guys who stays out of politics as much as possible, and I would hate to think that any political ideas raised in my book hampered your ability to enjoy the story or relate to the characters.

Because really, this is your story.

These characters are your characters.

When you read the book, no one knows what the characters look like, what they sound like, or what they truly think and feel, but you. It's your story, written for you, and the experience of it is created by you when you read the words and flip the pages.

I write about people who work for the federal government. The nature of their work brings them up against issues of national security and politics, but apart from that, I truly do try to keep any views I might have to myself. So please, don't let any of my words offend you, and if you spot anything in my writing that you feel is unfair, or biased, or off-color in any way, feel free to let me know.

My email address is below, and if you send a message, while I might not get back to you immediately, I will receive it, and I will read it.

saulherzog@authorcontact.com

Likewise, if you spot simpler errors, like typos and misspellings, let me know about those too. We writers have a saying:

To err is human. To edit, divine.

And we live by it.

I'm going to talk a little about some of the true facts that this book is based on, but before I do, I'd like to ask for a favor.

I know you're a busy person, I know you just finished this book and you're eager to get on to whatever is in store next, but if you could find it in your heart to leave me a review, I'd be truly humbled.

I'm not a rich man. I'm not a powerful man. There's really nothing I can offer you in return for the kindness.

But what I will say is that it is a kindness.

If you leave me a review, it will help my career. It will help my series to flourish and find new readers. It will make a difference to one guy, one stranger you've never met and likely will never meet, and I'll appreciate that fact.

Now that those formalities are out of the way, let's talk about some of the events in this book.

The book opens with an accidental nuclear detonation off the coast of the Svalbard Archipelago, north of Norway. This fictional incident is caused by Sacha Gazinsky sabotaging a test launch for a fictionalized nuclear-powered cruise missile called Petrel. It is, however, based on an actual incident that is strikingly similar.

On 8 August 2019, an explosion, now referred to as the Nyonoksa Radiation Accident, really did occur near the village of Nyonoksa, outside Severodvinsk in Arkhangelsk Oblast.

The Russian Government had previously confirmed that, since 2017, it was conducting tests for a nuclear-powered cruise missile named 9M730 *Burevestnik*. According to the US military, these tests were all near-complete failures. Russia disputes this, saying the tests are progressing on target.

The base from which Sacha and Natasha Gazinsky flee to London is based on a factual Russian facility. In reality, Nyonoksa is home to the State Central Navy Testing Range, the main rocket launching facility of the Russian Navy.

The explosion that took place at Nyonoksa in 2019 immediately killed five Rosatom scientists and was so powerful that it was picked up by the Bardufoss Infrasound Station outside Narvik, Norway, a thousand miles away.

The cause of the accident was initially unclear. It was confirmed by the Russians as being related to the development of an "isotope power source for a liquid-fueled rocket engine," but whether that was *Burevestnik* or another, as yet unannounced, system was unclear. It was also unclear whether the explosion resulted from a failed test flight or the attempted recovery of a previously failed prototype from the seabed. In support of the latter, US satellites had spotted Rosatom recovery vessels capable of handling nuclear material in the area.

In any event, the seismic data showed an explosion that must have resulted from contact with land or water--it was not consistent with a solely airborne explosion--and this was supported by local fishermen sighting a hundred-meter column of water rising out of the ocean.

Immediately after the explosion, Arkhangelsk's two principal medical facilities, the Semashko Medical Center and Arkhangelsk Regional Clinical Hospital, began receiving survivors. Victims were suffering the effects of radiation poisoning.

The hospitals had not been warned of this risk beforehand, and soon afterward, medical staff were being flown to Moscow's Burnazyan Federal Medical and Biophysical

Center for radiation exposure testing. The paramedics escorting them wore hazmat suits. The staff was forced to sign non-disclosure agreements, but it is known that at least one tested positive for Cesium-137 exposure.

In the days following the explosion, background radiation levels were measured that were sixteen times higher than normal, and all Russian monitoring stations stopped sending data to the Comprehensive Nuclear-Test-Ban Treaty Organization. Norwegian monitoring stations detected isotopes consistent with a nuclear detonation.

On 14 August, four-hundred-fifty civilians were evacuated from the village of Nyonoksa. A few days later, three US diplomats were forcibly removed from a train headed for Arkhangelsk, accused of attempting to enter a closed city. This was the train Lance Spector avoided by taking the bus from Vologda.

Two months later, the US delegation to the United Nations officially referred for the first time to the "Skyfall Incident." The NATO reporting name for *Burevestnik* is Skyfall. According to the US delegate, the incident "was the result of a nuclear reaction that occurred during the recovery of a Russian nuclear-powered cruise missile [which] remained on the bed of the White Sea since its failed test early last year."

What makes the Nyonoksa Accident so noteworthy is the context in which it occurred.

The accident came just one year after a remarkable speech, delivered at the Manezh Central Exhibition Hall on 1 March 2018, that was widely reported in international media.

In his annual state-of-the-nation address, and in front of an audience of lawmakers and military and government officials, the Russian President announced a slew of new Super

Weapons programs that the Associated Press described as "a stunning catalog of doomsday machines." And just like President Molotov in the book, he truly said the words, "No one has listened to us. You listen to us now." He also said, "Today isn't a bluff. It's not a bluff, trust me."

The stated purpose of the weapons was to counter the growing effectiveness of American missile defense systems that "devalue the Russian nuclear arsenal if we sit with our arms folded." He claimed that NATO and the United States have sought to "win unilateral advantages over Russia" and summed up by stating, "You have failed to contain Russia."

In delivery and style, the event was not dissimilar to a PR junket thrown by a Silicon Valley tech company. The loud applause, the rapturous fans, the massive screen showing slick, computer-rendered animations of new products, was reminiscent more of Cupertino than of Moscow.

The weapons announced were essentially those portrayed in the book as the Five P's, although their real-life names differ.

There was the nuclear-powered cruise missile with near-unlimited range that could reportedly fly "like a meteorite." Apparently based on discarded US Air Force research from the 1960s for the Supersonic Law Altitude Missile, this rocket would use a nuclear-powered ramjet as well as conventionally fueled boosters to allow it to remain airborne for weeks or months at a time. An animation showed it flying at will around the globe, taking turns to avoid certain countries, adjusting its trajectory via a two-way comms link, and eventually striking a target in Hawaii. While commentators expressed doubt that the system is feasible, the message was clear.

Then, there was the hypersonic boost-glide vehicle called *Avangard* that could reach speeds of Mach 20, making it all but unstoppable. The President said it would strike targets, "like a meteorite, like a fireball," and it was speculated that it could be intended as an upgrade to the future RS-26 Rubezh ICBM, as well as the RS-28 Sarmat ICBM, which had both been previously announced. The President's words were accompanied by animations of a cluster of independent warheads striking Florida.

Another treat, referred to by commentators as *Kanyon* or *Status-6*, was a submarine-launched, nuclear-powered, underwater drone that could deliver a nuclear dirty bomb to coastal targets. The animation showed it being launched from an altered Oscar II class submarine and detonating beneath a fleet of US surface warships.

There was also a hypersonic cruise missile, launched from a MiG-31 Foxhound interceptor, capable of Mach 10, and a laser weapon that was visually similar to the US Navy's own AN/SEQ-3 system.

I mention these weapons, which truly are being developed by the current Russian government, not to scare readers or to drum up any ill-will against Russia, but to highlight that the plot of this book is not really so far-fetched. I would say that while these weapons are terrifying, they are no more hideous than those of countless other nations, including my own.

I should also point out that experts have raised varying degrees of skepticism as to whether the Russians could even pull off these designs, none of which has yet been successfully demonstrated.

What is clear is that they are a challenge--to the West, to America, to NATO, to the human race as a whole. They embody the demands of a dangerous regime not to be ignored, not to be underestimated, not to be written off.

As Moscow continues to demonstrate, while many

regard it as a spent force, a dwindling second-rate power, its leadership still refuses to *"go gentle into that good night."*

Finally, I'd be remiss if I didn't tell you that Book Four in the Lance Spector series, *The Sleeper,* is now available for pre-order.

So grab your copy now. I promise, if you enjoyed the first three, you're only going to be drawn into these characters more deeply!

God bless and happy reading,

Saul Herzog